UNBREAKABLE

Written by K.A. Knight.
Edited By Jess from Elemental Editing and Proofreading.
Proofreading by Norma's Nook.
Formatted by The Nutty Formatter.
Cover by Opulent Designs.
Art by Dily Designs

For my mum, who walks through the darkness with us

...and also because she was jealous that my sister had a dedication. There, you happy now?

TRIGGER WARNING

Please note, this is a dark book and as such contains scenes that some may find triggering. Mentions of sexual abuse, torture, murder, mutliation, death, suicide, sexual violence and much more can be found within, please be mindful if any of that may upset/trigger you.

If you have any concerns please reach out.

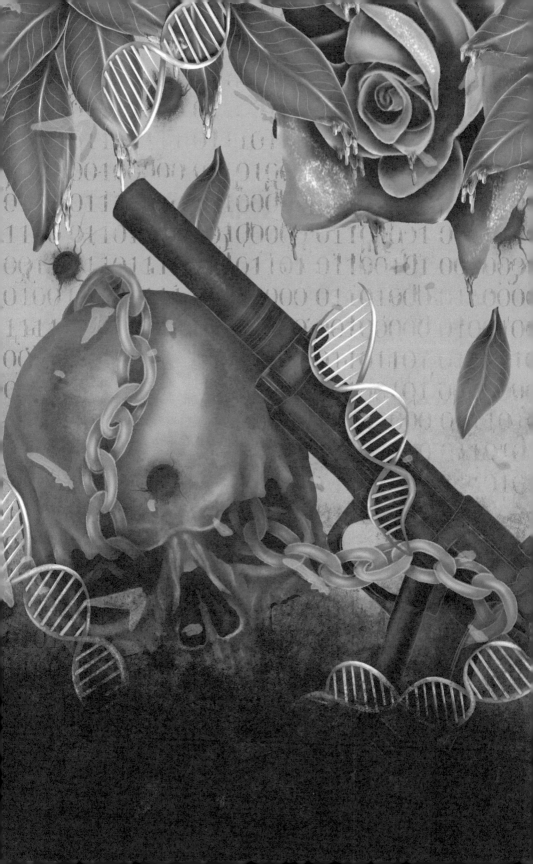

PROLOGUE

NOVA

G ritting my teeth, I swallow the taste of my own blood, my nails breaking as I claw at the rails of the bed. My legs thrash against the restraints, my arms too.

My head is thrown back in agony as it blisters through me like a flame.

The blade slides deeper into my stomach, and I lift to watch the blood well on my abdomen before I glare at the scientist above me.

He doesn't spare me a glance.

"You're dead," I warn, my voice choked.

He ignores me as he plunges his hand into my stomach, making me fall back, and finally, the trapped howl of agony rips through the lab before I pass out.

When I wake up, I feel him above me, watching and judging.

He pulls me apart just to put me back together again like a cat playing with a spider. Forcing my swollen, grimy eyes open, I find my stomach stapled, but I'm still tied down and coated in sweat and blood.

My father stands there with a pen poised above a notebook. "How do you feel, Novaleen?"

"Fuck you," I croak, my voice raw from screaming.

His eyes narrow impatiently before he repeats the question harder.

"How do I feel?" I echo, my tongue thick. "Like when I get free, I'm going to rip you apart to see how you like it."

Dropping the pen, he leans in with a cruel twist of his lips. "Oh, but you won't be getting free, will you? Not again." With those parting words, he departs.

He leaves me screaming and fighting, trapped again.

Once again, I have been reduced to an experiment.

ONE

NOVA

Stumbling from the plane crash, I vomit whatever is left in my stomach onto the grass. Hands rub my back, hold my hair for me, and pass me water. I accept it all as I straighten and wipe my mouth, and when I turn to them, I know my gaze is ice cold.

The same ice moves through my veins.

Numb.

"We need to go back to the base and search for signs of my father, gather all the research, and destroy what is left," I order. Louis watches me worriedly but nods, and then I sweep my gaze over all of them. "And we need to see to Isaac's wound."

"I'll be fine," he mutters, but he's favouring one leg, his face is shiny with sweat, and his eyes are pinched in pain.

"If we are going after my father, we need to be better than fine," I snap before I soften my voice, stopping before him. "Please, I can't lose anyone else. I can't deal with anything else right now."

He searches my gaze, those grey eyes worried, before nodding. "We've got you," he murmurs. "Are you okay?"

"Not one fucking bit, and I won't be until my father is dead." I grab my gun, throw it over my shoulder, and pick my way through the plane crash, heading back to the base.

I know they will follow.

They are worried, I sense it, but I can't put them at ease. I can't even speak anymore, not without wanting to scream. I thought . . . wondered if he was really dead, but after seeing the video and then hearing nothing from him, I thought he truly had passed, that he was buried and I was safe.

I was so fucking wrong.

My father is alive, and not only that, he orchestrated this whole thing. I am nothing but a puppet once more, my strings being pulled by him. He brought me home, ensured I met the other fucked-up kids like me, then sent me on missions to stop his partner who clearly still worked with him.

I wonder if his partner knew that was the endgame or if my father lied to him too.

Either way, I'm done playing his games.

I'm done being an experiment.

I'm going to find him, and when I do, I'm going to kill him once and for all. This time, there will be no doubt, no burial, just his rotting corpse at the end of my gun. I'll free us all, I'll keep us safe, and I'll do whatever it takes because this isn't just about me anymore.

Or about us.

This is about every single person he has experimented on. He was right, this brought us together, but he should have realised then that he fucked up because we won't rest until he's stopped. The very same super soldiers he created will be the ones to end his life, and there is nothing he can do to stop that.

It's a quick journey through the forest, as the plane didn't go too far, and with our enhanced speed and strength, we are back in a few hours. The sky is starting to lighten as we approach the base.

"Nico, Jonas, Dimitri, sweep the whole area and look for any soldiers who have not fled or been killed yet. We want no surprises. Nova and I will help Isaac," Louis orders.

I let him take charge because I wouldn't know what to say right now.

I'm not reliable.

My anger conflicts with my disbelief.

My idealistic future, the happiness I had felt was just on the horizon, was ripped from me. I should have known it would happen. People like us don't get happily ever afters, and to think that just makes us pretty little liars.

Pain is a constant, Novaleen. It is how a person deals with it that interests me. Some conquer it and wield it, while others crumble and fall.

So tell me, daughter, when I make this hurt, and I will, are you going to conquer or fall?

His voice in my head makes me gnash my tongue until I taste blood as old memories and wounds resurface—ones I thought long since buried.

He's right, though, pain is constant, but I will conquer it. I will never fall, not with so much on the line.

The pain he instilled in me will be wielded as the blade for his death—he can bet on that. He wanted to watch his experiments in action and see what we are capable of? He's about to, and he has no idea what I am truly willing to do to finally stop the man who started all this.

I will end this with one of us in the grave.

I don't enter the labs. Instead, I sit just beyond, watching Isaac instruct Louis on how to help him. They check the wound for bullet fragments before stapling it closed and dressing it. He also takes some antibiotics and pain relief. I admit he looks better, but we leave him to rest a little. Louis comes out to stand near me, drying his hands, as I watch the stairs, protecting their backs.

His bright blond hair is tinted with blood and ash, and it's streaked down his face as well, but those bright eyes are sharp and locked on me.

Tossing the towel away, he crouches before me, places his hands on my knees, and says nothing. I am unable to meet his all-seeing, bright-green eyes for too long, so I glance away, scared of what he will see.

"Nova," he says, our unit leader demanding attention.

I can't give it to him.

"Baby," he pleads, changing it up. The worry I hear in his voice has me looking at him.

I feel my lip tremble before I bite it, refusing to fucking cry. I won't be so goddamn weak. "He's alive," I whisper.

"I know, and he won't be for long," he vows. "I will fucking kill him for what he did to you and my brothers. I'll bring you his fucking heart on a goddamn platter if it will stop this." I must look confused because he slides his hands up my body to cup my face. "This vagueness, this nothingness, you pulling away from us to protect yourself and drive off the hurt—guess what, Nova? It hurts, so fucking let it. Do not shut everyone out just because you're scared."

"I'm not scared." I get to my feet, pacing away.

"You are. We all are." That makes me stop as I turn to look at him. "You don't think I still have nightmares about him? I see his face every single day of my fucking life. I wear his cruel intentions on my skin as scars, and my heart is heavy with dread and the idea that he could hurt those I love again."

"I failed," I admit, finally acknowledging what is wrong.

I was so sure I was right and that it would end, but now I've failed them, Annie, and the soldiers.

The whole fucking world.

"You didn't fail, Nova," he begins, but I shake my head. "You didn't. I did!" he yells, and when I turn to face him, his eyes are brimming with tears. The sight shocks me into silence. I've never seen Louis cry, nor did I think I ever would.

His hands are fisted and his chest heaves as he watches me.

"I failed," he repeats.

I step closer, and he reacts as though he doesn't believe he deserves comfort. Wasn't I thinking the exact same thing when I pushed him away?

"Louis," I start.

"I failed them, Nova. Don't you see?" he rants. "When Bas died, I couldn't protect D, and he withdrew, not feeling anything. He was like a machine, and I couldn't stop that. You did! You brought him back! I couldn't stop Jonas from descending into madness, but you did. I couldn't stop Nico from blaming and hating himself, cutting himself up every day, but you did. I couldn't get Isaac to look after himself and let the guilt go, but you did. I couldn't figure out what I was doing wrong, and yet, you did."

Ignoring his retracting steps, I pull him to me as tears drip down his handsome, heartbreaking face.

"And you couldn't begin to look in the mirror and maybe see that it's not all on you to save them? That you can't protect them from everything? You were so focused on saving them, you were losing yourself." I grip his face. "I see it, Louis, and I refuse to lose you, so I'll fucking fight for you, for them, but don't you ever lessen what you did for them. You've looked after them. They are alive and a family because of you. Neither of us has failed, nor are we to blame, and together, we will do this. You're right, I was withdrawing, but I won't. I won't hurt you like that. I'll endure the pain for you, for them, because I love you."

He gulps, his Adam's apple bobbing.

"What if I don't deserve your love?" he murmurs.

"You do, and the fact that you even ask that proves you do," I retort, gripping his face harder. "You deserve to be loved and so much more. We all deserve to be happy, but we know we have some things to do before then and we will. When we survive, which we will, we'll do it together. It isn't all on you, Louis. We follow you because of our trust in you, but that doesn't mean it all weighs on your shoulders. Let us help. Let your family share the burden."

I feel them before I see them, and Nico, Jonas, and D silently press to Louis's back as we hold him.

"Let us help you, my love," I murmur as Isaac stumbles in, probably waking from our shouts, and wraps his arms around us.

All of us stand together, holding Louis as he sobs.

I don't know what flipped in me. Maybe it was seeing such a strong man break before me, believing it was all his fault and all on his shoulders, but now I am confident and strong once more.

I refuse to lose him or anyone else.

"She's right. We let you take on too much, but it's not on you, Louis. This is a burden we share," Nico murmurs. "You are not in charge of saving us. You never were."

"He's right," Jonas says seriously. "No one blames you for anything. We owe you our lives. You brought us together."

"You made us a family," D murmurs. "And what Bas did is not your fault. It's not anyone's. No one could have saved him, Louis. No one."

"We will always have each other," Isaac adds.

"And we will never lose another," I promise as I kiss away his tears. "We will protect this research, we will destroy my father and the legacy he built, and we will do it together. Wherever this road takes us, I know that for certain."

He nods, blowing out a breath. "I guess I take on too much."

"You think?" I snort, making him crack a grin.

"Want me to suck your dick to make it better?" Jonas asks, making us all laugh.

"Hey, you never offered to suck mine." Dimitri grins, making Louis's grin grow, which is why they are doing it.

"I was trying to make him feel better! I'm not good at lovey-dovey shit, but fine!" Jonas drops to his knees, pushes his hair back, and smacks his lips, making D laugh as he shoves him away.

"Give me the dick!" Jonas yells, crawling after D, who runs away laughing.

"Boys," Louis and I say at the same time, and we share a secret grin. "Go get packed up," Louis finishes.

"Nico, you help them. Isaac, go back and rest."

"Yes, sir!" Jonas leaps to his feet, dragging D with him. "I will if you want me to, though I think Nova is better at it."

Nico sighs and gives us a look as if to say, *I'm stuck with these idiots?* before he lumbers off after them. Isaac squeezes us both before moving stiffly back to the bed to lie down until we are ready to leave.

"He's right. It might cheer you up. Want me to suck your dick?" I grin.

Louis rolls his eyes as he drags me closer, kissing me softly. "Later, baby. For now, let's get our family out of here." Nodding, I help him start to pack up.

The more I find, the darker my mood gets.

All joy disappears as I remember what happened to us and what will continue to happen.

Louis begged me to not shut down, so I don't, and I feel every hard, sharp edge, even as it cuts me to ribbons on the inside.

I endure it for them—for him.

When we are done and all loaded with bags, Jonas sets explosives on the compound to destroy everything else, meaning my father can't come back here and no one else can find this.

As we leave the base, there's an explosion on the horizon. Turning my head, I see the plume of smoke coming from the direction of the plane, and I watch it wind throughout the trees and into the sky, knowing it's burning the evidence of what transpired.

Of us, of my father, of it all.

I want someone to find it, but it would only make them hunt us. I know it's for the best. Turning away, I meet the shadowed eyes of my men and know they feel the same. They are anxious for what's to come, even though they are determined and ready to do whatever it takes.

"Let's go," I murmur, glancing back at the smoke once more. "We'll get this research back and then we'll hunt. We'll hunt him to the ends of this fucking earth, and we'll stop him."

"Too fucking right." Jonas grins, his expression wicked and filled with anger.

"I'm with you," Isaac offers solemnly, but I see hints of anger in his gaze directed at the man on the phone—my father.

"We all are," Dimitri responds.

"We will do whatever it takes. We are the only ones who can stop this, and we will," Nico adds with a glance at me.

"Let's end this," Louis agrees.

After all, they have their own pasts with my father, their hatred matching my own.

Hiking back to our trucks, I hold onto the hatred, letting the anger in my heart warm me and keep me moving so we can stay alive.

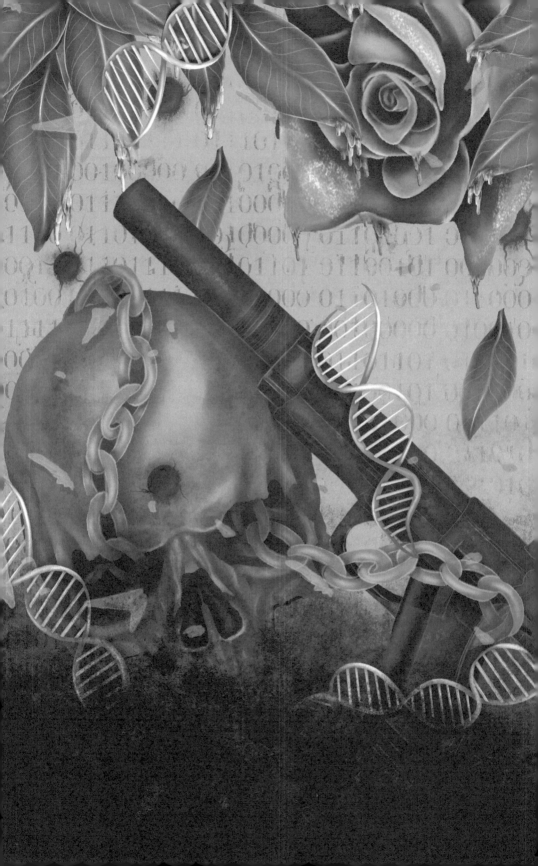

TWO

NOVA

Even the plane ride home is quiet, all of us lost in our own thoughts —or exhaustion from the marathon we have been on over the last few weeks.

"Where to?" Louis asks, seeming as lost as all of us, and when I speak, my voice is hoarse from not using it.

"We go home to my sister. We regroup, lick our wounds, and seal his research away. Then, we kill him."

Louis nods, but I sense his worry. I ignore it as I head to the shower. My head hangs as I wash the blood and death away, only it ends with me sobbing on my knees.

I thought it was over.

I thought we were safe.

I was wrong and all along, I was so sure.

It was just another test, another experiment.

I willingly walked into his lab, but this time, I'm not a child.

That's how Jonas finds me. Water sprays down on me as I cry, my arms locked around my knees as my bruised body shakes with my sobs. I lift my head and meet his forlorn eyes.

He slowly steps into the room and shuts the door, holding his hands out like I'm a spooked animal. I have to bite back my cry as he crouches before me. "I've got you," is all he says. Reaching up, he switches off the shower and lifts me out, holding me tight as he dries me off and dresses me. All the while, I cry silently, leaning into his strength.

With a soft kiss on my forehead, he carries me to the bed, where he lays me down and carefully covers me with the duvet before curling around me. "I've got you," he repeats, and I know he does.

The door opens, but I don't even lift my head, knowing they are all there. Jonas must silently communicate and I let him, choosing to close my swollen, raw eyes as they join us, sprawling around me. All of us touch each other, needing the comfort for what is to come, remembering what the man we now hunt is capable of.

What he did to us.

What he has continued to do.

"I fell for it," I croak sometime later, the hum of the plane's engine almost swallowing my words. "He did it to bring me out of hiding, and I fell for it."

"We all did," Dimitri murmurs.

I sniff. "I hate him."

"I know. We will find him, Nova. I promise that. We will end this. He will not get you. Not ever," Nico states firmly, his hand squeezing my ankle.

Why does some part of me feel like he already has and he's already won?

Ana and Bert stand at the front door as we pull up, and I'm out of the car before it stops moving. She's nervous but smiling. However, when she takes a look at my face, it falls away.

"Nova, are you okay? What happened?" she demands.

Stopping before them both, I search them for wounds. "He's alive."

"Who is?" she asks, sounding confused.

"Dad," I mutter. "Dad is alive."

"Nova, we buried him," she scoffs.

"I spoke to him." That falls into the silence like a lead weight as I hear the car doors slamming behind me. "He was behind this all along. It was to bring me back, to bring us back, and to experiment on us once more. We fell for it. He's alive, Ana."

She's pale, and I spare Bert a sad look before I focus back on her.

"And I'm going to stop him. I'm going to kill him for good this time." Unable to watch the twisting emotions crossing her face, I move around her and head inside.

I never thought this place would feel like home, but as I step into the foyer, I'm almost glad to be back.

Despite the horrors and the bad memories here, I have good ones too—of Annie, Bert, and my guys—and I need that. I will need all the strength I can muster for what is to come.

Heading straight to the kitchen, I grab a bottle and pour myself a healthy helping of whisky, grimacing at the taste as it goes down.

"I'll make some tea," Bert murmurs as he joins me.

I just nod jerkily until his hand lands on my shoulder, making my eyes close as the alcohol burns down my throat.

"I am sorry, Miss Nova, but you are not alone."

"Thank you," I murmur as I turn, watching him move around to make some food and tea. Annie comes in and sits heavily at the table, staring at it. Dragging the bottle over, I pour her a glass and push it to her. Without sparing me a look, she tosses it back.

She groans at the taste before meeting my eyes. "Part of me is angry, disgusted, and sad, but part of me is glad, Nova." She searches my gaze as I flinch. "I'm so sorry."

Reaching over, I take her hand. "You are allowed to be happy your father is alive, Ana."

"But how can I be after what he has done?" she sobs.

"Because he is still your father, and you can't shut off love just like that."

"You did," she whispers.

"No, he beat it out of me through years of pain. There is nothing but anger for him in my heart, anger and hatred, but you need to know, Ana, that I can't—won't save him. He has to die, even if that means you'll hate me."

"I know," she says, taking my hand and holding my gaze. "You have to
stop him, Nova. You have to."

And so we sit, with a shared bottle of whisky between two sisters who
don't drink.

One who just wants to heal the world, and the other who only ever
wanted it to leave her alone.

THREE

NOVA

"**S**am, this is my sister, Nova."

"The one who helped save me." He slides to his feet with a wince, and Ana moves forward, holding him up with a grunt.

"Sit down now!" she reprimands him.

"Yes, doc." He grins cheekily at her, watching her as she helps him sit and then fusses over his blankets and IV drip. The look in his eyes can only be described as soft, even as she tells him off, and for a moment, I want to turn away and let them have this moment, but he glances up at me. Some of that softness remains, but it's different. That look was for her alone.

I know because I see it in my men's eyes every single day.

After a few drinks with Ana, where we mourned what has to come, I felt the need to get moving and she needed to check on Sam, so here we are. She's obviously been taking good care of him, and there is clearly a bond between them.

"Thank you," he offers. "Did you get them?"

Sighing, I lean into the wall. "Not all of them, but we will."

"Annie told me all about your father."

"Oh, has she?" I grin as she blushes and ducks her head, the nickname seeming familiar on his lips. Despite my frustration, my turmoil, and the emotions I feel about what has happened, I'm almost giddy about the shared look they exchange.

"If I can help in any way, please let me know," he finishes sombrely.

"You need to rest, not help," Ana hisses. "Otherwise, I'll chain you to the bed."

"Kinky." He winks, making her blush brighter, and I grin as I push away from the wall.

"I just came to check on you, but it's been a long few days so I'm going to rest."

And leave them alone, but I don't say that.

He nods, but they are both lost in each other as I saunter away. The whiskey still burns my stomach, since I'm not used to drinking. We had a few more and some of Bert's tea and sandwiches before she brought me to see Sam, but now I'm exhausted.

My legs almost drag behind me as I head upstairs, unsure where my guys are but knowing they are close. They are probably checking the perimeter since we now know my father is about and could be, and probably is, watching our every move.

I should do a million things, but instead, I find myself stopping at my sister's room, needing comfort. I slide between her sheets fully clothed and close my eyes as I breathe in her scent. The familiar fragrance fills my lungs.

My heart aches, and my emotions are all over the place, but I'm so very tired.

When the bed moves, I crack open my eyes to see her. She slides in opposite me, taking my hand and holding it in the bed between us. She doesn't have to say anything, she just holds my hand as I close my eyes once more.

She's supporting me, just like when we were kids and I would sneak into her bed when she had nightmares. Only now, it's her turn to protect me from the very real nightmares I know are still to come.

"I've got you, Nova, sleep," she whispers.

And I do.

When I wake up, the room is dark and moonlight streams through the window, illuminating Ana's sleeping face. Her hand is still in mine, holding it tightly like she will never let go, and the sheets are twisted around us.

So I don't disturb her. Knowing she hasn't been getting enough rest, I slide out of bed, pad around it, and stop above her, looking down at her too young, too innocent face. Tucking the blankets around her, I brush her hair back and lean down to place a kiss on her forehead. "He won't hurt you. I promise," I murmur before slipping from the room, pressing my back to the door, and sucking in slow breaths.

At least one good thing came of all of this—we are back together and a family once more, even if it is dysfunctional and healing. Pushing from the door, I use the bathroom before heading downstairs in search of everyone.

I expect them to be asleep, but I should have known better.

They are in the dining room with the research spread out around them, organised into piles. Louis is on the phone arguing with someone, and D is on his laptop.

"What's happening?" I murmur as Bert comes in with a tray of mugs, which looks like it's not the first time. He smiles when he sees me and hands me a coffee. Taking it, I warm my hands as I meet their gazes.

"We are finding your father and any kids or soldiers who may still be alive," Nico replies as if it's simple, and maybe it is. I told them we needed to, so now they are.

"But you need to sleep—"

"And you need answers and for this to end," Jonas retorts as he accepts a mug. Bert leans in and lays a gentle kiss on Jonas's head like a father would before sneaking him a plate of pancakes that puts a wide, childlike smile on his face.

"You did this for me?" I murmur.

"We are a team, a family. It's what we do," Isaac says as he pulls out a chair for me. I sit with my mug, and he hands me a folder. "Here, look for anything helpful. It's not easy reading, so if you need a break, we understand."

Looking around the table, I can't help but tear up. "I love you all."

"We know." D winks, glancing up from the laptop.

Louis hangs up and comes to me, leaning down and kissing my forehead. "We love you too, now get to work," he teases.

"Yes, sir." I grin, opening the folder and diving in.

Hours later, my head hurts and all of my good feelings have disappeared into nothing but anger and hatred. Shoving my black hair into a bun, I lean back to stretch, ignoring the looks I feel thrown at me.

I know they are worried about how I am taking all of this. After all, I thought we were so close to stopping all of this and finally destroying everything my father built, only to be right back at the beginning. It's hard not to feel dejected and angry, but I try to hide it from them, even as I plunge myself inside those feelings, knowing I will need to survive what's to come.

After all, what I told Annie is true: I will have to kill my father.

Despite everything he has done, there is a price for taking a life, and it will be steep, but I will gladly pay it to protect children and soldiers and to stop the abominations he calls experiments.

"Here, Miss Nova." Bert places a plate next to me. "You must eat."

I lift my head, and he frowns at whatever he sees there. "Please," he adds, his face contorted in worry. "I will go check on Mr. Sam to make sure he is okay so Ana may sleep."

"Has she not been?" I find myself asking.

He grins. "Like you, she is unable to rest when there is a job to be done, but you cannot do that job when you're exhausted, hungry, and weak, so eat." He infuses his tone with a command, the same one he used on me as a child, and I smile but turn back to the folder, feeling too sick to eat.

What they did to this man . . .

It's a crime against humanity.

Acts of pure evil disguised by the word "science."

I always knew my father was evil and that what he did was wrong, but I never really understood the extent of his reach and ability to hurt others to get what he wanted.

"Nova, eat," Nico snaps.

"I can't," I retort, glaring at him as he leans into me, ready to fight, his nostrils flaring.

I know it's only because he cares, but that dark part of me lights up at the prospect of releasing some of these emotions through a fight. Suddenly, Louis stands and rounds the table, kicking my chair back.

"Come on," he demands. "Nico, you too."

Expecting us to follow, he heads outside, and with nothing else to do, we file out after him. He turns to us, rolling back his sleeves as he watches me, and then gestures to the grass. "Well then, if you want to spar, then go ahead. If you want to fight us and take it out on us, then go ahead."

"I don't know what you mean," I mutter in shame.

"Nico, you're in," Louis orders, keeping his eyes on me. "Yes, you do. You need to fight. Nico does as well, so you are not the only one. Reading all that is not easy, and it leaves you feeling frustrated and useless, so get it all out, and then we will get back in there and you will eat." He grabs my chin. "Even if I have to force-feed you, you will fucking eat, baby, and then we will figure this out. You are not alone, Nova. You will never be alone, so stop acting like it. We are in this together, my love. You will remember that or we will remind you every single day we are alive."

Swallowing, I search his gaze. He lets me, shielding nothing and letting me see his own anger, frustration, and horror at what has been done.

"We've got you, baby. We've got you. If you need us to hold you while you cry, if you need us to burn the world at your side, or you just simply need this to help you work through your emotions, then we will. We will do anything because we are a family. We don't just get the happy emotions, but the bitter ones too. Nothing is ever too much for us, so stop shielding us and pushing us out. We want it. We want every brutal, raw edge. We can take it."

"What if I can't? What if I can't take it? What if I'm not strong enough?" I admit.

"Then we will be strong for you," he promises, stroking my cheek. "But, Nova, you are the strongest person I have ever met. Strength isn't measured by how tall you stand, but by how beautifully you break and get back up, and you, Nova, have been broken so many times, only to put yourself back together and keep going. You still believe in good, in love, in hope, and right and wrong despite the world never doing anything for you. Despite only seeing evil, you fight for good. We all do. We are all this world has."

"Then it's fucked," I joke, "because I'm not a hero, Louis. I never was. I'm just a scarred, angry woman trying to get back at her father."

"Maybe you started as that, but now you are so much more," he counters, angry at me tearing myself down. "Now you are one of us. You saved that man in there. You saved every single one of us. You walked into gunfire with our family to stop the experiments no one else cares about. You are magnificent, Nova, and not in the way your father always wanted you to be, but in the way that makes me love you more. You are real. You're flawed, emotional, and stubborn as hell but so fucking strong, I feel awe just being around you. No matter what is thrown at you, you never stop fighting, and that, Nova? That is what he can never take away from us or understand in all of his experiments. He wants to better humanity, but he didn't realise that by torturing you, by destroying you and letting you be reborn in the flames, he had already achieved that. You, Nova, are the best person I've ever and will ever meet. Now get your sexy ass on that grass and fight it out with Nico so we can get back to work, because like it or not, you're the only fucking hero this world fucking has, and we have to stop this. Together."

"Come on, beautiful, show me what you've got," Nico taunts, and I turn to see him shirtless and waiting. I know he needs this as much as I do. Both of us are angry at the situation we have found ourselves in once more, feeling dejected and let down, and we need an outlet. This is it for us, a healthy way of expressing it, and Louis is right. They can handle it. Nico can handle it. I need to stop testing them and pushing them away because I expect them to leave. It's easier for me to create distance so it doesn't hurt as badly.

But I'm beginning to realise that pain is the whole reason we live.

We hurt and love and do it all over again. Otherwise, why are we fighting so hard every day to make the most of the life we have? Love doesn't have to be grand and beautiful; it can be this, a man willing to fight for you, willing to show up every day and put in the work.

Life isn't perfect—fuck knows I know that better than anyone—and it hurts you over and over, but I truly believe it never throws more at you than you are willing to endure, and you'll find a shred of happiness in the chaos. You just have to be strong enough, brave enough, to hold on tight and fight for it.

Even if it hurts like hell to do so.

Even if in the end, you are giving them the power to hurt you back.

Trust, I'm finally understanding, is the scariest thing of all.

It's so easy to break but so hard to earn.

I have theirs, though, and they have mine, and if I let them . . .

I think they just might save me from myself.

"Come on, Nova," Nico teases.

Rolling my eyes, I step onto the grass and face him. He doesn't wait—there's no clean sweep here. No, he comes at me, swinging his fists. I duck his first hit and sweep my leg out, which he jumps over, and then there is no more thinking.

Louis is right. I let out all the emotions taking me away from them, and I use them to make my movements faster and hits harder, and Nico takes it all. His eyes are bright with glee as we spar, moving around the grass. We are evenly matched because what he has in bulk and weight, I make up for in speed and attitude.

I manage to connect a hit, and he stumbles back.

There are cheers, and when I look up, I realise everyone is gathered outside, even Annie with Sam leaning on her shoulder. "Kick his ass, Nova!" he calls, making me chuckle, but the distraction is all Nico needs.

He holds nothing back, hitting me like a freight train and knocking my breath clear out. I feel a rib crack as I slam to the ground. Grinning down at me, he blows me a kiss. "You getting slow, baby?"

"Nah, you're just getting bigger," I tease as I throw my legs up and flip back to my feet, circling him.

"You'd know." He winks, making me burst out laughing even as I fling myself at him.

The movements come easily to me as I fall into old practice routines, but Nico is just as good as I. I'm definitely more martial arts focused, whereas he fights dirty, but it works. We both take hits that would make the others fall and we keep going after each other, knowing we can take it. We exhaust our bodies and minds until we both start to slow.

I see an opening when his left hand drops. Slipping under his guard, I sucker punch him and sweep my other leg out, knocking him back on his ass, but just as quickly, he kicks my legs out and I fall beside him.

Panting, sweaty, and grinning, I turn my head and meet his eyes. "Better?" he whispers.

"Yeah, you?" I ask as he reaches over and takes my hand.

"Much." He squeezes as I hear footsteps approaching and look up to find Louis clapping.

Crouching over me, Louis pushes my hair back. "We are not your enemy, Nova. We love you, and we can take everything you throw at us. You can always work out those emotions with us without worrying. We feel it too."

He holds out his hand, giving me a choice to keep fighting alone or to let go and be with them.

I take his hand and let him pull me up, choosing to let him save me.

FOUR

NOVA

I'm able to eat, as if all my emotions have settled, and Louis kisses my head as he passes to take my now empty plate away. "Good girl," he coos, making my thighs clench as heat builds in my core. He knows exactly what he's doing.

Jonas grins at me, flipping a knife in his hand as he reads. D is lost in his computer, Isaac is helping Ana with Sam, and Nico is showering. I could rest, but I don't want to. We need to find something, anything, that links my father to this.

Louis has to debrief with command for a few hours, so I spend that time searching the notes and experiments, looking for his handiwork.

"Jonas," I murmur as I read one experiment. "Does this seem familiar to you?" I hand the file over, certain I experienced the exact same experiment, but it's more than that. The writing looks familiar, but I don't remember why. It's not Father's, that's for sure.

He takes the folder and scans it before I see him shut down. "The man who wrote this is dead. Move on."

"Really? I recognise it—"

"He's dead!" he roars, his eyes wild, and my head jerks back automatically as I prepare for an attack.

D looks up. I nod to let him know I have this and stand carefully, like I would with a wild animal. I round the table with my hands out, ignoring my adrenaline to focus on him. His chest is heaving, and his eyes dart everywhere.

He's been triggered. I know the signs.

Crouching to make myself smaller, I keep my hands to myself and just let him see it's me. "Jonas, it's okay, babe. It is just me. It's just your Nova."

"He's dead," he repeats. "Dead. Dead."

"Okay, this file is dated a while ago," I say, and he nods jerkily.

"Dead, he's dead," he repeats.

I share a worried look with D as Louis comes into the room. D urges me to carry on, so gently I lay my hand on his thigh. He jerks and grabs me, slamming me to the table with his hand on my throat.

It happens in a split second, but I ignore my instincts and relax into his hold.

I hold up my other hand to the others who want to break us apart, stopping them. Jonas is attacking but not killing, and he doesn't see me. I need to make him see me before they hurt him.

"Baby, come back to me," I purr, feeling his hand tighten on my throat as mine drifts up his chest to his face. He shakes his head, but I hold on tight, digging my nails in. "It's me. It's your Nova."

"No," he whispers raggedly.

Leaning up, I lay kisses along every edge of his face I can reach. "It's me," I promise. "Come back to me."

His hand slowly loosens as he blinks, and I see realisation dawn in his eyes. I don't let him pull away in shock or fear, instead wrapping my legs around his waist and holding on as I continue to kiss him. "If you wanted to choke me, all you had to do was ask." I grin, teasing him.

He smiles shakily as he lifts me and sits heavily. Curling up on his lap, I stroke his chest and hair and whisper teasing comments to him as he works through this. The others relax slightly and at my nod, they drift out of the room to give us some space.

"Sorry, so sorry, baby," he mutters, burying his head in my neck. "I'm usually okay and better prepared for the triggers, but the writing took me off guard."

"It's okay," I murmur. "I understand, you know that. You could never hurt me, not really."

"I could though. I could kill you." He shivers, clutching me tighter.

"We would never let that happen. Trust me, Jonas," I murmur, lifting his head so I can meet his eyes. I hesitate. I don't want to push this, but he needs to talk about it. I need to know what to avoid so I don't trigger him again. "What happened? You said they are dead."

I see the vulnerability in his eyes. Whoever this person is, it's someone he fears, which is not something I ever thought I'd say about Jonas.

"I killed him. I hunted him down. The others helped, knowing I needed to. I couldn't sleep knowing he was still out there. He was my first kill. I was seventeen."

"You killed him because he deserved it." I have no doubts. "He's dead. He can't hurt you."

"But he did so badly, Nova. He was my tormentor. When they left me to go insane, it was on his orders. Your father left him in charge of me. He was not a good man. He was not in it for science or experiments, but because he liked to hurt people. He was cruel, Nova, and he broke me. I still barely cling onto my sanity. Sometimes, I wake up thinking I'm back in the cage like the animal he called me."

"But you aren't, you are here with me, and they can't have you ever again. Do you understand?" I demand.

"He watched me, beat me, tortured me, left me alone in a pitch-black room for days, and shocked my brain over and over. Nova, what if he truly did ruin me?"

"Then he ruined me too," I snarl. "You, Jonas, are not ruined. You are fucking perfect, and I love you. You believe that, right?"

He nods sadly.

"Good, and I don't love someone who doesn't deserve it. Fuck what they did, fuck them, fuck them all. I'll kill every single one if it will help you sleep." I lean in. "But you have to stay with me, fight with me. He's dead, Jonas, and soon they will all join him for what they did. I can't change the past and what happened, but I promise I will never let them hurt you again."

"Promise?" he whispers trustingly.

"I promise. I promise you all. I will never, ever let them hurt you." I search his gaze until he nods. "Come back to me," I plead, still sensing the distance and hating it. I lean in and kiss him. When he kisses me back, I pull away, watching him rebuild himself.

Sometimes I forget how fragile Jonas can truly be. Unlike the rest of us, something in his mind shattered from the torture, and he fights every day to not let it consume him, but sometimes it wins, and I'll be there every time to help bring him back and put it back together for him.

The writing . . .

As I hold him, I realise where I've seen it.

The same man had come here once, writing on his pad and observing my father. When my father left, he leaned into me and promised we would have some fun.

Jonas was right; he deserved to die. I only had moments with him and I saw the evil in his gaze. I'm glad Jonas got to face him in the end and take back that power, but I couldn't hate my father more than I do right now as I hold the man I love.

The others slowly trickle back into the room, and I spend the rest of the day on Jonas's lap, teasing him and making him laugh until he's somewhat back to normal.

I feel the others' worry for him, for us, for me.

For what is to come.

I feel it, too, like we are on a precipice and none of us know what is coming next.

It won't be good, so we hold onto the moments we have in hopes that it will be enough to get us through.

"Nova, I don't care if you're getting freaky, get dressed! We are having a family meal!" my sister yells up the stairs.

I, in fact, was getting freaky, or about to, with Jonas pinned under me, chained to my bed.

He snarls, "Ignore her."

"Now!" she yells.

"She will just keep yelling." I grin.

"Then we can be quick," he says, tugging on his chains to try and get to me.

"If I come up there and see some stuff that scars me, I'm blaming you. Come on, everyone is coming. It's a family meal like we used to have."

Well, shit, the guilt trip gets me moving as I ignore Jonas's complaints. He peers down at his hard cock sadly. "Sorry, little J, maybe later."

Laughing, I throw his pants at him and quickly unchain him before I slip into my loose shorts, a tank top, and a cardigan before walking downstairs to meet my sister. "Bad timing," I mutter.

She grins at me so widely, it makes me grin back. "I don't care, come on. When was the last time we had a family dinner together?"

Taking her hand, I follow her after. "Long time," I admit.

"Yep, well, we are having one, all of us."

I let her pull me into the formal dining room, where everyone else is already seated. The table has been laid with candles and fancy china and more food than even my guys can eat. They all grin as I sit with Ana to my right, Sam next to her, and Louis to my left. Jonas comes in with a groan, rearranging himself as he glares at my sister.

"Not the right way to get us to like you," he complains as he huffs and sits down, but then he spots the meal and claps like a kid. "Yay, chicken!"

Laughing, I watch Bert bring in more plates. "That is everything. I hope you enjoy."

"Uh-uh, sit down, Bert. You are family," I order.

He freezes at the door, searching our gazes. Louis instantly moves from my side, patting the empty seat. "Come on, she's right. You're family."

Tears form in his eyes, but he blinks them away as he carefully sits next to me. Grinning, I lay a napkin in his lap and start to dig in. He scans everyone, watching them laugh and talk before a soft smile curves his lips.

"You are correct. You are my family."

Squeezing his hand, I smile up at him. "You are ours and always have been. Thank you for taking care of us."

I feel him watching me as I eat, but I let him work through his emotions, knowing he needs to. The food is delicious, and the conversations flow. Everyone is having a good time. Sam tells everyone stories of his army days.

The others chime in and all the while, he holds Ana's hand and keeps putting food on her plate.

I wink when I catch her blushing, and she flips me off, making me laugh.

It's honestly one of the best nights I've ever had. My entire family is in one place, and after taking down the amazing desserts Bert brings out, we all just lounge around the table, too full to move, and enjoy each other's company.

"Oh, I forgot. Something came for you earlier." Bert drops an expensive white envelope before me as he begins to clear the table with some of the guys' help. Frowning, I turn it over to see a red-wax seal. I rip it open, and a thick piece of cardstock drops out, clearly letting me see my father's handwriting.

Everything screeches to a halt inside of me as I stare at the note.

"Nova?" Isaac calls, noticing my silence, and everyone else turns to me.

"It's from my father," I murmur, and you could hear a pin drop at the sudden silence.

"What does it say?" Ana asks.

Swallowing, I pick it up, already feeling sick.

I don't want to read it, I really don't, but that won't solve anything. Being brave, I clear my throat and begin to read it out loud.

Dearest daughter,

For all of my wrongdoings, I have done something right. You. I watched you become the very thing I was aiming for, and now it's time to come home to me—where you belong, where you will only ever belong. Only I can understand you. The others are just holding you back. Think of all the things we can do, Novaleen. Ana was my control group and she has failed me. I no longer need her or the others.

Only you.

So come to me before it is too late.

Yours,

Father

Looking up, I see Ana wrapped tightly in Sam's arms like he can protect her from his words. Louis is already on his feet, and the others are coming towards me.

"It's a threat, a promise," I whisper, looking around. "If I don't go to him, he'll hurt you all."

"He won't be able to," Louis snaps. "You are not going to him."

"Maybe I should?" I suggest. "But not in the way he wants. We will all go to him to kill him."

"Did he say where?"

I shake my head and Louis sighs.

"Then it's moot at the moment. He thinks you can figure it out, though, so think hard, Nova. Meanwhile, I want patrols. Two of us need to be awake at all times, and no one is to go outside of the grounds alone. We watch each other's backs, stay close, and ride this out until we figure out our next move."

I nod, but my eyes go back to the note.

Before it's too late . . .

What is he planning to do?

FIVE

NOVA

My father's letter hangs over my head the entire day. I barely slept the night before, debating his meaning and trying to figure out where he is, but it's no use. Clearly, he thinks I can, but I'm drawing blanks.

Not only that, but he ruined the family meal we were having, the atmosphere becoming tense afterwards. All that laughter disappeared into stone-cold determination. We put the house on lockdown, and now we are taking turns to sleep and patrol.

I feel responsible. He wants me, while the others are merely in his way. I know how he thinks. He will hurt them to get to me, so I need to figure out his riddle before that happens, but my mind is blank, hence me beating up the punching bag.

I've been down here for a few hours, beating the shit out of this bag and taking my frustration out on it.

I did my patrols this morning, and after lunch, I came down here, and here is where I will stay until I can figure it out.

Sweat pours from me, my black plaited hair slapping my shoulders with my movements. I watch the others come and go, checking on me, before Nico stops the bag and jerks his head. Without a word, he takes a fighting stance, and we spar. There is no laughter, teasing, or flirting.

We don't hold back, trying to hurt each other. Both of us are annoyed, frustrated, and feeling useless, so we take it out on each other until he pins me with my leg thrown over his arm, his other arm banded across my throat as his lips tilt up in victory.

His dark eyes shine with triumph before desire sparks in his gaze, something neither of us will act on while so much hangs over our heads. "Better?" he asks as he releases my leg.

"Not really," I admit, closing my eyes as my head hits the mat. "I can't find him, Nico."

There's a sharp inhale. "Nova—"

"No, don't comfort me. I'm failing. He basically fucking spelled out his location and I can't find him! I can't even save my own fucking family or protect you."

"Shut the fuck up." His hand covers my mouth as my eyes snap open, filled with fury, and meet his own angry ones. "This is not just down to you. Even if you knew where he was, we wouldn't let you go. It's not on you to save the world, Nova. When will you realise that? Think it through. Your father loves to play games, and this is just another one. We were playing along unknowingly, and enough is enough. We don't play anymore. We break his fucking rules and play by our own."

"How?" I murmur against his palm.

"We change it up and do the unexpected. He wants us to find him and expects us to react to the threat, so instead, we'll lie low. We'll wait and watch, and when it's time, we'll kill the bastard. Stop putting the world on your shoulders and locking yourself down here. It's not good."

"It helps," I mutter.

Sitting up, he holds out his hand. "I know, but we worry." He smiles. "Plus, I'm sick of dealing with Jonas. It's your turn."

Laughing, I let him haul me up, and together, we go back upstairs. I have a new pep in my step. He's right. All this time, we were playing my father's game without even realising it, and I refuse to walk into another one. Instead, I'm going to play my own game.

He wants a perfect soldier? He'll get one.

It will be the last thing he sees.

Days pass the same way, filled with patrols and silence as we work hard to figure out the riddle. We are all determined to work through this. I try not to take it all on my shoulders like Nico said, but with each day that passes, the darkness inside of me grows.

I become restless from the sense of impending doom we all feel, and even Ana is affected.

She's been working around the clock, going through his notes with D and Louis. Nico, Jonas, Isaac, and I take most of the patrols, knowing they need as much time as possible to come up with answers. No more letters arrive, but the first sits proudly on the table.

It's a mocking reminder.

I'm lounging in my bedroom, debating what I could do to pass the time before I'm on patrol, when there's a knock at the door. It opens before I answer, and Jonas ducks inside, laughing to himself. I smile, knowing whatever he's up to will be trouble. Tilting my head, I watch him as he turns, and then my eyes drop to the object tied around his waist.

"Where the hell did you get a strap-on?" I demand as Jonas models it for me.

"Unimportant." He smirks. "The question is, do you want to play?" He wiggles his eyebrows as I continue to stare at him, a slow smirk curling my lips.

Getting to my knees on the bed, I crook my finger, and he walks up to me. "You want me to fuck you, Jonas?" I purr, dragging my hand up his chest and gripping his neck. His eyes flare, and his lips part in hunger as I tighten my grip. "Is that right, baby? You want me to shove this massive cock up your ass and fuck you with it?"

"Baby, I want you every way I can get you." He groans. "Ride me, use me, fuck me, claim me, do whatever the hell you want. I'm yours."

"Is that right?" I purr, leaning up until my face is level with his. "How about we test that out, shall we?" Dragging my lips along his, I bite the bottom one before falling back with my arms and legs spread. "First things first, we need that cock nice and wet, don't we, baby?"

33

The smile he gives me is wicked. "That we do, so be a good girl and come all over it for me. I want your cream in my ass while you fuck me."

"Make me," I taunt, tilting my chin up.

With a flick of his wrist, he produces a huge knife and advances on me. He presses one knee to the bed and with his eyes on me, he cuts through the thin material of the biker shorts I wear. I don't flinch, not once, and the heat in his eyes only grows. As he drags the sharp edge of the blade across my exposed stomach, I quiver under his lethal touch. My eyes drop to track the movements as it wiggles under the edge of my sports bra.

"I love it when you look at me like that, all needy and demanding." He groans. "I love it even more when you're all marked up for me." With a quick twist, he cuts my bra away, and it flutters to either side of me, freeing my breasts. Groaning, I arch my back, offering them to him.

My frustration turns into desire. It's what he wanted, and what we both need to keep us occupied.

The hard edge of the metal slaps one of my nipples, making my eyes close as I cry out. Desire surges through me as he teases my nipple into a stiff peak with the cold edge of the blade, only to do the same to the other.

"So pretty, so needy, you love this, don't you, baby? You love the threat. You love that you never know what I will do next."

"Yes." I groan, arching higher, begging wordlessly. My thighs clench together and rub for friction.

One of his hands delves between them and rips them open as he drops between my splayed thighs, the cool rubber of the cock pressing against my overheated, wet pussy. He lays it against me as he toys with me, the sharp edge of the knife circling my nipple.

His hips move slowly, nudging the strap-on across my pussy until the blunt edge hits my clit with each shallow thrust. Pleasure builds within me as my eyes snap open and meet his wild gaze.

Glancing down, I see the pink marks across my breasts from the knife, and I can't help but moan and reach for him, but he slaps my hands aside. "I'm playing, behave," he snarls, "or I'll turn you over and slam this cock into your ass instead."

Huffing, I drop my hands and roll my hips to grind against the fake cock, the rubber warming with my body until we find a quick rhythm. I hump it as he plays with my breasts, tweaking my nipples until they are sore and achy from the attention, but he still doesn't stop.

"Nova, baby, you're so goddamn beautiful. I love you like this, begging for me to make you come. You are all soft curves, hard edges, power, and muscle, and yet you are so pliant for me, wet and wanting. You're such a good girl when you want to come." He groans, moving faster as he winds me higher and higher.

"I fucking love you. I knew it the moment I saw you, but I fall harder each and every day. Our life is going to be like this, baby, with me coming to you with toys and you dripping to play with them. Fuck everyone else. Fuck normal. This is us, baby, and I'm loving it, so be a good girl and come for me so you can bend me over and I can feel you fuck me."

I writhe below him, jerking with my pleasure, and it causes the blade to slip. The quick slice across the top of my breast makes me scream as my release slams through me, leaving me gushing over the rubber cock. Jonas snarls, and while I'm still fighting the aftershocks, he shoves my thighs open farther and thrusts the fake cock inside me.

My hands scramble at the bed, gripping it as I try to move away, but his arms pin me in place as he starts to move, fucking me with the toy. I tilt my hips until it hits that spot inside of me that has me crying out wordlessly.

"Fuck, baby, look at you, taking these ten inches so well. You're getting it nice and wet for me. Goddamn, you're so beautiful. You love this, don't you? Love me fucking you with this dildo. Love coming all over it for me, knowing you're going to use it on me."

"Jonas," I purr, reaching up to grip his shoulders. Tearing at his shirt, I pull him down and slam our mouths together. He kisses me hard and wild, our tongues tangling. It's sloppy and delicious as he works between my thighs faster, deeper, and harder, making me lift my hips rapidly to keep up. The wet slap of our bodies is loud as he takes me, and the bed creaks with the force as he rips his mouth away. His lips are puffy and red from my attention, and his eyes are crazed as he slaps the knife across my heaving breasts. Groaning at the sight, he does it again and again. The sharp sting fades into a pleasurable burn, almost sending me over the edge once more.

It's only when I lift my leg and wrap it around his hips to take the strap-on deeper that he shows me he was only playing. His thrusts turn brutal, almost pushing me from the bed with the force. He snarls above me as he rains hits down on my breasts until it hurts too much and feels too good.

I scream his name as a release rolls through me, taking my senses with it until all I feel is pleasure.

When I come down from the high, I'm twitching and moaning beneath him. Leaning down, he laves my sore tits with his tongue before slowly pulling that huge fake cock from my body. Groaning at the almost painful feel, I lift up on shaky arms to see it dripping with my cum.

He slides his fist down it then drags it along my messy pussy with a moan. "Fuck, baby, you come so prettily for me."

"I love you too," I rasp as I push myself up, forcing my muscles into action even as my legs spasm from how hard I came. I tug him back down and kiss him as I roll my hips, sliding my pussy over the length to get it nice and wet. When I pull back, he's panting harder. "Now be a good boy and get on all fours for me. You wanted my cock, and now you'll get it. No safe words, no backing out. You'll take it and love it until you come so hard, they all come up here thinking I'm killing you."

"You better." He reaches behind himself and something clicks before the strap-on falls off, then he stands. With his eyes on me, he reaches back and rips his shirt off, exposing his exquisite chest. "Keep looking at me like that, baby, and I'll come before you're even inside me."

"We don't want that, do we? Pants too," I order.

He shoves his shorts down, his huge, hard cock springing free. Biting at his lip, he fists his length and strokes himself as he watches me.

Climbing onto shaky feet, I smack his hand away. "Uh-uh, the only way you get to come is with my cock in your ass, darling. Get on all fours now or I'll make you suck it instead."

He quickly drops to all fours, his perfect peachy ass pointed towards the door. Smirking, I quickly strap the cock on, liking how it feels. Moving towards him, I drop to my knees on the hardwood floor, ignoring the sting as I part his cheeks and rub the dripping head across his ass.

He jerks forward, so I grip a hip and pull him back. "Now I get what you mean. I love seeing you like this, begging for it and so easy to control. You want this cock inside you, babe?"

"Yes." He groans, his head falling to the floor as he pushes back. "Please fuck me, Nova."

"I didn't hear that," I tell him, dragging the cock across his ass as I reach down and palm his balls, rolling and squeezing them until he cries out. "Louder."

"Fuck me!" he snarls. "Please, baby, fuck my ass and make me come."

"Since you asked so nicely . . ." I release his hip and part his ass farther. "Now, just like you all say to me, relax and take it." I slowly start to push the huge, wet length in.

He jerks, trying to escape, but I pull him back and work his tight asshole around the length a couple of inches before pulling out.

"I promise it will feel good, babe. Just relax for me and take it."

"Shit, shit, shit." He relaxes slowly as I work it back in again, a few inches at a time, until I reach down and palm his cock. I stroke and squeeze it to the point of pain, just like he likes it, until he cries out, and then I slam the cock all the way inside him. My hips meet his ass as he shakes below me, his cock jerking in my hand.

"Not yet, baby," I coo, leaning down to kiss his back. "You're doing so well. It's all in. How does it feel?"

"Good, wrong, good." He groans. "Move, please fucking move."

Chuckling, I release his cock, grip his hips, and start to move. It is hard to find a rhythm at first, but when he starts pushing back, I get the hang of it. I pull out until just the tip is seated inside him, and then I slam back in as hard as I can. Each time I do it, he moans, and I see his precum dripping to the floor below as he fucks the cock, his arms and legs shaking.

He's already so close and I've barely started.

"You like it, baby?" I purr.

"Yes, there's a spot . . . Oh God, it feels so good."

I make sure to twist my hips and hit that spot that has him screaming and clawing at the wood.

There's a noise, and I turn to see the door opening. Isaac stands there, and his mouth drops open. With a confused chuckle, he starts to shut the door. "Nope," is all he says and then he's gone, so I focus back on Jonas, on fucking my lover.

Reaching down, I palm his cock and make a circle with my hand so he's fucking into it as I take his ass. He whines, his precum spilling over my fingers as I speed up. He screams, and his cock jerks in my grip as his cum shoots out, spilling over my fingers and onto the floor. I see his asshole clenching around the cock as he yells, still fucking into my hand and pushing back onto the cock until, suddenly, he stills.

"J, did I kill you?" I tease, but he doesn't reply.

Frowning, I pull the cock out slowly, hearing him moan, and then I flip him. His eyes are closed, his mouth is slack, and drool runs down his chin. His chest is heaving and covered in sweat, and his whole body shakes.

"Jonas!" I slap him, and his eyes slide open lazily.

"We are doing that again," he mutters with a full body shudder.

Laughing, I unclip the cock and crawl into his arms. He tries to wrap them around me but they fall back to the floor with a thump. Kissing over his racing heart, I lie beside him, just soaking in his warmth. "Sure thing, baby, you can take my cock anytime."

SIX

NOVA

The distraction with Jonas only worked for so long before I found myself in the gym again, working my body to forget my anger and frustration.

Just like the last few days, I'm sparring with Nico, but today, we are both frustrated. We are all on high alert, and it is taking its toll. I'm snappy and I know it, and he's reacting to it, his hits coming harder and faster.

"Pay attention," he orders.

"I am," I retort.

"No, you're daydreaming," he growls.

"Asshole," I hiss as I slam my foot into his side. He blocks my second attack and spins me away.

"That's right, baby, I'm an asshole, an asshole who's kicking your ass. Come on, is that really all you got?" he mocks. "Want me to be blindfolded?" He covers his eyes and with a snarl, I throw myself at him. It is clear he was expecting an attack, but not like this, so he stumbles and falls back. Despite it, he quickly wraps his arms around me to stop me from hurting myself, and once we hit the mat, he flips us.

Gritting my teeth, I slap my hands out, but he quickly catches them and pins them above my head, his thighs holding mine down. Even as I buck and twist, I know it's useless. Nico is a powerhouse and he pinned me. His eyes are hard and hungry as he watches me fight him.

"Finished?" he asks when I slump.

"Never." My eyes narrow before I flip the switch. I won't win outright on strength, so I play dirty. Lifting my head, I slam my lips to his, swallowing his groan as our tongues tangle. My chest presses against his bare, sweaty one. For a moment, I forget my plan as desire courses through me, mixed with my anger, but his hands slowly loosen on mine and I wiggle them free. Sliding my palms across his shoulders, I rip my mouth away and twist us. My knees land on either side of his head, and I grin down at him, his hair mussed, his eyes tight, and his lips puffy from my attack.

"You got me, baby. Now what are you going to do to me?" His hands slide up my thighs, tugging me down until I'm almost sitting on his face. "I know, how about you sit that pretty pussy on my mouth? I'm fucking starving."

"Fuck you," I snap angrily, still fighting my emotions. I go to stand, but he sweeps my leg out and I tumble. My face hits the mat, and my arms are twisted into my back.

"You're too angry, too worked up. I think we need to work some of that frustration out," he mocks, grinding his cock into my ass. I can't help it. I push back even as I wriggle to try and get free of his hold.

"I'll fight you every step of the way," I growl.

His mouth meets my ear as he pins me once more. "Good. Fight me all you want, baby, but I'm still getting my cock deep inside this wet little pussy until you scream, and we both know it, so thrash, scream, and fight because it won't matter. You're mine, Nova."

"Asshole." I throw my shoulders back as he pulls away before I make contact.

"You love it." Keeping my hands pinned, he lifts up slightly and tears off my legging and knickers, tossing them aside so I'm bare below the waist. I manage to flip to my side, and he quickly turns me over and pins me once more, grinning down at me.

His huge erection tents his workout shorts, his tattoos stark against his tanned skin. His dark eyes remain locked on me as I lift him, wanting him badly, even as I'm angry at myself, at everything.

"There she is," he purrs. The sports bra I'm wearing has a front zip, and I narrow my eyes as he reaches for it. My hands are pinned under my back and his weight, so I kick out at him. He grunts as my foot hits his side, but he still unzips it, my breasts tumbling free under his hungry gaze.

Panting beneath him, I narrow my eyes on him. "Don't you dare—" I groan as he leans down and sucks my nipple into his mouth. He either doesn't notice or care as I fight him, sucking hard on it before popping his mouth free and blowing his warm breath across it. I fight the pleasure blooming inside me, the ache of my pussy, and my throbbing clit. I focus on my anger and he laughs against my skin as he turns his head and gives my other nipple the same treatment until they are both hard and aching.

With one hand, he pushes my breasts together and licks and sucks them both, leaving bites across them as my eyes close. I stop my fight as he presses his thigh against my bare pussy and rubs it back and forth.

"I wonder if I could make you come like this," he murmurs against my breast. "I think, considering that you're dripping on my leg, I could. Don't you, baby?"

"Shut up," I snap, and he hums, biting my nipple. I cry out, arching up without meaning to. The pleasure is too much, and he's right. I'm already on the verge of coming, which annoys me. He easily changed my feelings from frustration and anger to need and want.

"Good girl," he purrs. "Ride my thigh and make yourself feel good, and when you've come enough, I'll give you my cock and let you fuck out your tantrum."

"Bastard," I mutter as I roll my hips into his hard thigh, whimpering at the feeling. I'm going to do exactly that and love it. Nico and I have never really been alone to fuck, and I'm so excited and ready for that huge cock.

Frustration ebbs from me, turning to blazing desire as I roll my hips into his touch, chasing my release as he chuckles meanly. He edges and taunts me with what I want. "Say please, Nico, make me come."

"No," I grumble, and he stills, his mouth hovering over my breasts while his hand pins my hips so I can't even get the friction I need. "Nico," I whine.

"Say it, baby, or I'll leave you here naked and wet," he replies.

"Then I'll find one of the others," I retort, fighting again.

"No, you won't. I'll warn them. The only way you are going to come

41

tonight, baby, and get a cock is with me. So, say please and be a good girl for once."

Smashing my head back, I try to move my hips again, but he has me well and truly pinned. He's just that fucking strong, and he waits patiently. Grinding my teeth, I blow out a breath. "Please, Nico, make me come," I mutter.

"Was that so hard, baby?" he purrs, sliding his lips over my nipple again. He pulls his knee away, and I go to shout at him when his hand covers my pussy. "Fuck, you're so goddamn wet for me, but you're going to need to come a few times to take my huge cock. I don't plan on fucking you softly, baby, so come for me." He slams two thick fingers into me and rubs my clit with his thumb.

I tumble over the edge with a scream.

"Good girl, keep going," he purrs. "That's it, milk my thick fingers and show me how good it's going to feel being buried deep inside you. Shit, baby, look at you, so goddamn pretty."

Groaning, I shake from the force of my release until it ebbs. I open my eyes and meet his dark gaze.

Grinning, he slides down my body. "If you behave and don't fight me, I'll lick this pretty pussy until you scream."

"Fine. Only because I want your tongue," I retort with a small grin. Chuckling, he presses my thighs wider and tosses them over his shoulders.

"Whatever you say, Nova," he murmurs, rubbing his nose up and down my wet pussy with a groan. "You smell so fucking good, baby. I can't wait to have you dripping down my throat."

"Then you better make me," I order, reaching down to grip his dark hair, tugging at the roots. He groans, and it vibrates through my pussy. Luckily, he doesn't taunt me this time because both of us are too needy now. His tongue lashes out, lapping at my pussy as he moans.

My head falls back and my eyes slide shut as I grind into his mouth, those two thick fingers working in and out of me before he adds a third. My moans reverberate around the gym as I lift my hips and grind into his face.

His other hand comes up and pins my stomach down for his attack as his tongue sweeps down and around my asshole before moving back up to my clit. "Nico," I whisper, riding the pleasure that's growing once more.

His tongue speeds up, lashing my clit as his fingers fuck me, sounding wet and loud in the gym. It's so fucking filthy, I groan. My heart skips a beat as I tumble over the edge once more, screaming my release as my thighs clamp around his head, keeping him against my pussy.

He licks me through it, keeping his fingers inside me until I relax. I push him away, my pussy oversensitive.

Sitting up, he pulls his fingers and mouth from my pussy and pushes his shorts down, fisting his hard cock. "Say thank you, Nico."

I narrow my gaze, and he smirks as he strokes his huge length, making me lick my lips hungrily.

"Say thank you, Nico, and you can have my cock like we both know you want."

I know he's serious, and my need for his huge length outweighs my pride. I'll beg if it gets me what I want. I need him inside of me so badly, it feels like I might die if I don't get him. "Thank you, Nico, now fuck me."

Shoving his shorts farther down, he strokes his cock as he crawls over me, his other hand grabbing both of mine and pinning them to the mat above me as he nudges my thighs wider. He rolls his hips to tease me, and I'm about to start shit when he presses to my entrance and slams into me.

I cry out his name as he slides all the way inside me. It hurts so fucking good, my eyes cross and my legs wrap around his hips to take him deeper.

"Baby." His head drops to mine as he starts to move with slow, rolling thrusts that have me gasping before he speeds up, his hips slapping into mine. Each time, he hits so deeply inside of me it hurts, but it's so good.

"Faster," I demand. "Harder." I need everything he can give me.

I manage to get my hands free, so I reach down and grip his ass to urge him on. He pushes them away, so I slap him hard. His head snaps to the side, and when he slowly swings it back to me, he's snarling.

Oh shit.

Flipping me onto all fours, he slams his hand down on my ass. "You want to act like a brat? I'll fuck you like one."

"Nico—" My response ends in a scream as he hammers into me, pushing me across the floor with the force, his hand slapping my ass again.

"You want to slap, baby? Then you'll get the same." He smacks me harder, making me clench around him.

"Please." I claw at the mats, pushing back. His hand comes down harder, and I know it will bruise. He fucks me hard and fast, hitting that spot inside of me that has me seeing stars, and then his hand comes down across my clit.

I scream as I explode, milking his cock for his release.

Groaning, he works through my fluttering pussy, fucking me as I pant. I collapse forward after the pleasure releases me, my pussy, ass, and tits aching.

Still recovering from the release, I remain boneless as he flips me again and slams back into my pussy. He hitches my leg up as his other hand pins my wrists above my head, keeping me restrained for his attack. He fucks me hard and fast, his teeth gritted and his veins bulging in his neck.

It's too much. I can't take it.

I feel him losing control, moving with wild, erratic thrusts, so I turn my hand and lace my fingers through his. "Nico, I love you," I say, and it sends him over the edge.

He roars his release as he spills inside of me, shoving his cock as deep as he can. It triggers me again, and I am close to blacking out as I clench around his huge, invading length.

When I can finally breathe and see again, I'm panting below him. He is breathing heavily and covered in sweat as he leans down and presses his lips to my forehead. "I love you too, Nova. Feeling better?"

"Much," I admit. "Thank you."

"Always, baby," he murmurs as he collapses, half on me and half next to me. "Just give me some time to recover."

I laugh, and we both groan at the feel of the vibrations. Closing my eyes, I wrap my arms around him and just hold him. My mind is quiet for the first time in a long time, so I soak up the peace, knowing the real world will invade soon.

But not yet, not here with us.

Sam is still healing, but he begins to train in the gym while I beat the shit out of the bags, growing angrier every day. He watches me with an impressed arch of his eyebrow, so I start to train with him. I have to take it easy since he's still seriously injured, but when he's tired or hurting, he sits out and watches, giving me pointers and refusing to leave me alone. I find that I don't hate it, however, since it distracts me from my eternal struggle.

Taking a break, I sip my water as I stretch out my muscles. He holds his side with a wince. "I hate being this weak."

"But you like Ana babying you," I tease, making him grin widely.

"That I do." He chuckles. "She's something else, your sister. She's . . ."

"Annoying." I laugh.

"Incredible," he adds. "I've never met such a strong, smart, sexy woman."

"You like her," I tease, nudging his foot, and he rolls his eyes.

"More than that. I don't know, it sounds crazy, but it's like I knew who she was to me when I met her. I think she feels the same too," he admits.

"It doesn't sound as crazy as dating six mostly crazy men," I reply, making him chuckle. "Ana has always known her own mind. She's already made her decision, but as her big sister, I have to warn you—if you hurt her, I'll kill you painfully, and we both know I can make that happen."

"I'd be disappointed if you didn't." He nods seriously. "But I have no intention of ever hurting her. It would be like cutting into my own chest. She's been my rock through this which reminds me. I better go check on her. She's been working too much and not eating."

"Whipped," I cough just as Isaac appears with a plate of food.

Sam eyes me. "You were saying?"

I kick him, and he laughs as he slowly climbs the stairs, holding his side.

Isaac comes over, handing me the plate of salad, cheese, and bread. "Just some snacks. It's been hours." He eyes me worriedly. "It's my turn to ask you if you're okay."

"I am now that you are here," I tease. Tugging him closer, I kiss him before melting into his chest. He wraps his arms around me tightly and holds me. "I'm scared," I admit softly.

"I'd be worried if you weren't," he replies, the vibration of his laughter causing me to shiver and hold him tighter. He pulls back and frames my face, searching my eyes. "Whatever happens, Nova, we do it together, okay? You're not in this alone. Tell me you understand."

"Together." I nod as he kisses me softly before deepening it. I moan, the plate falling to the floor as he reaches down and hoists me up. Desperation and need dance between our lips as I claw at his shoulders, but then there's a crack and the lights go out.

Isaac drops me to my feet, and we both sprint for the stairs. I've just reached the top, breathing heavily, when the sound of a crash comes again.

"Find the others, I'll bring Ana!" I yell at Isaac. Sliding down to the lab, I grab the knife I set on the table earlier. Trusting Isaac to check in, I peek around the lab. The house emergency lights flicker on, throwing us into a dim glow that's barely enough to see by but enough to clear the hallway.

There's another crash upstairs, followed by the sound of shattering windows, footsteps, and yelling.

I ignore it, trusting my guys, as I duck and roll into the lab. There's a scream when I come up swinging. Ana is huddled under the desk, clutching a book, tears streaming down her face. Covering her mouth, I cock my head to listen.

I was sure I heard something beyond her screams.

Creak.

It comes again.

I press my finger to her lips and she nods, sniffling. Leaning in, I kiss her forehead in reassurance and move silently to the door in a crouch, peeking around into the corridor beyond.

I watch as booted feet appear at the end, coming from upstairs. It's a tall man, and he has goggles and a mask on. Wearing all black, he holds a gun in his hands as he sweeps the entryway. The house is silent now, and I know my men will be hunting. They trust me to get Ana and myself to safety, just as I trust in them.

I watch as the man turns to the corridor and heads down it, his flashlight sweeping around.

Pressing my back to the wall, I wait and count his footsteps. I feel calm and prepared and very much in my element.

When the man walks past, I pounce. I slap one hand over his mouth and slam the knife into his jugular with the other before dragging him into the lab as he fights and screams. I wait until he stops moving and lower him softly to the floor. Glancing back at Ana, I hold out my hand. She drags her eyes from the body and scrambles towards me. I keep her behind me as I check the corridor and slide out, keeping her to the wall.

"Nova, who are these people?" she whispers. "Are we under attack?"

"Yes," I murmur, glancing around the entryway. They haven't breached the front door, which makes sense. Who walks straight into an enemy's lair? I'm betting they came through the upstairs windows, maybe even repelled down.

I hear a soft thud upstairs and nothing else.

"I don't know who they are, but I need to get you to a car before I return for the others."

"No, I won't leave you or Sam," she hisses, trying to push me. I slam her back to the wall and wait as I hear footsteps pounding across the landing. Once they are gone, I get in her face.

"We are all trained to handle this and you are not. Ana, I can't concentrate when you are in danger. I need to keep you safe so please, let me look after you."

She wipes at her face, glancing around. "No, we face this together. Give me a weapon. I'm not leaving you."

"Ana!" I hiss, but she snaps her hard gaze back to me.

"No, together. Weapon." She holds out her hand. A familiar gleam of determination enters her gaze, and I know it's pointless to fight her on this. We are only wasting time.

I hand her my only knife and tell her to wait there as I go back, grab the semiautomatic rifle the attacker was carrying, and check that it's loaded. When I return, I nod at her. "Stay behind me at all times," I order. "I mean it or you're out of here."

"Fine." She nods as I swing around the stairs and keep low, moving silently up the steps. I hear her breathing behind me but other than that, she controls her panic, her feet only making a soft slap on the stairs as she watches my back.

At the top, I crouch lower, putting my hand up to stop her, and swing my weapon each way, searching. When nothing jumps out, I move and press my back to the wall, tugging her with me.

Heading down the corridor, I check each room as I go. Nearly every window is broken, making it hard to guess how many men there are or where they are.

I don't like this, I don't like that Ana is here, and I definitely don't like that I can't see the others. I've just stepped past the doorway of a room I thought I'd cleared when a gun swings out, aiming for my face. I barely duck it in time, but when I jerk up, there's a knife embedded in the man's chest. I glance back to see Ana's shocked face.

"He was going to hurt you," she whispers.

Nodding, I slam my gun into his face, pluck the knife free, and hand it back to her. "You did good," I praise her.

I drag the body away and we keep moving, but at the next door, a hand wraps around my mouth and jerks me in. I slam my foot back, and I hear a grunt before I break free to see Jonas, his expression showing his annoyance.

"How many?" I hiss. "Where are the others?"

"I don't know. They pulled Nico and Louis through the window before I could get to them and dragged them away. Sam was trying to find anyone else, me too."

"Isaac?"

He shakes his head as Ana moves hesitantly into the room. He looks at me and I shrug. "She's helping. She saved me actually."

"Okay, they seem to be coming from this floor's windows. We'll work together, take them down, and find the others," he suggests.

"Sounds good." I lift my gun and grin. "You got a weapon?"

"Baby, I am the weapon." He smirks but shows me his pocket, which is filled with a knife and a . . . yup, a grenade. "Let's do this. Oh, and Ana, nice knife."

"Thanks," she squeaks.

"Make sure to keep it out of us," he offers softly, warning her. "I'll take the back, you take the middle, and Nova, you're in front. We work as a team. You're one of us now, kid." He ruffles her hair, and she smacks his hand away, smiling slightly, and I know that's why he did it.

I mouth, "Thank you," and then head to the door, needing to move and make sure the others are okay. Louis, Nico . . . God, I hope they are okay, but I know they would want me to keep moving, so I do. I focus on saving my family, on keeping them safe.

48

That's all that matters now. I should have trusted my instincts before and got us to safety, but that's moot. It's in the past, and all I can do now is keep moving forward and remind them why they should fear us.

They'll regret coming after us, and my father will regret standing against us.

He wants proof of the effectiveness of his experiments? Well, he'll get it tonight.

This house will be filled with screams and run red with blood like it did when I was a child.

I move down the corridor. In Ana's room, my trainer-covered feet crunch over glass, but beyond that sound, I hear breathing that isn't ours. Smirking, I turn and joke, "Clear," before heading to the door. Once there, I slam it shut and leap over the bed, slamming into the man crouched there.

He's out before he even saw me coming. Grabbing his gun, I toss it to Jonas, hearing him catch it, and then I tie up the bad guy before standing and opening the door again.

Ana is blinking and shaking her head. "I didn't even see you move," she whispers.

"Kind of the point, babe. Super soldier, remember?" I tease as we head out into the corridor again. Each room has more broken glass, and I can't help but think about how annoyed Bert will be when he sees it.

Bert . . . I hope he's okay. Hopefully, he's hiding in the pantry or something.

I have no time to worry, though, because as we approach the next door, I get a bad feeling and nod at Jonas. He moves me out of the way, flipping open a knife, and with a wicked grin, he stabs through the wood. There's a groan as the door swings open, and Jonas descends on the man like a wild beast. He beats the shit out of him before plucking his knife out and throwing it at a man sneaking through the window. Once there, he rushes to the window and looks out. "Ropes," he mutters as he tugs it down and throws it at me. I use it to tie both men together, taking perverse pleasure in their sixty-nine position. It will be a nice surprise when they wake up.

Chuckling, Jonas kisses me on his way by. "Good one, baby. Two more rooms."

I nod, and luckily, the next two rooms are clear, but there are more ropes, meaning there are more men somewhere. At the end of the hall, I gesture to the attic, and Ana and I crouch as Jonas sweeps it.

When he returns, he's brushing the cobwebs from his hair. "Nothing but spiders."

"Then they are downstairs," I grumble, throwing him a narrow-eyed look, "probably with the others. How about we switch up this game?"

He grins. "What do you have in mind?"

Dropping my gun, I nod to the side. When he sees what I'm looking at, he winks. "Fuck, you're a genius."

It's a tight squeeze as Jonas and I head down in the dumbwaiter first. Once there, we yank open the door and roll out into the kitchen. As we sweep it, we find the back door is open, and there are tracks leading out. They are probably checking the perimeter. Locking the door, we wedge a table before it to give us notice when someone tries to get back in.

A bang makes me spin to the cupboard next to me and yank it open. I find Bert hiding inside, a frying pan in his hand. "Miss Nova," he whispers gratefully, looking me over worriedly.

"Stay in there, okay? We are going to get them all."

"Miss Nova, I saw them take Isaac and Samuel past. I am sorry I couldn't stop them."

"Don't be sorry, but I need you to wait for Ana to come down here, okay? Keep her safe," I instruct him.

He nods seriously. "Of course, Miss Nova, be careful."

Jonas picks up a butcher's knife, and we move out of the kitchen, ready to sweep the rest of the downstairs and find our family.

Oh, and kill the bastards invading my fucking house.

SEVEN

NOVA

The entryway is empty. Jonas and I sweep every nook and cranny and find . . . no one. There are no footsteps or people. Sharing a confused and slightly worried look, we head to the closed double doors of the living room.

As soon as I touch the wood, I know something is behind it. I shoot Jonas a look and he nods, lifting his gun higher to watch me. Taking a deep breath, I rip open the doors and roll inside in case anyone starts firing. I might be fast and strong, but a well-placed bullet could still take me down, and I don't plan on dying today.

Nobody is.

No one shoots, however, and when I jerk my head up, I freeze as fear pounds through me.

Dimitri, Louis, Nico, and Isaac are lined up in a row of chairs, tied up and gagged. Their eyes are wide, and Nico shoots fire at me with his gaze. Louis's expression is demanding, Isaac looks worried, and Dimitri seems sad. Jonas slides inside behind me and pulls out a knife, hurrying over to them as I climb to my feet and look around for Sam. I don't see him. I hope he got away.

I don't know how they captured my men, other than taking them by surprise and drugging them, which is possible since they look sluggish, not to mention the number of bodies in the house.

"Get them free, and let's get the others. We can regroup—"

I blame my own stupidity and shock.

Dumb, Nova, so fucking dumb.

"I'm afraid that won't be happening."

His voice is like a boulder, slamming me back to reality, and I actually gasp as I spin to see him. Every bad memory, nightmare, and moment I have thought of him pounds into me until I stagger back.

He is just a man, but the power he has over me is that of a god. Fear and pain return until I no longer feel like Nova, their Nova. Instead, I feel like that scared little Novaleen, staring at her father.

"Hello, Novaleen." He grins at me. Four masked men stand behind him, their guns aimed at us. "Sorry to drop by like this, but it is my house, after all."

"Father," I spit, finally finding my voice. "I would say it's good to see you, but I preferred you dead." I grin. "Not to worry, though, I can rectify that." I raise my gun, and he yanks something—no, not something, someone into view, holding them before him like a shield.

Ana.

Fear dawns on her face as she watches me, her eyes searching the room for Sam. Panic threads through me, but I try to mask it and come up with a solution that will get us all out of here alive.

"Uh-uh, we need to talk, Novaleen. Do not be so brash." He huffs, his eyes narrowed in displeasure as my hand with the gun hesitates.

"It's over," I spit and look Ana over. "Are you okay?"

"I'm fine, but Bert . . ." Sobs rack her body. "I think they killed him while he was trying to protect me."

I startle, resisting the urge to kill them all as I breathe through the grief of losing a man who was never supposed to be more than staff but took in two little girls and tried to make their miserable existences worth living. The gun wavers and falls as I stare at a shaking Ana.

"That's a good girl. Behave, Novaleen, or should I say Nova?" he spits. "Though I must say I much prefer your true name."

"Yeah, well, fuck what you prefer," I retort, feeling Jonas moving behind me.

"Tell him to stop, Nova, or I will kill her and the others." He grins, and the expression is slightly deranged, but the intensity in his eyes shakes me to my core.

"You won't kill your daughter," I hedge. No matter how much of a monster he is, Ana is still of his blood.

"Try me," he replies, and for a moment, we just stare at each other in a test of wills before my shoulders sag. I'm unable to put any of them at risk, least of all my sister. "Jonas, stop."

I hear him stop instantly. "Baby," he murmurs.

"Don't," I snap at him, glaring over my shoulder.

He nods in understanding. I will not risk my sister or my men, knowing how sadistic my father is. He would relish our pain. More than that, he would cause it to understand the aftermath then study us.

"You did this all to talk?" I gesture around. "Then talk."

He releases Ana, thrusting her towards me. I grab her hand and haul her behind me, but she stops at my side, gripping my fingers in support and fear. We are two sisters standing together against their father. His men stream into the room, taking up position, their weapons aimed at my men to make sure I do not go back on what I said.

"Look at you." His eyes move over me as mine move over him.

The sharp edge of panic and fear disappears the longer I'm in his presence. The projected version of the man from my childhood fades, and standing in his place is an older man. His hair is grey, short, and styled. His eyes are the same, sharp blue, but surrounding them are crow's feet that weren't there before. His lips have sagged slightly, and they are surrounded by lines. He's plumper than he was before, maybe stress eating, and his shoulders are slightly rounded as if from stress.

He looks older and weaker.

It just reminds me that he is nothing but a man, and something about his decaying appearance makes my chin tilt up as I face my maker—the man responsible for all of this. I always worried about how I would react, but I truly feel nothing except . . . pity for him.

"Look at you. You're older, a lot older. You look weak." I see him flinch and know I've landed a hit. For all his research, all his gifts, he cannot stop himself from aging.

"And you, you look stronger every time I see you. You are impeccable, everything I imagined and more. I cannot wait to see what is going on in your body." His eyes go far away for a moment. "Though you are surrounding yourself with . . . strange company."

I ignore that, unwilling to let him land any more blows, even as I search for a way out of this, inching us back to my men. "I feel sorry for you," I comment, trying to distract him as I tug Ana with me.

"For me?" He laughs.

"Yes, for you. All these years, you wasted your life on research that even your own government has turned its back on. You have no one to trust, no one to share it with. You are completely alone. These people follow you out of fear or obligation, nothing more. Everything you have done will be for nothing. No one will remember you, and no one will mourn you. You will simply disappear like specks of dust in the light."

"Oh, that's where you are wrong, Novaleen." He grins, and alarm bells sound in my head. That smile would appear right before he would do something so horrible, I cannot even think about them. "They will remember you. They will remember I made you, created you, and changed everything. And you? You're the key to that."

"I will never help you," I snap. "This is my family. This is where I stand. You'll have to kill me."

"Never." He shrugs. "I need you, like you pointed out; however, I don't need them."

Fear stabs through me, but I tilt my head back at his bluff.

"You won't turn us against each other. We stand together," I snap, squeezing Ana's hand.

One sister who just wanted to heal the world and the other who wanted to watch it burn are finally united and standing together.

Father sees it, and with a cruel grin that sends shudders down my spine, he looks to Ana. "Look at you, Ana. You are incredible. I have been following your research. It is very good, but think of everything you could do. Join me and help me finish my research, and we can change the world. We can help those who need it, heal them, and make them better so no one ever has to suffer again." It's a lie, but he's appealing to her soft caring side and he knows it.

For a moment, I panic, thinking she will try to help him simply to defuse the situation or protect me, until she looks up with a determined expression. I realise the days when Ana trusted or would help our father are long gone.

"Never. I'll never help you. You are nothing but a psychopath who craves power and fame. You split us once, but it won't happen again. I'm with Nova every step of the way."

Pride fills me as I stare down at my little sister.

"Then you are useless to me," he spits.

I see it too late.

For all my training, for all my strength and abilities, I'm too fucking late.

The gun flashes in the dark living room, and I watch in slow motion as the bullet heads for Ana. I throw myself towards her, but when she screams, I know I'm too late.

Too fucking late.

Too fucking slow.

We slam to the floor, where I cover her with my body as Jonas lunges at my father. A scream escapes my lips when one of the men slams their gun into his head and he collapses in a heap. Lifting up, I meet Ana's gaze as she blinks rapidly.

She's alive.

"You're okay," I whisper, cupping her clammy cheeks. My mind screeches to a halt, my heart frozen. "You're okay."

"Nova?" she whispers raggedly. "I'm cold."

"No, no, you're fine," I promise as I sit back, but everything freezes inside me when I see the bloody state of her stomach. There is a large hole in her clothes and skin. Pressing my hands to it, I feel tears dripping from my eyes. "You are okay," I tell her as I apply more pressure, making her whimper. I lift my head, searching for something. Anything.

"Help me!" I scream at my father.

"Nova," Ana whispers, her body shaking underneath me.

"Fucking help me!" I beg him as he stares at us. "She's your daughter!"

"She's useless to me," is all he says.

"No, no, no," I say. "I'll do anything, please, please fucking save her. Please don't take her from me, not now. I just got her back. Please!"

"Nova." Ana's voice is firmer. I swing my head down to see her smiling shakily. "I love you."

"Don't you dare say goodbye," I snap. "I can save you. I can—"

"Nova." She reaches up with a bloodied, shaking hand and cups my cheek. "You can't save everyone."

"I can save you," I protest, lifting my hands and whimpering at the blood pooling around the wound. I turn my head to see Isaac fighting in his restraints. "Tell me how!" I tell him.

"Nova, stop it," Ana demands, a wheezy breath rattling her lungs. "It's okay. I love you, please know that. I'm okay with dying to protect you. Tell Sam . . . Tell him I love him too," she pleads as I hang my head, sobs racking my body. For all my power and all my strength, I'm lost and useless in this moment.

"Tell me how to save you," I whisper to her.

"You can't. It tore something important. Even if you operated now, it would be too late," she admits with a cough, wincing in pain. "I don't fear death, Nova. You taught me that, but please don't let this break you."

"I can't lose you. I just got you back," I sob, lifting her into my arms. She's so fragile and pale.

"You'll never lose me," she whispers, blinking rapidly as her face pales even further.

"Don't you fucking dare close your eyes. Stay with me. Please, stay with me." My tears drip into her face, mingling with her own as her body shuts down.

I know the signs.

"Sorry . . . Love . . . you," she gurgles, struggling to breathe.

"I love you. I love you so much, Annie," I croak, holding her tighter and rocking her in my arms. Her blood covers us both.

I wish I could say it was quick, but she struggles to breathe before her body gives out. All the while, I plead to a god I don't believe in not to take her. I feel the moment she dies, the moment she lets go, her hand dropping between us as her head falls back.

I rock her back and forth, singing to her like I did when she was a child.

When the song ends, I squeeze my eyes closed. "No, it's not real. Please, please, don't leave me all alone. Please don't leave me, Annie."

"Nova, it is time to go or I will kill the rest," Father snaps, tired of me.

I drop my head back on a ragged scream, then I gently lay her down, brushing her hair from her face as I position her arms and legs so they are straight. "I'm so sorry, Annie. I'm so very sorry. I love you so fucking much." Leaning down, I press my trembling lips to her forehead, my tears splashing into her unseeing eyes. "I will make this right," I tell her softly before turning away.

Blinking through tears, I turn my head to my father, no longer scared. I feel empty and cold. "You're a dead man walking."

He opens his mouth to respond when there's a roar and a body flies into him, smashing him to the side. Sam scrambles to his feet, his chest heaving and blood coating his head, but then he spots Ana.

"Ana, no!" he croaks, stumbling towards her. He falls to his knees next to her unmoving body, and I choke on my tears as I watch. "No, baby, wake up. Look at me!" He slaps her face before looking up at me. "Why aren't you doing anything? Save her!"

"I'm sorry," I sob.

"No, no, you're okay. You're okay, baby." He pulls her into his arms, kissing her face as I cry. "Please, baby, I just found you. Please, don't let me lose anyone else."

"Sam," I murmur, reaching for him.

He screams and pulls her away from everyone as I stumble to my feet, his back bowed as he cries, trying to get her to wake up.

Everything in me is cold and broken at the same time.

It's as if I can't breathe and I'm swimming underwater.

I can see my guys fighting to get to me. I see my father raising the gun again and hear a shot go off. It hits Sam, but he doesn't move except for a flinch and a yell. He shoots again.

Four more bullets are shot until Sam slumps over Ana, their blood mingling together, and I still can't move.

A girl bound to heal, a soldier bound to die, I think idly.

My eyes are locked on their bodies. Someone screams my name, but I don't move as the soldiers board the windows and something starts pumping into the room to knock us out.

Let them kill me.

What is the point of living without her?

I look at Sam and for a moment, fresh agony spills through me before it, too, is swallowed up.

My grief is not loud like his.

It is silent, deadly, and cold.

"It's time to go, Nova." Father holds his hand out to me. He took her from me. "I'll kill them, Nova."

That's what jerks me back to reality.

"If I go with you, you'll leave them alone?" My voice sounds strange, even to my own ears.

"Yes," he promises. "I never needed them, only you. They are failures. I will let them live if you'll come with me now."

For a moment, my eyes go back to Ana's unseeing ones. "No more death, not for me," I whisper as I turn. I can't bring myself to meet their gazes.

Nico roars behind his gag, his chair creaking with his struggles. Louis pleads with me, his eyes darting around as he tries to look for a plan. Dimitri is silent, watching me with understanding. He is the only other person who has felt my grief. Isaac cries as he reaches for me. Jonas, still slumped on the floor, remains silent.

Six men who love me and would give anything for me.

They would die for me.

"No more death," I tell them as I step back to my father. "No more."

Turning away, I put my hand in his as he grins down at me. "We are going to do great things, Novaleen."

At the threshold, I look back, meeting their eyes. "I love you. I love you all. I can't watch anyone else—" For a moment, emotions slam through me before I lock them away. "Stay alive." With that, I let my father lead me from the house in a daze, and when he injects me in the car and knocks me out, I welcome the oblivion, drowning in the darkness and hoping I never wake up.

EIGHT

LOUIS

My eyes start to water, and my body tries to give into the toxins being pumped into the room, but I refuse. I fight against them to get to her.

I am so fucking angry at her, I want to tan her hide raw for sacrificing herself for us. I know why she did it . . .

Nova. I hear the engines as they speed away.

Fuck! I rock harder, trying to break the chair, when I hear a cough. Jerking my head up, I see Bert opening the front door. He stumbles into the living room, batting away the smoke and shoving open the windows to clear it. When he sees us, he squints, his eyes watering too.

His mouth is twisted in agony, and his hand is pressed to his chest where he's bleeding. He's pale and clearly in danger, yet he heads towards us. "Nova?" he croaks.

I try to shout and warn him, but I can't, and he stumbles over Ana and Sam.

Falling to his ass, he sees the bodies and screams before covering his lips with his hand.

I shout his name, trying to get his attention. With each second that passes, they take Nova farther away, but his eyes are locked on Ana as he cries. "Ana . . . Oh, God." Turning his head, he throws up.

Somehow, I manage to work the gag down. "Get us free!" I roar. "Nova!"

Nodding, he crawls to us as he cries, grabbing a knife from my boot and slicing my bonds. After, he moves back to Ana, stroking her face. I leave him there as I cut the others free, all of us rushing out the front door to go after our love.

Our girl.

However, our cars are destroyed.

"No!" Jonas roars, going to run, but I grab him.

"Don't," I snap. "We need a plan."

"No—"

"We will get her back!" I yell at him. "Isaac, get Bert and check him over. Everyone else, clear the building now!" I see them hesitate, and I turn on them. "Now!" I roar, and they rush inside as I turn to stare at the driveway. "We're coming, Nova, I promise."

"I failed her," Bert whispers, his sad eyes focused far away. "I failed Miss Nova, and I failed Miss Ana."

"You got us free so we can rescue her."

"Ana is dead. I should have protected her better. I should have protected them both better."

"We do not have time for regrets," Jonas snarls.

"Jo—" Isaac starts, but he shakes his head.

"We don't! Each moment we waste puts him that much farther away from us. Regrets don't change what happened, only actions do."

"He's right," Bert murmurs. "Go get her and bring her home."

"How the fuck do we do that? We have no cars."

"There's one in the garage." Bert sits up, wincing in pain. "Bring Nova back. I will not lose them both."

"You need blood and surgery," Isaac begins.

"I need my girls!" he snaps, angrier than I've ever seen him. "Screw me. Leave me to die and go get her. That's an order."

"Isaac, stay with him," I demand.

"No." He stands. "I'm going too."

"I need you to keep him alive," I implore. "Nova loves him. She can't . . . I won't let her lose anyone else."

The weight of my failure sits heavily on my shoulders, but I push through it, knowing I need to be smart. They need answers and a leader. They need me, so I don't break, not yet.

Nodding, Isaac sits back down.

"Everyone else, grab your weapons. Let's get our girl."

Storming from the room, I load up. Dimitri pulls the SUV around front, where we all hop in.

"Which direction?" Dimitri asks nervously.

"Drive," is all I say, because honestly, I don't know. I need to think.

Where would he take her?

It can't be close. He'd want her far away from us just in case. "Airport," I mutter. "The son of a bitch will either take her to a boat, which is too far away, or a private jet. Clearly, he's moving around with them, so get us to the airport."

"Step on it," Nico growls, the only words he has spoken.

"Louis," Dimitri whispers, sharing a look with me as he guns it.

"Don't. We are getting her back," I snap at him. "Now focus on driving."

We are all alert, watching the road as he drives like a madman, covering the distance in half the time we did last time. Leaping from the car, we sprint through the building, only to see a plane taking off with a car parked before a hangar. I hurry over and search inside, freezing when I see a note on the seat.

I unfold it, only to realise it belongs to Nova.

I miss you—Nova.

"She was here." Slamming the door closed, I look at the plane. "She's on there."

"Fuck!" Nico roars, punching his fist into the car before whirling on Dimitri. He grabs him and slams him into it too. "Work your fucking magic. Track her!"

"I need my laptop."

"Nova," Nico roars.

"Nico!" I demand. "We need to calm down. We need a plan."

"Fuck your plans!" Jonas hisses, clenching and unclenching his hands. "Look where it got us."

I slam my fist into his face before he can react, and everyone freezes. "I am just as lost as you," I tell them honestly. "I am just as scared and panicked, but right now, Nova needs us, and acting like buffoons will not help. Instead of fighting each other, we need to work together to bring her back. We will find her," I promise. "We will bring her home, but right now, we need to take care of Bert, look at Jonas's head, regroup, and come up with a foolproof plan to get our girl back."

"And then?" Dimitri asks.

"Then we kill her father."

NINE

ISAAC

My heart hurts.

I've lost the only woman I have ever loved, and more than that, I couldn't even save her sister for her. The one time she actually needed me, I couldn't do anything, but I can save Bert for her. I can and I will. I refuse to let another person she loves die.

It's the least I can do.

He's knocked out at the moment. Luckily, he didn't need surgery, but it's going to take a long time for him to heal. He's had two blood transfusions, and I'll keep him sedated for a while to make sure he doesn't spring up and hurt himself more.

Scrubbing my hands of the blood, I hang my head as tears fill my eyes.

Her screams echo in my brain.

God, I saw the moment she broke and actually felt it in my soul. Tied to the chair, I could do nothing but watch the love of my life lose everything, shut down, and give up. I hated the defeated expression she wore. I hated the fact that she was struggling to even breathe and talk.

Even then, though, she protected us and made a deal to keep us alive.

She should have let him kill us because living without her is not possible.

The only thing that is worse is knowing she's out there somewhere, all alone and hurting. I failed her. I failed them all. I should have seen this coming when they knocked me out, but I did nothing. I let Bert get hurt. I let them kill the sister of the woman I want to spend the rest of my life with, and then I let her leave.

That moment haunts me as I finally break. Sobs rack my body as I remember the dead look in her eyes as Ana's blood coated her cheek and hands.

She looked weak and raw—not words I would ever use to describe Nova.

Now, she's with him, the man willing to kill one daughter and hurt the other, and she's all alone and hurting. Yet here I am, feeling sorry for myself. I smash my fist into the wall, and the throb of pain cuts through my self-pity.

It feels good, so I do it again and again.

Even as my knuckles split and my bones crack, I keep on hitting the wall, letting it all out until I fall to my ass, cradling my broken hand. My heart hurts as I pray the others have found her and that they are coping better than I am.

Usually, I'm the one in control, helping and containing them, but not now.

Not this time. I cannot even think clearly.

When they come back empty-handed, I know we failed. One look at their heartbroken expressions and I know we've lost her.

"He took her on a plane," Dimitri says where we stand in the foyer, covered in blood. "We will find her. I'm going to right now." He rushes away, no doubt heading to his laptop. I turn to track him when my eyes catch on Ana's and Sam's bodies curled around one another.

Sharp, piercing agony rips through my chest for everything my girl has lost.

"We should bury Ana," I whisper. "It's not right that she's lying there. We should put her to rest and give her peace. Nova would want that and a place where she can go to see her sister."

"We will," Louis replies softly. "We'll bury them both."

"Together. They'd like that, I think," I say.

"Together." He squeezes my hand.

NICO

I need to keep it together for the others because they are falling apart. Guilt, agony, and stress wreck them. I have to be strong.

Jonas and I dig the graves. We picked a spot under a big apple tree we think Nova would like. I take Ana into my arms and carefully carry her over as Jonas holds Sam. Bert drags himself out front as we bury them, knowing we can't call the police or offer them a proper burial without drawing too much attention to ourselves.

We can do this, however, for our girl.

Once they are in the ground, we silently cover them up, and then Bert clears his throat. "We should say something." Tears stream steadily down his face as he stares at the side-by-side graves.

"Miss Ana . . . She was a force to be reckoned with. She was kind, funny, and very talented. When she was a kid, she would come up with the most profound things, and I knew she was going to change the world." He hiccups but straightens with purpose. "She saved me, an old man with nothing to live for. Those two girls became my world. I watched her grow into an incredible woman who was so kind, generous, smart, and determined, but she was aching. She missed her sister. I never saw her happier than when she got Miss Nova back. They were always destined to be at each other's side. Without her, there will be a hole. I'm so glad I got to see you grow up, Miss Ana, and fall in love and stand for what you believe in. I'm so very proud of you. I have loved you since the moment you took my hand and declared us friends when you were four years old, and I will love you until the moment I lie in the ground at your side. I will find your sister, our Nova, and I will bring her home. I will uphold your dying wish. I hope that in the next life, you find the peace and happiness you deserve with Sam, Miss Ana, and now I will wait for the day when I pass on and into your waiting arms."

I know we all wear matching expressions of pain. We barely knew Ana, but we know how much Nova loved her. Stepping forward, I clear my throat. I hate speaking, I hate being vulnerable, but for my girl, I will. She can't be here to offer peace to her sister, so I will do it for her, and when she comes home, she can say her goodbyes and I will be there to catch her.

"Nova loved Ana more than anything in the world. Everything she ever did was for her sister, to keep her safe and give her a chance at a normal life. I never knew what true love was until I saw them together."

Bert starts to sob, and Jonas catches him, holding him as he cries.

"I will never forgive myself for failing you, Ana, or your sister, but your death will not be in vain. I promise you that. We will make them pay, and I will spend the rest of my life trying to heal your sister's broken heart with every ounce of love inside me. We can never fill the hole you have left, but we will keep her happy and loved until you two meet again."

"The world is a cruel place," Dimitri says. "I hope now you have peace. If you can hear me, find a man named Bas. He will love and protect you, and when our time comes, we will meet you both on the other side."

"Love lives on in those who love you, who outlive you. I know Nova will never let your love or your life fade, Ana," Isaac adds softly.

Jonas nods. "I'm sorry we couldn't save you, but we will save her."

"Together," Louis adds.

We stand around her grave, each saying our goodbyes and offering her our hopes and apologies until, with a wince, Bert gently lays a flower on each of the graves. "I will stay here with you until the very end," he vows, and then he lets Jonas lead him back to the house.

"We need to find her," I say as I watch them go. "We all know what he's doing to her right this moment." I focus on Dimitri. "Find her." I stomp off, needing a moment to hide the tears in my eyes, the horror in my soul, and the fear that I have lost the love of my life.

TEN

NOVA

I wake up slowly, feeling groggy. Every inch of my body hurts, but it's the pain in my soul that has me crying out. Once, where my sister existed, there is nothing. She was ripped away, and the pain is so acute, I pass out again.

I'm dying from a broken heart.

She's gone.

I drift between consciousness and sleep, struggling with the pain.

She's gone, and I don't want to wake up again. I don't want to live in a world without her. Out of all the things my father has done, he finally did what he always wanted—he broke me.

I would gladly beg and give everything I have to get her back. All the pain I endured as a child was to protect her, and now she's gone, and it was all for nothing. We changed nothing, and we saved no one.

She's gone.

I can almost hear her laughter here and feel her chasing me through the woods. I want to stay here forever with her in this place where she exists, where she didn't die for me. We are happy here, and we have a normal life.

The world doesn't give a fuck about my pain, though, so it drags me back, kicking and screaming. I wake with a gasp, jerking upright before struggling against something binding me. Panic slithers through me as I twist and turn blindly, fighting whatever it is.

"You are going to hurt yourself if you do not calm down."

Lights blare to life, and it's then that I realise I'm strapped to an operating table. The room is sterile, half empty, and clinical, and my father stands at the door. He watches me with an impassive expression as he wanders over.

"You killed her," I whisper.

"She was useless to me. Let that be a reminder, Nova. Do not become the same. If you want to live, then do as I say and we won't have a problem, little girl." The smile he gives me is pure evil.

"Did you ever love us? We were your children," I ask numbly.

He hesitates, his gaze going far away. "I suppose I did, in a detached sort of way. I loved the attention you brought me, the normality, the cover, and the accolades. Is that the same thing? I suppose not. I always knew I was not capable of such emotions. They are a hindrance, after all, but if it makes you feel better, Nova, I will miss Ana. She had a very capable brain."

"She was your daughter!" I scream at him.

He watches me struggle against my restraints with a patient and cold expression. "And now she is dead. It is a pity. Had I known the strength of your attachment, I would have kept her alive to make you more . . . compliant. Nevertheless, we will find a way."

"Fuck you! I will kill you all!" I scream, the numbness morphing into pure fury for a moment.

"I hope you keep your fight because it's most entertaining," is all he says. "Now, shall we carry on where we left off?" He picks up a collar, and I close my eyes in horror.

I'm dragged, limp and covered in my own blood and vomit, down the white tiled corridor. It's dark and when we step through each section, bright overhead lights flicker on. I cannot even lift my head, legs, and arms as I hang between two men who haul me over to a door, grunting as they open it.

Every part of me hurts just as much as my soul aches. I deserve it, and it almost takes away from losing her. I wish I passed out, but I didn't. I felt every incision and test he ran on me. I felt it all, and now I'm suffering from my father's cruel touch.

The door beeps and unlocks, and they drag me in, dumping me unceremoniously onto a single cot screwed to the back wall. The room is small, barely enough to walk in, with just a bed, the door, and another door to the left, which is open to reveal a small bathroom. A camera blinks its red light in the corner, pointing at me.

"I don't understand the fascination. She broke as easily as the others," one says with a laugh as they step out. The door slams shut with a click, letting me know it's locked, and then the lights go out, plunging me into darkness where I can finally break.

I bet they are listening, so I cry silently, tears tracking down my face as I turn and bury my head against the wall. Grief and agony rock through my body as I drag my legs to my chest and bury my head in my knees as I shake and cry.

I don't even know if the guys are alive or if they are okay, and the thought sends my heart plummeting to my stomach. What if he killed them? What if they are all gone?

What if I'm all alone in the world once again?

ELEVEN

DMITRI

The plane isn't registered, but to take off or land, even on a private airstrip, they have to let somebody know. It will take some searching, but I'm confident I will find where they are flying to. I just hope it's in time.

I don't sleep or eat.

I leave the others to clean the house so Bert will rest. They want it to be perfect for when she comes home. Jonas even makes him pancakes. They are all confident in my abilities to find her, even when I'm not. If I find where she flew out to, they could have travelled again, yet I know I have to find her. The look she gave us when she left haunts me, and it's all I see.

I can't lose her, not like I lost Bas.

I refuse to let another person I love drift away when I can stop it. I know the pressure is mounting on me, but I keep moving. I have four computers open, working at all times. One scans any international data with her photograph, looking for her, the second looks for her passport—which is a long shot but worth trying—and a third searches for her father's.

"Anything?" Jonas demands from behind me.

I ignore him, using the fourth computer to search through the data of all incoming flights today.

"Dimitri, anything?" he snaps.

"Not fucking yet!" I spin. "Just fuck off and let me work. I'm trying my best."

"Hey, we know you are." He moves over, crouching before me and taking my hand. "We know. This isn't all down to you."

"I have to find her," I murmur, dropping my gaze to the floor in shame. "I have to. I couldn't save him, but I can save her. I can. I will."

"We will," Jonas promises. "This isn't like Bas. Nova will fight to get back to us. She's so strong, stronger than any of us. We have to trust in that just like she has to trust in us right now to find her, but blaming yourself will not accomplish that, okay? So focus, find her, and give me a fucking target to destroy because right now, I'm fucking useless and I hate it."

"Scan the bodies." I jerk my head up. "If we can find out who they are, we can trace their payments back to the source and we might just find her."

"Got it, I'll do that." He stands. "You good?"

I nod, even though we both know it's a lie. "We're going to get her back," I murmur.

"We are, and when we do, we'll burn the fucking world for her."

JONAS

I feel useless as I pace near the front door. All the bodies have been checked, and we are running their IDs to see if we can find any links. We are tugging at every thread, unravelling the game he has set before us so we can find our girl, yet there is nothing more I can do. There is nothing I can shoot and nobody I can fight. I'm stuck waiting while my girl gets farther and farther away.

It's clear we are all feeling the pressure. Isaac is working around the clock to get Bert fixed and back to health, as if making sure he's absolutely fine will bring her back. Louis is on the phone with every military contact he can think of, screaming at them. Seeing him lose control really hammers home just how fucked we are.

Nico is in the gym, beating the shit out of the equipment to stop himself from going on a killing spree, and Dimitri? He's barely slept or moved, his eyes are bloodshot, his clothes are rumpled and stained, and he hasn't moved away from the computers since the moment he woke up.

And me? I'm standing guard, as if they will come back. I know they won't. He doesn't want us. No, he wants her—the only experiment to succeed. He wants his daughter and what her mind holds, and the idea of what they could be doing to her right now makes me feral.

I'm like a wild animal, but the only person who is able to soothe me is gone.

They have backed us into a corner, but don't they know that only makes us more dangerous? After all, we have something to fight for now, which we never did before—our family, our heart, our reason to live.

I remind myself that she's survived his treatments before as I pace, ragging at my hair. She's survived so much pain at his hands. We promised her she would never be taken again, but we broke that promise. I hate it, and I hate that she's alone again. I hate that she's hurting, grieving, and in agony, and we aren't there to hold her.

I need my Nova, and if I have to kill every single person who gets in my way to get her back, I will, and when I find her father?

I'm going to torture him to death for hurting the love of my life.

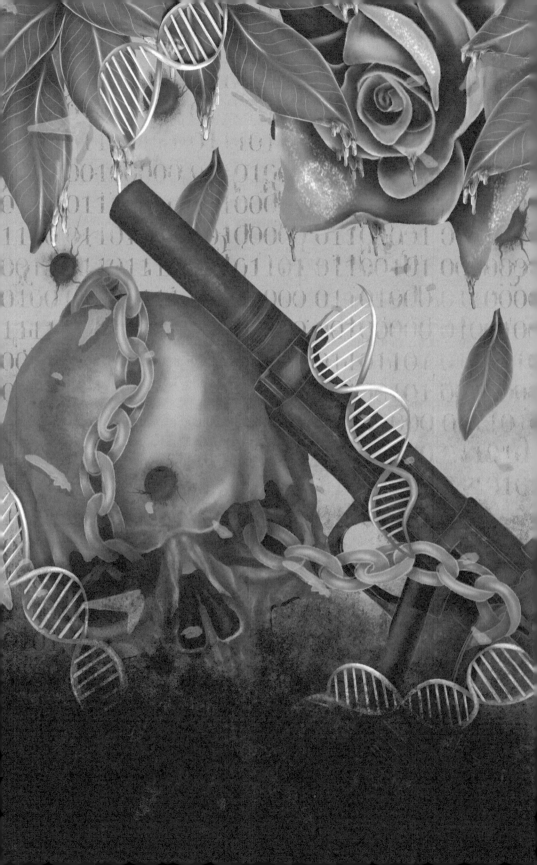

TWELVE

NOVA

T he days pass in a cycle of pain and passing out. I don't know if it's night or day, and the rest I do get only occurs when my body gives in and I fade into the darkness. When I wake, I never feel better. My body is slowly breaking down, and every inch of me hurts.

This is so much worse than ever before, as if he knows he's racing against a clock and needs to get what he can before it's too late. Is my father worried? It's the only thing I hold onto. He's worried he's not as safe as he thinks and that they will come for him.

My family.

They will come for me.

I don't want them to, though, because all I want is revenge. I want to wring the life out of my father's old, wrinkled body for what he took from me—my sister.

Even thinking of my sister has my eyes closing in pain. Doesn't he see that no matter what he does now, he can never replicate that kind of pure horror and agony again? He took the only person in this world I have ever risked everything for and loved so completely. I'm a shell, existing in nothing but physical pain. I revel in it, however, because it's better than the pain in my heart.

I don't know what he expects to gain from this experiment, but I no longer care about the thought process of his sick mind.

All I care about is killing him and joining her once more.

I lie on the bed—maybe for the fifth time, but it's hard to tell—and my body won't move on command at the moment. It's due to the sedative that is still in my system from the last test. I don't know what they did, only that I fought them before the needle went into my vein and then it was lights out. When I woke up here, I had a new incision on my back and agony racing through my spine. I don't bother asking since they won't tell me. The scientists here are butchers, nothing more. I spotted other cells when I was dragged back here. They didn't seem to be occupied, but that doesn't mean they aren't now or haven't been in the past. Knowing them, this place, wherever it is, was or is full, and they are just running one giant experiment ring.

It's clear all their attention is on me at the moment. My father thinks I hold the key to his successful research or some shit. It means I'm important, which means I get the brunt of his attention and experiments. I guess that's something.

The door opens, and I don't even bother looking up, knowing it will be the guards once more. They sent five to begin with, but now I'm too sluggish to even lift my head, so they only sent two. It's insulting and pisses me off. I want them to be afraid of me. I want them to be scared.

They should be.

I'm going to rip every single person here to pieces and then burn it down with me inside.

Grabbing my arms, they drag me from the room. I don't fight them, but I let my anger grow until it blinds me. I let it push away the numbness, exhaustion, and sleepiness in my body until I'm practically on fire with it. Now, they are dragging a loaded weapon without even realising it.

My father wants a weapon? He wants a soldier?

Then he got one.

It's time to show him that. It's time to make them all pay in any way I can.

I don't even look where we are going, since I know it will be a lab of some sort. When I get inside, I see it's not the operating lab, which means no sedative. That provides me with more opportunities to hurt them. They don't even bother tying my wrists down, as if expecting me to be compliant. They band my shoulders, waist, and legs and, with sneering looks at me, they leave me there.

I wait and roll my eyes as I look around the room, mostly out of boredom and to stop my mind from wandering to anything else.

Boom.

I watch her fall again before squeezing my eyes shut and pushing the memory away. Torturing myself by watching my sister die over and over won't help. I need to stay focused. I need to keep my mind sharp. I can't give in, not yet.

And the guys . . .

I can't even think of them. The last time I saw them haunts me even in my sleep. I love them more than I've ever loved anything apart from Annie. They gave me a family, they gave me a home and a purpose, and now I will never see them again. I tell myself it's for the best because this is my problem to handle. I can keep them safe, and I can end this, even if it means I die.

They still have a future.

I just hope they understand that and let me go.

Focus, Nova.

I snap back to attention, scanning the room once more. The table I am on is metal and resembles every other one I have been tied down to. There is a computer on a desk to the left with files spread out across it. I'm too far away to see what they say, but they won't help me anyway. There's a surgical tray to the right filled with tools. It's too far to reach for now, but I note the scalpels and scissors that could be useful. The wall before me is glass, and not much else exists here.

Pure white.

I can't wait to see it splattered with blood.

Just then, the door opens, and a scientist in a lab coat comes bustling in. He doesn't even look at me. His grey hair is combed back perfectly, and his bright-blue eyes are hidden behind thick-rimmed glasses. He's fit, clearly in shape, and slightly smaller than me, but right now, he's in charge and he knows it—not that he looks up from his tablet as he moves around the room, muttering to himself. My eyes track him like he's prey, and when he stumbles and knocks into the tray, I almost smirk in victory. It spins closer to me, and he rubs at his hip as he moves to the computer. Keeping my eyes on him, I reach out as far as I can, my pinkie catching on the edge of the tray, and with gritted teeth, I pull it closer until I can reach the top and grab a tool. It happens to be a medium-sized scalpel, but I grip it tightly, sliding it up the inside of my arm to hide it as he lifts his head and frowns at me.

I simply raise my eyebrow as he stands, heading my way. "Shall we begin?" he asks formally, as if I have a choice in the matter. I want to say as much, but he's already turning away again, so I take my shot. I swipe out, stabbing the scalpel into his middle. He falls back with a scream, blood gushing from the wound. His face is pale and sweaty as he stumbles around, shouting for help. The idiot yanks the scalpel out and blood spurts everywhere.

I guess I hit an artery.

Good.

Ripping the bindings from my body with the last of my strength, I grab the dying man and slam him into the glass as the alarm sounds. The door locks as the guards fight to try and get in. Grinning as my father appears, harried and confused, I slam the gurgling man into the glass. His blood splatters across it, and with my eyes on my father, I rip out the scientist's throat before dropping him to the floor. I step back, covered in blood and gore, wearing a maniacal grin on my face.

"You are behaving like a feral animal!" Father yells as the alarm cuts off.

"That's what I am," I sneer. "You caged and tortured me, and you expect me to be civil? No!" I scream. "You wanted an animal? Now you've got one."

Slamming my hand into the glass, I laugh when the guards jump, my bloodied handprint remaining behind like a promise. Laughing, I grab one of the bone saws when the door opens and the guards stream in.

I throw myself at them, fading into the anger and ignoring everything else, even the pain in my heart and body, as I hack and kill. They are trying to subdue me, but I'm trying to kill them. I see them drop, I hear their screams, and I feel their blood splatter me, but I still don't stop.

Not even as I'm thrown onto the table once more and pinned down by five of them as I twist and laugh, seeing their shocked expressions above me.

I see a fist heading towards my face, along with their shock, their horror, and their dawning understanding.

They underestimated me.

They won't ever make the same mistake again.

I pay for what I did. Father calls it conditioning, but I know the truth. It's punishment. He's angry he underestimated me and that I fought back instead of being the good little experiment he always wanted. He can never dull the spark of rebellion, but he sure tries. He keeps me awake for two days with drugs and pain until I'm delirious, but I still continue to laugh and struggle, even as they torture me until, finally, he gives the order and I'm tossed back into my room.

I lie where they threw me on the floor, and my laughter finally turns to tears. Curling around myself, I push through the agony and focus on my memories.

I'm back at the dining table with everyone laughing around me.

Annie is sitting on Sam's lap, love in their eyes.

Bert is smiling at me.

Louis is holding my hand, and Nico is under me. I'm safe, and I'm warm. Dimitri winks at me, Jonas throws food, and Isaac watches me. I'm loved. I'm safe. I'm happy.

I lose myself in that memory, uncaring that my body is slowly wasting away. Let it, he can have it, but he can never have this. He can never take away the love and happiness I found in a short amount of time.

He can never have them.

They are mine, my secret, and the reason my mind doesn't break.

In there, I am with them, and they are holding me tight and telling me they love me. I think of what our lives could have been like had it been different. We'd have a farm somewhere warm, with no more fog and rain in that manor. No, the sun would shine, and we would work the land. Our lives would be simple, but they would come home to me every day. We would live in the kitchen, dancing and singing. Bert would be there with us, making pancakes for Jonas. There would be horses and goats and maybe a dog or two. I'd never be in pain. I wouldn't even know what that is. I'd be so loved, I would choke on it. Their bodies wouldn't bear the scars of their past, and they wouldn't know what it means to lose everything. They'd be happy.

That's all a dream, but I hold onto it to get me through this.

To give me the strength I need to endure.

To survive and finish this.

Maybe they will get that farm one day, and maybe they will find peace. I'll make sure of it.

I'll make sure, even though I won't be there, that Dimitri won't have to stare at the screen anymore. I'll make sure that Isaac never has to worry about not being okay, that Jonas gets the passion and room he needs, that Nico finds peace, and that Louis is finally unburdened.

I'll make sure of it. I have to.

Even if I burn in the ashes of what I desire, I'll do it for them.

I know I can do this. I can do anything—anything but go home to them.

I stay inside my dream. It's the only time I will be home with them ever again.

THIRTEEN

NICO

I find myself in her old room. It's sparse. Other than a few books and clothes, there are no pictures or anything else to indicate it was her room. I hate it, yet it's the closest I can get to her right now, so I stride in and drop onto the bed, sucking in her scent. I finally break, and the tears fall.

I failed her. I failed them all.

I cannot even breathe around the guilt and pain I feel. I don't let the others see, knowing they will worry, but here, I cry silently and beg for her forgiveness. I couldn't stop him from taking her sister and I should have been able to. What's the point of all this power and strength if I can't use it to stop the one person in this world I love from suffering any more than she already has?

I need her. I need her so badly.

I need her in my arms. I need to hold her tight and reassure myself she's safe.

Instead, I feel sick, knowing she's out there right now and probably in pain.

My heart aches so much I struggle to breathe. It's my job to protect them, to keep her safe, but I failed, and now she's all alone.

I stare out of the window and wonder where she is under the night sky.

Can she see the stars? Is she thinking about us too? I inhale her faded scent, needing it to calm me. My heart won't stop breaking or hammering until she's back in my arms, but this will have to do for now.

For a moment, I close my eyes, imagining she is here with me—her soft hands sliding across my body, the smile she gives me that ruins me. She is strong, but she needs us.

Needs me.

I often wondered what it would be like to lead a normal life, but I know with certainty now I would take all the pain, torture, and imprisonment just to have her again and be given a chance at happiness by her side. She's worth it.

My eyes open, and I look at the stars again. "Stay strong, my love. We are coming for you," I promise her. We will not stop until we do. This isn't the end of our story. Our girl will get the happy ending she deserves, and she'll get the peace she needs. I'll make sure of it.

We all will.

She might be willing to give her life for us and her sister, but so are we. Every one of us would die for her without hesitation, and without her here, we have nothing else left to live for.

"Nico, she needs you to be strong," Louis murmurs behind me. It's a testament to how lost I am that I didn't even hear him come in. I stiffen and don't turn to face him, not wanting him to see my tears, my weakness.

The bed dips and arms wrap around me, offering comfort, and I struggle to pull myself together. "Break now, then tomorrow you will be strong again. We are going to get her back, we have to, but I need you to do that."

"I failed her," I croak.

"No, *we* failed her, and it won't happen again," he replies. "We will get her back, and then we will kill every single one of them for taking her. We will beg for her forgiveness and spend the rest of our lives following her around, but for that we need you."

"What if I'm not strong enough?" My eyes lock on the stars. "What if he was right about us . . . about me? What if I failed his tests because I'm not good enough."

"That's fucking bullshit and you know it, brother." I turn, and he grips my chin, pressing his forehead to mine. "He failed us because we didn't fit into his little perfect box—nothing more, nothing less. Our girl thinks we are fucking perfect, and we will not dishonour her by proving otherwise. He thinks we are failures, so let's show him we're not." Wiping the tears from my face, he smiles sadly. "Then after, we can deal with all this. Until then, let's shove it all in a fucking box, okay? It is the only way I—we can keep moving."

I realise then that this is for him, not just me. He's faltering and he needs me.

Wrapping my arms around him, I hold my brother as we break in our love's bed, our silent promise drifting to the stars. We are coming for her.

Nothing will stop us.

FOURTEEN

NOVA

I t's like my rebellion broke that last line between prisoner and captors. They are brutal with round-the-clock experiments. Father is almost frantic, his hair out of place and dark circles under his eyes. Is he feeling pressure or guilt?

I almost laugh at the idea.

Since I'm not a child, he's not holding back, and the idea that he held back previously scares me—not that I will ever show him that. I slowly lose myself in planning how I will bring this place down. I go through many plans and ideas. I hear Louis's voice in my head, making me discard ideas that won't work. I can't just outright escape because there are too many guards. I would be drugged or knocked out instantly, and then I would lose my shot. No, I need to let them relax again and think they have broken me. I need maps and schematics, and I need to hack into the cameras and alarm systems. Then and only then can I make a move. It seems insurmountable from my position, restrained to a table as they run electrodes across me. An armed guard points his gun at me, but all I have now is time.

Time and nothing else.

I bare my teeth at him like an animal and watch in satisfaction as his eyes widen in fear.

"Now, Novaleen, that is not very nice, is it?" my father calls through the two-way mirror.

"I was never the nice one. That was Annie. You know, the daughter you killed," I retort, and his expression turns cold.

"Today we are going to be testing your mental fortitude and how it affects your body—"

I tune him out, imagining leaping across this table, taking that fucking tablet he holds, and shoving it up his ass.

Two hours later, I find out what he really meant—mental torture to see how my body reacts and if my emotions heighten my strength and speed.

Snarling, I lunge at him, but the chains hold me down. He makes a tutting noise. "It seems your past is a trigger and heightens your skills. I wonder what else is? It's evident your emotions are tightly tied to it. Would speaking about Ana be one as well?"

I freeze, my heart slamming in my chest, and the machines note it for him. Not even my pain can be my own. I had been playing with him and winding him up for hours, but now I stare, begging him with my eyes not to go there.

Not to rip out whatever remains of my heart.

But of course, he does.

"How did her death make you feel?" he asks, sounding clinical and cold.

"Don't," I snarl, but even I hear the devastation in my tone.

"Did it bring up those instincts in you?" he continues, ignoring me completely, his eyes going to the machines. I see my heartbeat race on them, just like it pumps in my chest. Each breath is agony until I'm raggedly breathing, my hands shaking where they are chained to the table. I want to rip off the lines, smash the machines, and cover my ears like a child, but I cannot protect myself from this, just like I couldn't protect her.

"Novaleen, we require your answer. When you felt her dying, what happened inside your body? Can you talk me through it?" When I just stare, fighting back my anger, he frowns. "It was almost too easy to kill her, you know?" He switches tactics. "She was so trusting and still expected her father to protect her. She never could understand the need in me to succeed no matter what. It never mattered how many degrees she got or how much she succeeded in our field, she could never turn her emotions off. She was soft. It got her killed. I felt nothing as she fell—"

"Stop," I beg, whining like an injured animal.

"It was nothing to me, like watching the results of an experiment. I suppose I did expect to feel something, but I didn't. She was useless to me. She was corrupted by you, and she outlived her purpose, but you loved her anyway, even when she hated you. Did she know you protected her all those years?"

My heart is exploding out of my chest, and my head aches and spins. "Did she understand how much of a martyr you were and how easy it was to get you to do what I wanted? I just had to threaten her. It's why I kept her all those years. I knew you would never leave her, not really. Did you tell her, Nova? Or did you just let her hate you? Did you think you deserved it?"

I fight against my restraints but it's useless. Baring my teeth, I feel my anger and pain explode as I yell at him wordlessly.

"Did she die hating you, Nova? Or did she forgive you? Did my bleeding-heart daughter die thinking you would save her?"

Closing my eyes, I try to block out his words, but it's useless. They burrow into my brain, ripping every part of me to pieces. Ribbons of my heart and soul die from his sharp-edged prodding.

"I think she did. I think, even at the end, she expected you to save her and you couldn't. At that moment, you wanted to kill me, so why didn't you? I would like to understand."

I try to breathe through it, choking on my blood and pain. For a moment, there's silence as he watches the monitors.

"Interesting. That simply breaks you down. It's a weakness. Let's switch gears then, shall we, Novaleen?" My eyes flutter open, and even that small act hurts because he's right.

She expected me to save her and I couldn't.

I have to live with that, but not for long.

"What about the others? The failed experiments you had grown so attached to?" I become ice cold all over. "Maybe I should bring them here to be used as . . . incentives."

I lift my head slowly to meet his knowing eyes.

"Do you think you are more inclined to love them because you are so desperate to be loved since you were not as a child? Or are you simply so desperate not to be alone, you convinced yourself to love those people like yourself?"

No, he does not get to ruin this.

He doesn't get to taint them and what we have.

"Do you think you are more likely to keep losing all your hair because of stress from your experiments never working out? Or is it from the realisation that you will never again be able to accomplish anything?" His eye ticks, and I grin evilly. "Does it upset you that no one will ever remember you? That all of this will become nothing but a warning to those who come after you? That everything you have done is for . . . well, nothing? You're old and weak, Father. You're slower, your brain is not connecting like it used to, and your skin is wrinkled and sagging like cottage cheese. Who knows what lies in your future? Wouldn't it be ironic if you lost all your memories or something as simple as a mortal disease killed you before anything could ever be finished?"

"Novaleen, let us get back on track," he says, his voice tight.

"Oh, I am on track. Do they all know that you are legally dead and you are slowly losing money? Do they know that no one will ever support you and this vision you have? That's why you are so desperate to finish this now and find the answers, isn't it? Do they know it keeps you up at night, wondering if the scientific community will ever accept it?" I know I'm on target when his knuckles turn white on the tablet, gripping it tightly. The guards shift slightly. "Do they know you sold your soul to the devil only for it to mean nothing?"

"Enough! Punish her!" he yells and turns to depart.

"Do they know how weak you are, and that's why you crave my strength?" I scream after him before descending into laughter. I even welcome the pain as the guards close in around me, needing it to forget his words, his truth.

"Hello, boys, ready to play?" I jangle the chains. "How about you take these off and we play fair?"

One sneers at me. There are two types of guards here—ones who are desperate for the money and look the other way and others who enjoy their orders and dish out pain. Luckily, I get the latter today. Their fists smack into my head on the left and then the right. Laughing, I spit my blood onto the table, watching in satisfaction as it drips across the brilliant white floor.

Let it stain it like it stains my soul.

They pummel my body, the temporary physical pain briefly driving back the heartache until it comes roaring back.

You couldn't protect her.

I bare my teeth. "Is that all you got?" I demand, needing them to knock me out so I don't have to think or remember for a little while.

"Oh, I'm going to enjoy this," one spits, and then his hands wrap around my throat. He adds more and more pressure.

Black dots dance in my vision and my lungs scream. On the verge of death, of passing out, and I race towards it, needing oblivion.

"P-Pussy," I croak out, and he grips tighter, then my vision fades out.

All I hear is the trapped fluttering of my heart and then nothing.

I go with a smile on my face.

When I wake, I know I'm not alone. I turn slightly to see Father sitting on a chair, watching me. Groaning, I flop onto my back. "I haven't had enough sleep to deal with your fucking face," I sneer.

"Does your hatred keep you happy?" he asks, observing me. I swallow, and he watches the movement. "You loved me once," he declares as if it confuses him. "Even though you knew you shouldn't, you loved me."

"I was a kid," I whisper, staring at him, "just a kid. You were supposed to love me."

"I did in a way."

"Someone who loves you wouldn't have done what you did. I feel sorry for you. You'll never know loyalty, love, or friendship."

"No, just riches and great success. How horrible of me. Nova, think of the great things we could do together if you only helped me. When I get the information I need, I can let you go back to them if you wish."

For a moment, I'm tempted to give in before the reason for his presence dawns on me, and then I laugh.

"You're desperate. You can't get what you need. Really, Father? A bargain? Pleading? It's below you. Pathetic," I spit.

"If I have to hurt them to get what I need, then I will, Nova," he snarls.

"You will never find them." I smile. "You will never get your hands on them. They are safe from you and so much fucking stronger than you could ever believe." As I talk, my sore throat starts to fade back to normal thanks to my healing. I know by tomorrow, the only evidence of my brush with death will be the bruises on my neck.

"They were failures." He frowns. "They didn't meet the required—"

"That's your problem, Father." I force myself to sit up, not wanting to be lying down before him. "All you see is data and numbers, not the person. You failed them, not the other way around. They are stronger than I am and better too. They are the very things you have been working so hard for, and you let them go. Don't worry, though, because I found what you never did—their souls, and they are mine. Rip me apart, burn me, cut me, or shoot me, but you will never have them. You can't." I bare my teeth.

"We shall see about that." He stands, looking me over. "Rest. We need you to be strong, not weak like you are now. I shall allow you a day to recuperate."

"How fucking kind," I snap.

"You will remain here and sleep." The door shuts and locks after him, and a plan starts to form, leaving me grinning.

I have a whole day. I can do a lot with a whole day.

FIFTEEN

LOUIS

Two days have passed, and I'm having a hard time keeping it together. I struggle to eat and sleep, but I know I need to. I check in on the others all the time. Bert is doing better, but it's clear he's struggling with the loss of Ana and Nova. Those two were like his daughters, and I cannot imagine how he feels. He's back in the kitchen, cooking up a storm as if they are going to walk through the door at any moment and will need food. I think it gives him something to focus on. Jonas and Nico take turns eating all the food, making themselves sick, knowing Bert needs that. Isaac keeps checking on him, too, and like Nova would want, I check in on Isaac, but it's Dimitri whom I'm the most worried about. His skin is bleaching from being indoors, and staring at the screens day after day is creating purple bags under his bloodshot eyes. He's jittery with all the caffeine he has consumed, but he won't listen to me. I know I will eventually have to ask Isaac to sedate him so he can rest before he kills himself.

He's worried, and he can't physically handle losing someone he loves again.

Not like Bas, not when he feels like he can do something, so for now, I help as much as I can. When he snaps and gets annoyed at me, telling me I'm doing it wrong, I don't take it personally.

Like now.

"D, calm down."

"No, you are doing it wrong. We will lose the file," he snarls, his eyes narrowed on me. "Are you that fucking dumb?"

"Dimitri, breathe," I order.

His nostrils flare before he covers his face, scrubbing it with his hands and turning away. I see his shoulders droop. Disappointment and guilt are in every line of his body. When I move in front of him, his eyes are filled with mortification. "I am sorry, Louis. I know you're only trying to help."

"You need to sleep."

"Not yet. I'm so close. I can feel it."

"You cannot help anyone if you are bedbound and sick because you did not rest and eat."

"Not yet," he murmurs, dismissing me once more.

"At least have something to eat and drink," I demand, pushing the plate at him. The forgotten ones have been taken away. "Nova needs you to be strong." It's wrong to use his love for her, but it works. His eyes close for a moment before he snatches up the sandwich and starts chewing, not even tasting it.

"Good. I'll come back in a bit. I want it all eaten. I am not playing anymore, Dimitri. I will keep you alive, even if it makes you hate me." I go to check on the others, knowing he needs a moment. I do as well because even mentioning her name hurts.

I miss everything about her—her laughter, her sarcasm, and the way her eyes would glint as she challenged me. I miss the way she loved and supported me. I miss the way she kept my family together.

She belongs here, with us.

If this is just a snippet of what our lives will be like without her, then we won't survive it. It will break us, and our family will wither and die without our heart.

I'm just planting flowers around the graves when Nico jogs over. "Dimitri needs us."

I jerk to my feet. Fuck, I knew I should have pushed him to rest. Nico must see the panic in my eyes because he claps my shoulder and says, "He's fine. It's good news. I think he's manic. We could barely understand what he's saying, he's so excited."

"Then let's not keep him waiting." We jog inside to find Dimitri pacing in the living room. A worried-looking Isaac watches him from the sofa, and Bert flits around Jonas with a plate of pancakes, watching Dimitri with interest.

"You're here!" he practically yells when I enter, and I know my eyebrows rise. "Sorry, sorry, this is important. Sit."

I do, perching on the edge of the sofa and exchanging a worried look with Isaac. His eyes let me know that he will take care of Dimitri after this. I hate putting that on him, but it might do him some good to have someone else to fuss over.

"Dimitri, take a breath and talk to us," I tell him.

His hands shake as he closes his eyes and calms his breathing. "Sorry, sorry, but I found something. You see, I was looking into his bank accounts to see if we could follow the money trail as another avenue, but then I started to think he's too smart to use his accounts. I thought maybe blind funding, but then I checked Ana's name just to be sure and there, in bank accounts she would never know to check, were purchases, so I started to track them down." He speaks so rapidly, it's hard to follow, but I try. "I've managed to track one all the way back to the source. It's a manufacturing company based in China. He spent a considerable amount there. When I looked into what they manufacture, it seemed to be lab equipment. If you weren't looking for her father, you would assume she bought it for her own research," he finishes with a grin.

I blink, and it finally clicks. "You think it's the equipment for whatever lab he has taken Nova to?"

"It was made just a month ago when Ana was with us, when he was dead. Yes, I think so. If we go there and put some pressure on them, we can figure out where the equipment was shipped to or at least find the next step. I have the guards' IDs and their friends' and families' funding, as well as trying to decrypt the other purchases, but it's somewhere to start, right?" He deflates then, looking anxious, but I grin and nod.

"You did good, Dimitri. Let's get the plane fuelled and go check it out before he realises we are onto him and tries to cover his tracks." Slapping his shoulder on the way past, I offer him a nod. "You did good, brother. Get it all started and then sleep on the plane. That is an order." Turning to the others, I clap.

"Pack up, brothers. We are going after our girl."

"Finally," Jonas cheers around a mouthful of pancake.

SIXTEEN

NOVA

L ike Father promised, they leave me alone. It's clearly the middle of the night, and the lights are out. I crawl from the bed and into the bathroom, where there are no cameras. Why would they be necessary when there is no escape route? Or so they think.

Shutting the lid on the toilet, I ignore the ache in my body. Above the toilet is the vent for the room. It's a square that will fit my body at a squeeze. I'm taking a guess that the air ducts are beyond, but it's worth a shot. I need to get around without being seen.

I stare at the screws for a moment until I spot the shampoo bottle. Ripping off the lid, I twist the plastic, and with frustrating patience, I slowly undo the screws. When enough are out, the top swings down. I leave the bottom attached in case I need to hide quickly and recap the bottle of shampoo, even if it is bent, and then I peer into the vent. Well, here goes nothing.

Gripping the edge, I lift myself up and into it. It's a tight squeeze, and I think about Nico and how he would freak out right now. Pushing thoughts of them away, I use my arms to crawl through the vent as quietly as I can. It's straight for about three feet before it branches left and right. Closing my eyes, I remember the hallways I was dragged through and choose right. The motions allow my mind to settle. If they find me, they will punish me, but they already are so it doesn't bother me.

I peer down the first open vent I come to and see a corridor, so I keep going. I stop over the fifth vent when guards sweep the corridor, relaxed and chatting away. I wait as they pass, not wanting to give my position away. When it's quiet again, I carry on, coming to a four-way junction. I haven't seen a control room on this floor, and I've seen a lot of it, so I'm guessing it's either up or down. If it were me, I would have it near the entrance, so I head that way. I squeeze and twist until I can stand up, and then I press my back to one of the metal duct walls and my hands to the other, watching it dent slightly, before I begin to climb. I grit my teeth as my muscles strain, thanks to the beatings I have been taking and the lack of exercise, but the burn is good because it clears my mind and takes it off my itching throat and worry for my guys.

Sweat beads on my forehead, but I continue to climb until I come to a junction once more, this one going left and right. I pick left this time for no other reason than I went right last time. It's a squeeze as I wiggle up and into the tunnels. I hit some of my bruises and cuts and have to breathe through the pain, but it keeps me alert and awake, so at least that's something, I shimmy down the tunnel, and it eventually stops at a dead end with a grate. I peer through the slats to the room beyond. It appears to be empty, so I open it and drop down onto an unmade bed. It cushions my fall, and I roll onto my feet, glancing around.

I got lucky. It seems to be an unused medical room with another two-way mirror. Moving to the door, I look out to see the numbers in the corridor. This one seems to be empty, but there's a camera in the upper right-hand corner. Blowing out a breath, I look around and find what I'm looking for. Grabbing a metal pole, I open the door a crack and swing the opposite door open, activating an alarm, and then I wait. Not too long after, guards come surging down the hallway, opening the door and stepping inside. With them distracted, I hurry out and along the corridor. When no alarms blare, I figure they are focused on the room. I make it to a junction, looking left and right, and find what I want at the end on the right—a nearly white door with a word saying, "Security."

Bingo.

The door is slightly open, so I hurry inside and shut it. The guards must have gone to the room to investigate. There are rows upon rows of monitors, and I quickly memorise the camera locations before moving to the unlocked computer.

Idiots.

I scan through the contents as quickly as possible, finding the alarm map. It shows me the layout of the building we are in, which seems to be a three-story industrial unit above and a bunker of five levels below. I memorise it and click it all shut before focusing on the cameras. I carefully turn some just a few inches to create blind spots, knowing I might need them in the future. Without much else to do, and knowing I'm running out of time, I slip out and into the closet room just as the guards storm past, muttering about idiot newbies. I dart out after them and back to the room I climbed out of. Jumping, I catch onto the vent, haul myself up, and shut it after me.

It's like I was never there, unless they watch the cameras.

They seem almost bored with this job, however, thinking it's too easy, so that works well. As quickly as I can, I make my way back to my room, shutting the vent. I use my fingers and nails to slide the screws back, but not all the way. My fingers bleed after, and my nails are jagged and broken, but I wash them and ignore the pulsing pain and ripped skin as I slide back into bed.

They will come to check on me soon.

It's almost all too easy.

This is going to be fun.

Not five minutes later, the door opens, and a guard peers in before it shuts again.

I lie back in bed and wait, knowing I need the rest, so I shut my eyes for a few hours.

I wake up with a groan when the door opens. My eyelids are heavy, and my body is sluggish from the lack of sleep and the round-the-clock torture and experiments, but I force myself to sit up as a guard throws a tray on the bed next to me. I glare at him until he huffs and leaves, then I pick up the tray. I know they could have drugged the food or done something to it, but I also know I need to eat or I won't be at my full strength, and that outweighs the other risks.

There's chicken with mixed veggies, some bread, and yogurt. It's not Bert's cooking, but I use my hands to eat it because obviously, why would I need cutlery? Fucking assholes. I have to use the lid of the yogurt for a spoon, and when I'm done, I toss it at the door, watching it clatter, the mess bringing me great joy.

It's the little victories.

The same guard comes back and cleans it up, glaring at me the entire time before he stomps off. He lets the door swing shut behind him, but I hurry over and put my foot in it. When he doesn't reappear, I peek out to see the corridor is empty. The camera here is one I moved a few inches to give me a blind spot, so it will work when I need it to. Not right now though.

Ripping the bottom of my shirt, I ball it up and stick it in the lock, so the door shuts but won't lock properly. Unless they look closely, they won't notice, which is exactly what I want. I begin to stretch out my body, flipping off the camera as I loosen up, and then fall into a usual routine—one I haven't used since before I was alone and moving constantly. Jumping jacks turn into burpees then sit-ups and push-ups, and then I stretch out my body and do it again. I'll need to keep my strength and speed up. I finally collapse onto the bed, panting and covered in sweat, with that telltale burn in my muscles.

I eventually manage to drag myself to the shower and wash off all the sweat and dried blood. Watching it circle the drain, I trace the bruises across my body. There are older, yellowing ones and bright black and purple ones. I let the shower spray hit the laceration on my side and peel off the gauze. It's healing well, and I shouldn't need it anymore, so I gently wash that before doing the same to the one on my hip and then turning to scrub my back. I wash my hair a few times to get the feel of their hands and leers out of it, and then I stand under the spray, letting the lukewarm water take me away to a different shower, where hands slid possessively across my body.

Jonas loved joining me in the shower. I press my hands to the wall, wishing he were here touching me, loving me, and making me laugh.

I wish they were all here.

And Ana.

Fuck.

The tears start, but I let them fall, washed away by the shower until there are no more, and then I dry off and slip on some grey shorts and a matching shirt they provided before collapsing onto the bed and turning away from the camera.

The lights go off shortly after, and in the dark, I imagine a body behind me in the bed, never letting me sleep alone. I envision their comfort and lov and not for the first time, I wonder what they are doing. Have they stopped looking? Have they let me go?

Fuck, I hope so. I would hate for them to end up trapped here once more. I'm not worth it. I want them to trust in me to finish this and find the life they deserve, but even as I think that, I know they won't. They are loyal, and they love me. They have proven over and over that we are in this together and that they will always come for me.

I just hope that when they do find me, it's not too early.

I want them to arrive when this place is up in flames and understand it's over. Then, they can mourn me and move on.

I hope they find the happiness they deserve. I send it as a prayer as I stare into the darkness.

SEVENTEEN

NOVA

Morning comes all too quickly, and I know my day of rest is over. The lights flicker on, and I sigh as I turn over, knowing they'll be coming for me soon. I quickly use the toilet, wash my face, and brush my teeth before tying my hair back, slipping on some trainers and socks as I wait on the bed. I place my hands on my knees like a good little girl, even as my heart fills with fear and determination.

As soon as the door opens and the guards step forward, I know today will be different. They have cuffs, so I hold out my hands, letting the guards chain them together before they silently drag me into the corridor. We don't go to the labs, and I quickly work through the map forming in my head from my days here and the cameras to figure out where we're going, but I draw a blank. I soon realise why when we head down two levels in an elevator and through a secure door.

I've never seen this section before.

Yay, this will be fun.

"Oh, spooky and dramatic with the long hallways and cameras. Would it kill you to put some art somewhere? Haven't you ever heard of happy worker —" I grunt as an elbow meets my gut, making me double over, then I glare at the guard. "Touch me again and I'll break your arm," I hiss in warning.

I might have a plan, but that doesn't mean I'll take their pain.

With a sinister smile, he slams his arm into my gut again, only this time, I let him, and instead of doubling into the pain as the air whooshes from my lungs, I use it. I lunge for him and grab his arm, and even with my cuffed hands, I manage to slide behind him and slam his arm down over his shoulder. I hear the bones snap before he howls and drops to his knees, cradling his arm.

I hold up my bound hands as an alarm is triggered. The other guard points his weapon at me, glancing between me and the downed man who has tears falling down his mottled face. Through gritted teeth, he says, "You are fucking dead!" He surges to his feet, but more guards pour down the corridor with their guns pointed at me, blocking him.

I smile sweetly at all of them. "I warned him what would happen. Now, shall we continue on? We all know Dr. Davis doesn't like to be late."

For a moment, nobody moves, so I just smile with my hands up as the broken-armed guard is led away cursing. I'm the most dangerous person here, and they all suddenly realise it. Their eyes are sharp and wary, and their guns are held aloft, ready to be used.

They are truly understanding the depths of the experiments now and just what I'm capable of.

"Well?" I sigh like they bore me.

A guard slowly moves toward me, circling me and pointing his gun at the back of my head. "Walk," he barks, and I do just that, surrounded by a platoon of guards.

That's how we enter the giant room I am led to, with the guards blocking most of my view bar my father who turns and spots us with a frown. "Is that really necessary? Novaleen, you will behave, won't you?" he questions.

"Of course I will." I practically ooze sincerity.

"See? Put the guns down. You don't need them." When nobody moves, his face clouds in anger.

"Oh, you've done it now," I whisper. I know that look.

"I said now, unless you want to be on the next garbage rotation!" he yells. All too quickly, the guns are pulled away and the guards step back, melting to the sides of the room. Their eyes remain on me, and they are ready to act, but they are following orders.

"Good boys," I purr and hold my wrists up to my father. "Can we get these off now?"

"Yes, of course," he replies like we are civilised people, and he moves over to grab the key as I look around our location today. It's not a lab, that's for sure, and as I see what's in the room, I get a really bad feeling and all my cockiness evaporates.

There's a giant mat covering most of the space, clearly for sparring and training. To the left is a gym with floor-to-ceiling mirrors, and to the right of the mat is an extreme obstacle course.

There is a man in the middle of the mat I don't recognise. He has on army cargos and a black T-shirt, but his feet are bare as he does push-ups. He's well-muscled with a buzzed head and intense black eyes. I watch how he moves, fast and hard, his body a well-oiled machine. That would give him away if his clothes didn't.

He's a soldier, not a guard, and he's clearly fast and capable.

"Ah, I see you've noticed Sergeant Joel," my father comments as he undoes my cuffs, and I flex my hands. "One of the successes of that batch. I believe you met or found some of the other unsuccessful members of his unit."

I swallow hard as I eye him, thinking about Sam. This man knew Sam? When he leaps to his feet and rolls out his muscles, his eyes land on me. They are cold, dead, and cruel. This man is nothing like I am, and he's embraced whatever they have done to him.

"Yes," is all I say.

"Good. He will be part of your testing today. You are always asking for more of a challenge, so I figured someone on your level would be more beneficial for your results. I'd like to see the difference between the outcomes of the experiments from adulthood to childhood."

"How?" I ask, knowing the answer deep down.

"By testing you against each other, of course," my father answers, turning away to grab his tablet as I eye Joel. He's tall and built like a brick shit house, and he clearly likes what he's being ordered to do.

I don't know if they suspect it was me last night, or if they simply want to punish me, but I have no choice but to perform for them. I can't endure another punishment so I need to be smart. I need to make them relax.

I need my father to think he's won.

That means defeating Joel. A spark of excitement rolls through me. I've had to hold back for so long, even with my guys. I worried about what I would become if I let go, but with this sergeant, I won't have to. He's changed, like me and my guys. He can take it, and unlike my guys, I have no loyalty to him, and getting rough and winning is what I need to do to survive.

He moves closer, nodding at my father, but his eyes are all for me.

Like recognises like.

He sizes me up like I did to him, and there's a gleam in his eye I don't like as he surveys me. It's hard to pinpoint, but when his eyes drop to my body, I almost shudder in revulsion.

"So, you're the prodigal experiment?" he sneers. "You don't look like much." He has a thick Irish accent, and sure, he's attractive, but that gleam? I watch him more carefully. "In fact, you look like a lost little girl. Is this really who you are pinning all your hopes on?" he asks my father, ignoring me.

"She has shown the best results under pressure and seems to have accessed more of her brain than any other, including you, even if she wastes it," he tells Joel without even looking at me.

"Happy to waste it." I salute my father, and Joel throws me a glare.

He grinds his teeth, but like a good soldier, he ignores me and focuses on my father. "Orders?"

"I want her fully tested. Push her to her limits."

"I'm right here," I mutter, but they both ignore me.

"And past them. Show me exactly what she is capable of, and I will make my decision about how this will proceed." My father looks at me. "I am rooting for you. You were my hope for the future, for what we could become, but if you fail me again, I will allow Joel to put you down and proceed with his strand of research. Is that understood?"

I swallow hard. So far, my father's need for me has kept me alive, but he's telling me that if I fail today, it won't. I need to push harder than I ever have because I know Joel will not let me do anything else. This will be a true test. I'm not a child anymore. I'm a full-grown adult with abilities others could only dream of.

I hate what my father has done to me, so I never explored the full depths of my abilities, and the darkness in my brain scares me, so I always shied away from discovering exactly what I am capable of. I only ever pushed as hard as he made me and never any further, truly scared of what he had done to me.

When I'm pushed, what if I'm not even human anymore?

I guess we are going to find out.

Joel nods and smirks at me. "Gladly. Start on the course, and we will compare times. Go," he orders.

I hesitate, wanting to smash in his smug face in and ignore his orders, but I have no choice. My father is watching me right now, and I am at their mercy. I need to play nice and give into the side of me I fear to survive.

I remind myself I am doing this for my men as I turn to the obstacle course, Joel sharply on my heels. He is almost silent as he moves, but I can feel him behind me. I stop at the beginning of the course and eye it, my brain working a mile a minute to plan the best route for the fastest time.

"Begin when you're ready," Joel snaps. I bend my knees slightly, closing my eyes for a moment as I centre myself. I imagine his smug face if he wins and know I can't let that happen.

He thinks I'm nothing, and my father is expecting me to fail.

I won't just to prove them wrong.

When my eyes snap open, I give myself over to that force deep inside me. Strength surges through me, as does speed, purpose, and determination.

I let all my worries and thoughts flee until there is only action.

Adrenaline pumps through my veins as I push off the floor and leap at the first piece of equipment. A rope hangs down to help me climb the wall but I ignore it, leaping up and grabbing the lip of the vertical wooden block. I hang there for a second, easily six feet in the air, and then I haul myself up and roll over, flipping to land with one knee down on the ground, then I'm moving again. There's a rope strung between two poles, and I quickly ascend the ladder to it and drop forward. I use my hands to pull me across it, with one knee pressed against it while the other hangs. When I reach the other side and descend, I race across a small sprint section to a cargo net suspended twenty feet in the air. Pushing off, I grab the ropes and climb diagonally, since I noticed they are shorter distances for my shorter legs, and it makes the ascent quicker. I can feel them all watching, but I ignore them as I reach the platform at the top and race across it. The platform ends, and there are twenty-foot poles dotted at random intervals to a bridge on the other side. I leap across them and race down the slope back to the ground.

The next piece has four poles in staggered heights before each other. I duck under the first, climb atop the second, and hop to clear the other two. After all, he never mentioned rules; he just said to get through it the quickest.

Before me are monkey bars and I jump, grabbing onto the first and swinging easily to the second. With my legs locked together, I keep up the momentum, moving so fast I barely see the bar before I move onto the next, and then I drop to the ground at the other side.

There's a tire with a line at the end. It's huge and easily weighs six hundred and fifty kilograms. I crouch and flip it, grunting at the weight, but then, just to be an ass, I pick it up and with gritted teeth, I carry it to the end, knowing even most army people would struggle to do so. The next obstacle is a round sprint track, and I push myself to run faster, and then, without stopping, I drop to my knees, crawl through the tunnel, and pop to my feet on the other side before I sprint back to the first wall I started at. I race up it and drop down on the other side, sliding to a stop beside Joel who has a watch in his hand.

Smirking at him, I fight back the need to bend over and pant, but then I realise I don't actually need to. It didn't even wind me. What the fuck?

"Well?" my father calls, and there's a smugness in his voice that tells me he knows the answer.

"Twenty seconds faster than me," he reluctantly admits, and my father's laughter fills the air.

"It's not over yet," Joel snaps, dropping the watch. "Weights next."

Joel forces me to lift the weights he does, watching my form carefully. Next, he has me run on the treadmill next to him. When he ups the speed, so do I, always doing one better. After that, I'm forced through cardio until he finally calls it quits. I sip the water I'm given and watch him talk with my dad before nodding and heading back my way.

"Last test of the day," he mutters, glaring at me. He's clearly angry that not only can I keep up, but I can beat him.

"Sure, what is it? Want me to lift you until you cry? Or maybe beat your ass on the course again?"

"No. This time, I'll be beating your ass." I narrow my gaze, and he grins. "It's time to test your combat skills."

Great, he literally meant kick my ass. For a moment, Nico's face is on top of Joel's, smiling at me and urging me to fight him before it's gone. Nico is nothing like Joel. Joel wants to hurt me. This might be a sparring session, but it will be no-holds-barred. He will break bones and rip me apart if he can. It's in his eyes and the tension in his muscles.

Dropping my water to the floor, I kick off my shoes and step onto the mat. I shake out my arms before taking up my stance. I'm heavily trained in mixed martial arts, but I can already tell from the way this man moves that he knows exactly what I do and maybe more, which means I need to play dirty, and I will do just that.

I have to win.

He circles me, and I watch him carefully for signs of his moments, but unlike most, he gives nothing away. His arm just suddenly swings and his fist catches me in the chin. My head whips to the side from the strength of his punch, which is so much stronger than I have ever felt. I almost go down. My chin instantly aches, and my whole mouth locks up as he smirks.

"You're weak and sloppy. You care too much about being normal to fully give in. You will never win." He launches at me, holding nothing back. I have to fight just to stay on my feet, blocking his fists and feet. One connects with my ribs, and I feel the healing bones crack again. A fist hits my shoulder, and it goes numb as I stumble back under his assault. My heels almost catch on the edge of the mat because he's pushed me back that much.

I hear my father sigh. It's one sound filled with resignation and disappointment, but coupled with the glee in Joel's eyes, it ignites something within me. Something clicks, and I duck his next swing, leaping at him. I wrap my legs around his neck and flip us both, getting back to my feet and circling him as he stands and watches me.

The predator just became the prey.

He's right. I do hold back because I am so worried about what is inside of me. I am scared of myself, not my father, but I can't hold back, not if I want to survive this.

I have to let go.

Cocking my head, I smile slowly. "My turn," is all I say.

This time, I drive him back. I attack him with more speed than I've ever used before. Each movement is clean and so fast, he can't anticipate it. Years of training and honing skills flow back to me until he has to dance back out of my reach. His chest heaves slightly, while I'm not even sweating or panting. After all, brute strength isn't everything.

I'm faster than him, I realise, when I duck under his punch and come up behind him, kicking out his knees. He stumbles forward, but he flips back and over me, wrapping his arm around my throat. His muscles bulge as he squeezes, almost breaking my neck. Most people would struggle, so he's expecting that, and when I relax and go limp, he loosens his hold enough for me to slam my elbow back into him. I hear something break, and then I drop completely. He wasn't expecting that, and I'm free. I slam my hand up, right into his nose, and it explodes as he groans and steps back.

Ignoring the blood and busted nose, he comes for me again, but this time, his movements are wild with aggression. It makes him unpredictable and as fast as I am, so a few of them catch me. We both fight without holding back, each of us landing hits. Blood splashes across our skin, and bruises and broken bones make us cry out in pain.

His fist catches me in the face again, but the force of it knocks me down and he's on me in an instant. I narrow my gaze on him as his hands wrap around my throat.

"Why?" I ask him, voicing what I've been curious about this whole time, even as I wrap my legs around him and buck, trying to dislodge him. "Why are you helping him despite what he did to your unit?"

"Do you know how many soldiers die on duty, or even after? He can help stop that by making us harder, stronger, and faster. Why wouldn't I want to protect my people by doing that? We can be better."

"He will sell it to every army, and then you'll still be in the same predicament," I snarl as I thrash.

"I do this for my people. Why do you still fight, lost little girl?"

I meet his eyes as my nostrils flare and my lips curl in disgust. "For my people." I smash my head into his and roll out from under him, leaping to my feet and then kicking my foot into his balls. "And you will lose."

He falls forward with a cry, cupping his balls, and I smash my elbow into his head. He hits the mats hard, knocked out.

Panting, I look over at my father, feeling my split lip pour blood. One of my eyes is swollen, and one ankle aches.

He smiles at me, and I hate the spark of pride I feel at that. "Take Joel to the infirmary," my father calls, then he picks something up and heads my way. "I knew you could do it. I was always betting on you. We just have a few more things to test and then you can rest, okay?" he says kindly, but I grind my teeth. He gestures for me to turn and I do.

A blindfold wraps around my head, blocking my sight. Blowing out a long breath, I loosen my stance, my arms hanging at my sides as I wait for instruction.

"Please show us your senses so we may test each. You will face multiple opponents," my father says, and I hear him move away.

I hear more movement as guards come towards me, and I wait as they spread out, and then it's silent.

Finally, there's a squeak, a scent, and I move quickly. I am fast, but so are they.

There has to be at least three of them. One knocks my leg out, but I jump back up and slam my own into something hard. There's a grunt, then arms wrap around me from behind. I kick and smash into another body coming from the front. They fall back, and holding onto the arms around me, I push off and up, rolling to my feet.

I lose myself in the fight. I can't see, and the darkness seems to unlock something inside me.

It's as if that darkness was always waiting to come out. I hear more than I ever have. I hear the air whooshing in and out of their lungs, the beating of their hearts, and I can almost smell their fear as I attack.

I lose myself in the rhythm. There are at least eight of them now, and I know as soon as I knock one out or hurt them too badly, they are dragged away and replaced by another. There are no words, just actions. I don't know how long I fight for, but after what feels like hours and I start to slow, a punch lands that I wouldn't have let make contact before.

My body is tiring. I'm still healing, and it's taking its toll.

Another punch slips through, then another, until I'm finally kicked down. Suddenly, several booted feet slam into my body. I drag my knees to my chest as they slam into me over and over. I groan, managing to crawl from them and get back to my feet, but then something hard hits the back of my head.

The last thing I see as the blindfold slips away is my father turning away in disappointment.

EIGHTEEN

ISAAC

The flight to China was uneventful, and we find the manufacturing plant easily enough. We survey it for a while, watching the workers come and go. The trucks leave and arrive, and D tracks each one in case we need to know where they go, and then we wait for Louis to give us orders and let us know it's time.

Bert was worried when we left, but he was also determined. His final words reach me even now. "Bring her home!"

We will. We have to. This is a good lead, I remind myself, even as I shift for the hundredth time. I need to move, to do something, anything. As the clock ticks, I can't help but wonder how much more damage is being done to the woman I love while we sit here.

"Soon," Jonas reminds me. He is struggling too. I feel it as he sits next to me, crammed into the car. Louis is at the store opposite the plant, Nico is on the roof of the store for a better angle, and D is in the front of the car with his laptop open.

"Not soon enough." I scrub at my face, no doubt messing up my hair, but I don't care.

"I prefer it when you're the happy-go-lucky doctor," Jonas grumbles.

"Well, tough shit. Not everybody is happy all the time, Jonas. I'm allowed to be upset," I snap, and he watches me with wide eyes. "Sorry," I mutter.

"Don't be. I've been waiting for that outburst. It's good. I like it when you're happy, but this? This is real. I was getting sick of you holding it all back," he mumbles, glancing out of the window to make sure we are not compromised.

"What do you mean?" I feel my brows draw together in confusion.

He snorts and grins at me. "Come on, Isaac. You act so calm all the time, so put together and like you're ready to face everything. You take in everything we do and say and never complain. That takes its toll, and I always saw it lingering under the surface. I'm glad it's finally coming out."

"What?" I whisper.

"Madness," he says calmly. "It's the same madness we all have, including Nova. Let it out, brother. We are going to need that to get her back."

He turns away like he didn't just drop a bomb. Is he right? Nova always asked me if I was okay. She worried about my reactions and how I was dealing with everything. What if I kept such a tight grip all along because I was worried about what would come out?

Jonas wears his madness proudly, Nico channels it, Louis embraces it, and Dimitri fights it, but me? I hide it.

What if I've made it worse?

Is he right? Do I need to embrace it and therefore burn myself?

Have I been holding back who and what I am?

Yes, I realise with sudden clarity.

"Who knew you were so smart?" I mutter as I stare at his profile.

"Nova." He shrugs. "She sees us all clearly."

Isn't that the sad truth?

Taking his hand in mine, I squeeze it. "You're right. Maybe you can teach me how to embrace it better and I can teach you how to be calmer, brother."

"Nah, she likes me when I'm manic, and so do I." He winks. "But welcome to the club."

Louis slides into the car along with Nico and turns to us. "We'll wait for most of the workers to leave, but not the boss, and then we'll go in. I want as few witnesses as possible. We go in silently. I want no alarms, no police, and no footage of us being there. We do not give the doctor any reason to suspect we are on his trail. Is that understood?"

We all agree since we don't want to do anything that could jeopardise us not only getting to Nova, but also keeping her alive. He's right. We have to do this silently and carefully without tipping off her father.

We wait until the shift ends to make our move. I go with Louis right through the front door. D is at the electrical board outside, cutting off cameras and alarms and fielding any phone calls that might happen from mobiles. Nico repels in from the roof and slips through the open top-floor window on the right, while Jonas is on the left, although we all hear him squealing softly in our earpieces as he goes. We are covering all of our bases. We shut and lock the doors behind us. The warehouse is massive and filled with shipping containers and lab equipment in the process of being made or tested. We move past them, looking for any stragglers or workers.

"Security guards are up top, Nico, coming your way," D says.

"Got them," Nico murmurs, and there's a barely audible grunt down the mic. "Taken care of."

"There are three workers on the late shift coming in early in the canteen. I can auto lock the door from here, but avoid it so they don't see your faces. They haven't noticed as of yet, too busy talking and drinking coffee."

"Got it," Louis murmurs down the mic as we move to the stairs. They lead up to the second floor. Nico is already there, and all of us converge on the office on the second floor. The door has no window, so Louis smashes it open and we surge inside. Nico instantly shoots the phone as the man jerks up from a nap, imprints of the wood from the desk across his cheek.

His eyes widen in fear, and he leaps up, but I push him back down into his chair.

"Sit," I demand.

"What do you want?" he asks in English.

"Just some information," Louis replies, sitting in the opposite chair. "If you tell us what we need to know, we won't harm you, but you will forget we ever existed. In fact, we are more than happy to pay for this information." He smiles charmingly, and the man relaxes but glances at Nico and pales. He plays the part of muscle well—not speaking, just glaring.

"What information?" the man finally mutters.

"Just about one of your buyers and where the last shipment went. That's all." Louis lifts the bag he is carrying and throws it on the desk. The man glances at it and slowly reaches out and undoes the zipper, seeing the bills inside.

He blinks owlishly at us. "I have a family," he says randomly. "You can have the information you want. I'm just trying to provide for them."

"We know, hence why we did this here and not at your home. You're innocent in this," I reply softly, "but you're supplying equipment to a very bad person, and we want to talk to him. No one will hurt you or your family so please, just tell us what we want."

"Okay, can you tell me the date? I will find out for you," he asks, sitting up taller. I'm surprised by how easily he wants to help us, but when I glance around, I see why. It's in the hard glint in our eyes. Anyone can see we are getting that information one way or another, and he's simply choosing the best way out.

Smart.

Dimitri informs him and watches carefully as he pulls information from a cabinet. It's paper, which surprises me, but he hands the folder over. "That's everything we have on the buyer. It was his first time with me. I remember speaking to someone who mentioned their usual supplier did not have what they wanted. It's the credit information as well as the delivery address. I remember because it was very far and random. Do you need anything else?"

"He hasn't bought again?" Louis asks with a frown.

"No, only that once. I guess he went back to his regular supplier after," the man replies with a sincere tone.

"Thank you so much for your help." Louis stands then carefully tucks the chair under the desk. "Forget you saw us. I would hate to have to come back and visit you and your family. Here, take the money and our apologies." Louis turns, and we all follow him out like we were never here.

Dimitri turns the cameras and alarms on once more, unlocking the door like nothing happened. For a while, we watch the man in the office, but he doesn't make any calls or ask for help. He stares at the money. His shoulders slump, and he seems both resigned and relieved.

"He won't tell," I murmur as I watch him, noticing the signs. "He needs the money too much."

"Are you sure?" Louis asks, looking over at me in the car.

"Yes." I watch the camera, but I'm sure, and then I look at Dimitri. "Do we have it?"

"Yes, he's right. It's a weird delivery address. It's an airstrip. Give me an hour and I'll have more information."

An airstrip.

Fuck, are we still on a wild-goose chase?

NINETEEN

NOVA

W hen I wake up, my whole body aches like one giant bruise. I trap a groan in my throat, just feeling out my situation. It wouldn't be the first time my father has taken advantage of my passed-out state, and it feels a lot like that now. I'm lying on something cold and hard—a medical table perhaps. There's that air-con noise that only happens in the lab and the whirring of machines. I'm not in the gym anymore, but I'm also not tied down.

That's a plus, not that I'll need to make a move yet. I need to play the long game.

I take stock of my body. Nothing is broken. There may be a few fractured ribs and some bruised bones, but nothing feels completely wrecked, which is good. I undoubtedly look like shit, but I don't care about that.

I'm about to open my eyes and scan my surroundings when I hear booted feet entering the room. I relax my body despite the fact I want to stiffen, keeping my breathing nice and slow. It's a moment when they might give things away unintentionally.

As expected, someone comes over and checks on me. I feel them hovering above me before they wander a little farther away. "Dr. Davis." I almost snarl at the voice. It's Joel. I guess I didn't kick his ass hard enough if he's awake.

"Feeling better?" my father responds, and there's a thread of disappointment in his voice. I want to laugh.

"Much. I will not make the mistake of misjudging your daughter again. She is a lot stronger than she looks."

"That she is. Watching you two spar, though, gave me the results I expected for you, and it also gave me some ideas," Davis murmurs, and a horrible feeling starts to build inside me, like the moment before a car crash when you see the vehicle coming towards you. That's how it feels. I want to knock myself out. I want to run. I know it's going to be bad, but instead, I lie here and listen.

"An idea?" Joel queries.

"Hmm, yes. I always thought Nova would be the start and end of my research, the key to it all, but what if she is in a different way? She reached peak human potential, and she has begun to access her mind more than any other. It is changing not only her brain, but her physical abilities and structure. She is adapting, to put it mildly, but she started out like the rest of us, and that will give her some limitations. If we were to use that and create a being, a child, perhaps, born from two individuals already enhanced through experiments, then the possibilities would be endless."

My heart freezes.

"Are you saying what I think you are?"

"Yes, you and Nova will breed. You will make me a child, which will be the future of us all. Just think how strong it would be with two almost perfectly enhanced parents."

"I . . ." Joel hesitates, and for a moment, hope fills me that he won't agree and he sees how wrong this is.

"You can do this, yes? She isn't bad looking. If not, we can offer stimulants. She will, of course, have to be sedated, and although there are other ways to do it, this would be the fastest."

No, no, no.

"I-I can do it. Of course." He sounds unsure, but I know that won't stop him. "The child, what will happen to the child?" I guess he's not as big of a monster as I thought. My mind is numb to what I am hearing.

They want to impregnate me.

No, they want to rape me and implant a child in me, which they will use as a test-tube baby.

"It will become the next step of my research. The first one or two always have mistakes, but Nova is in her prime, as are you, so we have plenty of time to get it right."

Annie, he's talking about Annie. Calling her a mistake.

I'm almost sick at the implication of what he's saying.

He's going to force me to breed children for him to experiment on.

My eyes snap open, but the men are too focused on each other. My head is turned to face them, my cheek pressed to the metal table. A tray, as usual, is next to the metal table, ready for his next sick experiment.

I can tell by his face he means it. He'll do it.

Oh, God, no.

I'm numb and cold as he turns and finds me awake. I can see his mouth moving, but his words don't register. Other doctors join us, and my head turns to look up at the ceiling. Something cold touches my stomach, but I still don't move or make a noise. I can't or I'll scream.

Or I'll break.

Something sharp pierces my stomach and starts to drag, causing red-hot agony to shoot through me.

They are cutting me open.

It's like everything snaps back into place, and the noise in the room comes rushing back with the agony. Air fills my lungs with a gasp. I lie here as he cuts me open, and when he turns back, I stare at the man I thought I couldn't hate more but do.

Looking into his eyes, I know he'll do it. He will force him to breed with me or worse. I can't have that. I won't. I will not become a vessel for his sick games. That child would be a pin cushion, tortured and ripped apart like me. I will not put another person through what I went through, but I cannot stop him. I'm weak, powerless . . .

Or so he thinks, but he doesn't understand the lengths I will go to in order to stop this and make sure it never happens to another, even at the risk of my own body.

He will never get my womb or get a child from me.

I'll make sure of it, even if it ruins me for life or kills me.

It's better than the alternative.

There is a table next to me holding the hot sealing prong they use to cauterise my wounds. I don't think, just act. Grabbing the red end of the prong when he looks away, I slam it into myself, into my open stomach wound, screaming in agony. My skin is on fire, and the pain courses through me, but I carry on. I fight them off when they try to pull me away. It's only when I start to pass out that they manage to rip it from me, but I know the damage is already done.

I smile shakily as I begin to die.

That wasn't my aim though. My womb is ruined. I smile at him. "Now you'll never get what you want. Now you will never get my children."

Then, once more, everything goes dark.

I welcome it like an old friend.

TWENTY

LOUIS

W e watch the private airfield for hours. Only one flight comes in all day and by the looks of them, they are not your regular businessmen. No, this is a don't ask, don't tell kind of place, which means there will be no records.

It's another dead end . . . until we see her.

A tiny, curvy blonde leaves the building after locking up. A manager maybe? "Follow her," I instruct, and so we do. This town is small, so there isn't much, and she heads right to a bar.

Dimitri follows her in, reporting that she's sitting alone at a table in the corner.

"Find me everything you can on her," I demand. She was the one meeting the clients, so maybe she knows something.

"On it," he murmurs through the phone, and a few minutes later, a document is on my screen. I scroll through it as the others spread out to watch the back. Jonas remains at the airfield with Isaac, searching just in case.

Lives alone, thirty-five, divorced, and has worked there for five years. She has a huge bank account, one dog, and one cat. No family, nothing else. She's also alone on a Friday night in the bar looking lonely. No listed address, shit.

She's the only link we have, the only choice.

She's lonely and desperate for attention. I hate it, but I know what I'm going to have to do to get the information we need. It makes me feel sick.

"I'm coming in," I tell him. "I'll get the information."

"How?" he asks, but I hang up, ignoring the clenching in my gut and the deep feeling of betrayal. If Nova found out, she would kick my ass, and the thought makes me smile as I cross to the bar. I'd let her since I'd deserve it, but I have to do whatever it takes to get my girl back. After that, she can beat me and then kiss it better. Taking a deep breath, I paste on a fake, overly friendly smile. I hang around the bar for a while, ordering a beer and taking a sip before approaching her. She's reading a romance book, and when I stop before her table, she is so engrossed she doesn't even notice at first.

I clear my throat, and her head snaps up, her eyes widening and cheeks heating. She looks around nervously.

"Hi." I grin. "I'm Reggie."

She blinks and then blushes harder. "Oh, God, I'm sorry. Hi, erm, hi, yeah, I'm Sarah," she blurts out.

"I'm new to town, and I don't really know anyone," I tell her, leaning in like this is a secret. She smiles and giggles as she looks around. "Can I join you? I really don't want to sit alone, drinking my beer."

"Oh, of course."

I slide into the booth opposite her before she can change her mind. Her eyes scan me and heat, and when she meets my gaze, I see desire and curiosity. Good. I can use that, even as the sight of another woman lusting after what belongs to Nova makes me want to gag. This body is hers, every inch of it.

"What are you reading?" I ask, leaning back and purposely flexing my arm as I drape it on the back of the booth. Her eyes follow it like I knew they would. "Sarah?" I murmur silkily. I hate this. I hate every fucking second of this.

I can feel Dimitri judging me, but I'll do anything for her.

"It's just a romance novel." She ducks her head. "I love them. They always get their happy ending. I don't know why I said that."

Laughing, I reach out and eye the cover. It's of a lady and a dragon, and I make a note to read it to Nova later. She would probably love it. "I love happy endings. I'm hoping for my own," I say softly. "Is it sexy?" She laughs nervously, and I chuckle. "I take that as a yes. I'm curious, do you enjoy reading it? The sex scenes?"

"I . . . Yes," she admits, eyeing me through her lashes. "Most women do."

"How come?" I ask with genuine curiosity and no judgement.

"I guess it's how we want to be loved. It's more than the mind-blowing sex they get, which if we are honest, not a lot of women get, but it's the love. Did you know romance is the biggest selling genre in fiction? Let that sink in. Women are so desperate to be loved right that they buy books about it because they know it's the only way most of them will get it, and men? They make fun of it. They make fun of women wanting to read a book about being loved and cared for like the idea is ridiculous."

"Because men are idiots. You want to be loved?" I ask.

"Everyone wants to be loved, Reggie," she replies, sitting up straighter, bolder in her passion. It's cute. "Every single person, no matter what they say, wants that. They want to be loved deeply and stop being hurt over and over. They want a happy ending without pain. Many don't find it, so they find it through this, fiction, until they do find their happy ending. Other people already have it and love relearning the feeling through others. Some simply want an adventure. They get it through books. Like me, a small-town girl, I've got to visit the stars, see other planets, and go to the deepest depths of the oceans. I'm a soldier, a sailor, a mermaid, a pirate . . . I can be anything I want in these books, and for the hours that I indulge and read, losing myself between ink and paper, the shitty world around me doesn't exist. I'm free."

"That sounds amazing. I never thought about it that way. I guess I never really gave myself the time to explore reading. I'm always so busy planning for the future or what comes next."

She smiles. "You should."

"I will." I'll explore it with Nova, if she desires to find the kind of freedom pages can offer. She will always have that deep love this woman loves reading about, but I like how happy it makes Sarah, and I want that for Nova.

She's a lovely woman, and she deserves to find happiness. She's clearly smart, kind, giving, and optimistic, but she isn't my Nova. There is only one woman for me, and I'll use and hurt this kind woman if I have to.

I take a deep breath, hating myself for what I'm about to say. "If you want, I could help you find that freedom."

"How so?" she asks obliviously.

Smiling secretly, I stand and offer her my hand. "How about you take me back to your place and I'll show you? We can even act out some of those scenes."

Wrong, so wrong, so very wrong.

She hesitates, but then she lays her hand in mine. I pull her to her feet, and she clutches her bag as I lead her to the door.

I tell myself to hold her hand. Even if it looks odd, I drop it in the ruse of opening the door. She hesitates again but ducks through, and I wipe my hand on my trousers, the wrongness of it sticking with me. I need Nova to replace it. Sarah's hand was too hot, and it didn't fit right, not like my Nova's, which fits perfectly.

At the parking lot, I look around and back at her with a smile, draping my arm around her coat-covered shoulders so I don't have to touch her.

"You drive?" I offer. "I don't have my car."

Liar, but that way Dimitri can follow us.

"Of course." She fumbles with her keys, and I grin. When she gets them, she blushes and leads me over to her car. It's a nice brand-new model, and I slip into the passenger seat as she hits the ignition, and then we are on the road. I glance into the side mirror to see lights a few cars behind us. They are not noticeable to anyone else but me.

Dimitri.

I make small talk until we pull up in front of her house, and then I get out and follow her up to it.

Her house is adorable, a single-story cottage set before the woods. The lights are on, and there are flowers bordering the stone paths to the door. Once inside, we are greeted by a purring black cat and she blushes. "This is Romeo." She laughs as I chuckle.

She heads in, strips off her coat and bag, and drops them onto a side table. There is a kitchen to the left, a farmhouse style one that's cut with a few steps into an open-plan living room. Sofas face a huge fireplace with bookshelves on either side, and the back windows are floor-to-ceiling to show the forest.

It's cute.

"Do you want a drink?" she asks nervously.

"Sure, a drink would be great," I reply.

I wander around, pretending to look at things, but really, I'm scanning the house. Beyond the kitchen, there is a door that clearly leads to a bathroom. There's also a short flight of stairs to an open loft up top with a bedroom and an office. That's where the information will be. Maybe locked?

"Here." Sarah offers me a tumbler of what smells like vodka and something fruity. "Oh, let me just let Juliet out." She blushes again and calls, tapping her leg, and an older Labrador trots in. Juliet spares me a glance as she goes outside. I use the opportunity and pour the drugs into my cup, using my finger to stir, and then I swap mine with hers, which sits on the table, all before she turns back.

"Sorry," she offers, and heads over.

I sit on the sofa, and she copies me, clearly nervous.

"So, what's your favourite book?" I ask, sitting back on the sofa, trying to gather as much information as I can in case we need it.

She hesitates. "At the moment or in life?"

"Both," I reply, and she seems to struggle for her answer.

"Right now, probably *Touch of Frost Queen*. I don't think I could pick one in general because there are so many good ones." She grins. "What about you? I don't know much about you, so tell me all there is to know."

"There isn't much," I answer, and she looks worried. "I live a pretty boring life." I take a sip, but she doesn't. "We can spend all night talking if you want, or we can spend our night having fun. Which one would you like?"

"Fun," she whispers.

"Good." I smile. "Down the hatch." I wink. "And then into the fun."

She quickly downs the drink and reaches for me. I let her straddle me, but just as she leans in to kiss me, her eyes grow fuzzy. Thank God. I don't think I could stand feeling her lips on mine.

It doesn't take long before she's out, and I turn so she falls into the sofa.

I lay her down slowly and cover her. Romeo jumps onto her chest, purring. Her dog, Juliet, barks at the back door, so I let her in, and she snarls at me but moves over to her owner. Juliet whines and nudges Sarah, and then she crouches before her, snarling at me when I get too close.

"Good girl," I tell her and move to the front door and open it, finding nothing but darkness. Dimitri slowly materialises, glaring at me before slamming his fist into my stomach, and then he steps past me. "You deserve that." He stops at the sight but turns away, scanning the house as I rub at my aching abs.

"Search upstairs. There's an office there, get everything," I demand.

"What if the information isn't here?" he mutters.

"Then we wait, and when she wakes, we get it out of her," I snap.

"Seduce it out of her, you mean," he retorts angrily.

"You think I enjoyed that?" I go toe to toe with him, snarling. "I hated every single fucking minute, but it if gets us closer to our girl, I will. I will do whatever it takes, and then I will beg on my fucking knees for forgiveness."

"I can't wait to see her kick your ass." He smiles, and I smile back.

"Me too. Now go, we don't have very long." My phone rings and I answer it. "Report," I tell Jonas, ignoring the other missed calls from the general. I don't have time to deal with him. I've debriefed him as much as I can, and he's angry, but there are more important things than handing over the research.

Like getting my girl back.

"Nothing here, boss, only a few flight numbers." It's clear he's frustrated.

"Text me them all, you never know."

"Got it," he offers as I hang up.

"Anything?" I call to D.

"Give me a second!" Dimitri snarls.

I wander to the kitchen and do the pots while I wait—it's the least I can do—then I fill up the cat's and dog's water dishes since she will probably feel groggy.

"Nothing." Dimitri comes back down.

"Fuck." I slam my fists down, and my eyes go back to where she stirs. "Then we go to plan B."

We wait for her to wake. Dimitri leans against the wall, and I sit on the coffee table. When her eyes flutter, I wince. She sits up groggily and rubs her head. When she sees me, she frowns. "Reggie, what happened?" she slurs, looking around. When she notices Dimitri, she screams and scrambles back on the sofa.

"We will not hurt you, Sarah," I promise. "I'm sorry about drugging you."

"You drugged me? What the fuck? God damn it, I knew it was too good to be true. A ridiculously hot man hit on me then drugged me. Come on, what the fuck? You couldn't just live with your mother or something?" She seems to be talking to someone else, maybe God, so I ignore it.

"I need information," I begin, and she laughs hysterically.

"You could have just asked like a normal person," she snaps. Is it bad that it didn't even occur to me until she mentioned it? Maybe.

"You wouldn't have told me. You would have screamed and called the police, and it would have cost precious time," I reply logically with my hands splayed, showing I'm harmless.

She watches us carefully. "Get out," she demands.

"I can't. Please, we just need your flight records for this date." I show her the date, and she frowns harder, her nostrils flaring.

"Get out before I call the police or worse." She tries to throw herself over the sofa, so I move quickly and block her, sitting her back down. She slumps, realising she is outnumbered. I can see how terrified she is, but she holds it in check well. She's brave, this girl.

Very brave.

I hate that I'm doing this too. She is a good person and doesn't deserve it.

"I should have taken that Italian mobster up on his fake marriage offer," she mutters. "But no, I had to be independent, and look where it got me."

"Please, Sarah," I plead. "You can hate me and call the police, but I need the information. Not for me. For her."

"Her?" She hesitates.

"My girl. The love of my life. She was on that plane. She was taken. You said you read about men doing everything they can for their love, and that's what I'm doing. I love her more than anything in this world. She's my family. She's my everything. I can't lose her." I know my voice cracks, but I let her hear the truth. "Please, Sarah, I just need to know where she went, I have to find her."

"I'm fucking crazy," she mutters as she stands and moves over to a small bookshelf I didn't notice. She roots around for a while before ripping a paper out and handing it to me. "I don't ever want to see you here again; do you understand me? And if this girl isn't who you say she is, I hope she hurts you badly."

"She will, no doubt," I admit. "She's crazy like that." I chuckle. "Thank you, Sarah. I mean it."

She simply nods, and it's clear it's time to leave.

As we head for the door, she calls out, "Reggie, or whatever your name is, I hope you find your happily ever after."

"So do I, Sarah, and I hope you find yours too," I reply as I shut her front door and look down at the note. "Ready the plane. We are wheels up. It's time to get our girl."

Hold on, baby, we are coming. Just hold on a little longer.

TWENTY-ONE

NICO

"I s he sure this is where his contact is meeting us?" Louis asks for the hundredth time. I scan the busy market, on the lookout for any threats. The sunglasses and scarf wrapped around my head obscure who I am, but I'm still on alert, waiting for Davis's men to pop out. Jonas is inside the bazaar a bit farther up, and Dimitri is in the van with Isaac, while Louis and I are close in case this goes wrong.

"He's sure. We need the weapons before we get there," I reply, and Louis nods, knowing I am right. Not only is Jonas's contact going to sell us everything we need gear-wise, but they will also get us the false identities we need to get into the labs. Obviously, with one look at most of us, Davis will know who we are, but that's an issue for another day.

Picking up the small, green-quartz elephant figurine, I let the sunlight catch it. "Do you think Nova will like this?" I ask Louis.

"Here he is."

"Louis," I demand, "do you think she will like this?"

He blinks, coming out of his work, and looks at the elephant and smiles. "Why does it matter?"

"It matters," I say as I look down at it, curling my fingers around it. "I want to show her we didn't forget or let her go. I want her to know that I thought about her every minute of every single day and that she will never be alone."

He's silent for a minute. "It's perfect, Nico. She will love it."

Nodding without looking at him, I hand over some money, and we get moving again, scanning the streets as we wait for word that Jonas got what he needs. A plan has started to form from the location information we received from the airfield. It's going to be next to impossible to break in and free her.

We need to be smart, hence this meeting.

This won't be an overnight job. We are planning for every possibility so we never lose our girl again.

We wander around the market for hours before Jonas finally joins us. "All good," he says, carrying two duffle bags over his shoulder and another two on his wrists. I take some, and so does Louis. "Let's get going." We weave our way back to the van, and as soon as we are inside, we head back to the plane, ready to get to the location.

Once onboard, I sort through the weapons with Jonas, my eyebrows rising at the explosives inside.

"You never know." He shrugs.

"Jonas, this is enough to blow up a city," I say carefully, knowing he's always a little unhinged, but since Nova has disappeared, he's become very unhinged.

"Good." He nods.

I share a look with Isaac but shrug. Jonas is good with explosives. He won't blow us up, right?

"Okay, now that that's all sorted, we have one last decision left. Who's going in?" Louis asks as he joins us.

Everyone volunteers, but I wait for them to quiet down. "It has to be me. I was one of the first to fail, which means their files on me are old. Davis didn't pay much attention to me along the way or even at the house. He would probably recognise me up close, but I won't let him. It has to be me. I look the part and can act it. Dimitri needs to be on the outside as our point of contact. Louis, you need to direct us and put us in position. Jonas would end up killing too many people, and he needs to be our backup plan. Isaac is too kind and would try to save everyone. It has to be me." I know I'm right, and as they share a look, it's obvious they clearly know it too.

"It means going into the belly of the beast, Nico, and probably facing a lot of your past and fears," Isaac remarks carefully.

"I know." I nod. "I'll be fine. I have to be, for her. Beast or no beast, nothing will stop me from getting to our girl."

And that is what it comes down to.

I would face every single bad memory, fight a million armies, crawl through a million tiny spaces, or face torture and imprisonment again if it meant freeing my girl and kissing her.

Isaac said the belly of the beast, but they haven't seen a beast, not yet, so I'll show them one.

And they took the beast's girl.

TWENTY-TWO

NOVA

I don't know how long I'm out for. I vaguely remember waking as my father screamed for his surgeons, his doctors, everyone. I remember masked men running in, IVs, and sedation. After that? Nothing.

I'm in one of the side rooms now. The bed is uncomfortable, and my wrists are manacled to the bed. It's dark bar the light through the gap in the door to the corridor, and I'm alone, the beeping of the machines attached to me the only sound filling the room.

My whole body, from chest to pelvis, feels raw and pulverised, but whatever drugs they have me on are keeping me a little numb to it for now.

I remember what I did. I even remember why, and suddenly, the ramifications of my actions take root in my brain. My eyes lock on the plain ceiling above me as my heart rate speeds up, the beeping growing louder as panic winds through my chest.

I ruined my body. I no doubt destroyed any chance of ever having kids.

Good, that means he can't use me to hurt them. They will be safe. He will have to find another way. I protected many innocents from having to go through what I and the others experienced.

I can't have kids.

I never thought I wanted to bring a child into such a fucked-up world and a fucked-up family, not to mention I would be a terrible mother. No, I was better going without, but as my hand covers my stomach, tears fall silently from my eyes, rolling into my hair as I bite back my pain. At least I had the choice, the chance, and as my eyes close, the images of tiny versions of Louis, Nico, Jonas, Dimitri, and Isaac fill my head, running around with a smile. It's something I will never have.

Our world is crazy and dangerous, but it doesn't stop the bone-deep longing from suddenly appearing because I will never be able to give them that now. I don't regret my choice. I did it to save the child that would be born into a test tube, even if it meant my death, but it doesn't stop the pain.

I seriously maimed my body and my future to save something worse from happening, and it hurts.

It fucking hurts.

Haven't I given enough?

Haven't I suffered enough?

When is it my turn to be happy?

How much more can I truly give?

Grief for a child I will never have now aches alongside the grief for the sister I lost, and I hold onto it as I sob silently, my body racked with pain. I thought I was so strong, and I thought I could handle anything, but for the first time, I don't know if I can survive this.

I don't know if I want to.

I'm so alone, so very alone, and so very tired of being covered in shit I can't scrape off. I struggle to even breathe and open my eyes. I'm so very tired of being alive.

Is this how Bas felt?

It would hurt Dimitri and the others to lose another like that, but the thought to end this all is there. Almost selfishly, I realise I wouldn't have to be around to see it.

I already planned not to make it out of this alive and to end this once and for all. Maybe it would be for the best because they wouldn't know I didn't try to make it out. They would only know I died stopping this, and that might make them hate me less.

I know I'm spiralling and going to a really dark place, but I can't help myself.

I can't pull myself out this time.

The door opens and my father stops above me, a scowl on his lips. "Well, I hope you are happy and got what you wanted. You will never be able to have kids, Nova. Do you know what you have done? You have ruined my research!" he hisses as he leans down. He wipes away my tears, and I flinch, knowing it wasn't an act of comfort. He eyes them clinically and then smiles. "There are other ways to make you into what I need though, and now you have removed any barrier that meant I needed to keep you healthy." He turns and leaves.

When the door shuts with a click, I allow myself to sink deeper into that dark hole.

I did it. I stopped him from getting my kids.

It doesn't matter what happens to me.

That's all that matters. They will never hurt innocents.

Only me.

I deserve it.

It's good because it means they might finally kill me, and I will be free of this pain. This world is a shitty fucking place but for a moment, I had hope for a better life. I got a glimpse of happiness and love, only for it to be taken away, and I can't keep pretending I will get it back.

Wherever the guys are, they are safe from him, and that's good. They wouldn't want me now anyway.

I'm not just broken this time.

I'm ruined beyond repair.

TWENTY-THREE

NOVA

They leave me alone for several days to heal. I'm checked on every few hours by a doctor who refuses to look or speak to me properly, and I am forced to eat and drink as if they think I will try to kill myself that way, which lets me know how bad I truly look. On day five, I've had enough, so I slide out of bed, crumpling to the floor in pain. Gritting my teeth, I stand and bring my IV with me as I shuffle to the toilet, hating the weakness and the pain.

I cannot stand another day lying in that bed and pondering how much I hate life and how unfair everything is. I'm over it. I'm over the pity, and I'm just angry.

Flicking on the light, I shut the door behind me and take a steadying breath, then I turn to the LED lit mirror. I wince at my reflection. The lighting is harsh, but I look like death warmed over. Hanging my head, I close my eyes and pull in deep breaths, trying to pep myself up. I need to look on the positive side. I've had days to rest, no torture, and three meals a day, and the food could be worse.

It falls flat, and I look back at my reflection with tears in my eyes.

There are purple and black bags under them, my lips are chapped and raw, and my skin is pale and lifeless. My hair is greasy and hanging in unbrushed strings around my face. I can't do anything about the wound or the pain or even about my situation right now, but this? This I can fix as much as I can. Maybe when I look like the old me, I'll have more confidence too.

I turn to the walk-in shower cubicle. There isn't a curtain, like they think I might hang myself with it—or them, I can't decide. Looking down at the IV line, I think about ripping it out, but I know better. Instead, I tug off the tape, slowly slide the needle out, and then toss it away. As I strip off the gown, I don't allow myself to look in the mirror to see the gauze covering my wound.

I flick on the shower and don't even let it heat before I step in, the sharp iciness making me gasp in a good way. It wakes me up and reminds me that I'm still alive. With my blood pumping faster, my heart awakens from its slumber, and I slick back my hair and just stand here, letting the water wash everything away—my tears, my defeat, and my hopelessness.

I finally turn and start to wash my body. I carefully avoid the gauze and wash my hair twice before deciding to tackle it. It needs to be changed, so it might as well come off, but am I prepared for what lies underneath?

Refusing to look won't change anything, but I still just stare as if that will make it better. It's best to see it now when I'm alone, I rationalise, so that he can't monitor my reaction and use it against me. *Just do it, Nova,* I tell myself, getting annoyed all over again.

I despise weakness, so I reach for the gauze.

The water dampens the gauze as I peel it off, and I stare at the scar while the spray hits my back. A choked noise escapes my throat, and I cut it off instantly. I know why I did it, and my sacrifice is proven on my body by a mark. I am strong, but that doesn't stop the agony I feel at seeing my raw, red skin stretching from either side of my belly button and carved into my abs. It's almost clean, but it's going to scar badly, and there is nothing I can do about that.

I remind myself that I have many scars, and all are proof of my victories and survival, but it doesn't stop me from mourning the loss of innocence with each and every one that mars my skin, and this is no exception. It hurts more because of what it stands for and because I realise the guys haven't touched this one and made it better. For the first time since we have been separated, I no longer look like the woman they love—another connection to them severed. This isn't skin they have kissed, tasted, and loved. This is raw and brutal. Like me.

I carefully wash the edges. Despite how fresh the wound is, it looks weeks old thanks to my healing, so I guess that's something. Once I'm done, I get out and dry off, putting on a fresh set of grey underwear, joggers, jumper, and socks that were left in here. I have to roll the joggers down so they don't press on the wound and they sit on my hips, and then I shuffle back into my room, exhausted just from that movement after days of being bedbound. I shuffle over and slowly sit, refusing to lie back down and choosing to rest just for a little bit to catch my breath.

I need to heal faster. I can't exercise because it will rip the wound, but I need to do something, anything, rather than just sit here with my pitiful thoughts.

As I'm about to get up and figure out a plan to keep myself busy, the door opens. I freeze when I see who it is. Instantly on alert, I search for a weapon. He holds up his hands in a placating gesture, his expression cold. "I'm not here to hurt you."

"Then why are you here, Joel?" I snap.

He steps inside and shuts the door, keeping his back to it as he watches me. He ensures there is space between us since I'm practically vibrating with tension and the need to act. I shift closer to the IV pole, ready to use it as a bat if he comes closer.

"To talk," he answers simply. I just carry on glaring, and he glances at my stomach. "How are you feeling?"

I fight not to wrap my arms around myself protectively, feeling sick at his presence. After all, he was going to rape me on my father's orders to create their super babies or some shit. When I don't respond, he sighs. "For what it's worth, I'm sorry it has come to this and that you saw no other way out."

"Apology not fucking accepted," I snarl. "Now get the fuck out."

He ignores me and moves closer, walking around the room as he inspects everything. I keep my body tense, ready to move, tracking every tiny movement just in case. They can't use me for my womb anymore, but my father has made it clear that my life will be hell and this man is his sidekick, his minion.

"It won't change anything, you know," he finally murmurs and glances over his shoulder at me, not surprised that I'm watching him so intently. He turns and moves closer. He's fast, with controlled, coiled movements. Pure soldier.

"What won't?" I find myself asking, and then I snap my mouth shut to stop more questions from coming out.

"Your sacrifice." I flinch at his words, but he carries on. "He's just going to take it out on you even worse now. You thwarted his plan. He needed you alive and somewhat functioning before, but now? He will make it hell for you."

Tilting my head back, I smirk at him. "I've lived in hell since I was a child. Bring it on."

He watches me carefully before a smile curls his lips. "Good. I was afraid your spirit had been broken. Where would the fun be in that?" He moves towards the door then stops to glance back at me. "There's nothing to save you anymore, girl, so I hope you are ready for the repercussions." Then he's gone and I slump.

All my adrenaline vanishes, becoming bone-deep exhaustion, and despite my mind screaming protests, I curl up on the bed and close my eyes, hoping to leave this place the only way I can—in my dreams.

He's right. There is nothing to protect me now.

There is nothing to save me.

I won't leave this place alive, but neither will they.

I'm escorted back to my room that night, and there is a terrible glint in the guards' eyes, like they know something I don't. I hate it. Alongside dickhead's earlier warning, I know tomorrow will be very fucking bad. It's time to move my plan up and fast.

Ignoring the agony ripping through my stomach, I pull myself up and into the vents again. I crawl towards the control room once more and wait for the guards to grow lazy, drifting off into a nearby room where I hear them making food, the fools.

I drop down, wincing as each step sends pure agony splintering through me. My stomach is healing faster than humanly possible, but it's still not fast enough to be doing this.

Once inside the control room, I quickly turn off the camera and the alarms, and then I head back down the hallway. The only issue I'll have is if I run into guards, but still, I don't hide. I walk like I know exactly where I am going, and maybe I do from the map I've been creating in my head. I find what I need on floor four, and I know I need to hurry before they find out what I've done and turn it all back on. Opening the unlocked door, I slip inside, scanning the shelves with a grim smile before yanking down the chemicals I need.

I feel my stitches rip, and blood starts to drip into my trousers, soaking the material. Glancing down, I see it seeping through the grey fabric, turning it red, but I still keep going.

I mix most of the chemicals together in the steel mop bucket, and then I drop the last one in and hurry back to my room, racing against the cameras. Once there, I quickly shimmy under the quilt to hide the blood on my clothes that show I've been moving.

Ten, nine, eight, seven, six, five, four, three, two, one . . .

I count down in my head and right on schedule, the chemicals mix together and explode. Alarms start to blare, and I hear running feet as they try to contain the fire. My main mission is to cause chaos and make them suffer before I kill them, and that starts tonight.

Just like I expected, my door slams open and a guard peeks in. I tilt my head towards him. "Problems in paradise?" I tease.

He points at me. "Behave." He slams the door.

Grinning, I slide the sheet off and hurry to the bathroom. Peeling the bloody clothes off is harder than I expected, but I manage to get them off and soak them to get as much blood out as I can before replacing the grate and checking the wound. It's red, raw, and angry, and I nicked the skin and popped a few stitches, but there is nothing I can do about it now. I cover it with more gauze and redress it before slipping into another top and pants, and then I climb back into bed as the alarms continue to blare.

I smile as I close my eyes.

One step closer.

I'm one step closer.

TWENTY-FOUR

NOVA

I t's a testament to how much the wound knocked me on my ass when I'm jerked awake as hands grab me. I didn't even hear them come in or see them turn on the lights. I was sleeping, and it pisses me off. I start to fight before agony slams through me from my wound, and then I stop. I can't do any more damage to myself than I need to.

I need to heal so I can kill them, so I let them drag me away even though I hate it.

I'm brought into one of the medical rooms, but instead of a bed, there is a chair one would see in a dentist's office. I'm tossed into it, and my arms and legs are quickly strapped down. Struggling against my need to fight, I relax into the leather and blink.

"What, no breakfast?" I taunt.

The guards ignore me, stepping back against the wall, and look at the opposite wall as if to avoid even looking at me. I'm forced to wait, and I grow bored. I test the restraints. I could snap them if need be, but for now, I leave them on, and sometime later, the door opens, admitting my father.

"Novaleen," he snaps in annoyance, the door shutting behind him. His tone is angry, and he looks tired, probably from the fire last night. His suit is slightly wrinkled, which tells me all I need to know. He's stressed and hasn't slept.

"Looking bad, Pops," I taunt. "Now, what's on today's agenda? Teeth pulling?"

"There was an explosion last night."

"I did hear something." I shrug as much as the bindings will allow. "What's your point?"

"We know it was you." My father sniffs, looking irritated.

"Are you sure?" I smirk. "I was in my room, you know, being a prisoner and all."

"Are you trying to make me believe that one of the most intellectual minds of our time couldn't have timed that?" he snaps.

"I think you have a problem in your house, Father, and it isn't me. After all, I'm injured and a prisoner. Maybe you should look at your staff." I see him falter just for a moment, but it's enough to let me know he's worried about that, worried about being betrayed from the inside.

It's another crack in the armour, which is something else I can use.

"Punish her!" he snaps as he turns and storms out.

The guards step forward almost as one, and I let out a low breath and force a smile. This is going to be bad, but I can survive it. "So, what do you guys think about—" My breath whooshes out of my lungs as one man slams his fist into my stomach. I feel my stitches rip, but not enough to cover the tearing of the wound from yesterday. It hurts like a motherfucker though. That's when I realise that if I can make him do it again, I can cover my ripped stitches.

"Pussy," I rasp, and just like I expected, he winds his fist up and slams it into my stomach, rupturing the wound. Blood pours from my flesh, and agony courses through me, but I smile as I wheeze. He played right into it, giving me exactly what I wanted.

"I'm going to enjoy this," another says as he steps up, and my heart stills as he grins. Winding a cloth between his hands, he kicks his foot into the chair, and my head slams back. He places the cloth he was holding over my mouth, and then ice-cold water pours across it, spraying over my mouth and face. I can't see, and my ears buzz. I struggle to breathe, my lungs on fire as I writhe in the straps, feeling blood slide across my stomach and chest. Just when I'm about to pass out from choking on water, he stops, allowing me to suck in desperate, painful breaths, only to repeat the action again.

It continues until my throat feels like razors are cutting into it from the inside and my lungs are so desperate for air each breath hurts. My stomach competes for a close second. Drenched, shivering, and coughing, I force my eyes open, waiting to see what will happen next.

He called it a punishment, but this isn't punishment.

This is a lesson.

This is a warning.

Their warnings come back to me. I have no buffer anymore, and this shows me just that. A scream slips free as something red-hot presses into the bottom of my foot, making me contort in the bindings. My toes burn and throb like pins and needles but a hundred times worse. All I can do is just lie here as they beat the bottoms of my feet with something hot. I could break free and kill them, but it would be for nothing, and I would be punished more.

No, I need to bide my time.

Never before have I come so close to breaking as they tear my body apart one sensation at a time. After my feet, I'm woozy, but I refuse to pass out.

"They say she's strong, so let's see how strong." A guard laughs, but I can no longer tell them apart. I jerk when my shirt is ripped away, leaving me in a grey cotton sports bra, and when I lift my head, I watch as they tear the gauze from my injury and dig their fingers into the wound, tearing it back open.

The howl of agony that leaves my lips is animalistic, and despite my best intentions, blackness claims me.

I wake with a jerk as something sharp pierces my stomach. "Fucking animals. This was sewn perfectly, now look at the mess," someone mutters.

I blink, trying to bring the room into focus, but it takes too long and my brain is sluggish. Eventually, I realise I'm in the same room, still shivering both from shock and temperature. Rolling my head down, I see the guards are gone and there is a man in a lab coat bent over my stomach, stitching up the mess they made of my wound.

"Such a waste," he mutters as he starts to staple me.

"I know you." My voice is little more than a whisper, but he jerks and looks up, freezing. I cough, clearing my throat, and he watches me struggle. "I know you," I repeat stronger once I catch my breath.

"I would hope so." He looks back down at his work and carries on. It hurts, but it's clear he is here to help, not to cause pain. "You spared my life once."

Blinking, I stare at his face until it comes to me. He was the head of the lab, the one we let go free before the plane crash. "You bastard!" I surge towards him, but he pushes me down with a glare at me then the door.

"Shut up. If they hear you are awake, they will come back in and hurt you. I was only supposed to stitch you up so you didn't die," he hisses, and we both stare at the door before he sighs and hurries to seal my wound.

"You bastard. I let you live, and you came back to him," I snap.

"It's not what you think," he mutters, ducking his head. "We don't have time to discuss it." He quickly cleans my stomach and looks me over, shaking his head. I see something almost haunted and sad in his eyes before he shakes it off. "Believe me, if I had any other choice, I would take it."

"You do."

"No, I don't, Nova," he replies sadly. "None of us do, least of all you. You, more than anyone, understand obligation and chains that bind us." He stands quickly, shoving his stuff back into his bag before pulling out a needle. He sticks it into a bottle, drawing up a dose and testing it before turning to me.

"This is all I can do. I'm sorry." He injects me with something, and I gape as he hurries to the door and rushes out.

My blood heats, and the guards step back in. "Look who's awake." One grins. "Time to continue with our punishment, shall we?"

Lying back like I'm at a spa, I smile like I'm in charge. "Of course, where were we?"

They have to bring the doctor back in three times before he announces that if I lose any more blood or am hurt again, I will die. It's a lie, well, close to a lie. I do feel like I'm dying, but I wouldn't give them the satisfaction. I can't decide if he's trying to help me or if he just feels guilty since he won't meet my eyes as I'm carried back to my room and tossed onto my bed.

I lie here, unable to move or feel thanks to the meds the doc keeps pushing. I'm guessing it's morphine. It let me drift while they tortured me, but it pissed them off more since they didn't get the reaction they wanted, so they had to get more creative. The last time the doctor came in, they did too, and he couldn't give me anything, hence the agony now.

But anything is better than the pain in my soul and the fact that I almost slipped away.

My men never would have known. They are all I think about. I hate it. I hate that I can't see them. I hate it and miss them, hoping wherever they are, it's better than this. It's all that keeps me going. I close my eyes now and imagine them here, needing their warmth and comfort.

It dashes away when the door opens. I groan and try to sit up, expecting more guards to haul me away, or even my father or a doctor. What I don't expect is him.

It's one single guard, and with one look into his cruel, mocking eyes, and I know his intentions. I leap to my feet, stumbling as I try to head to the bathroom to put a door between us, but I'm slow, the drugs and pain slowing me down.

He grips my hair and yanks me back until I'm pinned beneath him again.

"You know what your daddy said?" he says into my hair, pulling me back tighter to let me feel his hard cock against my ass. "That you are free game now. He doesn't need your cunt for anything, and he wants us to feel motivated, so I figured why don't I sample it? It seems like such a waste, don't you agree? Be a good girl and take it, and I'll get you extra food and some pain meds."

"Fuck you!" I yell, slamming my elbow back. "I'll fight you every step of the fucking way, you disgusting pig."

His fist slams into my face, the force knocking my head into the floor, and for a moment, my ears ring and my vision blurs. He rips at my clothes and when his hands reach into my underwear, I come back online. I turn over and slam my foot into his face. He falls back with a roar, so I do it again, blood pouring from his nose as we stare at each other, breathing heavily until his radio crackles.

"Omar, we need you in Lockdown One. Omar, repeat, where are you? He's mad you aren't at your post."

"Better get going, Omar," I choke out.

With one last look at me, he climbs to his feet, wiping his nose on his sleeve, and answers the radio. "I'm on my way." He grins at me. "This isn't over. There's no one to protect you, little girl."

"I don't need them to, but the next time you touch me, I'm going to cut your hands off and shove them down your throat," I promise.

He leaves me, slamming my door shut, and I curl into a ball, unable to move as the reality of what almost happened hits home.

Screaming, I slam my feet into the floor, roaring out my agony as tears begin to fall.

Sobbing on the floor, I wrap my arms protectively around me until anger starts to take over. I crawl to the bathroom, drag myself up by the sink, and stare at my reflection. I have one black eye, a split lip, bruised cheeks, a gaunt face, and . . . my hair.

I once loved my hair. It almost falls to my ass, wavy and black, but now all I can think about is how he used it against me. It could have been the difference between me getting away or being trapped.

Smashing my fist into the mirror, I watch cracks form, splintering like my soul, so I do it again until it shatters. Picking up a shard, I start to hack at my hair. Clumps of the black mass fall into the sink with the shards until I drop my shaky hand. My head hangs forward as tears slide down my cheeks.

I lift my head and meet my eyes once more.

My hair now falls to my shoulders in black waves, and I smile through the curtain. It's a bloodied, wavering smile, but it's there.

They will not break me.

TWENTY-FIVE

LOUIS

"How are you doing?" I ask into the comms in Nico's ear. We are all perched in different areas around the base, but he has to enter for his new job an old acquaintance we bribed got him at the lab. He shaved his head and with that, the guard's uniform, and the fake scars we added, he shouldn't be too noticeable unless they look closely. Dimitri even created a very convincing background as a marine and paid mercenary. He just went inside the compound, and I hate not having eyes on him.

I remind myself it isn't for long, since he's going to plant the external remote so Dimitri can hack into their systems. From there, we can come up with a better plan, but none of us are willing to leave Nova alone another day, so we need someone on the inside.

His grunt echoes through my mic, and I smirk as I peer down the scope, watching the guards' movements up top.

"This way. What did they say your name was, grunt?" another voice says through the mic.

"Jones," Nico mumbles, lowering his voice even more to make it less familiar.

"Right," someone retorts with a sarcastic tone and lowers his voice, but I can hear it through the mic. "All fucking muscle, brawn, and no brain. Like we don't have enough of them already."

I wait, counting the seconds of the guards' rotations as they patrol from one side of the fence to the other. When I do, I scan the jungle, but I can't spot any of the others at all, even though I know they are there.

"Right, this way, Jones. I'll take you to security, who will check you all over and give you your job rotation. Bunks are up top if you are stationed here. You'll get a number, you'll either be nights or days, and we all eat in the cafeteria."

"What about days off?" Nico asks haughtily.

The man snorts. "Not for a while, dumbass. They are on the verge of something big here, and it's all hands. And don't go asking questions. It's a sure-fire way to get us all in trouble. Do your job, keep your head down, and get the massive paycheque you've been offered. After all, that's why we are all here. Got it?"

"Got it," Nico responds, seemingly put out, but it appears to assuage the man.

"Okay, here is the upper security office. There is another one deep within the compound in the underground structure. You will receive a tour if you are assigned there. I know they wanted more guards after a . . . security breach."

"What kind?" Nico asks.

"The bad kind," is all the man replies. "Yo, T, I've got a newbie for you." I hear the sound of retreating footsteps.

"Name," a bored sounding woman with a thick accent says.

"Rob Jones, Robert for full," Nico replies, and then there's typing and no more conversation until Nico breaks it. "Been here long, T?"

"Long enough," she mutters. "Okay, lucky you, you have been assigned to the underground, or as we call it, hell. Here is your key card. Show it to the security officers down there and they will get you settled. Usually, you would bunk up here, but some officers get to bunk underground if they don't mind it—most do."

"I don't," he says quickly, too quickly.

"Play it cool," I snap down the mic.

"Fucking military weirdos, always so eager," T mutters. "Fine, I'll assign you one underground. You'll get a tour and all the other information down there. We don't have many rules here, but stay silent. You see and hear nothing of what happens there except for security. Also, the only way out is in a body bag, got it, Robert?"

"Got it."

"Here. Take the elevator all the way down. Oh, and Robert? Welcome to hell."

NICO

The elevator is a service one, big enough to fit equipment, beds, or even a small army. The buttons tell me I'm at level one, and they only go down, so I hit the very bottom one labelled B10 and scan the key card. I checked the cameras as soon as I got in here, so I make sure I look bored, and I don't speak into the earpiece, although I can hear the others wondering what it's like. The small screen shows me the numbers as we drop, and I make sure to stand at attention, my hands clasped behind my back and legs spread. My duffle bag is tossed over my shoulder, and I'm wearing a black button-up to hide my distinctive tattoos as well as boots that are slightly platformed to change my height ever so slightly. I want to itch my head and the lack of hair there, but I ignore that too.

I wonder what Nova will think. She loved my hair, but it will grow back. I would do much worse things to be near her again.

The door dings as it slides open, and I don't know what I expected, but it isn't a plain white corridor leading farther into the underground laboratory. A guard turns the corner at the end and hurries my way.

"New guy?" he asks as if anyone else would have gotten down here. Plus, I know they checked me via camera before they even let the lift descend.

I incline my head, and he jerks his. "Follow me. They didn't want you getting lost."

Or wandering around, more likely, and seeing things I shouldn't.

I follow him down the hall, my eyes bouncing around in fake interest, but really, I'm clocking all possible areas for attack and exits, needing to memorise it for the others.

"Nico, you good?" Jonas asks.

I can't respond with the man walking at my side, peering down at an iPad, so instead I clear my throat. "This is far underground. What kind of research is conducted here? I wasn't told."

"For a reason." The guard snorts and doesn't even look up. "It's our job to keep it that way, so no one outside of these walls knows anything, understood?" He looks up at me. "Don't go getting a conscience, merc. There is a reason we hire certain kinds here. We don't need your morals or brain, just your brawn, got it?"

"Got it," I respond slowly as if having to think about it. "Do you get reception down here? I want to watch the games." I shrug.

He chuckles. "Oh yeah, we do. We have the best connections in the world here, all thanks to the trusty scientists. You take care of them, they take care of you, if you know what I mean." I nod like I do.

We turn a corner, and I peek into open doorways, but they all seem to be empty labs.

"This level is mostly just for the entrance. All the fun happens below, and those levels are only accessible by stairs. This is level one. Level two has living quarters as well as some medical rooms, and level three is the security base, as well as more labs and medical rooms. Level four is recreation and offices."

"Is there a level five?" I ask.

He peers at me and clears his throat. "No questions," he reminds me, and I bite my tongue. He leads me to some stairs at the end and down we go. The concrete walls are only interrupted by cameras, lights, and black stencilled level numbers beside sealed doors we have to scan to get into. At level three, we exit into a corridor. Most of the doors are shut, and I only see some guards milling around in a small kitchen, living room area, but to the right is a security office, which I'm led into.

"New guy. Jones. He's yours." The guard I'm with slaps my back. "See you around, man." I just nod and quickly scan the room as the bored guard turns to the computer and starts typing, ignoring me too. The whole wall is filled with screens of all the floors and labs. This is where I will need to plant the bug, so I step forward, knocking into the chair he's sitting on as my hand slips into my pocket. When he turns to yell, I practically stumble back into the desk, placing it underneath and holding up my hands. "Sorry."

"Clumsy bastard," he snaps, turning back to the computer.

I click my fingers twice to let Dimitri know and then refocus on my surroundings. This might be the only chance I have to look around in here, so I need to make the most of it.

I'm scanning the cameras for any signs or traces of her when a conversation from guards outside has me stiffening.

"Did you see the beating she took? No wonder the doc is so interested."

"I saw her fight that military guy. She kicked his ass."

"She's hot as hell too. I might try and sneak into her room."

"Don't be stupid. The doc is her father." He lowers his voice then, and I can't hear more, but it's enough.

She's here.

Nova is here.

I hear the others cheering down the mic, and I smile but quickly school my features as the guard turns back to me with the rotations schedule. My heart hurts at the beatings they mentioned, but my girl can take it. She can survive anything, and she isn't alone anymore.

I'm here.

TWENTY-SIX

NOVA

"N ow, Novaleen," my father begins as he sits down opposite me. This could almost be called a meeting if you overlooked the fact that my hands are strapped to the electric chair. "Shall we begin?"

"It's Nova," I reply conversationally.

He frowns, his eyes roving over my hair like they did when I was first dragged in here. "I was told you broke the mirror in your room and cut your hair. May I ask why, Novaleen?"

"I felt like a change. You know how it is, got to spice up your life a little. The round-the-clock torture can get a little tiresome." I'm hurting all over, mind, body, heart, and soul, and yes, I'm taking it out on him. I don't know what he wants from me this time, and I don't fucking care.

He won't get it.

"I thought your punishment might make you more amenable, Novaleen. I simply wish to talk today."

"Of course," I mock. "Hence the electric chair."

"I have learned that sometimes you need to be persuaded. Do not make me the bad guy." He leans back, his arms crossed. "I'd like to talk to you about what you did while we were apart."

"When I ran away from home so I wasn't your prisoner, or when I thought you were dead, or both?" He goes to answer, but I cut him off. "Oh, I'm sorry, time's up, and I simply do not give a fuck."

The buzz zaps me, short and quick, and I narrow my eyes.

"I had one hell of a party when I thought you were dead, with Jell-O shots and a bullseye with your face on the board—" My words cut off with a snap of my teeth as the electricity pulses through me again, harder this time. When it cuts off, I sag a little.

"Now, how about we start elsewhere since you seem averse to talking about anything with your past, your . . . friends, or your sister."

"Do not speak her name," I warn, nostrils flaring as my nails dig into the chair, wishing they could carve into his face instead.

"You are still upset about her death. While I do hate the force I had to use, and she was very bright, it was necessary, Nova, you must see that. I had to free you from that bond. She was holding you back. You could never reach your full potential while you were worried about her or her reaction," he explains as if it's a logical decision.

I simply look over his shoulder to the glass screen where some other scientists are monitoring us. "Novaleen," he snaps, hating when I don't give him the attention he thinks he deserves.

"Did you spend years building this little hideout of yours?"

"Yes," he responds carefully.

"And white paint was the best you could go for?" I taunt.

The chair buzzes again, and when it cuts off, I laugh.

"Fine, let us talk about those men you are with. Failed experiments. I looked into their files. Most of them offered a lot of potential, but in the end, they failed, unlike you. Why do you think you felt so connected to them? Was it simply circumstance or because you felt like you could be somewhat free with them when it came to your past and abilities? Do you think that affects the way you saw them? Did it create an artificial bond?"

"It was not artificial," I snap. "They are my family."

"I am your family," he murmurs. "We do not have a bond."

"You are a sadistic fuck who dresses like a person in a toothpaste commercial," I spit. "They knew that. We had been through the same things."

"Ah, trauma bonded." He makes a quick note, which I hate.

"No, it is more than that," I hiss angrily at him before blowing out a breath and calming myself, knowing he wants a reaction. "I do not need to defend my relationships to you or explain them. It was fate that brought them to me, and what we have cannot be replicated or explained with science."

"Ah, that is where you are wrong. After all, I brought them to you, and I plan to repeat it. If we are to create solid, cohesive units of soldiers, then they will need a similar bond of trust. Maybe I should have taken them after all." He sighs. "A pity we can't find them."

I jerk at the slip of information, hanging onto his every word. I want to know more. Why can't he find them? Are they lying low? Hiding? Or worse, hunting?

"I would be interested to see what curated a bond faster—fear or loyalty," he murmurs to himself then blinks at me. "Never mind. Tell me how you have been since leaving me. Stronger? Faster? What other changes have you noticed?"

"Well, there was that time I felt a burning sensation when I peed, but that turned out to be an STD—"

Zap, and so it goes.

He asks question after question, which I answer with angrier and sassier answers, infuriating him. I just suffered a particularly bad shock when my head lolls back and my eyes go to the glass, and I swear I see a flash of a familiar, haunted gaze, but it is just wishful thinking, so I close my eyes, not wanting to hurt my heart more than it already does.

After the shock therapy, as Father called it, there is a cruel twist to his lips. He is angry that I refused to play his game. I know whatever comes next will be a punishment that I have no choice but to take. I'm escorted to a lab and tied down on the examination table. My eyes close for a moment as I try to rein back my panic, remembering the last time I was like this and I burnt out my insides. Still, I'm sore and healing, so surely they wouldn't—

A scream escapes my throat.

Their warnings were correct. They don't need me alive anymore, and the proof is in his eyes. His gloved hand slices open my healing stomach, cutting right through the stitches and tearing me open once more. There is a dangerous glint in his eyes. This is more than a punishment. This is a warning to give him what he needs or I will beg for death just like those other kids did.

When his gloved hand starts to force the wound open, I can't control my reactions anymore.

Gritting my teeth, I swallow the taste of my own blood, my nails breaking as I claw at the arms of the bed. My legs and arms thrash against the restraints, and I throw my head back in agony as pain blisters through me like a flame.

The blade slides deeper into my stomach, and I lift to watch the blood welling from my abdomen before I glare at the scientists and Father above me.

He doesn't spare me a look.

"You're dead," I warn, my voice choked.

He ignores me as he plunges his hand into my stomach, making me fall back, and the trapped howl of agony finally rips through the lab before I pass out.

When I wake up, I feel him there, watching and judging.

He pulled me apart like a cat playing with a spider, ripping off its legs to see if they still kick. Forcing my swollen, grimy eyes open, I find my stomach stapled, but I'm still tied down and coated in sweat and blood.

My father stands there with a pen poised above a notebook. "How do you feel, Novaleen?"

"Fuck you," I croak, my throat raw from screaming.

His eyes narrow before he repeats the question harder.

"How do I feel?" I repeat, my tongue thick. "Like when I get free, I'm going to rip you apart to see how you like it."

Dropping the pen, he leans in with a cruel twist of his lips, his familiar eyes meeting mine. "Oh, but you won't be getting free, will you? Not again."

And then he leaves.

I scream and fight, trapped once more.

I have been reduced to an experiment—again.

TWENTY-SEVEN

NOVA

I'm stitched back up and pumped full of a drug cocktail that instantly makes me feel better. I overheard the scientist say that what they did was to test my healing, but that's bullshit. It was a warning through and through, and it has only made me angrier, but I have to play this smart. Even though I want to tear through them, I have to stick to the plan, which seems stupider the longer I'm down here.

I should just make my move, but I worry I will fail.

I hear Louis's voice in my head, telling me to be smart and plan.

Jonas tells me to gather weapons.

Dimitri advises me to gain access to their systems and tear them apart from the inside.

Isaac's voice says to allow myself to heal.

Nico tells me to use their weaknesses against them.

The only problem is, I don't know their weaknesses.

I'm escorted back to my room where I lie on the cot, debating my thoughts. They have to have a weakness, and I have to find it, which means action, because today taught me that they won't be happy until I'm ripped apart. I need to end this and soon.

Tilting my head, I see the door lock is off-kilter, so I get to my feet thanks to the drugs and I hurry over, sliding my nails between it until it catches. The dumbasses didn't even lock it properly. I could have gone through the tunnel, but it will hurt more, and honestly, they don't even seem to care. Surely, they have to know it's me fucking with them by now.

What else could they possibly do to me?

I need to find a weakness, which means going deeper into the facility than I ever have. I can't use the elevator because it requires a key card I don't have—I heard them mention it once. They force the guards to use the stairs, and I know they are for emergencies and will no doubt register if I open them.

I hesitate before rounding my shoulders and stepping out. When no guards come running or alarms go off, I walk down the corridor. Maybe they don't see me, or maybe they are just curious about where I will go. Either way, I have time.

I don't bother going down to the security room or the labs, since they hold nothing I want. Instead, I move to the elevator and press the button. It opens. Once inside, I look at the cameras and grin. It wouldn't surprise me if Father was watching as another test.

Determined to find something before he cuts me off, I jump and catch the ceiling tile. Pressing my feet to the wall, I push up and slide it to the side, and then I swing up into the elevator shaft, hoping there are no cameras. There's no way out that I can see. The cables for the elevator go all the way up, but there is only darkness. However, there are metal beams to the left and they go down, so I leap onto one. Ignoring the pulling in my stomach, I begin to climb down. I really hope the elevator doesn't move and crush me while I'm doing this. I have to walk across to the end of one beam. There's a gap where the elevator goes and then the door. Judging the distance, I step back and leap, catching the lip and forcing the door open. The weight makes me sweat, but I manage to get it open far enough for me to roll through and out onto another floor.

This one seems empty, and even the lights are off until I step farther in and they flicker on. The first two doors are locked, but I peer through their windows to see sheet-covered objects inside, clearly not in use.

Worried I won't find anything, I hurry down the corridor. I need to find a weakness to make this worthwhile. The farther I go in the corridor, the weirder this floor gets. There are no labs, bedrooms, or experimentation rooms that I can see, but at the end of the corridor, there is a huge glass window, and a terrible feeling starts deep inside of me.

Flashbacks of a similar window, of a dead kid in the middle of a blood-soaked experimentation room fill my vision. The guys were with me then, so I had their support. I was on the right side, and I had the power to stop it. Still, I am fearful of what I will find, but fear won't stop it from happening or make it better. Burying my head and pretending I don't see anything won't stop the truth. It just makes me weak, and I refuse to be weak.

On slow, unsure feet, I step closer to the glass, alarm bells screaming in my head, but I ignore them. I ignore it all. I am so focused on the glass that I don't even notice anyone else is here until a hand catches my arm.

I react on instinct, turning and smashing that person into the wall, snarling into the face of the man in the guard's uniform. He has a hat pulled low over his face, but when I get a good look at him, I freeze. "Nico?" I whisper, unsure if I'm seeing things or if I'm high or finally dead.

"Hey, baby," he murmurs, but he doesn't touch me.

"Are you real?" I whisper, my arm still pressed to his throat, pinning him to the wall.

"I'm real, baby. I want to fucking touch you so badly to prove it, but if they see on the cameras, I'll be useless and they'll know who I am. I have a role to play, so make it real, baby, and knock me out or some shit."

"No." I start to back away, and he snarls.

"I'm not leaving you alone here, baby. We have a lot to talk about. The others are close, but right now you need to make this look real. Smash me in the balls and then I'll escort you back." His eyes are telling me to play along, while my heart is leaping in joy. I want to collapse into his arms, sob, and let him make this all better, but he's right.

He winces. "Sorry. The guys are blowing up my ear trying to talk to you. She cannot fucking hear you, idiots," he hisses.

I grin, ducking my head to hide it. Tears form in my eyes, but the longer I stand here, the weirder it looks. "Sorry, babe," I whisper as I drive my knee up into his balls.

I step back, smirking like I'm happy as he crumples to the ground, cupping his cock and groaning. I want to help him, but I quickly step to the window like I'm worried about him stopping me. It's all about appearances now. We were caught before, but we won't be ever again.

Despite how angry and worried I am for what their presence means for my plan, I'm also relieved and happy that they came for me.

But that all fades when I get a look into that room.

Hundreds of bunk beds fill the room, with perfectly fitted white sheets and one single pillow. A lot of them are empty, while some have kids sitting atop them—kids of all ages, sizes, and races. Drawings are scattered on the walls, and some are even sketching now. One is reading in the corner, and one is asleep. Two are playing chess. I count fifteen altogether.

Fifteen innocent children are locked up in a gilded cage.

Is he experimenting on them?

Oh, God.

I cover my mouth as I look, my hand going to the window. They wear the same jumpsuits I do, but smaller. They seem clean and healthy, but that doesn't mean anything. I know how looks can be deceiving.

A hand grips my arm.

Nico.

I feel him freezing next to me as he gets his first look in the room. "Fuck, we have a problem," he mutters to the others.

"Nico!" I gasp in horror.

He shudders next to me, his grip tightening. "I know, baby, I see, but we have to get back. We'll help them, I promise, but we can't if we are caught."

He's right, I know he's right, but I'm also a zombie as he leads me back to the elevator, knowing my father wanted me to see this. I feel over-whelmed, and sickness claws at my throat. The pain starts to seep back in a little, the bone-deep, soul-wrenching pain. I was so dumb to think he would stop now that he had me.

I was going to blow this place up, and they would have been killed. I'm so thankful something stopped me. Maybe deep down, I knew, but this changes everything.

"Nico," I whisper in the elevator, and he tightens his hand, lowering his head so the camera can't catch his lips.

"Not yet," he snaps.

Knowing I'm pale and probably in shock, I let him drag me from the elevator.

A guard approaches. "Boss wants her back in her room." He looks at me and smirks. "Saw what you wanted, did you?"

I was right. He let me find that.

It was all another game.

I simply stare through him, my brain overloaded.

He will do what he did to us to those kids.

I have to swallow back my vomit, but then I think fuck it and heave forward, spilling it on the other guard's shoes. He yells and stumbles back.

"That's my girl," Nico mutters before tightening his grip. "I'll take her back and remind her to behave."

"You do that before I do," the guard snarls. "Fucking animal. Make it hurt, but not where they can see, if you know what I mean." He picks up his radio. "Turn off the cameras in her room. It's time for payback."

Payback, right. At least this works in our favour, but holy shit.

Nico smirks. "Thanks, man. Don't want to get fired too quickly, you know?"

Without waiting, he drags me back down the corridor to my room. Once there, we both glance at the cameras before he looks at me. "Fuck it, let them catch me." I'm in his arms in a minute. He turns me and presses me to the wall, his lips descending on mine. One hand comes up and rips out his earpiece, and he tosses it away—even I can hear shouting coming from it. Groaning, I grip his hat and rip it off, only to freeze at his shaved head. Pulling back, I gawk and he winces. I can see the worry there, so I rub my hand across it and grin.

"I like it. You look meaner," I murmur.

"I've missed you so much, baby," he says, dragging his lips across mine again as if he can't decide if he's going to kiss me or talk, so he does both. "So fucking much. I'm so angry at you for leaving, and when we blow this joint, I'm going to spend the rest of our lives proving it. But fuck, I'm so fucking happy to see you."

"I missed you too," I reply, but it cuts off as he kisses me again. I whimper when he pushes me back and my stomach protests. He pulls away immediately, dropping me.

"Nova," he says, his voice shaking.

"It's fine. I'm okay," I promise, but I wince as the pain slowly trickles back in. Before I can grab my shirt, he pulls it up and hisses. He goes to rush out of the door, but I stop him.

"Breathe, big guy, and think smart. I promise I'm okay."

"You have a massive fucking wound on your stomach, and you are covered in bruises. How is this okay?" he snarls. "I was so happy to see you, I didn't even notice your hair or how skinny you look. Nova, I'm going to fucking kill them. Tell me who did this, or is it all of them? Either way, they are dead." He rushes to the bed, picks up his earpiece, and puts it in. "Yeah, I'm here. Get in here, we are killing all of them."

Laughing, I take the earpiece. Luckily, he lets me, clearly worried about fighting me. "Hi, guys," I say nervously. It's silent for a second, and then there's a rush of voices all at once. Tears form in my eyes as I smile. "Okay, one at a time."

Louis's voice comes first. "What does he mean you're hurt?"

"I'm okay, just a procedure. I'll tell you later." I worry then, eyeing Nico. They came after me, but what if they are too angry at me?

Even just looking at Nico reminds me of that night, the one that stained my soul.

Ana.

"Fuck, I missed you so much," Jonas says.

"Talk more, I need to hear your voice," Dimitri murmurs.

"Are you okay?" Isaac asks.

"Tell us everything," Louis says before his voice softens. "We've missed you so much. We haven't stopped looking, not even for a second, and after this, we will be sitting down to discuss you sacrificing yourself for us and the appropriate punishment." I shiver from his tone and the promise in the words, and a spark of desire forms in me despite everything.

Sitting heavily on the bed, I sigh when Nico wraps himself around me, his big arms feeling like home. We don't have long, we need to use the time wisely, but I ache to hear their voices too. Seeing him and hearing them made it all real, and I just want them here with me, but that's foolish.

"Before I forget, there's a hole in the cupboard on this level. It leads to the ducts beyond to get in and out. I blew it a few days ago. I turned the cameras to avoid it and I will make sure to note some access points."

"Clever fucking girl," Dimitri purrs.

"I dropped a bug so Dimitri could access their systems and give us control," Nico explains, making me nod. Of course they did. Of course they planned.

"Louis, there are kids here. Whatever you have planned, it has to change, okay? They come first. We need to save them."

"Nova—"

"No, they come first, promise me. I can live with pain or staying longer or being punished by them, but I can't live with knowing kids are being hurt or worse. Promise me."

"I promise," he responds reluctantly, and I slump in relief.

"We don't have long." I grip Nico tighter, not wanting to let go. "It's not usual for them to punish me like this, and if Father finds out, he won't be happy, even if he will let it happen. There's a soldier here who survived the experiments. Avoid him at all costs. He's good, very good, and completely on Father's side." I have so much to tell them, but some of it won't even come out. I choke on my words. Right now, those kids have to be our first priority. "Whatever you have planned, I want in. I have access to the ducts through this bathroom, and I'm pretty sure they are watching me. Whatever timeline you have thought out needs to be moved up. He's losing his patience with me, and I don't know how much longer he will keep me alive when he can't get what he wants."

"What do you mean?" Isaac asks. "Are you okay?"

I hesitate, and Nico glances at the wound, a worried look in his eyes. "Baby, tell me they didn't . . ."

"They wanted my kids," I whisper before hardening my voice. "I stopped them from ever getting that from me."

There's silence then, and I wait with bated breath. Nico lifts his eyes, and I see so much pain there it staggers me. "I'm so sorry, Nova." He grips me tighter, kissing my stomach. "I'm so sorry you had to do that. You're so strong, baby. We'll make them pay."

"Nova," Isaac whispers.

"Don't, okay? Please." I can't afford to break down now. "I'm okay. I

165

made a decision, one I can live with. I couldn't live with knowing that they would use my body and my children for his gains. I would never let another go through what I did. I'll probably break down after." If I survive, not that I planned to, but I have a feeling they don't want to hear that so I leave it out. "But for now, I need to be strong, okay? It's the only way I'm getting through this."

Luckily, Louis chimes in, giving me the escape I need. "Okay. Dimitri is accessing their system now. Nico, go back to guard duty and give us the information we need. We are coming, baby, just hold on, okay? Just a little bit longer. Then we will stop this bastard once and for all, and then I'm taking you home and never letting you out of my sight again."

I swallow. "Louis, I need you to promise me." My eyes are for Nico though. I know they will all fight me, but I need them to hear this. "If it's between saving me and saving the kids, save the kids."

Voices explode in my ear again, and Nico snarls, ready to fight me. "No. I mean it. We all make sacrifices. I will never forgive you if you choose me and they die. Promise me that they'll come first and you will save them. I can't—" I look away. "I cannot lose anyone else, so I need you to promise me this."

There's a moment of hesitation where I don't think they will. "I promise, Nova." He seems determined. "Nova, I'm sorry about An—"

"Don't say her name," I snap before I close my eyes. "Please, I can't . . . I can't, okay?"

"Of course, Nova," Isaac says, his voice reassuring. "We are right here, okay? You're not alone now."

"We're coming, baby, just hang on, and I will kill every last motherfucker in there for you," Jonas adds. I can't help but smile.

"I didn't want you to come after me, you know?" I hear them responding angrily, so I quickly hurry on. "I didn't want you to get caught or be in danger. I just wanted you to be happy, to find a life."

"You are our life, and we can't be happy without you," Nico snaps. "Do not ever think otherwise. There is no us without you. Baby, where you go, we go. There is no happiness, no life, and no future without you. I would suffer a hundred years of torture and die a thousand times simply to be at your side. Live or die, we do it together."

"He's right. Before you, we were a team, then after you, we became a family, and you are the heart of our family, Nova. We cannot function without you. You beat for us, so don't you even dare," Louis warns. "Now give Nico the mic, baby, kiss him, promise him you're okay so he doesn't go off the rails and kill everyone for the marks on your body, and remind him we will do that together."

"Yes, sir," I tease, handing the mic back over. My spirits are lifted, and love for them runs through me, along with worry. Nico puts the earpiece back in and grunts at whatever they are saying.

"I've got to go, baby."

Leaning forward, I cup his cheeks and kiss him soundly. "We will end this together. Louis is right. No killing anyone yet."

"No promises," he mutters, but I can tell he won't risk me or the kids. Standing, he gives me one last lingering look before turning away, but panic winds through me.

Catching his hand, I tug him back. "Don't you dare get caught or no one here is safe, do you understand me? I'll kill them if they so much as think about hurting you."

"Back at you, baby," he murmurs, kissing me hard before hurrying out the door like he doesn't trust himself to stay.

I'm alone once more, knowing they are out there. They are close, and that gives me hope.

It gives me renewed determination.

This isn't just about me or ending this or even the kids. It's about keeping my lovers safe.

I will not lose anyone else.

TWENTY-EIGHT

LOUIS

Ripping out the earpiece, I give in to a moment of weakness, my head pressed to the sniper rifle. I know my position, and I know what I should do, but it wars with my need to see my girl and protect her. She's hurting beyond the wounds she has suffered since we have been apart. I heard it in her voice. The others might not have, too focused on their own joy, but I did. I heard the truth in her words.

She's struggling, and part of her wants to die there, but I will not ever let that happen.

If she dies, then I die. It's that simple.

I quickly come up with a different plan, putting the earpiece in once more.

"Fuck this, I'm going in," I snap, not as collected as I wish, but it's too late to take it back.

"What?" Dimitri demands. "What about the plan?"

"No, he's right." I bet Isaac knew it the moment he spoke to her. "She needs him. She needs someone with her right now even if she won't admit it. I think she had a plan that we interrupted, one we wouldn't have liked very much, and I think, given the chance, she will still follow through."

"What do you mean?" Jonas snarls.

"No," Dimitri mutters, "she wouldn't. She knows how much that would .

. . after Bas."

"She felt like she had no choice. She's grieving and not thinking properly. Coupled with whatever they are doing to her, she was doing what she thought was best with no way out. I will not allow that to happen, but someone needs to be there to remind her. Nico can't be compromised; we need him. Dimitri needs to stay here to get us in. Jonas wouldn't control himself, and Isaac would be taken away for his brain. It has to be me. It makes sense."

"He's right. So what's the plan?" Jonas sounds calm, which worries me, but I have no choice but to roll with it. I can only worry about so much.

"I'll get myself captured and make it look like I'm poking around for her. They might keep us together if they want information and for us to behave. I won't give them a choice. This will also mean that there are two working from the inside. Nico, I want you to check out that opening she mentioned. Jonas, when he relays where, I want you inside the perimeter and making us an exit. Dimitri, I want in that system now and I want complete control. Isaac, research every fucking option for our girl and what she mentioned about her choice. Do you understand?"

"Yes," they reply instantly.

"And I want safe spaces for the kids when they are out. You know your jobs, so do them." I rip out my earpiece, stowing it with my gun and other weapons, knowing they won't be allowed inside. I do keep a few knives and a small gun, just to make it look real.

I'm coming, my love, I tell her, even though she can't hear me.

I will not lose her, not like I lost Bas, Ana, and Sam. Fuck the mission. She comes first.

It doesn't take me long to get into position. I don't dare do it too close to their base in case they start to look around for the others. I can't draw attention to the guys. Instead, I head into the nearest town and begin to ask questions like I'm a forward scout, knowing it will get back to them. Nico already mentioned some guards live and work from here, so it's only a matter of time.

Four hours later, they take the bait. "I know the place you're looking for," a stern-faced man in jeans and a big coat says. "Follow me."

Dumb move, but it's exactly what I want, so I finish my drink at the bar and hurry outside after him. "Where is it?" I demand, trying to play the part, scanning the area. I can't go too easily or they will know it's a trap.

"This way. We can't be too careful. You never know who's listening," he mutters with a smirk. It's blatant, but I let it slide as he leads me around the back of the tiny pub. There's a black Escalade idling there, and five men jump out, their guns aimed at me.

Snarling, I quickly pull mine and grab the man leading me, pulling his back to my front as I press my gun to his head. After all, I have to give them a good show. "Where is she?" I demand.

"Come with us and you'll see," one says, his gun still aimed at me. "You're an idiot for coming alone."

Good, they fell for it.

"Don't move," I snap as they inch forward, "or he's dead." I start to back away. I hear the crunch of the gravel behind me as another approaches, but I pretend not to notice. Fuck, I'm a good actor. "You'll bring her to me."

"Now, let's talk about this," the leader says, holding his gun out in surrender, glancing behind me just for a second. The barrel of a gun presses to the back of my head. I could duck and shoot, I could win this easily, but I freeze instead. "You want to see her, correct?"

I simply grind my teeth as if debating my options, my instincts screaming at me to kill them, but I ignore it.

"I thought so. We can take you to her. Just stay nice and calm, drop the gun, and you'll be with her soon."

I hesitate, looking them over as if debating taking them on, and then the gun prods harder into my head. "Now!" the voice behind me snaps.

Releasing the man in my hold, I drop the gun, and they quickly bind my wrists and shove a black bag over my head before tossing me into the SUV, and then we are on our way. Even disoriented with the bag, I keep track of the turns we make to ensure they are, in fact, taking me to the base and not somewhere else. I'd have to kill them and try this again, which would waste precious time.

The general is getting itchy for updates, and Nova needs to be out of there. So much is riding on this plan. I have to trust the guys to do their part as well. It's up to Jonas, Dimitri, and Isaac now to find us a way in and out and to bring their systems down. Keeping Nova alive and okay is my job. Nico has infiltrated the inside.

Hopefully, this will work because one way or another, this ends now.

After thirty minutes, we turn up at the base. This time, I'm inside the SUV and driven straight to the front door. I overhear them talk about how glad the boss will be. Idiots. After a few stops and starts to check security, we come to a complete stop. Doors slam, and then I'm yanked from the vehicle. I stumble before righting myself. My eyes strain, so I shut them and focus on my other senses. I feel a burning sensation on my neck that lets me know my men are still out there watching.

Good.

My boots hit hard concrete which suddenly changes as we pass into a warmer area inside. There's some muttering as I'm groped, and then a few minutes later, we are moving again. When a woosh sounds and we start to descend, I realise I'm in an elevator.

The same one Nico went in?

I guess only time will tell. Hopefully, it means they are bringing me where I want to be. These idiots are so excited to bring me to the boss, thinking it's all their idea, that they haven't got a clue they are playing right into my hands. The elevator jerks to a stop, and they yank my arm. The air is cooler here, and it has a clinical scent, one I'm familiar with from my child-hood. It's almost stuffy under the hood, and the bindings dig into my wrists, but I don't speak as their boots echo with mine down what I assume is a corridor. Another door opens, and I'm led inside what seems to be a room. It feels closed in, the air almost stale, as if it's not used much. I'm pushed into a chair, and my hands are rebound behind me, then the boot steps fade away as I'm left here.

Time passes oddly under the hood, and instead of trying to figure it out, I run through my list and plan. Convincing them to pair me with Nova should be hard but doable. Then, I'll ensure she is okay and check in with Nico—again, hard but doable. After that, we just need to find the research, destroy it, kill her father, and get out of here.

Easy, right?

I run through the pros and cons of my options since I have nothing else to do, and that's when I hear the door click, followed by soft footsteps. Not boots, more like soft-soled shoes. A scientist? A worker? A chair screeches in front of me, but I don't move, focusing on the sound to pinpoint the person. The breathing is soft, slow, and calm, and the scent is familiar.

Like pine needles and bleach.

"Hello, Dr. Davis," I murmur.

He chuckles, and the hood is pulled away. He's sitting before me, wearing a lab coat and looking exactly the same as he did when we saw him in the house, except now he has no blood on him. "Louis, I would say it's nice to see you, but . . ." He shrugs.

I roll my shoulders as I watch him, glancing around the room, noting the camera, the one exit and entrance, and the two guards behind me with guns and batons before I focus back on him. "The feeling is mutual."

"I'm sure. But then again, you were looking for me, not the other way around." His eyes narrow slightly as he works through my motivations. He could never believe it's just because I love his daughter since love eludes him. It makes him blind to how far people are willing to go.

It's something I can use against them.

"I wasn't looking for you, but for Nova."

He snorts, clearly not believing me. "Leave us. Keep the door open but stand outside." He waits for the guards to do just that, and he doesn't even spare them a look because he believes they are so beneath him. It gives me some hope that Nico will slip through without detection if he plays it smart.

"Why are you here?" Dr. Davis asks me, eyeing me warily.

"I was looking for Nova when your goons found me," I snap, repeating myself as I tug on the bindings. "Where is she? Is she okay? Is she alive?" I demand, pretending to panic when I know full well she is. Still, there's a moment of hesitation inside of me. What if he hurt her between the time I took the earpiece out and now?

"She's alive. I need her, after all, but I never needed you." He opens a folder. "You did show great promise though, and she clearly cares for you and you for her, so maybe we can still use you and get her to do what we need by hurting you. She's been somewhat . . . uncooperative."

That's my girl.

"But then again, you were always problematic. You had issues following orders." He shuts the folder with a dramatic sigh once more as if I've displeased him. "Sad really, you showed great promise. I was almost reluctant to end your experiment and label you a failure, but . . ."

"You did." I shrug. "What a shame. I want to see Nova."

"Yes, well, I need to decide if I'm going to kill you or use you. It has to be a thought-out decision, you see."

Shit, we have no time to waste. I lean back, projecting calm and mirroring him—a tried and true psychological movement.

"I did, but I never had anything on the line. We both know I am clearly willing to risk everything for her. She would do the same for me. You want us both to cooperate? Put us together." I shrug like it's easy.

"And why would I give you what you want? Neither of you have any options."

"You think we have no options truly? I thought you were smarter than that, Dr. Davis," I mock. "You created us, after all. What was it you used to say? To expand the human potential? You think the reason that you explored and widened to new possibilities truly could not outthink you? Either you are dumber than I imagined or simply not very imaginative. I could kill you right now and be gone before your guards even get here." Leaning forward, I watch him lean back. Fear flashes in his eyes for the first time as he understands the truth of his creation. "You created it, so don't doubt us. Put us together if you wish for us to cooperate. Otherwise, life will get very, very hard for you."

He doesn't like to be outplayed. He will find a way to take it out on us, but for now, he has no choice. He can't be sure I don't have something up my sleeve, and he's already admitted that he needs my help with Nova.

Standing, he glares down at me. "You're a means to an end. I'll make her aware of that. Soon, I won't need either of you. Remember that, Louis."

Stiffening at his clear threat, I incline my head as he storms out the door. If he doesn't need us anymore, then that means he got what he wants, or he's close to replicating the process without years of mental and physical torture and stimulation.

Not good, not good at all.

"Take him to her cell. Make them both aware of the consequences if they are to misbehave."

"But, sir," one of the guards begins, "I think—"

"I don't employ you to think! Do as you are ordered or you will be gone in a blink."

I watch the guards enter, ready to unbind my hands. I simply stand, yanking my hands apart and snapping the bindings. I take great joy in watching them pale in fear and reach for their guns. "Shall we?" I mock.

They share a look, and one pulls out his baton and presses it to my chest. "Try something, I dare you," he mutters. "I'd love to beat the shit out of you like we did that girl of yours."

I stiffen, my eyes narrowing. "You touched her?" I ask.

"Touched her? Oh, I would do so much more—"

Before he can speak his next words, I take the baton and slam it against his windpipe. He crumples to the ground, choking as he dies. Dropping the baton, I look at the guard pulling his gun. He glances from me to the guard and sighs, putting it away. "I haven't touched her. I don't get paid enough for this. Come on." He jerks his head.

He's smart. He can live for now.

Needing to check on her myself, I follow him. No one even mentioned the dying guard, so I guess they don't really care. It makes me wonder how much I can push it but first, I need to see her.

I'm led through a maze, but I memorise it, and then we stop before a closed door. After leaning in to open it, the guard lowers his voice, his mouth turned away from the camera. "If you love this woman, find a way to get her out. He's not going to stop until she's dead. It's been bad." With that, he opens the door, stopping any questions I might have, but I'll remember his face. He can live.

Stepping in, I almost drop to my knees right then and there at the sight before me.

"Nova."

TWENTY-NINE

DMITRI

I watch Louis be led inside with a soft sigh. He's crazy, but I understand why. It doesn't stop me from wishing I were him, though, so I could be at her side, but I know my place. I'm the best bet for getting into their systems, and that's how I help them. It's what I intend to do even as I listen carefully to Nico's conversations with the guards as they take a break. He's prying for information without being obvious. He's good; I'll give him that.

Glancing back down at the laptop on the grass, I refocus on getting into their systems. I have the cameras and alarms so far, but there are firewalls around folders and files that I want to break. I want full access, and anything less than that is not acceptable. There is no room for error when it comes to my family.

We all have our roles. Louis's phone rings then, and I purse my lips. I must groan out loud because the earpiece crackles with their voices.

"What is it?" Jonas mutters as I swear. "Are they okay? Is Nova?"

"Yeah, sorry, it's the general again," I mutter.

"Again?"

Nodding even though he can't see, I work through the responses to him. "Yeah, Louis had me feeding him false leads so he didn't get suspicious and try to stop us from going after Nova. He also didn't want them following us and giving away our positions. This isn't sanctioned."

"But why?" Isaac asks, sounding confused. "He trusts them, doesn't he?"

"As much as you can trust the government." I cough, relaxing back into my computer once it's done. They will eventually come looking, maybe even at the manor, but for now, we are safe. "How's it going, Isaac?"

He's taken the spare laptop to follow Louis's orders while we wait for me to get into the systems and for Nico to report back on the opening for Jonas. We need to wait for the night to sneak in anyway, so we have time—time Isaac is utilising for Nova's benefit. After all, he's the doctor, so he knows best.

The long silence tells me all I need to know. It's not good. "Without seeing the damage, I'm not sure, but . . . It is probably permanent."

"Fuck," I mutter.

I never asked her if she wanted kids. I never thought about it. I was always too focused on the mission, on the next invention, the next moment, but I won't ever admit to her that the idea of a little Nova running around doesn't appeal to me. What would our child be like after all we have gone through? Maybe it is for the best, but if it hurts her, I will find a way.

Come hell or high water, money would be no option. I will give her what she wants.

No matter how impossible it seems.

"And for the kids when we get them out?" I know he's looking into that too. He's locating the best safe places for them. It's important to us and to her that they are safe and happy and that they never have to suffer again. Who knows what they are doing to them in there. I mean, look what they did to us. The cycle stops with us.

"I have some options. I don't know if they are orphans, but I am assuming they are since either no one is looking for them or he paid to adopt them. Either way, I'm assuming they have no family, which makes it easier. Psychologically, he uses patterns to repeat his experiments. There are homes we can get them into, although it might be hard without revealing why they have no details or documents, but I'm still looking."

"Okay," I murmur. "I can always erase their pasts, but they might talk about it."

"True, kids are kids. You remember what we were like?" He chuckles before going quiet. "Do you think they are okay?"

"Of course," Jonas responds. "Dimitri can see them. He would tell us—"

"I mean mentally. Who knows what she has been through again, and coupled with the loss of her sister, I'm worried," Isaac admits.

"We will get her out, and then we'll have the rest of our lives to heal her hurt and help her," I offer. "We will not lose her like Bas."

"Want me to just storm in there and kill them?" Jonas mutters. I can hear him moving, no doubt changing to a better position to be near the base.

"Later maybe." I grin as I scan the cameras. I can see Nico in the break room, and then I flip through and find Nova. The door opens, admitting Louis. The pure shock and happiness on her face lets me know she's going to be okay. I want to stare, to memorise her face and reaction, but I turn that camera off for a moment to give them their privacy, not letting anyone else see. They won't know, but I do.

I refocus on the alarms and reprogramming them to do what I want. They don't even know I'm in their systems, destroying it all from the inside out while also trying to crack into their mainframe files. I'll get there eventually. It will just take some time.

"I'm hitting the head," Nico calls to his friends and moves away. Instead of the toilet, however, he moves down the corridor. "Okay, heading to the hole," he mutters to me. "Is she okay? Is Louis safe?"

"They are both good, brother. Keep going forward, and I'll call out any issues." I track his movements on the camera and tilt the one away from the janitor's door so they can't see him coming and going. It's not enough to draw attention, but enough to satisfy us.

"Yup, that level." I watch him ride the elevator. "Okay, forward. If Nova was correct, two lefts, one right."

Tracking him, I spot some guards ahead. "Slip into the next room." Silently, he moves into the room and we wait. "Okay, go." He's back out. "Hurry. Rotation changes soon," I say, and he speeds up without running. Finally, he reaches the door and steps inside. I scan the cameras for any issues while he works. "It's a mess in here. Whatever she used, she did a good job. They tried to board it up. If I can get the boards off, I think I can get an opening, but I will need a noise to cover it."

"Got you." I trigger a fire alarm, covering the noise. I hear him grunting, snapping, and yanking as he removes the boards. I watch the guards run.

"Almost disabling," I tell him when I see the guards in the control room, trying to switch it off.

"One more," he says, and just as the alarm cuts out, he speaks again. "Got it. Shit."

"What?" I demand.

"Erm, nothing, nothing. I've got this."

"Nico?" I ask, confused by the sudden tightness of his voice.

"Just keep checking on everyone else. Buy me time. I'll be there soon."

"Got you, man," I say even as I frown, wondering what is wrong.

THIRTY

NOVA

"Nova," he murmurs as he stares at me. I'm sitting on the edge of the bed, hardly able to believe it's him.

How?

Why?

"Louis?" I murmur, rubbing at my eyes as if to wipe away the vision of him. The door shuts behind him, the noise snapping us into motion. He rushes to me as I rush to him. We meet midway, our lips coming together in a sloppy kiss as he lifts me into the air.

"I've got you, baby. I've got you," he promises as he kisses me and holds me tight.

"What are you doing here?" I murmur as I rain kisses across his face, unable to stop touching him.

"You needed us, you needed someone here, so I got captured. Don't worry, we have a plan." His grin is wide as he holds me tight, as if he will never let me go again.

I hope he doesn't.

Pulling back, I eye him in shock. "You got kidnapped because I needed you?"

"Of course, baby, I'd do anything for you." He groans, gripping me tighter and kissing me.

"I love you. I love you so much," I mumble against his lips. "I've missed you so much."

I'm slammed to the bed, my legs thrown over his arms. "I know you're hurt, my love, so stop me if I make it worse, but I need to be inside of you. I need to feel that you're alive. I've been going out of my mind."

Gripping his face, I tug him close as he rips at my pants, his eyes desperate. "I'm yours," I tell him, and I am. Fuck the pain. I want him to remind me of who I am and that I'm more than this living, breathing wound. I'm Nova. I'm okay. Just for a moment, I want to lose myself in his body.

Groaning, he yanks off the cheap underwear. His eyes flick back to my face and with a dirty grin, he spits on his fingers. He thrusts them into me, making me cry out as he works them inside of me, stretching me while his lips meet mine and swallow my moan. His thumb rubs my clit as desire slams through me, making my back arch off the bed. Grunting, he pulls his fingers from my wet pussy then shoves his pants down, and with one hard kiss, he thrusts into me. His cock stretches me as he sinks deeply inside me. The slight pain makes me groan as my body adjusts, and he moans as his head falls to mine.

"God, baby, I missed you so much. I was so fucking worried. Don't you ever do that again," he snarls as he pulls out and slams back in. "Say it, say you won't leave us again."

"Louis," I beg, biting his lip.

Snarling, he lifts and drops me on his dick as he reaches between us, rubbing my clit harshly. The sudden desire and pleasure makes my eyes close as I jerk.

"Say it," he orders, and just when I'm about to come, he stops. His cock is still inside me. Rocking, I try to get off, but he stills me and I slump. "Say it, Nova."

"I won't leave you again," I snap. "Please."

"Good girl," he purrs, kissing me as he rubs my clit while rocking into me, making sure to slide over those nerves that have me clawing at his shoulders and gasping into his mouth. It's too much. All the pain I've had fades into pleasure that explodes through me like fireworks. I scream into his lips, my body jack-knifing, and pain hits me from the movement in my stomach, but I don't let him stop.

I lock my legs behind him to keep him inside of me as he kisses me through my release. "Such a good girl, Nova," he murmurs as I shudder. He slowly pulls out of my pussy and shoves back in, hard and fast.

His other hand comes up and rips my shirt off to bare me to his gaze. I freeze then, and his eyes widen when he sees my new scars. I wait for his anger or disgust, but he slows, making sure I meet his eyes before he leans down and trails his lips over every single one until my throat is tight with tears.

"You are so perfect, my girl," he promises, "then and now. No matter what, I will spend our lives kissing these better and loving the story they tell of my girl surviving to get back to us."

Closing my eyes, I let him heal the wounds with his words and touch as his lips move up and down my chest. He licks my nipples before sucking them into his mouth. The zap of pleasure makes me fall back, and I grip the edge of the bed as he continues his assault.

His thrusts speed up. One hand holds me, while the other slides softly across my dripping clit. His mouth switches between my breasts as he murmurs, "Come for me, Nova. I need to feel it again. I need my girl's cum on my cock, and I need to fill you with mine so deeply, we can never be separated again."

"Louis!" I scream, uncaring who hears. Gripping his hair, I pull his mouth to mine as I fall off that cliff. He follows me this time, bellowing into my mouth as his hips flex, filling me to the point of pain as I feel him jerk and come inside me.

Shuddering, I suck in desperate breaths, my body alight with pleasure as he kisses my lips. "I love you. I love you so much, Nova," he murmurs. "I told you that I would always come for you, and I will. There isn't anywhere in this world where you could hide from me. It's you and me, Nova, forever. No matter what."

Whimpering, I fall into the kiss.

"I've got you, my love," he promises, our bodies still joined as pleasure continues to course through me. "I've always got you."

THIRTY-ONE

NICO

I tug out the earpiece for a moment, laying my hands on the cool, jagged metal of the hole our girl blew. I need to breathe through the panic because I don't want them to hear and make it a problem. There is no one else who can do this, only me, so I need to fucking get over it. I peer back into the black hole. It is a small, tight space.

It's the very fucking thing I fear more than anything.

It's another fucking scar, thanks to her dad, only this one is internal. If the others knew, they would try to figure another way out, but there is no other way. I need to do this for her and my family. Without giving myself time to overthink it, I cram myself into the hole, grunting and groaning as I contort my body into a weird angle until I finally fit. Closing my eyes for a moment, I slow my breathing like Isaac taught me. He has been working with me on triggers and how to control them, and although it hasn't worked, I wish I had tried harder now. I know I need to get moving, but I'm stuck, hesitating in the darkness. My body locks up with fear.

It's a stupid, irrational fear, but it doesn't stop me from sweating or my breaths from picking up even as I try to control it. Squeezing my eyes shut, I manage to lift a shaky hand and put the earpiece back in. "I need her."

I can't do this without her. I know she's with Louis, and I know she can't get here, but it doesn't matter.

"What?" Jonas asks, but Isaac is faster.

"Nico, why do you need Nova?"

"Tunnel is small," is all I can grit out. "I need her voice."

"Okay, that we can do," Dimitri responds, not questioning if I can do this. They simply hear my need and respond. My family, my brothers, always try to give me what I need. "So, it's a recording, but it's the best I have. Ignore the shit she's saying, since it is from when we were in the lab, but it's her, big guy. It's your Nova."

Her voice mercifully fills my ear then, the familiar cadence making my locked-up muscles relax as my shaking slows to a stop and I can finally suck in a lungful of clean, unpanicked air.

"How boring, yet another day—" She's talking. I don't even know about what, but it doesn't matter. She's here with me, and she needs me.

It gets me moving.

My panic over saving her takes precedence over my own fear.

"You want me to solve the problem? Fine." Even her sass translates, urging me on. Her anger becomes my own, and it's another reminder that I cannot leave her down here, not even for another day. I move faster, sliding my hands up the metal tubing, my back to the other side as I climb. I don't give myself time to think about where I am.

Instead, I focus on the motions of my body and her voice in my ear. It's an arduous process, and I don't know how much time passes until I reach a dead end. I turn to face what I presume is the outside world and blow out a breath.

"There, I'm done. Are you happy?" she snaps.

"I'll be happy when you're home, baby," I respond without meaning to and have to clear my throat. "Jonas, I'm here."

"Okay, the GPS signal in the earpiece should let us find you now that you are above ground. Here, Jonas, I have sent it to your phone. Go. Nico, you are going to have to wait there while he locates it, is that okay?"

Nodding, I close my eyes, realising he can't see me. "Yeah, just keep her voice in my ear."

"Got it, brother, hold on. You are doing amazing."

Her voice starts in a different clip this time. She's laughing, and then I hear Ana. "Annie, no, you'll get us in trouble."

"You are always in trouble anyway." Annie laughs, and then there's a bang.

"What is the meaning of this?" It's her father. "Well, who did this? Ana, was this you?"

"No, it was me." I can almost see my girl's defensive stance in front of her sister as she takes the blame. It switches again, this time to random clips of my girl's life from the labs and house footage. It's always her voice, and she's always calm or angry, never sad or screaming, thank God.

"One day, I'm going to get my revenge on you. You know that, right?"

I smile at that. That's my girl.

"There will come a day when there is nothing else you can do to me. You will look into my eyes as I make sure you can never hurt me again. One day, Father, you will regret your choices, and that's a promise."

That's my girl, and I intend to keep that promise with her. Before this week is through, this place will be dust, we will be home, and she will be in my arms where she belongs.

"Okay, drawing closer. Sorry, brother, I keep having to stop to avoid guards," Jonas mutters, no doubt moving through the base in the dark. I'm guessing D cut the alarms and turned the cameras away from him, or maybe Jonas just took it as a game and broke in—it wouldn't be the first time. "Question, if I blow you up by mistake, will you be mad?"

"Yes," I grumble.

He hesitates. "Okay."

"Jonas, you measured the explosives, right?" I demand.

"Sure, sure, totally measured them. This is the correct amount. I'm positive. Hundred percent. Okay, maybe like sixty percent, but it should be okay."

"Fucking hell." My eyes close once more. "If you kill me, Nova will kick your ass."

"Then she will kiss it better. I'm like forty percent sure this is the right amount. Maybe you should leave once I place it if you don't want to die because you're boring."

"I'm boring because I don't want to die in a fiery explosion?" I retort.

"Yep, exactly, think how exciting it would be—"

"I don't know if you're being serious or trying to distract me," I grumble.

"Maybe a bit of both. Me, personally, I'd like to die in a shark attack. I very much like being eaten, and those grey bastards are cute, so when I'm old and grey, feed me to the sharks."

Isaac sighs. "We are not feeding you to the sharks."

"I will," D adds.

"It's my dying wish!" Jonas snaps.

"You aren't dying!" I practically yell.

"Not yet, but one day, and when I die, I want to be surrounded by sharks. I want to die how I lived—with madness."

"You're mad, that's for sure," I mutter as something hits the side of the vent.

"See? All set. Oh, I forgot the timer. I better run, you too, Nico!"

Fuck!

I hear him sprinting away, so I release my hands from the side and let myself plummet, knowing it's the fastest way. At the bottom, I grab the side with a grunt and slide out of the hole, catching my shoulder and almost ripping the uniform. I've barely made it out of the hole when the base shakes.

It goes quiet for a moment. "Nico, tell me you're alive," Isaac demands.

"I'm good. Did it work?"

Coughing, Jonas replies, "Oh, it worked. There's a hole big enough even for your fat ass. Okay, let me cover it quickly before the guards get here. You better get back to work, soldier boy."

"Fucking idiot," I snap, even as I cover the hole but leave it loose enough for them to break through and slip out of the cupboard. The alarms up top are screaming, and I blend into the soldiers passing by.

"What was that?" I ask.

"Who knows? Someone said it was an attack, but it is probably just those idiot scientists experimenting again."

"Nothing to worry about then?" I question.

"Probably not. Better get back to your station. They will send up an alert if anything is wrong."

Nodding, I slip away. I don't want to just lie low in case they find the hole and realise we are close, but I have to trust that my brothers know what they are doing. "That's a good idea. Jonas, set another explosion in a bin and make it look like one of the scientists threw out chemicals."

I hear him moving to do just that, and after patrolling the corridor like I'm supposed to be doing, I see the guards heading back down and relax. It looks like they bought our ruse, and we are one step closer to getting our girl out of here.

"I'm fully in the system. I probably need twelve hours to plan, and then we'll make our move."

"Got it," I mutter.

Twelve hours until my girl is mine again.

Twelve hours until all this is over.

THIRTY-TWO

NOVA

I'm wrapped in Louis's arms, soaking in his warmth and strength. His hand is tangled possessively in my hair, and his leg is tossed over mine. The cot is small, not made for two people, but neither of us care. We are as close as we can get.

"Tell me everything I've missed," I murmur against his bare chest, rubbing my face there. I feel him hesitate and sigh. "Everything, Louis."

"There she is." He chuckles. "Okay, well, we tried to track you—" I listen as he tells me about their efforts, my heart squeezing as I realise they didn't give up once. They didn't even think about it. All the while I was here, numb, and hurting, hoping they had forgotten me as I planned how to bring this place down and, in the process, kill myself.

I'm a selfish bastard.

I don't want that now. Seeing them again has brought back my desire to keep going, but it hurts that I even thought about leaving them. It's clear my leaving really hurt them, and that's something I have to live with. I wouldn't change my decision, and I can't. The past can only hurt us if we allow it. Instead, I need to learn from it and learn to trust them, to love them, and know they will always come for me.

"I wasn't sure," I whisper when he's done. "Part of me hoped you would forget me and move on, be happy . . . It would have been easier."

"How could you even think that?" he demands, jerking my chin up until I peer into his eyes.

"Because I can't lose any more people I love," I admit.

"You won't, I won't let you, but don't you ever dare think for a minute that we will give up on you. We could never walk away from you. Never mind the mission, baby, you're our whole life. This might have started as five fucked-up kids seeking revenge, but it is so much more now, and you know that. We are a family. You are our fucking heart, and without you, we cannot exist. We need you, and you need us. I love you, Nova. I've never loved anyone the way I love you, and I will not lose you ever again. A month was long enough. It was fucking agony each day, even more than your father ever managed to cause us. I will not spend another second away from you, do you hear me? It's us, Nova. It's always been us. Tell me you understand. Tell me you won't ever think that again, that you will never leave us again."

"I can't," I reply, and he narrows his eyes so I rush on. "Not if it means saving you because I love you too. I love you so much I'm willing to die to protect you. I won't lie to you, Louis, and I know you would do the same, so it has to be enough. It has to be enough that we are here and that we are together again and that I love you."

"You are infuriating," he snaps but softens, pressing his head to mine. "I have our whole lives to convince you we are better together."

"I know we are." My breath brushes his lips. "Sometimes it just hurts so much because I know . . ." I swallow as my darkest fears come out. "I know if I lost you like I lost Ana, I wouldn't go on, I couldn't, and that makes me so fucking weak."

"You could never be weak, Nova, and despite what your father said, love isn't a weakness. It is our strength, and without it, what is the point? Without it, we would just be like him. Love makes us stronger than we ever could be. It makes us believe in a future, in a better world. Love is the reason we fight and never give up, even when it looks bleak. Love gives us a reason to be a better person."

"When did you get so smart?" I mutter. "But what if I love you all too much? I mean, look what my father is capable of. If he knows of my love for you, he will use it against me . . . against you."

"Let him try. It's us against the world, baby, and I'm not going anywhere ever again, believe that. Your father, the experiments, the military, and even the fucking end of the world itself couldn't tear me from you."

"You are so hot when you get all riled up." I smirk, making him chuckle.

"Good, remember that for when we get out of here and I tan your ass red for daring to leave us."

"Promises, promises," I murmur, dragging my lips along his. "But I'll hold you to that."

Things are just about to get interesting when the door opens. We both freeze and lift up, seeing the guards. "Time to go, love birds." One smirks. "The doc wants you."

"Of course he does." Slowly, I slide from the bed. Louis helps me, keeping a hold of my hand as the guard comes towards us.

"It stinks of sex in here." Another laughs. "Is she good?"

Before I can react, Louis knocks out the guard and is back at my side. The remaining two guards look from their friend to us, and each grab an arm and drag us from the room. "You'll pay for that," one mutters, and once we are out of sight of the cameras around the corner, he slams his baton into Louis's stomach, causing him to bend over, gasping.

Snarling, I elbow the man holding me but then freeze when Louis holds up his hand. "Don't. Let them, baby."

"Yeah, baby," the one in my ear croons, and Louis's eyes turn molten as he glares at the man.

"If you so much as look at my girlfriend wrong one more time, I'll rip you apart limb from limb, and we both know I can. I'm being nice so far, and you don't want to see me when I'm not."

The man listens, thank fuck, and instead, they drag us silently down the corridor and thrust us into a room with a few tables and chairs and then stand at the door at attention.

"You okay?" I ask, shooting the guard who hurt him a glare that promises retribution.

"I'm fine, baby," Louis mutters, but I still glare at the man.

"You're dead for touching what's mine," I warn him. He laughs it off with his friend but I'm serious. Nobody hurts my men and gets away with it.

Not even me.

My father makes us wait, and when he enters, he places his tablet on the table and sits, watching us for a while. "I have a different kind of experiment today. We are getting close to locating a better way to open the mind without—"

"Torture?" I supply.

"Experimentation. We are synthesising a serum, but we'll need to test it. However, I still want to know the exact parameters of what I am creating. You understand, yes?"

I want to ask if the serum is being used on the children, how he is creating and testing it, but I can't without looking interested, and that would give him exactly what he wants.

"Oh, of course," I mutter. "Quit the crazy mumbo jumbo. What the fuck do you want?"

"I would remain polite, Nova. After all, I let your friend survive when I could have killed him. Remember that."

Grinding my teeth, I don't respond, and he smirks.

"Good girl."

Pulling something from his pocket, he places a gun on the table between us, not even sparing Louis a look.

I glance from the gun to him, but his face doesn't even move. He knows I could kill him with it.

"Kill one of the guards," my father orders, "or I'll kill him."

I don't even hesitate. After all, he deserves it. I pick up the gun and for a moment, I aim it at my father. He doesn't even flinch, and I know then he has a fail-safe plan in place, so instead, I turn it to the guard and fire. I shoot the one who hurt Louis. I know he's doing it to use Louis against me, to see how far he can push me and get me to follow orders, but I got what I wanted, so I don't fucking care.

"You did not shoot me," he muses as I place the gun back on the table.

"It wouldn't do me any good yet. When I kill you, Father, it will not be at the expense of one of your games. It will hurt, and I will be there to watch the life drain from your eyes."

Taking the gun, he doesn't even spare the dead guard a look. "So you say, yet you need a weapon in your hand to even feel that level of commitment."

"I do not need a weapon to kill, Father," I tell him honestly. "I never did. I never needed anything to be strong, but you've given me more than enough reason to be now." I leave it at that, not giving away our plan.

"Come, I have some things I wish to show you, though I assume you already know." Louis and I share a look but stand, moving to the door where the other guard is pale-faced and glancing between his buddy and me.

"Let that be a warning to you all," I say with a smirk as I pass, and he actually flinches.

Pussy.

"So fucking sexy," Louis murmurs to me as he takes my hand, and we follow my father. We could overpower him right now, but it would be a mistake. I can almost hear Louis telling me, *We stick to the plan*, and a moment later, more guards round the corner, waiting for us.

It's a trap. He was seeing if we would take our shot.

Once again, he's testing us. Good, let him think we are subdued. Instead, we follow blindly until we end up before the room where I found the children. The beds are filled with sleeping bodies now, and my heart stutters as I see them.

"These are my next line in experiments, naturally. Although the soldier aspect offered a good basis, since they were already trained, they were too . . . limited. Too many died from the experiments, but I think I finally have it right. For that, I had to go back to the beginning. To kids. To the malleable mind. They will be the next best thing in this world—highly intelligent and trained to respond. I will sell them to the highest bidder to fund my next line of experiments."

"Bullshit, you just want the money," I snap. "All this talk about science and expanding the human mind and saving mankind is bullshit. You just want money, you greedy bastard. I will never let you hurt those children the way you hurt us."

"You cannot stop me." He smirks. "Once I have what I need from you, you'll be useless. I just wanted to show you what you will be saving by following orders and giving me what I need. If I get what I need from you to make the serum successful, then I do not have to hurt them, do I? But let me show you how serious I am." He mutters something into a mic, and I watch, horrified, as a guard moves to the closest bed and covers the child's face with a pillow.

"Stop it!" I demand. He does, lifting the pillow only to repeat the action. He's not killing him, but he's making the poor, screaming, half-asleep child wish for death.

Something snaps deep inside me.

Before I've made the conscious decision, I've grabbed the pen from his pad and pressed it to his neck. "Tell him to stop now or I'll gouge out your jugular," I threaten. The place is silent bar the child's screams, the others huddling together and crying as they watch.

"You kill me and you are as good as dead," my father reasons, but his eyes are a touch too wide—fear.

"True, but I'll take you with me. Your choice, Father. Look at you. You're afraid. Do you like it? I'll admit that I like seeing the terror in your eyes, now see the truth in mine. I'm willing to die here, are you?"

Gritting his teeth, he nods, and I watch the man walk away. I should drop the pen, but I'm so fucking angry. Instead, I swipe it across his cheek, slicing it open as he shouts and falls back, covering it with his hand. I drop the pen as the guards surge towards me, and I grin at him.

"Now you'll always wear a reminder. Now you are as ugly on the outside as you are on the inside."

"Take her away now!" he howls, covering his cheek as I spit at his feet. Louis tries to grab me, but the guards drag me away as I see my father stumble down the corridor, no doubt looking for help. I laugh as we are thrown back into our cell.

Still laughing, I kick the door and then turn to the camera. "How do you like that, asshole? How do you like being on the other end? I will gut you!" I howl.

"Shh, I've got you." Louis wraps his arms around me and leads me to the bed. "Try to calm down, Nova. We have to be smart."

"Fuck smart. I want him to suffer now."

"Soon," he promises.

"No, now!" I yell, and before I know it, I'm flipped and pinned. His snarling face looms above me, and the strength in his grip makes my pussy clench, even in my anger.

"If you won't listen, then you clearly need an outlet. I will oblige, so be a good girl and come for me."

Keeping me pinned with one hand, he rips down the joggers, yanks my legs open, and slams his fingers into me. The bite of pain makes my back bow, even as I fight to get free.

He smacks my clit, making me cry out. The sharp pain brings my focus back to his snarling face. "That's it, love, focus on me. Take it all out on me."

His fingers twist inside me, curling around that spot that feels so good it hurts, all while his thumb rubs my clit. Against my own wants, I come with a cry, clenching around him with the force. Louis grins, not slowing as he continues to attack my body, forcing me to focus on him.

Use it, he said.

Use him.

Gripping his hands, I flip us and shove his joggers down as his head hits the bed, his eyes narrowed in desire. His blond hair is spread across my pillow, and his muscles clench. "That's it, Nova, use me. Come on, baby, I can take it."

I slide my hand across his abs and grip his cock. Tightening my hand, I stroke his hard length, feeling him jerk. His head drops back as he arches his hips up to thrust into my fist. "Nova," he groans needily. "Baby."

Feeling mean, I lean down and lick the tip of his cock, channelling all my anger and frustration into the desire between us.

His mouth parts on a moan, and he closes his eyes in bliss.

Seeing this huge, strong man weak below me is a heady feeling.

I lap at the tip of his cock, tasting his salty precum, and surrender. I suck the tip of him deep as he writhes with a bellow, and then I release him with a pop.

"Nova," he snarls, opening his glittering eyes. "Get your perky ass on my cock right this second."

"Or what?" I purr, leaning down and sweeping my tongue along his cock, keeping my mouth open so he can watch as I slide him to the back of my throat and rub him and his precum all over my mouth.

"I mean it, Nova. Don't be a brat or you'll be face down and my cock will be in that pretty ass instead of your pussy until you're screaming to come, and I won't let you."

"I'd like to see you try," I retort as I slide my tongue inside the tip of his cock with a hum.

"Last chance, brat," he warns, his jaw flexing.

Moving up his body, I press my lips to his. "Taste how much you want me, Louis."

"I always fucking want you," he says as he grips the back of my head, drags me down, and tangles his tongue with mine, tasting his own need. His other hand slides down my back and grips my ass, dragging my pussy along his cock, trying to get me to ride it.

Pulling away, I wag my finger at him. "Bad Louis."

Moving out of his grip, I slide up his body and seat myself on his face. "I'm sick of hearing you talk," I purr. "Use your mouth for better things and make me come on that silver tongue."

He grips my hips. "Gladly, love." He yanks me down, sitting me heavily on his face with a groan. His tongue instantly darts out and laps at my pussy.

I almost fall back from the bliss, one hand hitting the wall next to the tiny bed as it creaks with my rocking. I ride his face, grinding into his mouth as his tongue thrusts inside me, and his nose presses to my throbbing clit.

I circle my hips, finding the pressure I need, while I sit harder on his face as his nails dig into my ass cheeks, spreading it as he laps at my hole and thrusts inside it.

Moaning, I slap my hand into the wall, grinding down. I'm so close again, I'm already shaking. When he begins to hum, I'm lost. I cry out my release and fall forward to curl around him as I shudder, winding my hips through my release until I fall back.

Lifting my head, I meet his dark, hungry eyes. His face is coated in my glistening cream, and he laps greedily at his lips while reaching for me.

"Fuck, baby, bring that pretty pussy back here. Let me fucking suffocate between those thighs, drinking nothing but your cream for the rest of my life. They could come in right now and they would have to fight to get me off you."

Crawling up his body, I grab his hands and press them to my breasts as I rock into his cock. Lifting up, I grip his length and meet his eyes once more.

"How about I fuck you instead? I want to see you come. I want to feel it," I tell him as I press the bulbous head of his cock to my entrance.

"Then ride me, baby, and make me come," he growls. "Ride my big fat cock. It's hard for you, always for you, waiting to be used, to be fucked."

"That's because you're mine," I say as I slam myself down, taking his full length. His hands grip my breasts, squeezing as I start to move, chasing another release. I use him like he demanded, taking it all out on his body. My head drops back as I ride him, making sure to swivel and hit my throbbing clit.

Each thrust pushes me higher as he sits up, shoving my shirt up and sucking my nipple into his mouth. He pushes me higher and higher until I spiral and explode.

Snarling, he rolls us until we fall from the bed and my back hits the floor. He grips my hair and hammers into my body, taking what he wants. He takes the control away, leaving me breathless as I cry out.

He pulls out of my body, making me whimper, then he flips me over and yanks my hips up. Slamming back inside of me, he slaps against my ass with each brutal thrust. My head is pulled back by his hand in my hair, and the slight pain makes me moan loudly.

"You're mine, Nova, never forget that," he snaps, smacking my ass with an open hand. The sting makes me jerk before it fades into a fire that burns through me, scorching away my anger. "All of you. I'm never letting you go. I will always be here, protecting you. We will get our revenge, love, together. Until then, take your man. Take every hard inch of me and know it's all for you."

His voice is feral as he smacks my ass once more, pummelling into me. His hips stutter and I know he's close. I want to drain him dry. "Come, love, now."

"I can't," I admit, my body on the threshold.

"You can and you will," he growls.

Pushing me down, he grinds my pussy into the cold, rough floor, and I shatter once more as he moans, bowing over me as he fills me to the brim with his cum.

I'm boneless, my eyes closing as he turns us and wraps his arms around me. "Good girl, Nova. That's it, relax. We'll get him and our revenge together. Just hold on a little longer, my love."

Panting, I relax into his arms, knowing he did the right thing, but it doesn't stop me from feeling anger or guilt. What if he takes it out on the kids?

We need to move.

THIRTY-THREE

NOVA

That night when the door opens, I expect the worst, but when a figure slips in and Nico grins, I relax.

"Sorry, I had to wait. Your father was on a warpath."

"How's the bastard doing?" I mutter as Louis glances over at Nico.

"His face is cut up pretty good and he's angry about it. I heard it was your work." Nico smirks, running his tongue across his lips as I nod in response. "That's my girl."

"I thought I was your favourite girl. You lied!" I hear Jonas cry out, making me laugh as I fall back.

Pushing away from the door, he heads over. Louis moves away, sitting up on the edge of the bed so Nico can cup my face. He kisses me softly and when my eyes flutter open, I see his are closed and his head is pressed to mine.

"I just need a minute, baby, to soak you up so I can go back out there. I just need a reminder of why the fuck I haven't killed them yet and taken you away."

"A reminder?" Smirking, I cup his face, sliding my hands up into his hair before yanking his head back as he groans, his eyes fluttering open. "I'll remind you, my love."

I turn my energy, my anger, into this . . . into something good.

201

I know Louis is watching, but neither Nico nor I care. It isn't the first, nor will it be the last time, and he gives us a moment of privacy together even though he's close enough to touch.

"Shit, wait, I want the cameras on, Dimitri."

Nico yanks the earpiece out and puts it in my ear.

"Scream for them, baby, so while they are out there working, they will get a reminder, too, and they will remember what they are fighting for."

"Fuck, D, show me the cameras," Jonas whines in my ear.

"I'm busy." Dimitri huffs. "But do as Nico says, Nova. Give me a reason to work harder."

"I agree. It would be good for morale," Isaac says, and I can almost see his smile.

"You heard him," Louis murmurs, leaning back and getting comfy to watch.

They want a show? They'll get one.

Using his short hair, I yank Nico down to me. "Suck," I demand, and Nico gladly wraps his lips around my nipple through my shirt, sucking hard. I groan, my eyes sliding to Louis for a moment to see him smirking. When Nico turns his head to suck my other nipple, there's a wet patch over my breast.

Wanting skin on skin, I push him back and stand. "Get undressed. I want you naked. I want all that skin on me," I tell him, and meeting his dark eyes, I slip from my clothes and sit on the edge of the bed.

Snarling, he rips off his belt and drops his weapons. His trousers are next, getting caught in his boots. He toes them off and reaches behind him, tugging his shirt up and off as I watch the flex of muscles with a moan. Desire courses through me at the sight of all those muscles, hard lines, golden skin, and thick scars.

When he moves closer, I press my bare foot into his chest. His dark eyebrow arches and he steps closer, bending my leg at the knee until he's nearly touching me.

Bending down, he drags his lips across my foot before sliding back down with his teeth. "Show me that pretty pussy, baby. I've been dreaming about it since I last had you, and it doesn't fucking compare."

Smirking, I kick him back, and he allows me to. My foot hits the floor once more, and I spread my thighs nice and wide, letting him see my wet pussy. I slide my hand down to tug at my nipples, then over my abs to cup my pussy, where I grind into my own touch. "Is this what you want?" I purr.

His eyes are locked on my touch as he nods jerkily.

"Then get down on your knees. Show me how badly you want it. Crawl to me. Crawl to my pussy."

Without pausing, he drops to his knees, keeping those dark, wicked eyes locked on me. Nico is huge, and when he starts to crawl, I watch the pull and play of all that muscle. His arms and back flex and bulge. He doesn't stop until he can run his tongue up my thigh to my pussy, sliding it across my hand and down my other leg.

"Show me, Nova, show me why I fight. Show me why I can't sleep or look at myself. Show me what's ours," he begs, his voice needy. His huge, hard cock bobs for attention, and he wraps his thick, tattooed hand around it, stroking himself as he waits.

I peel my hand from my pussy and he groans, falling forward at the sight. His tongue swipes between my folds as I fall back with a moan. My hands slide up my body to play with my breasts, but then his big ones are there, smacking my own away as he tweaks my nipples.

"Shit." I hear someone moan down the mic. "Louder, baby. Make him suck that needy clit until you scream."

Panting, I close my eyes. I can feel Louis's eyes on me and Nico's touch. The others' voices express their own need to hear my pleasure and know I'm alive. I feel it as well. I need Nico to remind me.

I need him to touch every inch of me, to kiss me and make it better.

To remake me as theirs as if no time has passed.

To love me as they once did.

His tongue curls around my clit, lashing it as I groan, allowing every little sound to slip out. Two big fingers slide into my pussy, stretching me as he fucks me with them. He sets a fast, hard pace as he greedily eats me, licking every drop of cream as if he can't get enough. I cry out and grind into his face for more, pushed higher and higher until I tumble and fall with a scream, shattering for him.

With a beautiful moan, he pulls his fingers free and licks them clean before shoving them back into me and licking them once more.

"Nico," I whine. He tweaks my overly sore nipples, and electricity goes right to my clit.

Chuckling, he wets his fingers once more, but instead of licking them clean like I expected, he slides them down and circles my asshole before slowly thrusting them inside me there.

"I'm going to make you come on my cock, princess. I'm going to fuck you hard and fast, and then Louis is going to claim this pretty little ass, isn't he?"

"Fuck, please," I whine as he slowly fucks my ass with his fingers, only to pull away once more, leaving me needy.

Slapping my pussy with his other hand, he hoists me farther up the bed. "Hold on, baby," he warns as his cock drags along my wet centre, and when his lips meet mine, he impales me.

My eyes almost cross.

Nico is so big, it borders on painful but in the best kind of way. With that one thrust, I forget everything. I focus only on him, biting at his lips as he pulls out and hammers back in, fucking me hard and fast just like he promised.

The bed squeaks with the force as he hammers me across the bedding. Snarling, he slides down and bites my sore nipples until I whine.

"Nico," I beg, lifting my hips to meet his thrusts.

His hand slides up to grip my neck in a collar, a reminder, a promise that I am still his and he is still mine.

Nothing has changed, even though everything has.

The world could fall apart right now, and I would gladly stand in the decimation, begging him not to stop . . .

And I do loudly, for the others to hear.

Their pants and grunts of pleasure reach my ears as they no doubt touch themselves while Nico fucks me.

"That's it, baby. Fuck, you're so goddamn beautiful. Look at you, taking me so good. That's it, tighten on me, come for your man," he demands, nipping my nipple as he twists his hips to drag his length along those nerves that have me seeing stars. I am so close it hurts, but with one more brutal nip of his teeth on my nipple, I tumble over the edge, gripping his cock like a vice as I do, screaming into the mic.

I hear someone moan their own pleasure, but I'm lost, barely able to move or make a noise as Nico pulls from my clinging body and guides me to my knees on the hard floor. Placing a pillow under my head, he guides me onto Louis's waiting cock. I slide down his hard length and turn to see him as Nico slides his wet cock across my ass, taunting me as Louis stills.

When I push back, Nico slides his cock in an inch, letting me clench on his tip until I slam myself back, impaling my ass on his cock as he roars.

Gripping my hips roughly, he yanks me back, fucking me hard and fast. One hand slides up my body, collaring my neck once more, while Louis's lips find mine.

They work me between them, fucking me in tandem. Hands caress every inch of me, reclaiming my body for themselves and me.

I'm pushed and pulled between them, and another release builds inside of me. Louis rubs my clit and with a shout, I come hard, clenching around them and dragging them with me. Louis moans in my ear as he pumps his cum deep inside my pussy.

Nico roars, thrusting into my ass until I feel his hot release splatter inside me. We all pant, locked together.

"I love you," I whisper to them both.

Lips caress my back. "We love you too, and we always will, baby."

We lie like that for a while, them just holding me until they eventually pull out of my body and help me clean up and dress before holding me on the bed.

"So beautiful," Dimitri murmurs down the mic, reminding me they are there.

"I love you all too. I can't wait until I get to touch you again," I admit.

"Us also," Isaac offers softly, his voice tense.

"Are you okay?" I ask Isaac, needing to check on him.

He sucks in a breath and releases it slowly. "I will be, sweetheart, when you're back in my arms."

"How's Bert?" I ask, afraid of the answer.

"He's going to be just fine. I promise."

"Thank you," I murmur, "for saving him."

"I . . . God, Nova, I'm so sorry I couldn't save them," Isaac whispers, and my eyes close. "I'm so fucking sorry for everything he did to us. I couldn't save them, and I'm just so fucking sorry."

"I know, but it's not your fault, so don't feel guilty. My father did this, not you." Handing the earpiece back over, I curl into the bed. I'm suddenly exhausted and hurting at the reminder of my sister and Sam. Nico watches me carefully as he plugs it back in then crouches, taking my hand as he looks between Louis and me.

"So, here is the plan." Keeping our hands clasped together, Nico explains in detail every step of it. Louis asks questions, and they change little details until he's finished, and then they both look at me.

"Is that okay with you, Nova?"

I nod. "As long as I get to kill my father and we free the kids, I don't care about anything else."

They share a look before Nico leans in and kisses me. "It's almost over, okay?"

I nod again, unsure what to say. I feel like this has been a dream. Like I've been here underground for so long, yet I achieved nothing, then suddenly it's all going to be over. It has to be. My father won't forgive me for today, and if I survive the night, I will be dead tomorrow, my brain and body used for this final experiment.

Tomorrow, we'll end this lifelong mission.

But what will be left after?

"You just have to hold on a little longer, baby, okay?"

"Okay." I press my face to his side, just soaking in his warmth. "I can do that."

"I know you can."

THIRTY-FOUR

NOVA

I have no way of knowing if the guys are in position.

Today is the day.

Dimitri will bring down the alarms, Jonas will enter through the hole they made, and Isaac will come in after him. Isaac's job is to get to the kids, while Jonas's is to clear us a path. Nico will take down the guards and free us, and then we will finish my father. I know how wrong plans can go, though, and as soon as I wake up, I know this one will go wrong.

It's in the air.

All the guards come in pairs to drop off food, their eyes hard and wary as if they know something. Do they? Or am I simply overthinking all of this? Possibly, but after I shower and dress, doing some quick warm-ups with Louis to prepare for the day, I know I'm not wrong when the door opens and five guards storm in, their weapons pointed at us as if they are expecting trouble.

I share a silent look with Louis, in which we quickly adapt and allow them to take us. Nico will have to find us, but we can easily take these five out. We are led down the corridor once more, this time to the gym. Once inside, the guards spread out before the door, and then I realise they are in full protective gear.

Do they know something is wrong?

My question is answered when the door opens and Joel steps out. Unlike the guards, he's in simple jeans and a shirt, and he smirks as he comes to a stop a few feet away from us. "Your father asked me to question you while he's occupied."

"Occupied with what?" Louis asks.

No doubt he's worried that one of ours has been caught. I am too, but I have to trust them to look after themselves the way they are trusting me to be ready.

He ignores Louis completely and focuses on me. "Do you know anything about the loss of control over the alarms and cameras?" I just stare at him, waiting. "Nova, your father wants answers, and I have been given free rein to do anything to get those answers. Do you understand me? We both know you cannot survive another beating and round of torture."

Tilting my chin back, I smile tauntingly. "You want answers? Come and get them."

Joel smirks. "I was kind of hoping you would say that."

Louis steps closer, and Joel's gaze moves to him. "Don't worry, I'll let you watch. The guard can hold you. If you feel like giving answers at any point, just let me know."

He's trying to use us against each other. Clearly, they have noticed something is wrong, but they aren't sure if we are behind it or if it's something else. Father is taking precautions, but he should have taken more. This won't save him, and instead, he's given me the perfect opportunity to kill the one man I want to eradicate alongside my father.

Once we are given the signal, all bets are off.

Gone is the compliant prisoner, and in her place will be the super soldier he created.

Me.

I want revenge. I want to bathe in their blood. I want to drown in their bodies and screams, and I will have it. For a moment, my sister flickers in my mind, and I embrace it, letting her screams fill my head. It sends energy vibrating through me, and my fingers twitch at my sides, preparing to fight.

We need time, though, because if I fight now, I won't stop and the plan will fail. No, I need to be smart one last time, so when he advances on me, I don't move. I let him smash his fist into my stomach, curling around it for a moment and breathing through the pain before straightening. He meets my eyes, his own narrowing before he slaps me. My head jerks to the side from the force, and I spit out blood as I meet Louis's enraged gaze.

I silently tell him this one is mine and that I have to wait. I shake my head slightly. He wants to kill the man, but I can take this, and it will buy us the time we need. If they are focused on us, then they aren't focused on what else is happening, so for now, I accept the pain without fighting back.

Turning to Joel, I straighten and meet his angry gaze. "Fight back," he hisses in my face.

I simply stare coldly at him, waiting.

Shaking his head, he slaps his hands over my ears. The clap is loud, and my ears ring as I stumble. When his voice comes back, it's enraged, and he points at Louis. "What? So scared you won't even defend her? I thought you loved her. Isn't that why you came here? To protect her? Look at you just standing there. So weak. You won't even stop me if I do this." He slams his fist into my wound once more, and I grit my teeth to stop a cry from escaping my lips, narrowing my gaze on Louis who twitches. He's as still as a statue, but there is death in his eyes, and when he glances at me, his expression warns that he won't hold back much longer.

Despite the plan, despite the fact that Louis plans every move to the last second, he won't this time. He would ruin the plan simply to protect me.

If that isn't love, I don't know what is.

Fuck, I hope the guys hurry up or Louis is going to kill everyone before they get near us. When Louis doesn't answer, giving him what he wants, Joel turns back to me.

"Are you doing this?" he demands once more. Again, I say nothing, and his thumb digs into my wound. I bend inwards slightly, my eyes narrowing as agony spreads through me. He watches me from inches away, noting every expression. "Answer me and I'll stop. Make this easy on yourself. He doesn't want you dead just yet. If you answer, I'll make it quick when it's time, not like the brutal agony he will make you feel."

I say nothing, breathing through the pain, and he steps back with a snarl. I straighten despite the pain, and he attacks quickly, slamming his foot into the wound. I stumble back but right myself, knowing if I fall to the ground, it will be much worse. I refuse to fall ever.

"Fight back!" he roars as he grips my hair and throws me onto the mat. I'm just climbing to my feet when our signal comes.

An explosion rocks us, causing us to sprawl on the floor. I quickly leap up and know this is go time, so using their disorientation and confusion to my advantage, I point at the guards, telling Louis to take them.

Joel is mine.

"You want me to fight back?" I grin down at him. "You got it." I rush him with a silent roar.

He actually falls back as I advance, and I don't blame him. I let it all loose. All my anger, hurt, and grief. I embrace every dark part of myself. Power courses through my body, and my mind opens completely, making me work faster than ever before. I'm on him before he can even raise his hands.

I slam my fist into his face. "Fight back," I yell at him, mocking him as I slam my hands onto either side of his head, disorienting him before I bitch-slap him. He flies through the air, and I spare Louis a glance to see him ripping through the guards. He tears out someone's throat with his teeth before whirling to the next man, and desire and love pulse through me before I turn back to see Joel getting to his feet.

Wiping blood from his lips, he grins. "Finally, a fight."

I duck his punch and slam my fist up, breaking his ribs. He grunts but grips me and tosses me aside. I whirl, landing on my feet, and lunge at him. I wrap my legs around his neck as I spin upside down and then slam downward, rolling him to the ground. I hammer my fist into his face as he struggles and yells. Releasing him when his hand reaches for my wound once more, I roll back with a grin.

"Come on, is that all you've got?" I challenge.

"You're dead. Fuck what your father said. He doesn't need you. I'm the better one here," he spits.

"I'm the better one," I mock. "Yet you can't even beat a wounded female."

His nostrils flare, and he relies on emotion rather than logic as he rushes me. I know he's going for the face, so I duck, and then his knee comes up, but I was expecting it. I drive my own into his cock and when he stumbles, I leap up and ride him to the floor, hammering into his face. He brings his arms up to try and stop me, but he's slowing while I am only speeding up.

With a roar, I beat his face in, feeling bones break. Blood coats my split knuckles, but I still don't stop, not even as he twitches and then stops moving. Heaving, I sit back and take him in. His face is a bloody pulp.

"I think he's dead, love." Louis grins, and I look over to see him covered in blood, surrounded by dead guards. He tosses me a baton and a gun from a holster. I catch them and stand, and then I fire at Joel's face and chest at least five times.

"Now he is." Gripping the gun and the baton, I walk over to him, scanning for injuries. He does the same to me.

"I say we get out there. Fuck the plan, let's just hunt these bastards down. The more sides we attack from, the better. Fucking corral them like sheep." I expect him to turn me down but he nods.

"I say let's do it. We will meet with the others. Come on. Let's show them what they created."

JONAS

I hurry down the shoot that leads from the outside. I kick the boards Nico placed at the bottom, and then I wait in the cupboard with my eyes on my watch, and just as it hits zero, I whisper, "Boom."

The explosions I placed up top go off right on time. The gate goes down, and all the cars, entrances, and buildings explode. I spent all night crawling around the base, setting the charges with Isaac while Dimitri watched us and got into the last of the files. Thirty minutes before, he brought down all the cameras and alarms. Soldiers poured outside, looking for the source, but I was already inside.

"Damn, you should see the flames." Dimitri chuckles. "Okay, all systems are locked out permanently. Isaac and I are coming through the back gate while they flood the front. I'll be down in the elevator, but don't wait for us. Nico says Louis and Nova were taken somewhere and he can't find them. He's searching levels one and two, so you need to search the others. We will join you."

"Got it, and kill any I find on the way," I murmur, already pulling my gun before putting it back and palming two blades instead.

"Open season," he murmurs down the mic.

Grinning widely, I flip the knives happily and open the door. It's about time. I step out into the corridor and crack my neck. I plan to find my girl and kiss the everloving shit out of her, but first, it's time for a little payback.

They touched her.

They took her away from me.

I'll rip them to pieces until their screams echo through these corridors as a warning to whoever might try that again. Moving silently, I open each door to make sure my girl isn't in there, frowning in displeasure when I don't see anyone to kill. I want to give her a pile of hearts. In fact, I grab a bag and sling it over my shoulder just for that purpose, and then I step back into the hallway.

"Yoo-hoo, anyone home? Invader at the door!" When that doesn't work, I cock my head. "Oh look, I'm about to touch the experiments. Better come stop me!"

Still nothing.

What does a guy have to do to be attacked around here?

I mean, really.

Rolling my eyes, I pull my gun and fire at the wall, busting a pipe.

Whoops.

It does the trick, though, and I holster the gun just as two guards come skidding around the corner. "Only two, really?" I frown and point the knife at one. "Could you call the others on the radio? I'm starting to feel a little insulted. I need to show off for my girl."

Dimitri sighs. "Jonas."

"Can you record this for her?" I ask him as one calls into the mic. "Thank you, that was very kind. For that, you can die quickly."

He blanches and looks at his friend next to him, clearly scared. "Don't worry, we can wait for your backup. I want this to be fair," I tell them as I start to pick my nails with my knife, whistling as I wait.

"Erm, if you come with us, we won't hurt you?" the other offers.

I raise a brow at him, and he swallows.

"I'm sorry, that was stupid."

"It was, but it's okay. I bet it's your first time, right? Everyone is bad their first time. I mean, I wasn't, but I'm amazing." I shrug.

"I . . ." They share a look. "Maybe we can figure something out."

"Sorry, no can do. It's work, you understand." I wince as I hear boots before more guards emerge behind them and behind me, surrounding me. Grinning, I roll my neck. "This is more my speed. Don't shoot and cheat now, boys. Don't want to ruin the merchandise for my girl. Actually, she might give me head for a few bullet wounds. Feel free, but just avoid the face. She likes to sit on that."

"Doc says we can kill him," one calls, smacking his baton against his other hand as he grins at me. "Let's make it hurt. I've always wanted to kill one of these freaks."

"Oh, tough guy." I fake shiver. "I'm so scared. Please don't hurt me." Cackling, I crook my finger. "Bring it."

They surge towards me. Laughing, I dodge their weak attempts and slash. I twirl and slice through skin as I do. I hear screams as throats, arms, and legs are cut. I don't even see it anymore. I just keep moving as I dice them to pieces. Batons hit me, but I barely even feel them as I cut them down for my girl.

I do jerk as a bullet slams into my leg, but when I glance down, I see it's through and through and it hasn't hit anything important. It does, however, lodge in the femoral of a guard who goes down with a scream.

"Dummies," I chastise them. Spinning, I slam my knife into his neck and pull it out. Blood spurts across my face as I laugh crazily. Some are starting to retreat, and I follow them with my bloody knife held out.

"Here, here, scaredy cat," I call as they back away. "Do you want to know why the doc says you can kill me?"

When no one answers, I cock my head. "They called me damaged. Insane. I guess he wasn't wrong." Leaping onto the wall, I kick off it and come down on them. I slam my knife into one, turning my head and ripping my teeth into another. I use everything I have. When I turn back, there are only three left. One's hand is shaking as he aims a gun at me.

The other two are standing amongst the carnage in shock. Picking the one with the gun as my next target, I get to my feet. He shoots, and I duck under it. His hands are shaking so badly, he keeps missing as I walk calmly towards him, and once I reach him, I pull the pouch from my side, take the gun, and replace it with that.

"Can you hold this?" I ask him. He grabs the bag, his eyes wide as I race down the corridor and dive around the corner as it explodes. Laughing, I roll to my feet to meet the incoming guards.

The more the merrier.

There are ten of them in a pretty little row, all waiting to be killed.

"Duck, duck, goose," I call, pointing at one. "You're first."

I race towards them. They fire, but I manage to avoid being hit too badly, and I slide my knife in a figure eight fashion in the first man. He falls, and I turn to the next, slamming my knife into his thigh as I swivel on my knees and flip up and over him, ripping out the neck of another.

Ducking a punch, I turn and snap the neck of the next one.

I pull his baton and slam it across another's head, beating him until he falls, then I pluck the knife from the still screaming guard's thigh and make quick work of the others until they are all either dead or dying.

Crouching, I rip the shirt off the first male and stab him in the chest with my knife. He jerks, and his eyes widen. Oops, still alive. Oh well. Carving into his skin, I break his ribs, carefully extract his heart, and add it to the bag before moving to the next. I work my way through the ten soldiers. The last one is pressed against the wall, covering a bleeding wound on his thigh with his hand. With a grin, I uncover the wound and watch the blood squirt as he dies. Once he is gone, I do the same to him, carving out his heart.

I don't know which ones hurt my girl, but they are all complicit, so they died and will now be given to her as a sacrifice for their treachery.

Getting to my feet, I frown down at my bleeding leg. It's bothersome more than anything, so I use some of the ripped shirts to bind the wound. It will heal quickly enough and doesn't stop me from walking back to the other bodies and taking their hearts. I leave all their chests ripped open, the precious white walls sprayed with blood.

An idea comes to mind, so I move over to one wall and, after dipping my fingers into the closest soldier's neck wound, I begin to carefully write out words, stepping back once I'm done to check it out.

Perfect.

I LOVE YOU, NOVA.

There's a gagging noise, and I turn to see a soldier. They rip off their helmet and throw up. It's a female, her long, sweaty hair stuck to her face. She glances at me and then at the bodies. Her face is pale but determined as she straightens, pulling her weapon.

The woman stops before me, gripping her baton. "Look, I'm not sexist, okay? So I'm going to kill you the exact same way," I warn her. "I'll leave your heart though. I don't want my girl getting worried about me cutting through your shirt."

Before she can even speak, I slice her throat and watch her fall. I hesitate because I want more hearts for my collection, but I don't want Nova to be jealous, so I step over her and head off in search of more.

And my girl.

THIRTY-FIVE

NICO

The plan went wrong. I don't know how, but I blame Jonas. I was heading to Nova's cell when the alarms blared and the explosion rocked the structure . . . two whole hours early. Fuck. It doesn't help that the guards were all on high alert, but I didn't know why. I just knew I had to get to her. I bided my time, dressing in the gear provided and then slipping away when they started to move to their posts.

Pressing my hand to the wall to steady myself, I wait for the explosions to stop before ripping open Nova's cell door—only to find it empty.

Fuck!

Where is she? She has to be okay, I know that, but where did they take her?

Spinning, I search the corridor. "Any location on Nova and Louis?" I demand.

"They were being taken to the gym," Dimitri tells me. "Jonas is, erm, busy, but we are coming in. Meet you there."

"Got it. I'm free to take action?" I ask carefully. I've wanted to start taking them out since the moment I was brought down here. The things I have seen and the things they have done to my Nova have been burning in my gut since that moment, but I held it back and stuck to the plan.

"Free to act," Isaac tells me.

Smirking, I yank off the hat and toss it aside, rolling my shoulders. I might have been one of the guards, but I'm now their worst nightmare.

As I make my way to the gym to find my girl and make sure she is okay, I run into a mass of guards. "We are to report back to the doctor for protection. We've been breached," one tells me, clapping me on the shoulder.

Gripping the hand that touches me, I meet his eyes. "Yes, yes you have," I inform him, watching his eyes blow wide just before I snap his wrist. He screams, and I quickly break his neck. The guards scatter, trying to pull guns but unsure whom to shoot as I duck into their writhing masses and decimate them from the inside out.

I don't bother wasting my time because dead is dead. The longer I take here, the longer I am away from Nova—something I never want to be again. Pulling my gun, I fire again and again until it clicks empty. Bodies lie all around me, so I pick up a dead man's gun and continue until there is no one left standing but me.

Selecting another gun, I scavenge more clips and add them to my pockets, adding blades and everything else I might need, even a radio. The doc will want reports regarding his guards' whereabouts, and I'll be ready to answer when the time is right.

He's weak and scared right now, knowing we are coming for him.

Let him. He's our last point of call.

He's the end of all of this.

Stepping over the bodies, I carefully move through the maze of tunnels and head to the gym. Once I'm there, I find nothing but more bodies. "The gym is empty. No sign of her?"

"One sec," Dimitri mutters. "Let me check the portable camera."

I eye the corridors, debating which one I would take if I were Nova. She will want to protect the kids and get to her father—left to the kids, right to his main lab.

Blowing out a breath, I choose life or death . . .

Would her need for revenge outweigh her need to save innocents?

No, I don't think it would. I turn to the left and move to the elevator just as it opens for Dimitri and Isaac.

"She's in the labs," Dimitri tells me. "Isaac is heading down to the kids.

I'll go with him while you find her and her father. Oh, and if you see Jonas, stop him."

"What's he doing?" I ask, eyeing our surroundings.

"Erm . . . you know what? It's better not to ask," Dimitri says with a smile in his voice. "Get our girl. Let's end this."

Nodding, I step back and turn away as the elevator shuts once more. I have to trust them to protect the kids. They are the best at it. I would probably just scare them, and no doubt Jonas would terrify them. Isaac is soft spoken, and both he and Dimitri look kind and can talk with them. Moving through the halls, I stop when I find a mass of bodies littering the ground. There's something weird about them, and when I look closer, I realise it's because their chests are pried open and their hearts are gone.

Oh, God.

Running around the corner, I see the words written in blood and my head falls back with a groan. Jonas!

A noise has me lifting my head, and I see two guards come around the corridor, sweeping the area with their guns. Sighing, I fire and hit both between the eyes, stepping over them to continue.

"Trust me, it's better me than him," I inform them. There are more bodies with their hearts missing, and I follow the trail, needing to find him before I find Nova. She would never forgive me if I didn't.

The body trail lightens, with only one or two dotted around as if they were caught at the wrong time. They were probably sweeping or securing labs when he found them. I find one strapped down, his face completely carved away with a scalpel, and another is pinned to the wall like a bug, both hearts taken once more. How many has he taken, and what is he going to do with them?

I dread to think about it, but when I round the next corner, I have my answer. Jonas is whistling away, coated head to toe in blood, as he carves out the heart of a man who lies on the ground.

"Jonas!" I snap, seeing the open backpack next to him filled with the organs. His head whips up, his snarl turning into a welcoming smile.

"Hey, bro. Come help me. This one is tricky."

"Not a chance. Come on, Nova and Louis are in the labs," I order.

"But the heart . . ." Jonas pouts. "It's for Nova."

"Uh-uh, I think you have enough, come on." I clap his shoulder carefully.

He climbs to his feet, kicking the body before closing his bag and hefting it up. "Okay, let's go. You okay?" he asks me, smiling widely.

"Sure, are you?" I query warily. It is hard to tell under all the blood.

"Peachy. Isn't this great? It's been so long since I got to use so many skills." He sighs wistfully. "The only thing that would make it better would be if Nova was at my side. Do you think she will be impressed? I tried to get as many as I could."

"I think . . . I think she will be very shocked."

I grab his arm when he starts to wander away and pull him down the corridor to the labs where I hear smashing, and then I see her.

My raging fury.

My goddess.

My girl.

Her face is contorted in anger as she stands on a counter, smashing the shit out of computers with a metal pipe in her hand. Louis is gathering something into a bag, leaving her to it.

"Isn't she beautiful?" Jonas sighs before he rushes over.

Shaking my head, I decide to join them. After all, if you can't beat them, join them.

ISAAC

Riding in the elevator with Dimitri, I bounce nervously on my toes, worried about how everyone is. Nova in particular. I will need to talk to everyone individually, assess them, and make sure they are all okay. This is a tough situation, and it's clearly taken its toll on Jonas, whose sanity is questionable at the best of times, but right now, I need to focus on the kids. It's what she wants, and if it helps her, then I'll do anything, not to mention my need to save the innocent kids.

"Anything?" I ask Dimitri. He's trying to locate her father and check on the kids.

"Nothing. The cameras have either been destroyed or covered. They probably know we have access. Looks like we are doing this the old-fashioned way." He drops the portal computer and pulls out his gun.

I grip my own tighter, adrenaline pumping through me. This is what we are used to—working missions together—but this one has a high price tag and is more important than any other.

We can't afford to make mistakes. We must adapt to the situation and overcome it.

The ride seems to take forever, but it must only be a minute or so, and when the doors open, bullets fly. We flatten ourselves against the sides, and the doors shut as Dimitri hits the emergency button, keeping us stationary.

"What the fuck?" I demand. "How many are out there?"

"I don't know." He tosses me a mask from his hip. "Put this on. The gas will clear the immediate vicinity so we can get out and regroup." Tugging his own mask down, he pulls a gas grenade from his bag and when I nod, he turns off the alarm and allows the doors to open.

Tossing the grenade out, he jerks back as bullets whiz by us.

Our only protection is the shuddering metal of the elevator, which is being embedded with more and more bullets as the gas pumps into the corridor, fogging my mask.

We wait, our breathing loud as the hiss of the gas reaches us. Gradually, the bullets start to slow. The sounds of coughing reach us, and then we hear thumps. I nod at Dimitri and we roll out together. Luckily, no one is shooting. Most are passing out, and although it won't keep them down long, it still gives us enough time to clear it. They made a barricade, and there are at least ten guards here, their guns tossed to the floor when the gas hit.

As a doctor, I vowed to do no harm. I wanted to save lives, but they don't deserve saving. Not after what they have done.

No, my oath went out the window the moment they turned their devilish eyes to my girl.

Gritting my teeth as my instincts batter me, I raise my gun and fire with Dimitri, killing them as they choke and wheeze.

"Clear," I tell him. The gas starts to dissipate, but I keep my mask on for now as we peer over the barricade. It's made of everything and anything they could find, and I don't spot anyone over it. Dimitri told me the doors are at the end of this level, so we climb over and keep moving, but the next corridor is no better. Doors are ripped off, ready to be used as barricades, and guards quickly turn towards us.

Bullets fly and I roll, ripping off my mask and seeing Dimitri doing the same a few feet back.

"We have Nova and Louis. Everything okay?" Nico asks, his voice barking in my ear.

"We have run into a little trouble," I admit, taking shelter behind an over-turned door as more bullets fly.

I wait for them to reload and pop my gun over, firing into their masses without looking. I hear someone scream, and I know I hit my mark. Climbing to my knees, I peer over only to duck. I glance back at Dimitri, who's reload-ing, then hold up my hand and close it.

Ten.

He nods and gets to his knees, counting down on his fingers, and at zero, we both stand and fire as we move, working as a unit. He takes left, and I take right. We watch the bodies fall. A bullet grazes my cheek and my ear, but I still don't stop. My heartbeat slows as time seems to still as we fire, until my gun clicks empty, and then I duck behind the next door with Dimitri next to me.

"Only three left," I tell him calmly as I reload, then I speak into the earpiece where I hear them talking. "Guards before the kids. We are taking care of them. Any luck on the doc?"

"Not yet." Louis grunts. "Keep us updated."

"Got it."

I love how he doesn't ask if we are okay. He knows better. If we needed help, we would call for it. His trust is what has me sitting taller.

Dimitri and I wait. We can hear their feet crunching over broken glass as they head our way. I reload as we bide our time. When they draw closer, we pop up and fire. Three fall just as quickly as they came, and we keep moving. There are no barricades down the next corridor, and it's unusually quiet, which isn't a good sign.

"D," I murmur.

"I know," he mutters as we open empty rooms, needing to check every single one on our way. All it would take is one guard to sneak up on us and we would be fucked. We can't have that. I need to live for my girl. It's time-consuming though, and when we reach the next corner, the hair on the back of my neck rises. I hold out my arm to stop D and cock my head.

He narrows his gaze, and I shake my head, unsure.

There's only one way to find out. Playing it smart, I crouch and peer around the corner, my eyes widening at what I find.

A fucking army.

Shit.

Sliding down the wall, I sigh as I talk quietly into the earpiece. "Guys, we've found the doc."

"Where?" they all ask, making me wince at the mix of voices.

"Here, behind a wall of guards. He's hiding with the kids. It's a last fucking stand. Get your asses down here." I rip out my earpiece and check my mag. I don't have enough.

We're fucked.

THIRTY-SIX

LOUIS

I let her smash anything she wants. It seems to be keeping her occupied. She wanted to find her father, but I wanted to secure the research first, knowing they could hide it or get rid of it at any time. It's just as important as he is. We cannot let this fall into the wrong hands. She understands that, even though she's frustrated, hence the smashing.

Whirling, I bring up my gun when I hear a noise, only to relax at the sight of Jonas and Nico standing in the doorway of the lab. "Dimitri and Isaac?" I ask.

"Heading down to the kids." Nico tosses me an earpiece. "Baby, are you okay?"

Panting, she presses the pipe she was using behind her shoulders, covered in blood. Her gaze goes to Jonas, and then her eyes widen. I follow her gaze, noting the blood. "Jonas, what happened?"

"Oh, it's not mine." He grins. "Hey, beautiful. I've missed you so fucking much."

"Me too." She leaps down, destruction forgotten, and Jonas catches her. He lays her back onto the desk and kisses her hard and fast, while Nico moves over to me.

"Here, help me. We are locking up the research just in case."

Nodding in understanding, he helps me gather the paperwork and copy the drives, piling everything in the lockbox I found.

Finally, Jonas and Nova come up for air, and I see him swing a bag around. Frowning, I watch in confusion as he hands it to Nova.

He sighs in bliss. "For you, beautiful."

She opens the bag and then just stares.

"What's in it?" I ask Nico. Knowing Jonas, it could be anything. Guns, bombs . . . whatever he feels like.

"You don't want to know," Nico mutters.

I move closer and peer inside, and my mouth drops open. "Are those . . ."

"Hearts." Jonas grins at her. "Of every single guard I killed. I made them pay for everything they did to you."

"Jonas," I sputter.

"Told you," Nico says, laughing behind me.

"Jonas," Nova whispers, and I wince. "That's so romantic. Thank you, baby. I love you!" She throws her arms around him and yanks him down, peppering his bloody face with kisses as he grins at us.

"Fucking hell, maybe we are the crazy ones and he has it all figured out," Nico mutters.

Shaking my head, I move back over to help him, wondering how the hell I can beat a bag full of hearts to impress my girl, and it's clear Nico is thinking the same thing.

Moaning, Jonas climbs up on top of the desk and pins her down, grinding into her as he swallows her moans.

"Should we do something?" Nico asks, jerking his head at the pair.

"No, it's stopping them from doing something bad." I grin, adding more to the box and then locking it up before moving to the next.

I check in with Isaac as they kiss, and when he tells me he's okay, I keep sorting the research with Nico. When we are done, we both just stare at Jonas and Nova who are practically fucking.

Nico looks at me. "Break it up."

"No, you." I snort and share a grin with him just as my earpiece crackles.

"Guys, we've found the doc."

"Where?" we all ask, and it even breaks Jonas and Nova apart.

"Here, behind a wall of guards. He's hiding with the kids. It's a last fucking stand. Get your asses down here." Then there's silence, but I heard the panic in his voice.

They are in the line of fire.

"Time to go, kids," I order, reloading and grabbing my weapons before heading towards the door, trusting my family to follow.

It is time to end this.

DIMITRI

"They are on their way," I whisper to Isaac. "We should wait. We are good, but not good enough to take down all of them, especially without hurting the kids or ourselves."

Isaac nods just as a shot rings out. "We know you're there. Step out or we'll start shooting the kids one by one. Do you really want their blood on your hands?"

I share a look with Isaac and stand. Swearing, he stands too. With another shared look, we step out, unwilling to risk the kids. All weapons are trained on us, but they don't instantly shoot, which is their first mistake.

"Drop the weapons!" one yells.

I'm not sure why they haven't killed us on sight. Maybe he wants us alive or plans on using us to flush the others out, but it's working in our favour. They have a gun pressed against the head of a small girl in a blue outfit in the back. She's crying but she's brave, standing tall.

"Okay, stay calm. It's going to be okay." I soften my voice for her. She nods but winces when the gun digs in deeper.

"Now!" one roars as I scan them, counting and looking at entrances and exits, noting everything.

I share a look with Isaac.

"Stop looking at him and drop them now."

With my eyes on the girl once more, I release my gun from my hand.

I hear running footsteps and know the others are coming. They are close. Time slows as I grin at the guards, who are relaxing, thinking they have us.

Diving, I catch the falling gun, and before I even hit the floor, I come up shooting, hitting the two holding the kid, who runs, and then hitting three more before grabbing Isaac and diving back around the corner.

"Shit, that was epic." Isaac grins just as Nico, Louis, Jonas, and Nova skid to a stop before us, all panting.

Standing, I grab Nova and kiss her hard.

"Later," she murmurs, and I nod.

"Later," I promise as I look at Louis.

"Report," he demands. I move over so Isaac can have a moment with Nova.

"At least forty soldiers, now thirty-five. They are holding the kids hostage and know we are here. Two barriers to the left and the right. They have tactical rifles, helmets, and vests. I can't see her father, but for them all to have been called back here, I'm betting he's hiding with the kids, looking for a way out. He's not expecting us to risk the kids' safety."

"He's right though. We can't," Nova says, holding Isaac's hand. Jonas is in the corner with Nico just in case they move around or attack us while we talk.

Louis lowers his voice so they can't hear him. "I have a plan. It's crazy, but it just might work."

"Everything we do is crazy." I grin.

"True." He smirks. "So let's show them that."

THIRTY-SEVEN

NOVA

Dimitri nods at me, and I step closer, kissing him soundly. "Be ready."

"Always. I've got you," he tells me.

"I'm coming out!" I call. "It's Nova, Dr. Davis's daughter. Don't shoot."

I wait and hear murmuring. "Step out unarmed or we will."

"Coming!" I look back and grin, blowing them a kiss.

Trusting my guys, I step out with my hands up, no weapons on display. I stop halfway down the corridor, far enough away not to die but also close enough to do what I need to.

"See? Not armed. Where is my father?" I demand.

"We will search you," someone else yells. "The others with you will reveal themselves, also unarmed, or we will shoot you."

"That's rude." I frown, stepping closer. "Where is my father?"

"Step out!" he orders, ignoring me.

"Is he with the kids? Are they okay?"

"For now." He smirks. "If your friends want you and the kids alive, do as I order."

"Here's the thing." I grin. "They really don't like following orders unless they are mine and in the bedroom." Winking, I close my fist and drop.

Bullets whiz over me as the lights cut out, thanks to Dimitri. There's a

229

crash and I peer up through the door, seeing Louis and Jonas drop from the vents in the ceiling and onto the waiting mass. It turns the guards' focus inwards. I leap to my feet as Nico and Dimitri race past me, and then we leap into the fray.

Grabbing the gun taped to my back, I spray bullets at those closest to me before putting the gun away and using the knife I stole from Jonas. Screams ring out as the guns go off. I duck under a punch and keep moving until there is no one else but the darkness I'm fighting against.

Twenty men against five. They didn't even stand a chance. We are super soldiers for a reason, and the crazy plan worked. After all, they couldn't even imagine we would use one of our own as a distraction.

Morons.

The lights come back on. We are all panting as we stand in the mess of dead soldiers and guards. Smirking, I step over them and bang a bloodied hand on the window that looks into the glass of the children's room.

"Come out, Father. Your guards are dead. There is no one else to hide behind."

"That's where you're wrong." He steps out, holding a knife to a little boy's throat.

Snarling, I hit the button to open the door and descend the stairs, stopping before him, my men spreading out.

"Ah, that's close enough, Novaleen," he snaps, tightening his hold on the child.

Grinding my teeth, I scan the room, seeing the others hiding.

"Isaac." I nod and without a word, he and Dimitri head off to protect the kids. Jonas moves left, and Nico goes right, trying to circle my father, while Louis stands with me, side by side. My father cannot take us all, and his eyes flicker around as he realises that.

He wanted a super soldier unit, and he got one.

Shame it will be his death.

"Impressive unit," he remarks. "I guess I was wrong about them being failures. Maybe I was too harsh. We can sit down and talk about this—"

"Let the kid go." I ignore his silver tongue. His words mean nothing.

"No. You want me dead, Novaleen? Fine, but this kid will die with me, and you will have to live with more innocent blood on your hands. Just like Ana's."

"Do not!" I snarl. "You killed her! You are the one with blood on your hands," I yell. Anger flares inside me, along with guilt.

"No, Novaleen. I might have pulled the trigger, but you put her in the crosshairs. She was there for you. She trusted you to protect her. How foolish was that? You couldn't save her. All that training, all that money and time, and you couldn't even save the one person you wanted to. Maybe you were never what I needed. Never mind, I can start again."

"Shut up," I hiss.

"Don't listen to him, Nova," Louis mutters. "He's trying to make you react irrationally so he can get free."

I know he is, but it's working. Any mention of Ana and I become an unthinking, open, raw wound, and he knows it. He knows she is my weakness, alongside the kids.

"Let me go. Let me walk out of here, and I'll release the child," he offers, invading my conflicting mind. "Your choice, Nova. You can kill me now, but you'll be killing this innocent child, or you can let me go and save him."

"Nova," Louis snaps as I met the child's eyes.

All this time, blood, and pain got me here, but can I live with the stain on my soul if I do this?

It's a choice between life and death.

Between right and wrong.

Revenge and letting go.

I know what Ana would want me to do, and in the end, that's what I go with. I can live with him going free. I found him once, so I can do it again despite how angry I'll be. I cannot live with this child's innocent blood on my hands. I just can't.

I turn away from revenge and choose life instead.

I drop my gun to the floor, and he grins triumphantly. "Good, now I'm going to walk past you. Once up top, I will release the child and leave. Do not follow me."

He moves closer, and I turn with him as he starts to walk to the door, but when he's almost level with me, the kid drops to the floor and manages to slip his grip.

His only leverage is gone.

He quickly realises that and looks at me as I reach for another weapon to end this. Something settles in his eyes, and he rushes towards me.

Maybe he realises he's never getting out of this, or maybe he genuinely thinks killing me will distract them long enough for him to escape, but I see the knife rise, and then he drives it into my stomach, ramming it home. I let him, but I grab his hand as he tries to run, holding him to me as I snarl in his face. Using his hand, I yank the knife out, gritting my teeth at the agony.

His eyes flare as I pull the blade free and turn it. His hand resists and he struggles, but he's no match for me. I slowly drive it towards his own stomach, aiming for the kill shot.

He struggles in my grip. He's so weak.

"Nova, wait, Nova," he says, but I ignore his pleading as, inch by inch, I drive the knife closer until it starts to pierce his skin. His voice turns into a wail, and I slam it all the way home and let go. He stumbles back, covering the wound with his hands.

Even if at one time, he seemed like a god to me, now he is nothing but a weak, bleeding mess at my feet.

Isaac rushes over, putting pressure on my wound as I stare at my father. He peers down at the blade and then back to me in shock before falling to his knees. Despite knowing better, he pulls it free and drops it with clumsy, shaking hands before he falls back. Ignoring Isaac, I move to my father's side and kneel. My own blood mixes with his in a puddle beneath him.

Matching wounds.

Killing blows.

The only thing that saves me is my own healing ability and adrenaline as Isaac starts to inject me with something as I watch my father. His eyes blink rapidly, and his mouth opens and shuts as he covers the wound.

His hand lifts, reaching out, and I grip it. He thought he was unstoppable, but he was wrong.

"You thought you were unstoppable, but look at you now. You are weak and mortal. You are dying."

"Novaleen, please," he begs, coughing.

"You are just a weak old man surrounded by enemies. I'll leave your body here in the rubble to be burned and forgotten. No one will ever know what you did. I will make sure of it. All your research will be destroyed, and everything you did, everything you sacrificed, will be for nothing. Your life will be for nothing."

"Not nothing," he says. "You are alive."

"And I will never be anything but a normal person after this. Your research will die with us."

"No." He shakes his head.

Whatever Isaac injected me with is working. I feel nothing, and he's packing the wound and bandaging it as I squeeze my dad's hand to the point of pain to keep his eyes on me as he dies. I need to see it.

Leaning in, I press a kiss to his forehead.

"This is for Ana, Sam, Bas, and for every single person you have hurt and killed. They will be avenged here, and you? You will be nothing but a liar for all your bold claims and half-truths. Was it worth it? Was all the death and pain worth it, old man?"

He squeaks, losing too much blood.

"Was it?" I scream.

"Yes," he says. "You're alive and so is my research. It was worth it. I would do it all again."

Dropping his hand in anger, I sit back and watch as he dies scared, alone, and in agony. It isn't quick, and when his lungs rattle, I smile. When he takes his last breath, I almost laugh.

It's over.

It's done.

I check his pulse to be sure. "There's no coming back for you this time, Dr. Davis. It is over. It is done." Standing carefully, I lean into Isaac as weakness spreads through me. They are all watching me worriedly, the kids sheltered behind them.

"Let's go home," I demand. "Take me home, let me die, and then place me at her side."

I fall, my own wound getting the better of me.

It's too deep, and I lost too much blood.

The sacrifice was worth it, though, I think as my eyes close.

I am ready to be reunited with my sister.

THIRTY-EIGHT

LOUIS

The base has everything we need, so we move fast.

We will not lose her.

Not again.

Isaac barks out orders as Nico lifts her and rushes up the stairs to the lab. Isaac runs with him, holding pressure on the wound. "Stay with the kids."

"But—" Dimitri steps forward, looking heartbroken.

"Do it!" I order him and Jonas. I run after Nico, sliding into the elevator at the last moment. I don't have time to think about anything else. We reach the lab in under a minute and lay her down.

"Tell us what you need," I beg Isaac, swallowing my panic, knowing they are looking at me right now. I cannot afford to fall apart.

"Scrub up. I'm going to need to go in and cauterise what was hit, then we'll need blood. Luckily, she's the same type as Nico. Next, we'll seal and dress the wound." He starts putting an IV up and sliding it in as we quickly scrub up and gown, then he does the same. I take her hand as Isaac unpacks the wound.

"Nico, take your own blood. Louis, I'll need your help."

Nodding, I drop her hand and focus on the wicked wound he's unveiling. It is about five inches long, but it must be deep. He swiftly spreads it with a tool, and blood pours out.

"Wipe it," he demands. "I need to see."

I mop it up with the gauze on the table before he dives back in with some other tools, his eyes hard and determined.

"Don't you dare fucking die on me, my love," he grits out. "Don't you fucking dare. I'll bring you back."

"Isaac—"

"Don't, I can save her. I can save her."

"Tell us what you need," Dimitri demands, and I glare at him, looking over to see him in the doorway.

"The kids—"

"Are safe for now. What do you need, Isaac?"

"Help Nico," Isaac says, focused on his work.

Jonas hesitates in the doorway, tears dripping down his face.

"Is she going to die?" It's a heartbroken plea from the child inside him.

"Not today." I practically spit the words, speaking them into existence. "Talk to her, hold her."

Nodding, he hurries over and crouches at her head. He pushes her hair back, his voice low and soothing as he talks to her.

"Isaac?" I question. His eyes are narrowed on the wound I'm mopping up, his teeth gritted. His full concentration is on her, but I need to know.

"He nicked an artery somewhere. I need to find it," he mutters.

I quiet down then, looking at Nova whose face is pale, her lips growing blue.

She's dying. I know it.

"Isaac," I demand in panic.

"One fucking second," he barks. "Come on, baby. Where are you? Just show me." He digs into the wound and Nova screams, the sound echoing around us. Her eyes snap open for a second. I hold her down with Jonas as she struggles, her gaze completely unseeing until her eyes slide shut and she collapses.

Isaac doesn't even hesitate. He dives in harder, searching for the artery. "Isaac, we are losing her," I snap, needing something to do. "What do we do?"

"Give me a fucking second!" he roars before shouting, "I got it." He quickly clamps the artery before fixing it as I mop around the wound. He carefully pulls the tools out and drops the blood-covered metal onto the table. When he glances at Nova, his face pales at how still and weak she is.

She is close to death.

"Louis, attach the monitoring machines please. I need her blood pressure and heart rate, now. Nico, give me the line." He hurries around, quickly adding a line into her arm and directly pushing Nico's blood to her since she has lost so much. It drips down from her stomach and onto the floor as I attach the machines, the telltale beeping filling the air.

"Her heart is giving up," he whispers as he rushes to the wound, grabbing a staple gun. Pinching her skin, he starts to put her back together. "I'll need to recheck this, but for now, we need to close her and pump her with drugs and blood to keep her alive."

Every eye is on her, on her pale, sweaty face, until the machine suddenly begins to blare. Isaac's head jerks up, and he eyes her erratic heartbeat that suddenly stops.

Snarling, he rushes to her side and starts to perform CPR as I watch, feeling useless, my hand gripping hers.

"Don't you fucking dare," Isaac snaps as he gets in her face, even though her eyes are closed. "Don't you dare fucking leave me, do you hear me, Nova?" His voice is cruel, hard, and loud, unlike our soft-spoken Isaac, but I can't even protest around the lump in my throat. For all my plans and my strength, I cannot save her this time. "If you try to leave me, I'll bring you back from the fucking dead myself, so you hold the fuck on and help me save you, understood?" He rams his hands into her chest, his eyes going from her to the monitor.

"Come on, baby," I mutter. "You can do it."

"Don't you fucking dare," he says as he pushes on her chest. "Not today, not ever. You do not get to die."

Tears spill from my eyes as the machine continues to flat line. "Isaac—"

"No! She can't do this!" he roars, his eyes wild as he looks at me. "Mouth to mouth, now!"

I rush to do as he says, working in sync with him. He never stops working on her chest, and finally, a beep fills the air. We all turn, scared it isn't real, until it comes again.

Her heart is beating.

I must say it out loud because the room fills with joyous, relieved sighs.

"Nico will need orange juice," Isaac mutters as he double-checks the monitor and her pulse before cleaning the wound on her stomach. He applies something to it and then bandages it before covering her up. He's coated in blood as he rips the gloves off, tossing them into the bin. "I need a minute. Get me if anything changes," he mutters, and then he's gone, but I saw the look in his eyes.

I can't leave my girl though.

Not yet. My eyes go to Dimitri, who is hesitating near Nico, and he nods before going after Isaac as we work as a team to stay strong for her. Taking her hand once more, I lean down and brush a kiss over her forehead. "It's going to be okay, baby. We've got you. Just stay with us, okay? Please . . . Please don't give up on us. I promise we will never give up on you. We need you, Nova. Stay. Please, just fight one last time. That's it, Nova, one last fight. I promise."

DIMITRI

Rushing after Isaac, I find him around the corner, sinking to his knees, his blood-soaked face in his hands as he sobs. Turning away for a moment, I move to the closest room, grab what looks to be a bedpan and some cloths, and fill it with warm water before I return to find him in the same position. Dropping to my knees before him, I wet the cloths, and when he lifts his head, I smile sadly at him.

My heart aches. I want to be with Nova, to watch every single breath she takes, but my family needs me. She needs them. I need them.

When one of us falters, we have to be there for them. It's how we survive.

"Are you okay?" I ask. It's something I've heard her ask him a million times. Usually, he smiles that soft smile just for her, but this time, his eyes close for a millisecond and when they open, they blaze with agony. His lips tremble as tears carve a path through the blood on his face.

"No, no, I'm not." His voice is barely above a whisper.

"Me either," I admit as I start to wipe his face clean. "I've got you, brother. Let me take care of you for once."

"She . . ." His eyes close again as I meticulously wash his face. "She could die."

"She won't," I lie. I don't know if she will or not. I'm just praying with blind hope to a god I don't believe in.

He catches my hand, his eyes hardening. "She could, Dimitri. The wound . . . If she doesn't want to come back—"

"Shh." Twisting my wrist, I release it from his grip and continue to clean his face. When it's done, I sit back, dropping the cloth on the floor and taking his hand. "We have to be strong right now, okay? We are not losing anyone else." My voice hardens. "We can't. So, no matter how much it hurts right now, no matter how angry, sad, and worried we are, we keep it together for her. We give her a reason to fight. We keep our girl alive. We give everything for her like she did for us, okay? This isn't how our story ends. It can't be."

"What if it is?" he whispers dejectedly. I've never seen him like this before. Usually, he's the one who's comforting others and full of hope.

"Then we end it together just like it should be. No matter what, Isaac, we do everything we can. She deserves nothing less." Standing, I take his hand. "Come on, let's check on her."

I escort him back, and we all carefully watch as he checks her over. He hangs up the bags of Nico's blood. Isaac checks on Nico and covers him with a blanket as he grumbles before Louis orders Isaac to go shower. We can all see the toll this is having on Isaac, and I truly think this might scar him for life.

Nico and Jonas stay with her as I check on the kids and grab some food. They are all either asleep or in bed in the spare rooms we found. Despite what they saw, they don't seem overly upset. They are scared, that's for sure, but they are alive, and that's enough for now. We can deal with everyone else once we know Nova is stable.

I leave the food for Isaac and Louis, and then I head back to check on Nova.

I hesitate at the doorway. Nico is asleep next to her, or at least his eyes are closed, and Isaac is showering and eating under Louis's watchful gaze.

Jonas is holding Nova's hand and talking quietly. I should give them privacy, but I find myself leaning closer to hear.

"I know you're hurting, baby, not just your body, but your heart. I know you miss your sister, but please don't do this to us, okay? I can't live without you. I can't. If you die, I die. It's that simple. There is no place in this world for Jonas without Nova, so even though it hurts, even though it would be easier to give in, come back to us because without you, there is no us. Not anymore. Please, baby, don't break our hearts. They've been yours since the moment we met you. Where you go, we go, so if this is the end, if you go, so do we. You hear me?"

"J—" Moving closer, I lay a hand on his shoulder as he wipes at his face, dashing away the tears. "She'll be okay. I know it. She's strong."

I don't. It's a fucking lie. I'm terrified down to my very soul that she won't make it through . . . that she doesn't want to, just like Bas. I can't lose someone else I love. Like Jonas, I would simply lock us all down here and end us all so we could be with her again.

He's right—where she goes, we go.

Nova's heart skips a beat like she hears us and agrees, or at least I like to think so.

Sinking to the ground next to her, we sit and wait, watching our love and hoping we can save her this time.

This time, we won't lose the only person we love.

THIRTY-NINE

ISAAC

I t's been twenty-four hours since Nova last opened her eyes. I panic continually, thinking that I did something wrong, that I didn't do enough, that I missed something else. Louis informs me she probably just needs rest and time to heal. He's probably right, but it doesn't stop me from checking on her every thirty minutes. Nico is resting once more after giving more blood so we could do another transfusion since she lost so much. Louis and Jonas gently washed and dressed her while I put up more IVs. We've done everything we can, and it's up to her now. I know that, but it doesn't stop me from worrying.

Louis is staying busy, and between him and Dimitri, they have gotten all of the kids' information, as well as feeding them and checking them over, since I refused to leave Nova. Dimitri has started to look into their pasts. They probably won't have family, just like us, but I think it gives him something to do. They seem happy enough to be left to play in their new rooms, and as soon as we can move Nova, we can figure something out for them.

For now, we are here, watching our girl in the place where she nearly died.

Her father's body rots a few floors down. He doesn't get to be buried, after all. When we leave together, which we will, we plan on blowing this place sky-high, incinerating his body and every horrible thing he did here. Fuck, I'll even toast marshmallows in the fire with my girl.

Sighing, I tighten my hold on her hand, stopping myself from checking her vitals once more or uncovering the wound. She needs time, but it doesn't stop my constant need to assure myself that she is okay. Never before have I been more thankful to be a doctor, but I also know everything that could go wrong.

It so very nearly did. I almost lost her during surgery.

I will never forget that.

Not ever.

I must fall asleep because something makes my head snap up—a noise. I blink into the shadowed room, noticing a lamp is on in the corner that someone must have switched on. Nico is still snoring away, his blanket kicked off. Sighing, I close my eyes once more when the hand I'm holding twitches.

My gaze goes to Nova to see her blinking her eyes open and turning her head. Leaping to my feet, I grab a glass of water with a straw. "Shh, drink this," I whisper, holding both to her mouth. She sips it before turning away, and I put it back before checking her eyes and pulse.

"Is—" She winces in pain.

"It's okay, baby, just hold on," I murmur, my heart racing so fast it's hard to hear. "Vitals are good, no concussion or reaction in the eyes. I think you're going to be okay."

I almost slump at that. She's going to be okay.

"Am I dead?" she whispers.

"No, you are very much alive, sweetheart," I murmur, kissing the back of her hand and almost collapsing with relief. "You'll need to rest and take time to heal, but I think you'll be okay."

My eyes lock on hers once more, greedy for every word, touch, and look, which is why I don't wake Nico or shout for the others. I don't want to end this moment since I came so close to losing her.

"Are you okay, Isaac?" she croaks. Her eyes search mine worriedly, even though she is in a hospital bed in a bunker where she was tortured and kept alive to be experimented on.

This girl.

"Am I okay? Am I okay? You almost died on my fucking table, Nova, so no, I'm not okay. I almost lost the woman I love more than anything else in this fucking world. I almost . . . I almost couldn't save you and that killed me!" I laugh bitterly as Nico jerks awake.

"What, what?" He falls to the floor in confusion, searching for a threat before his eyes land on Nova. "Baby!" He rushes over and kisses her. She kisses him back, smiling as he hurries to the door to tell the others, but he turns back to focus on me.

"I'm sorry," she whispers, tightening her grip on my hand.

"Don't." I shake my head, trying to suck back all my emotions. I need to be okay, for her and for them.

"I'm so sorry you had to deal with that, Isaac," she whispers as I hear pounding feet. "I love you so much."

"I love you too," I promise. "Don't ever do that to me again," I order as I lean in to kiss her softly.

"Never," she vows just as the others slide into the room and surround her. There are so many voices, touches, and kisses that I end up pushing them back.

"Give her space. She needs to rest and relax, not be moved or jostled," I snap.

"Yes, doctor," Jonas teases, even as he grins brightly at her. "You missed so much." He hurries to tell her everything, and she smiles, but it turns into a wince, and he slows to a stop. "Are you okay?"

"Just tired and hurting," she admits. For Nova to admit that she's in pain, it must be bad.

"Let me give you something." I hurry to inject her, and she relaxes, smiling at us.

"I still can't believe you came for me."

"Of course we did," Louis murmurs. "We love you. There is nothing we wouldn't do for you, Nova."

"Now rest," Dimitri orders.

"It's over, baby. He's dead, and you're alive. Just rest. There's nothing else to do," Nico says, and under our watchful gazes, her eyes start to slide shut.

"Are you all just going to watch me sleep?" she mutters, making surprised laughter tumble from us.

"Yes," Jonas answers without a care.

"I was debating it," I mutter.

Huffing, she narrows her eyes once more. "Louis, get them to rest. They look exhausted, and that includes you. Oh, and fucking eat and shower, you stink." With that, she shuts her eyes once more, leaving me grinning like a madman.

Our girl is going to be just fine.

It looks like we finally get the ending we deserve.

FORTY

NOVA

I sleep for a while. I know because when I wake up, the big lights are on and the guys are milling around. Luckily, they look better. They've clearly showered and slept a little, even if Isaac is checking my wound when I wake.

"How's it look, doc?" I croak, my throat sore from sleeping and screaming.

He smiles softly as he covers it and moves to my side. "Good," he murmurs. "It's healing fast, though that shouldn't surprise me. I'd still like you to rest for a few days. I don't want to irritate the healing process or the staples, and your body has been through a lot of trauma, but you'll be okay."

I can see the question in his eyes. My body will heal, but will my soul and heart mend? I don't have the answer, so I look away, meeting Louis's eyes as he leans against the doorway, wearing a soft smile directed at me.

"Can I sit up?" I ask.

Isaac frowns but moves my pillows and helps me sit. It tugs on the wound, and I bite back a moan of pain. I'm used to it by now, after all, and I don't want them to worry. The quicker we can get the hell away from here, the better. Leaning back into the pillows, I eye them warily.

"The kids?" I ask. The last thing I remember is seeing them before my father attacked. "The one my father held?"

"All okay. They are a little shaken up, confused, and scared, but they will be fine. I don't know what was done to them yet, but I will find out. I promise," Louis murmurs. "Everyone else is fine, just focus on you."

"Where are they—"

"Nova," Louis and Isaac admonish.

Rolling my eyes, I relax as much as I can, but every look around at the white, sterile room makes me antsy. "Are we sure they are all dead, including my father?" I question, needing to know, needing to be sure.

"I checked and double-checked them all myself." Louis pushes from the door and takes my hand. "He's dead, Nova, for good this time. You're free; we all are. It's done. Our mission is over. We stopped him."

"It doesn't feel real," I admit.

"It will take some time. A lot has happened over the last few days," he says, kissing the back of my hand. "Just take a little bit of time to relax and let your mind and body heal, okay?" I groan, and he chuckles. "I know it's hard, but it's for the best."

"I hate bed rest unless it's for fun stuff," I mutter as Isaac grins at me, checking my vitals once more. I need to have a talk with him about those shadows in his eyes, but not with anyone else here. "The others?"

"Dimitri is wiping everything and copying all the files, Jonas is on patrol up top, and Nico is with the kids." My eyebrows rise at that, making Louis smirk. "Surprisingly, they seem to like him. He hates it, or so he says."

"Sure he does." I smile, closing my eyes. I am exhausted, but I know I can never fully relax while we are here. It doesn't feel like it's over while this place still stands. It's a reminder of what my father was capable of and can still do while his research exists. He might be dead, but his findings are not, which is something we need to discuss, but from the glint in Louis's eyes, I can tell he won't let me—not now when they are determined for me to relax and rest.

Isaac leans down and kisses me softly. "The more you rest, the quicker we can get out of here."

Grumbling to myself, I close my eyes once more, even though I hate leaving them to deal with everything. I expect to struggle to sleep, but before I know it, blackness claims me.

I jerk awake with a scream, the nightmare trapped on a loop in my brain until I fight against the hands on me, only to realise it's the bedding. Lights blare on, blinding me for a moment before I blink it away and realise I'm in bed, hooked to machines after killing my father.

I am not trapped by them as they cut me open.

My guys rush into the room, their weapons held up, and they only relax when I wave them away. Ignoring their protests, I sit up and suck in some air as hands rub my back.

"Are you okay?" Nico asks.

"Just a bad dream," I tell him, feeling embarrassed. "Sorry."

"Don't ever be sorry for that," he reassures me softly, wrapping me in his arms.

I fight it at first, not wanting to give in to the comfort and warmth, knowing I will break, but he's so hard to resist, and I slump into his hold. Tears form in my eyes. It feels like I've cried enough for a lifetime, but I can't stop them from coming.

"Annie and you guys were there, and I couldn't save you," I admit in a whisper, more tears flowing down. "She's dead."

"I know," he murmurs, kissing my head. "I know, baby. Let it all out."

"She's dead, and I'm alive. She's fucking dead." I smack my fists into his chest and he lets me. "She's dead. I lost her. I couldn't stop them. I couldn't do anything." I don't even know what I'm saying other than it all pours out. My nightmare brought on everything that has happened, and it spills from me like a tidal wave of pain. He holds me the entire time, stroking my hair. Their warmth, their comfort surrounds me, protecting me as I break, wishing they could take it away.

"I'm so sorry, babe," Nico whispers, his voice thick with pain. "We should have known. We should have protected you and Ana better. We are so very fucking sorry."

"It isn't your fault. It's his, and he's gone. We can't change it, but it hurts," I admit. "It hurts so fucking much that I feel like I'm dying sometimes." I lift my head to see his eyes filled with tears. "Will it ever stop? Will I ever stop feeling like my chest is in a vice and I can't get a breath without choking? Will it ever feel like I can live again?"

"No, but it gets easier."

I turn my head to meet Dimitri's sad eyes.

"Each day, it grows a little easier to breathe. There will still be moments where you remember them and it breaks you apart . . . Something little can catch you off-guard. But each day, it gets easier to get up, easier to move and carry on. You never truly forget them, not really. It's always there, waiting for you to remember, and sometimes you just . . . lose track of that for a time. It could be days, weeks, or even months, but then it's there again. The pain never goes away with time; it just gets easier to manage. Eventually, you'll forget all the bad stuff, and even though it hurts, you'll remember the good. You'll remember the happy times and smile and tell us about them to keep her alive within us. It doesn't mean you stop loving her by going on, Nova. It simply means you love her enough to keep moving despite losing her. That's how you keep her alive with us, and that's how you survive this. One foot in front of the other, one breath, one second at a time. Eventually, those seconds add up to minutes, hours, days, weeks, months, and finally years, until you've lived longer without them than you did with them. It still fucking hurts, but you're not alone. I wish I could change the past and save her, but I can't. I'm here though. *We* are here. You won't go through this alone. Even in the darkness, we will hold your hands, and I know Ana would want you to be happy. She loved you so much, Nova. You are her big sister, you will always be her big sister, and when the time comes, you will see each other again. Until that day, it's okay to struggle and forget what she smelled like. It's okay to let go, Nova. We will be right here to catch you."

Tears stream down my face as I take his hand, his own pain matching mine. It's the pain that only someone who has lost somebody they love so deeply can understand.

"You loved her, and she loved you, Nova, and that's all that matters," he whispers as he squeezes my hand. "I promise that we will love you until the very end. We will help you heal in every way we can, and one day, you'll tell me everything about her and I'll tell you all about Bas. Deal?"

"Deal," I croak as they shuffle closer, offering me their comfort as I cry for the sister I lost and the future she could have had and the torture I have experienced since childhood. I finally get it all out, enveloped by my men, my family.

My lovers hold me together as I break apart, giving me their strength when I am weak.

FORTY-ONE

NOVA

I let them look after me. I could say it's just to ease their nerves and stop them from worrying, but honestly, it's kind of nice. I've been through so much recently, so not having to worry about taking care of myself is . . . enjoyable. I love them for it even more. I still cannot believe they came for me. They could have left me and said fuck the mission. They could have even still carried on the mission, since I was never the priority, but they made me their priority because they love me. I see it in every touch, every look, and every action. I never thought about our future past this place and what it would mean.

I love them, I know that, but love hurts.

Love has the ability to destroy you. Look at Ana. But every time I think about pulling away to stop myself from being hurt in the future, they pull me back in. They won't allow us to end our relationship. They call us family. Didn't I call us that once as well? Can I have that again? I hope so. I hope I'm not too fucked up in the head to ruin this because this thing we have is good.

It's great.

It's not perfect, but it's a reason to live.

I loved them enough to sacrifice myself, but can I love them enough to keep living?

I guess only time will tell. There are some moments when I'm fine, driving towards the future and smiling with them as they flutter around me like nurses. Other times, the pain of everything I've lost and endured becomes too much and I drown in it, blinded to those helping hands reaching out to hold me.

They tell me time will help.

One breath, one second turns into minutes. Dimitri's words come back to me, and I force air into my lungs. I repeat it until I can see once more and I understand what he meant. Seconds can turn into minutes if you simply remember to breathe and let the pain wash through you rather than drown you under its waves. A mere second can change everything if we let it.

The darkness that plagues me won't be easily defeated. It will come back, and it will linger and wait for when I'm weak, but with them at my side, I hope it's enough that I will be strong enough to fight it.

I'm strong enough not to give in to its comforting lull, to not be selfish enough to take that leap that would destroy them the way my sister's death did me.

Death is easy, but living is fucking hard.

I have regrets, but when I look into their eyes, I wouldn't change anything I did because it brought me to them—these five, wonderful men who are so willing to travel across the world to find me and kill anyone who gets in their way.

I always thought being strong meant standing alone, just like my father thought, but I was wrong. Being strong means allowing others in, knowing they might hurt you. It's trusting them to stand at your back and catch you when you fall. We are stronger together than we ever could be alone.

We are just six fucked-up experiments with endless possibilities for a future.

It's kind of terrifying not knowing what we will be doing tomorrow.

For so long, surviving has been my mission, followed by stopping my father, but now the world is waiting for us.

"Hey, love," Louis murmurs, leaning against the door of the room they put me in. "You okay? Are you in any pain? I can get Isaac."

"Stop, I'm fine." I smile to soften my words. I know he's worried. His pinched features show his concern, as does the fact he checks on me every five minutes. If it wasn't so sweet, it would be annoying. "How's everyone?"

"We're fine, just worried about you," he admits, pushing away from the door and heading my way, cupping my cheeks with a sigh. Leaning into his warmth, I shut my eyes as I soak in his comforting, grounding touch. "The kids are leaving soon."

"What? Where to?" My eyes open as I struggle to my feet. With an annoyed frown, he stops me, preventing me from tearing open my wound.

"Somewhere safe for now until Dimitri can determine their backgrounds and what we should do to prevent this from ever happening again."

"We cannot leave them alone, Louis. They've been through enough," I argue.

For the first time since I woke up, his eyes flash like they used to. "We don't plan on it if you'd listen for one minute, brat." He huffs, a smirk playing on his lips. Desire flares through me, but I push it back because now is definitely not the time.

My eyes narrow on him, his narrow on me, and we just stare each other down until he grins.

"God, I missed that fucking look. I never thought I would see it again." His grin grows as I roll my eyes. "Dimitri hired a private plane with security. Bert is on the plane, and he will be escorting them to a safe house, ensuring they settle in. We have some of the best doctors available on staff to monitor them, and Dimitri has the place wired so we can watch them at all times."

"Oh." I relax at that. Of course they thought of everything.

"You really thought I would send them somewhere alone and scared?" he asks. It's a joke, but I see the pain in his eyes over the fact that I wouldn't trust him to sort this out.

Sighing to myself, I lean my head against his chest, listening to his steady, strong heartbeat and letting it ground me. "I didn't. You know that. I guess I'm just used to dealing with everything myself."

"One day you won't be. I cannot wait for that," he whispers, stroking the back of my head. "I promise they will be safe, Nova. I would die before I let anyone hurt them again."

"I know." I got so used to depending on myself down here, but Louis has proven himself over and over again. He's a capable leader, an excellent soldier, and a brilliant man. If he promises something, he will keep it. He's trying to help. It's just an old habit that I need to break so I can trust them to handle things without worrying about it. Fucking independence and stubbornness. "I'm sorry."

"You don't have to be, my love. I cannot begin to imagine what has happened to you since the last time I saw you." I start to stiffen, but he doesn't let me go. "We are here if and when you are ever ready to talk about it. If you never are, that's okay too. But know this, Nova." He tilts my head up to meet his gaze. "We are never going anywhere again. It's us and you, so get used to it, my love." He kisses me softly, making my eyes shut once more before he pulls away. "I'm going to check on them."

"May I come?" I murmur hopefully.

He frowns, and I know he's about to protest.

"You could carry me." It's a low move because I know he would give me anything I want, and honestly, Louis loves protecting me, so he scoops me into his arms, holding me tight.

"Brat," he mutters, but it is spoken in a loving way.

"You know it." I snuggle into his shoulder, wrapping my arms around him. How many nights did I wish I could have this again? I refuse to let my issues ruin this.

He walks confidently through the corridors, and I close my eyes. The pain is distant, thanks to the pain meds Isaac keeps pumping me with even though I say no, so I'm relaxed, and when we stop before the elevator, I see all the kids there, dressed in warm clothing, ready to go. They turn to us as we approach, and Nico steps from their masses. My mouth drops open with a laugh at the first sight of him.

He's covered in glitter and drawings, but it's the sheet tied to his waist like a tutu that causes me to laugh. The kids around him giggle, especially one little girl who hides behind him.

Not the least bit bothered to be caught like this, he winks at me. "I'll keep it on for later, baby."

Laughing harder, I slide down Louis's body and stay propped against his side. "You better." I grin as I look the kids over. They are all so young. I know they must have seen, heard, and experienced some horrible stuff, but looking into their hopeful, happy eyes, I'm reminded of why we did this. "I'm Nova," I introduce myself with a little wave.

"We know." The little girl peeks from behind Nico. "Nicky was telling us about you. He said he's going to marry you." She giggles harder.

"Is that right?" My eyes go to him, and Nico simply grins at me. "Do you think I should?"

"He's funny, plus he gave us piggyback rides and has juice boxes. I think you should," she replies.

"And what about me? Can she marry me?" Louis asks.

"I don't know," the girl hedges. "Do you have juice?"

"I have something better. I have chocolate," he whispers like it's a secret. She nods. "Then you can marry him too."

"Why, thank you for your permission." I'm unable to stop smiling, and my heart is light as I look around. "You'll all be okay. We promise. We'll take care of you now."

"We know," a little boy says, holding the hand of a girl at his side. "Thank you for saving us." He's clearly the oldest here, and although he's no older than ten, the way he looks at me as he speaks shows knowledge way beyond his age—one that is only put there by pain and horror.

"Okay, kids, the plane is here," Nico calls, clapping. "Remember what we talked about. Hold onto your friend until you're on board, and once there, what do we do?"

"Listen to Bert," they repeat in innocent voices with big, fluttering eyes. Something in my heart cracks, and I swallow my pain as I look at them, knowing this is as close to having kids as I will ever get, and although I'm happy, it hurts.

"Good, let's go!" The elevator opens, and they all file inside. Nico hangs back before darting over to me and kissing me soundly.

"I'll make sure they get on board safely. Bert is dying to see you, but he knows this is important to you. Go rest, baby." He steps into the elevator with the kids, bringing them up top and to safety.

"He's right. You need to rest," Louis murmurs, shouldering my weight.

"Not yet. Can we just walk around for a bit? I don't want to be trapped in that bed again. It reminds me too much of the beds my father tied me to." It's a low blow but true, and he jerks next to me.

"We will move you. What would be easier?"

"Louis, Louis, stop." He's about to go into leader mode. "It is fine. I know I need to rest, so it doesn't bother me too much, but I just want to be out of bed for a little while, okay?"

"Are you sure?" He frowns down at me as he lifts me into his arms once more. I could walk, but I don't protest, and he doesn't offer to let me.

"Yes." I press my lips to his neck, feeling him shiver. "Then I'll rest, and we can get the fuck out of here. The sooner I never have to see this place again, the better."

Louis falters but then turns. "I know a place." I let him take me without question, my eyes sliding shut as I soak in his love and warmth. I only open them again when he sets me down on a sofa in what looks to be a canteen. Jonas is stuffing food in his mouth, but he waves and grins at me before offering his plate to me. Grinning, I shake my head just as Dimitri comes in, holding a tablet in one hand.

"They are off. Nico is coming back down, then he and Jonas will wire the—" He jerks to a stop when he sees me. "You're out of bed. Are you—"

"She's gone! Where is she?" Isaac yells, frantically running into the room, his eyes wild until he sees me. "Oh, you're okay? You're okay," he says.

"I'm fine, I just wanted to see the kids off. I didn't walk, doc, so don't worry." I wink at him as he collapses next to me.

"Thank fuck," he mutters as I lean into his side, and he relaxes. Not too long after, Nico joins us as Dimitri looks between me and the tablet.

"You can carry on. I should know the plan," I grumble when they just keep staring.

"Sorry, babe." Dimitri winces. "Jonas and Nico are going to wire the whole facility. I checked everywhere and gathered all the data I could. The backups will be deleted and incinerated. No trace will be left behind."

"And we're sure there's no one else down here or up top?" I ask.

"We dealt with everyone up top after. They were preparing an assault team, which delayed them. Some had come down when ordered, so only a few remained," Louis explains. "We have searched every room down here for any others who might have hidden and found nothing."

"There was a doctor, the one we spared last time. He was here. He helped me," I tell them. "Is he okay?"

They share a look, and Louis sighs. "We found him. His neck was broken. It appeared to have happened hours before we even attacked. From what we saw, it looked like he was trying to gather his things to escape."

"Oh." I don't really know what else to say. He helped me, but that didn't make him a good guy, even if I know why he was doing it. There has been so much death here, it's hard to work through it all. He made his choice, though, and so did we. "When do we leave?"

"When Isaac says you're okay to travel." Louis narrows his eyes on me. "And I agree, no rushing this. We aren't letting you hurt yourself. A few more days won't change anything."

"It will for me. I want out of here," I mutter, but I know they won't budge, so I relax. "What can I do to help?"

"You've done everything, babe, just rest," Jonas says. "Or I can keep you occupied—"

"No sex," Isaac and Louis say at the same time.

"Spoilsports. I was going to suggest cuddling, or maybe I could carry her around while I wire up the place and she can watch my back." He becomes serious. "I know how badly I would hate doing nothing while being stuck in a place where I was held captive."

"Well shit." Nico chuckles. "Jonas is being all emotionally intelligent."

"Leave him alone." I point at Nico. "Or I'll kick your ass when I'm better."

"I can't wait," he purrs with a wink.

"Thank you, Jonas." I hold out my hand, and forgetting his food, even though I know it's a trigger for him, he hurries over. He sits at my feet, and I pull him closer to me. "You're right. It is hard to be here, but I've lasted this long, so I can last a few more days." Leaning down, I lay a gentle kiss on my lover's head. "Thank you for trying to protect me."

"Always, baby," he says, turning to kiss my hand and holding it to him, his eyes solemn for once until he suddenly perks up. "When we get home, I'll make you the biggest stack of pancakes with Bert. That always cheers me up."

God, I love this man.

"Alright, alright, she needs to rest," Isaac declares, his voice stern, leaving no room for argument.

"Can I rest here with you guys?" I plead with him. "I hate lying there." I hate the panic in my tone, but now that I'm fully awake, being trapped in that room feels too much like being trapped on those tables and cut apart.

"Of course," he tells me, "but you'll need to lie down."

"Sure thing, doc."

He stands, and they help me lie down, covering me up and giving me a pillow as Nico and Jonas kiss me goodbye and go to wire up the place. Isaac sits with me, checking my vitals and playing with my fingers as if he's loath to be parted from me. Dimitri watches the tablet carefully, but he brings me some food and water with a soft smile.

Louis is about to leave when his phone rings. He frowns down at it but answers, then he puts it on the table, pressing speaker as he leans back. "General."

"We have been trying to get ahold of you for days," the general snaps, making me roll my eyes. This might have started with them putting us on this mission, but it turned into much more.

"I have been busy," Louis drawls. "Would you like a report?"

There is a long pause. "You have one minute."

"We have located Dr. Davis and dealt with the threat. His experiments have ceased, and the research has been gathered for safekeeping." He leaves out anything else that's personal, and I send him a silent *thank you* for that. I don't want this dick knowing my business.

"Dr. Davis is dead?" His voice is carefully cold.

Louis frowns. "Yes."

"But you have the research with you?" he continues.

"We do . . ." Louis frowns over at me. "To keep it safe, although we will probably destroy it."

"No, don't destroy it. Bring it here with you," he says quickly.

Too quickly.

"For what?" Louis demands as I stiffen.

"Don't question things above your paygrade. Dr. Davis might have been a madman, but some of his research was cutting edge."

"It was insane and inhumane," Louis snaps. "Why do you want the research?"

"That is none of your business. I expect your team and the research at the bunker by next week. Understood?"

Louis's eyes harden, and he stares at the phone for a moment. "Understood," he replies then hangs up, meeting my eyes. "I don't like that."

"Me either." I look around. "You don't think he would try to use the research, do you? My father mentioned super soldiers. Hell, he even had soldiers. I never thought to question how he got them, but the general was against my father . . . wasn't he?"

"He said so from the get-go," Louis mutters. "That's why we trusted him. We even did our own background checks. He was clean, but I don't particularly want him or the government to get their hands on this research."

"Neither do I," I agree as Dimitri and Isaac nod. "So what do we do?"

Louis looks at the phone again before sitting taller. "We follow our plan for now. Rest, and then we'll go home when you're ready. Let me deal with this for now. I need to think some things over." Grabbing his phone, Louis strides from the room, and I share a look with Dimitri who quickly goes after him.

"Isaac, if he tries to use my father's research—"

"We won't let that happen. You know that, Nova," he promises, kissing my hand. "Rest, everything will be okay."

My mind whirls a mile a minute. I thought this was over. I thought this ended with my father. He never once mentioned any connection to the military, but how did he get soldiers? It could be a coincidence, and Dimitri said he's clean—they wouldn't have trusted him otherwise. The general said he thought my father was a monster, a traitor, but then why would he want his research?

To protect it or use it?

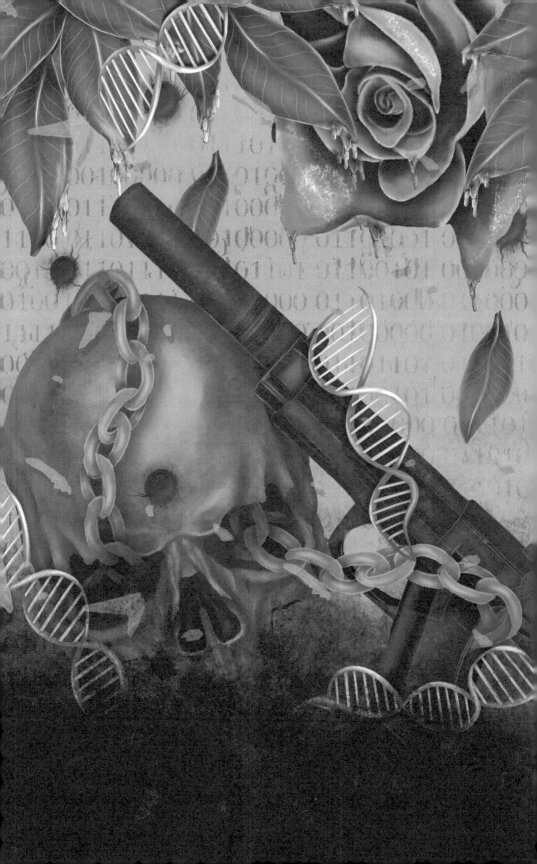

FORTY-TWO

NOVA

I'm over this shit.

I know they want to take care of me because they love me, but I'm over it. I want out. I want fresh air. I want away from this bunker and the stench of dead bodies that has lingered over the last two days. They've been so busy, I barely see them. Instead, I take the time to stretch out my body, careful of my wound since I don't want to stay here longer than I need to. I do some basic exercises. I walk and jog, I do some push-ups, and I eat and shower and repeat. By the second day, I'm going insane. At least I had a purpose before, and I had things to keep me busy. Granted, that was usually round-the-clock torture, but hey, beggars can't be choosers.

I'm fed up, to say the least, and when I stride into the kitchen we've claimed as our command post and find Louis, I decide it's time to tell him that.

He spins his chair around, and I watch his grin turn into a groan. "Baby," he starts.

"No, I'm fine. We are leaving. Today. Now. I want out!" I snap. "I will be fine on the plane. I will rest and relax and do everything you fuckers want, but if I spend one more goddamn hour down here, I'm going to go crazy—okay, crazier—and take it out on you bitches. So either be a good boy and give the order or I'm breaking out of here and you can follow. Either way, we are leaving, understood?"

"Nova, we are trying to take care of you," he says calmly, sounding completely rational.

"Aww, that's cute. I don't give a fuck. We are leaving," I retort unreasonably, but it doesn't stop him from chuckling or pulling me closer and kissing me, even as I keep my arms crossed, not willing to back down.

"If you are sure, I can tell the others," he begins.

"I am. I'm sure. I couldn't be surer. I need to get out of here, Louis." I let him see the truth. I'm afraid I'll go crazy if I stay down here another minute. There are too many ghosts, too much pain, and too many nightmares that plague me here. "Please." I'll beg if I need to.

"Okay," he says, standing and kissing my head. "I'll tell the others. Go get dressed and we can leave."

"Really?" I would leap up and down if it wouldn't tear my wound.

"Really." He grins. "We only stayed to help you. I would never ignore your desire to leave, my love. Let's go home."

"Let's." Leaning up, I kiss him harder. "Thank you."

"Always, Nova."

Now that we're standing down the road, the base looks small. How could one place house such horrors? Yet it did, and as I watch Jonas flip open the switch, nothing but relief fills me.

"Boom." He grins and two seconds later, the explosives they wired into the building blow it sky-high, incinerating everything.

The guards' bodies, my father's body, the labs, the results, and the rooms and all the pain they held.

The whole base goes up in flames, climbing into the sky. Nothing will be left but the scars on my body and soul from what happened here. It almost pisses me off. They should have suffered more, but I can't change that now. Turning away, I get into the Jeep we stole and watch the flames as we drive to the nearby airfield where Dimitri's plane is.

Nobody is waiting for me at home this time. There will be no little sister ready to welcome me back and share all my secrets with. It seems to hit me then, and tears fall from my eyes. I hide my face as we speed to the airplane.

Breaking down now will solve nothing.

Instead, I close my eyes and let the smell of smoke and the bump of the car lull me into a place between sleep and wakefulness where it doesn't hurt so badly.

I slept the entire plane ride home. I can see the worry on my men's faces, but I cannot bring myself to comfort them and let them know I'm okay. I'm not okay, and it couldn't be more evident than when we pull up at the manor and Bert opens the door.

I'm out of the car before they even stop, rushing into his open arms. "Nova!" he cries when he sees me, catching me as I fling myself at him. We sink to the ground as I bury my head in his chest, my tears falling once more.

"Miss Nova, I'm so sorry," he whispers, rubbing my back, his own tears wetting my hair as we hold each other. "I'm so very sorry."

"Me too," I murmur. "Is she . . ."

"We buried her." He pulls back, brushing my tears away. "I insisted on it. Your men dug the holes, and they made sure she was with Sam under the shelter of the tree so she wouldn't be alone. I made sure it was finished."

What does it matter? She's dead, but I simply nod, turning my head to see the two graves hidden under the canopy of the old tree. Pain splinters me apart, and I don't even notice him helping me to my feet and heading inside, not until I'm looking around the foyer, as if waiting for her to jump out.

She doesn't, of course.

This place is as empty as when I first arrived and filled with two more ghosts.

"I can make some food. I bet you must be hungry," Bert offers at my side but doesn't let go. "Or I can—"

"She's really gone." I don't know why I'm saying it. I knew she was.

I saw her die. I felt it. I held her.

Why did a small part of me expect to see her smiling face inside this house? Looking up at Bert, I see the same pain reflected in his eyes. Bert was never our father, but he sure as fuck loved us like one.

Loved Ana like one.

He lost two daughters that day, and now one is back. We share a grieving look for the good that was stolen from the world because she was the best. She was kind, sweet, strong, and sure. Ana was so intelligent, it was scary, and she was determined to make the world a better place. It should be her who's here, not me. She was going places, she had things to do, and she would have changed everything.

Me? I'm just a scarred, fucked-up individual who can take a lot of pain. Despite my father's beliefs, I'm nothing special. Not really. I'm just what he created. Ana? She was so much more.

But life is a bitch like that. I lived, she died, and it hurts.

They say that everyone was born with a purpose or they find their destiny, something they were created for, but if I believed that, then I would have to believe that my sister's reason for being born was to die. I refuse to consider that. It's a load of shit. We are born, we suffer through life, and if we are lucky enough, we find someone to suffer through it with us. I don't believe we are all born with a great destiny, I believe we make one.

Hers? Hers is in the legacy she leaves me with.

"I know," he whispers. "It's almost too hard to be here. I see a memory of her everywhere I look. It hurts, Miss Nova, but she wouldn't want us to stop. She wouldn't want us to be unhappy. She loved you so much, Nova. She loved you, and you did everything you could. If you couldn't save her, then nobody could, and she knew that. Your mission is over. You did it. Now it's time to live. We have to."

"I don't know if I can," I admit out loud for the first time.

"You can do anything you put your mind to. You always could," he responds with a squeeze.

"I spent my whole life protecting her and carrying on for her. Now what? What do I do, Bert?" I look up at him. "What do I do without her?"

"We remember her and honour her in the way we live."

Bert is right, and when he takes my hand, I let him lead me outside to the tree. There, chiselled in stone, is her name, right next to Sam's. The tears continue to fall as I struggle to breathe, holding Bert's hand tightly in mine.

"It's over, Annie. It's over. He's gone. He can't hurt anyone else anymore. I thought you should know." My voice is choked, and I swallow around my agony that is still as fresh as the moment her eyes closed. "I love you, Annie, and I'm so sorry."

I turn away because I can't take it anymore, then I leave Bert there and head back inside where my men are waiting for me, but if they hold me, I will break down further. I'm tired of crying. I'm tired of being weak.

"We should hide the research for now and check in on the children."

"Of course." Louis nods. "Are you okay?"

"I'm fine. I'll be fine," I reply. "I just need to stay busy, okay? Just let me do that."

"Okay, well, you can help Dimitri and Nico hide the research. Isaac and I will check on the kids." Nodding, I follow Nico to the car. He does let me help, but he carries the boxes in while I carry the hard drives with Dimitri.

"Any ideas?" D asks, looking around.

"One," I reply. It's a place I forgot about until now.

Grabbing a bag, I head upstairs, past my and Annie's rooms, to the formal sitting room on this level we never used. A panelled wall runs all the way around it. Moving to the bookcase on the right, I see the gap is still there. I used to fit behind it, but now I have to nudge it out of the way with Nico's help. Hidden behind it is a trapdoor Bert cut for us when we told him what we wanted, and it leads into the space that used to be a cupboard before it was sealed, so this is the only way in and out.

Crouching, I open the door and peek inside, seeing the torch waiting there. Books lie discarded in the blankets, and there are glow-in-the-dark stickers on the cupboard ceiling and drawings on the wall. It was a place for us to hide when we needed to. It was our place.

It seems only right that I hide this here, leaving her to protect it.

Crawling inside, since the others will be too big, I crouch and look around, a sad smile curling my lips. "Only Annie and I knew about this place. It was our hiding spot." Lifting my hand, I trace a drawing she made of us and Bert. Turning away, I drag my bag in and hold my hands out for the rest. "It will be safe here for now."

They don't question me, and I pile it all in here and cover it in a blanket just in case before sliding out. Nico helps me up, and Dimitri double-checks, adding something before straightening and moving the bookcase back. If you weren't looking, you wouldn't have a clue it was there.

"I set a camera and a motion sensor inside as well. It's not on the house plans, so that's good." He nods. "Okay, how about we get some food, take showers, and then crash? It's late."

"Sure." I look back at the spot as he takes my hand, and I allow him to lead me away. It's yet another reminder of what I have lost, but I know she's there, guarding the research for me.

I'm picking at my food. The table is quiet, and no one seems to want to disturb it, not even Bert. My eyes keep going to the two empty chairs opposite me. Is this what my life will be like? Sad, quiet meals with empty chairs?

I give them all a tight smile as I stand. "I'm going to bed. I'm tired."

"Are you okay?" Isaac asks worriedly.

"I'm fine, just tired," I lie and then move from the table. "Goodnight." I don't give them time to question me, nor do I ask them to join me, and they don't offer.

Are we broken beyond repair, or am I simply too broken to love anymore?

I don't know, but when I collapse, it's in her bed, not mine. I suck in her scent as I cry, wrapping her cold sheets around me and wishing she were here.

I wish they had taken me, not her.

Sam would have loved her through her pain. They would have stopped Father, grown old, and had kids. They would have made this place a home. She would have been happy. She would have been better than me.

But everyone is right. I need to live for her now.

I cannot change the past nor can I take the pain away.

I just need to learn to live with it if I can and hope they love me enough to stay by my side as I try to heal my broken heart and lonely soul.

FORTY-THREE

NOVA

The crack of lightning wakes me up, and I jerk upright in Ana's darkened room. There's a quilt over me, some water next to the bed, and clothes laid out. My guys were here, but they left me alone like I wanted, and I feel bad for a moment before my gaze moves to the window to see the rain coming down hard, the night sky lighting up with sparks of lightning as rumbles of thunder rock the house.

A storm.

Annie.

I jump up and walk out of the bedroom door, intent on getting to her.

I slip on some shoes at the front door and head outside without hesitating. Stilling as the rain lashes me, I feel it chill me to the bone as it causes the oversized shirt and shorts to stick to my body. Ignoring it, I hurry to the graves below the tree.

The cold makes me shiver, but I don't stop until I drop to my knees before her grave. The wet mud gives slightly, chilling me through.

Ana.

"Hey, Annie," I call softly, wiping the rain from my face as lightning arcs through the sky, lighting up the darkness like she always did for me. "I know you hate storms, so I'll sit with you, okay?" I whisper, the wind catching my words and taking them to her.

Pain bubbles in my throat until I choke on it and a sob breaks free. "I woke up and you weren't there. For a moment, I forgot you were dead," I admit, my voice cracking. Pain builds inside of me, and I have to let it out. "It's not fair." I slam my hand into the mud. "It's not fucking fair."

Tipping my head back, I release my pain in a scream.

The storm catches it, wrapping my pain and fury up in its depths and using it.

"I miss you so much," I whisper, crawling closer, shivering from the cold rain.

Sliding under the tree and the protection it offers, I lean against the trunk, watching the night sky for a while as pain swallows me. "I always loved storms. They reminded me of you and the times you would sneak into my bed and let me hold you through them, no matter how old you got. Whenever I see lightning, I smile," I admit, even as tears drip down my face, a smile curling my lips. "It reminds me that no matter what happens, love doesn't stop. It just changes. The lightning is my reminder you existed, Ana, and that you loved me and I loved you. Isn't that the most beautiful thing you have ever heard?" Looking down at her grave, I let my tears fall steadily, blending with the rain.

"Storms are my favourite thing now because of you. Every time it storms, I will be right here with you until the end, Annie, until the day they have to wheel me out here. Then, I'll be in the ground right next to you."

My head falls back to the wood, and I watch the sky light up with it, knowing she's right here with me. My hand curls around air where hers would be, my shoulder almost heavy from her head. I can feel her with me, and for the first time since I lost her, I breathe without pain.

I know it's going to be okay.

The storm tells me that.

She might be gone, but there will always be the memories and love I have of her. I close my eyes, letting the tears fall even as a smile curls my lips. She's right here with me as I say goodbye.

As I let her go and hold her heart with my own.

When my eyes open, I freeze.

My men stand before me, half asleep but concerned.

"She hated to be alone during storms," I tell them, shivering in the cold. "I couldn't let her be alone."

I worry what they will do, but I shouldn't have.

They don't complain or speak. They wrap me in a coat and blanket before sitting next to me under the canopy, keeping me warm with their bodies, and that's when I know they aren't going anywhere.

No matter what happens, we are family.

Forever.

They take my hand and settle at my sides, until we sit shoulder to shoulder under the canopy, protecting my sister through the storm. I break apart with the lightning and put myself back together again with their help.

Hours pass this way until my shaking gets to be too much, and then I stand, looking at them. "She will be okay now. The worst of the storm has passed, I think." I hold out my hand. "Take me inside."

Louis is the first to stand, covered head to toe in rainwater, but he never once complained. His hand is muddy like my own as he takes it. "Are you sure?"

Looking back at her grave, I nod with a smile. "I'm sure. She is going to be okay. It's going to be okay. I'm going to be okay," I reply, looking at him with a sad smile. "Take me to bed."

As he searches my gaze, I see lightning flash across his eyes, but I shudder again and he quickly herds me inside, the others following closely. The door shuts with a bang the thunder covers swiftly. Shivering, I kick off the wet shoes and drop the blanket and coat to the floor, watching them plop them into a puddle.

I run to the stairs and hurry up to my room, knowing they are following. Once inside, I turn to face them as they cross the threshold and shut the door behind them.

Sliding my wet clothes away, I drop them to the floor, shivering as they stare at me. "Nova," Isaac starts, but I shake my head and step back.

"Warm me up," I order.

"Let us get towels, and we can go back to sleep," Louis offers.

"No, I've slept enough. I need you to remind me I'm alive," I say. "I need to be held and touched. I need to be loved. I need you to remind me that you aren't going anywhere. I need you all so much. Please."

Nico is the first to move, following me to bed.

I lie back, shivering. "Warm me up," I call, and Nico crawls up the mattress, covering me with his body as his lips find mine in the dark. His kiss is soft, gentle, and loving. His hands slide across my naked body, infusing me with his heat and strong touch, offering me his comfort and love.

Other hands join his, gliding over my body, and I realise they have towels. They are drying and warming every inch of me until Nico pulls away and gets to his knees. "Up, baby," he orders. I kneel, and Louis slides behind me, drying my neck and face with soft, sure strokes before drying my hair as best as he can. All the while, Nico's eyes hold me prisoner, and when Louis reaches down with the towel and cups my breasts, I groan. Louis tweaks my nipples as pleasure sweeps through me.

Crawling to me, Nico runs his tongue along my thigh and up, chasing some water before stroking across my pussy. "Lie back, baby." Swallowing, I do as he says, lying back on Louis. He's naked and hard behind me, his hands still playing with my breasts, tweaking my nipples until they are hard and pointed, waiting for their touches and mouths.

There's a noise beside me, and I look over to see Jonas crawling up the bed on my right, his eyes on me as he lies by my side, wrapping his lips around my nipple. I gasp as he sucks. Another head joins his and I jerk, turning left to see Isaac doing the same on my other side as Nico traces my pussy with teasing licks, chasing water.

Dimitri is watching and waiting patiently for his turn, so I keep my eyes on him as they tease me and bring me back to life. "I need you all," I admit.

"You've got us, so just relax, baby, and let us look after you," Nico murmurs.

My eyes slide closed in bliss as they weave a spell around me. Pleasure mounts when Nico's tongue slides over my clit, and I almost come off the bed. He holds me down, and Dimitri slides in alongside him. My mouth parts on a moan as Nico moves farther down, leaving room for Dimitri as his tongue joins in, curling around my clit as Nico's thrusts into me.

I cry out, trying to pull away, but they don't let me. They up their assault until I moan beneath them, grinding back into Louis's hard cock.

"Please," I whimper.

With each of their touches, I come back to life, and when Jonas and Isaac bite my nipples, Nico thrusts into me with his tongue, and Dimitri bites my clit, I fly over the edge, screaming into the night.

"That's it, Nova. Give us everything. Let that big brain rest. I just want you to feel. Feel our love for you. Let us guide you. Let us love you," Louis murmurs in my ear. "Look at them, look at how much they love you and how much they want you."

My eyes open as I pant, seeing them spread around me.

"We are all yours, the best killers in the world, and you brought us to our knees. You made us obsessed with you. You made us wild with it and so crazed, we would kill anyone who took you from us. Let us love you as much as we can, let the storm feel it."

Oh fuck.

I can't even put into words how much I love them. I was dead before them. They aren't just bringing me back to life tonight, but every day since I met them.

I hear them murmuring, but I remain reclined, trusting them like they asked. When I'm turned, I open my eyes and peer down at Dimitri, who's below me as he smirks. Hands grip my hips and lift me, then they slide me down his cock, making us both groan. I fall forward, kissing him as she slowly fills me. Hands slide over my ass and lift me, then another cock is at my entrance, and my eyes widen as it pushes in, stretching me. They rock into me as I catch my breath and push back, and they work in tandem, thrusting into me. When I glance over my shoulder, I find Isaac there with love blazing in his eyes. Panting, I rock into their touches as a finger presses against my chin and turns my head. I roll my eyes up to Jonas, who smiles softly and kisses me before kneeling once more, holding his cock in his hand. I open my mouth, wanting to taste, and he obliges.

He slowly slides his length into my mouth. I suck, sliding up and down as they fuck me. Hands slide over my body, Louis and Nico no doubt, and I cry out around Jonas's cock. Dimitri groans, running his lips along my chest and neck. Others kiss my back and sides as we make slow, unhurried love.

Dimitri is the first to fall, groaning into my chest as I feel him come, taking me with him. Isaac groans as he and Dimitri pull out of me, then I'm turned. Isaac kneels before me, cock in hand, and when he slides back into me as I'm wrapped in Dimitri's arms, I cry out.

Jonas grips my mouth once more and fills it, my head turned.

"That's it. Good girl, Nova. Just feel," Louis whispers in my ear. "Just feel their love, feel the pleasure winding through you. Let it carry you away and trust us to be here to catch you."

Whimpering, I do just that, lifting my hips to take Isaac as he makes love to me, all while sucking Jonas's big cock as he speeds up, unable to resist. He takes my mouth hard and fast until he jerks, thrusting deeply as he explodes down my throat, and I have no choice but to swallow.

Panting, I become dizzy when I'm turned once more. Isaac is still in my pussy as Nico slides beneath me and working with Isaac, he slides across my pussy. When Isaac pulls out, Nico thrusts in, and then they are both fucking me.

"Louis," I beg.

"I'm here, my love. I'm right here. We all are, look."

Lightning arcs beyond the window, illuminating the room. The sight makes me cry out. My head falls forward, but I lift it when I sense Louis. He waits, but I'm ready for him, and he comes gladly. His leaking length slides across my lips, staining them and my soul with his need and love.

"Beautiful," he murmurs as thunder rocks the house. "Wild and unpredictable, but a goddamn beauty of nature, just like this storm."

I suck him into my mouth, needing to show him how I feel because no words will do it justice. I slide him across my tongue, hollowing my cheeks as he fills my mouth, working with Nico and Isaac to keep me filled while building pleasure once more.

There is nothing but love and need inside me.

I feel so alive, it almost hurts, as if electricity from the storm flows through me, guided by their touch and bringing me back to life.

Jonas and Dimitri wrap their lips around my nipples and suck as every single one of them touches me, loving me.

I can't do anything but fall once more.

I cry out my release, and just like always, they follow me.

Isaac and Nico groan, and Isaac splashes his cum inside me as Nico pulls out and sprays it across my legs and pussy. Louis grips my chin and takes my mouth hard and fast as I shake, trapped by the force, and with an audible bellow that matches the thunder, he fills my mouth.

Tears slide down my cheeks. I'm happy.

I collapse in their midst, my strings cut, but for the first time in a long time, I know tomorrow will bring nothing but joy.

How could it not with them surrounding me? They heal my soul with each touch.

Lightning fills the sky as I close my eyes once more, surrounded by my loves, my heart beginning to heal along with my body.

FORTY-FOUR

NOVA

I wake to an empty bed, warm and satisfied. I can hear them downstairs, though, so I don't worry. I roll over and just relax, soaking in their scents, thinking about everything we need to do.

We need to deal with the kids and find them someplace happy and safe to live. We also need to deal with the military.

They expect us to hand over the research next week, but I've already decided we won't. I need to broach it with Louis and the others, but I'm hesitant to break the peace we have found, so for a few more days, I will pretend and enjoy what we have.

Getting up, I head to the bathroom and crank on the shower. They warmed me up last night, but I still feel disgusting after sitting in the mud. Careful of my wounds, I wash my hair twice and scrub my body before sliding into one of their shirts and some leggings, adding fluffy socks. I leave my hair down to dry and head downstairs to find them.

I still at the kitchen door, a smile curling my lips. Bert and Jonas are cooking side by side. It's clear Bert is teaching Jonas how to make pancakes. Jonas's face is locked in concentration, his tongue caught between his teeth. "That's it, Master Jonas, just like that!" Bert praises as Jonas manages to flip it. "You'll be a chef in no time!"

My heart clenches with pure joy as Jonas grins at Bert, so carefree and happy.

"They better be for me," I call as I move to the dining table where Isaac is sipping tea.

He smiles at me. "Are you okay?" we say at the same time and giggle.

I sit in his lap, and he sighs as I snuggle closer, watching Jonas and Bert plate the food.

"I'm okay," he says. "How are you feeling? We didn't push you too much last night, did we?" His voice is quiet so we aren't overheard.

"I'm fine," I murmur, kissing his cheek.

"We haven't eaten yet. We waited for you," Bert tells me as he lays the food out with Jonas. "Master Louis is with Dimitri and Nico. I will call for them."

"Thank you, Bert." I catch his hand and kiss it. My gratitude is meant for so much more than the food he just gave me. He makes Jonas smile, and he is always here for us.

"Of course, Miss Nova." He smiles softly. "Quite the storm last night."

"It was." I look at the window where the sun is shining. "They say storms wash everything clean. I don't know about you, but I'm hoping that's true. I think it's going to be a beautiful day."

"I believe so," he whispers. "I truly do. I saw a rainbow this morning. That means good luck, but I hope it means a good future."

Meeting his eyes, I smile sadly. "I hope so too." Releasing his hand, I let him find the others as Jonas serves me a pancake and nervously hands me a fork.

"Well?" he asks hopefully. "Is it good?"

I hurriedly take a bite, and I don't even fake a moan. "So good." I lower my voice. "Don't tell Bert, but they might even be better than his, babe."

"I heard that!" Bert calls, making me laugh as Jonas grins, puffing up with pride.

Louis kisses me as he sits, sorting himself a plate before adding more to mine. Nico is sweaty when he drops into a seat, and Dimitri smiles at me as he sits and Jonas gives them pancakes. Bert sits with us, and we eat in comfortable silence. When I'm done, I lean back.

"So, what were you guys doing?"

"Updating security," Nico replies. "It means climbing all over the house."

"Ignore him, he drew the short straw." Louis laughs. "These pancakes are amazing. Congratulations, Jonas."

Jonas grins under the praise, sitting up taller as I blow him a kiss.

"How are the kids?" I ask.

"They are okay. They are settling into the apartment building well, so it should work until we find a permanent solution. Did you sleep well?" Dimitri asks.

"I did." I wink. "So, what's the plan for today?" I'm hesitant to bring up my suspicion about the military or what we will do, and it seems they are as well, so I let it slide for another day. It's not urgent, and I want to enjoy our time together since I spent so much time apart from them.

"We are going to finish updating the security on the house. It might take us a while, but you can help Dimitri organise it if you want. Isaac wanted to check you and Bert over once more, and then he's going to double-check all the research since he has the most knowledge. Jonas is working on a project for me," Louis explains.

I smile. "Sounds like a plan."

"Okay, so the new cameras will be here, here, here, and here," Dimitri tells me. "We are also adding motion sensors throughout the grounds. All the windows will eventually be replaced by the bulletproof kind the military uses, and we are also going to update the fence, gate, and alarms."

"Wow, sounds like a lot." It's clear they are doing this because of what happened last time.

"Nothing's too much when it comes to protecting my family." He grins at me. "Is there anything else you can think of?"

"Yeah, there is actually." I grab his face and yank him down to me, kissing him hard.

"What are you doing, Nova?" he murmurs as he tries to pull back. Sliding from my chair, I plop onto his lap, grinding against his hard cock. They brought me back to life last night, and it seems my desire came with it.

"I thought it was obvious. Maybe you need a demonstration," I tease as I reach down and unzip his jeans. He struggles between us, trying to move me gently, but I grip his hard cock and he stills.

I stroke his huge length while grinding into his jean-clad thigh. "Still confused?" Standing, I kick off my leggings, leaving the shirt since it's cold, and then I straddle him once more. Lifting the shirt, I meet his eyes as I slide my hand up my thigh to my pussy, circling my hole. "Your cock goes here—"

His hand darts out and grips my neck, making me groan. "Louis is right. You are such a brat."

"Very true," I retort, desire making my heart race and my thighs slick. "Why don't you fuck it out of me?"

He smacks my hand away as he yanks me back to his mouth. Kissing me hard and fast, he sweeps his tongue against mine as he dominates me. The chair creaks as we grind together, so he sits me on the edge of the desk, kicking my thighs open.

"D, I need your cock." I groan as he leans down and swipes his tongue across my clit.

"You get what I give you. Now, Nova, be a good brat and scream for me. I heard that through the mic while I was working and it drove me crazy. Do it again with my tongue buried in this pretty pussy and you can have my cock. You can ride it until you are filled with my cum and they realise what we are doing in here."

His radio crackles. "Dimitri, can you check the positions of the cameras?"

He completely ignores it as I tangle my hand in his hair, tugging his head closer as my torso falls back. My nipples brush against the fabric of the top, making me moan. His talented tongue curls around my clit, and he finds a quick rhythm that has my hips jerking up as I grind into his face, but just as I'm about to come, he moves down and thrusts his tongue into me.

"Dimitri," I whine, sounding just like the brat he accused me of being.

He groans, and the sound vibrates through me, making me jerk below him. When he pulls his tongue out, I meet his eyes. "I forgot that you taste like fucking heaven. I've changed my mind. Cover my face in your cum. I don't care if you scream or don't. I just want to taste you with every breath I take. I want to drown in it."

"D." I hold his hair tighter, watching his pupils blow in pleasure and pain. "You better make me then."

With a wicked grin, he grabs my thighs and throws them over his shoulders, eating me like a madman.

His tongue dips inside me, fucking me before rubbing my clit. The fast pace drives me crazy as I roll my hips, wanting more. He gives me what I want, thrusting two fingers inside me and stretching them as I cry out.

My release takes me by surprise. His fingers pull free then his mouth seals on my pussy, swallowing every drop of my cum before his fingers are back inside me, rubbing my G-spot. My legs jerk as one orgasm rolls into the next while he abuses my poor pussy, draining every drop of my release from me. When he sits back sometime later, his face drips with my cream, and he grins so broadly, it must hurt.

Legs shaking, I try to relearn how to breathe.

"Dimitri?" Louis snaps.

Reaching out, Dimitri grabs the mic. "Looking good, keep going," he says without taking his eyes off me as he stands. He pushes his jeans down and with a wicked grin, he wipes his hand across his face, gathering my cream and stroking his cock with it before stepping between my shaking thighs.

"Scream for me," he orders as he pulls me down and impales me on his length.

I do, my head falling back with a scream as he pounds into me. The desk creaks from the force of his thrusts as he grips my hip to work me onto his hard length. My legs are floppy, but I manage to wrap them around his waist and lift my hips for his punishing thrusts.

I want more.

He moans, gripping my hips as he drives into me harder, and the radio crackles again. "Dimitri? How about now?"

"So fucking good," he tells them.

"What?" Louis asks in confusion, and then he presses the radio against me and twists his hips, smacking my clit at the same time, and I cry out.

"Oh, never mind." Louis chuckles.

Dropping it, he smirks at me. "They all know you are in here getting fucked like the good girl you are, coming for your man. Fuck, baby, I can feel you gripping me. You're so ready to come again, aren't you?"

"Fuck, fuck, please, D." I can't help but beg as the pleasure inside of me grows.

"Good girl, just like that. You're taking me so well," he praises, spiralling me higher as he groans and hammers into me. "I'm close. That's it, baby. Now come for me. Milk my cock."

His words send me over the edge, and I cry out my release as he follows me, bellowing his pleasure as he thrusts into me, filling me with his cum just like he promised.

When he collapses over me, I wrap my arms around him, breathing heavily and grinning. He kisses my chest over my racing heart. "Isaac is going to kill me."

FORTY-FIVE

ISAAC

"I'm here for my checkup, doc!" Nova sings as she saunters into the lab. Unlike the first time we were here, she doesn't even glance around. Her eyes don't darken, nor is she held back by any ghosts, but her mental health is precarious at the moment with her sister's death and what she went through in the bunker. It's my job to ensure she is okay. She's all that matters.

Bert is healing well, and I'm happy with his progress, so now my sole focus is my love.

I pat the medical bed I moved in here, and she hops up, wearing a cheeky grin on her face. "Oh, kinky," she purrs. "How do you want me, doc? Want me to bend over and cough?"

Grinning, I strap on the BP machine and wait. It's great for someone who endured such a bad stab wound. I want to take some blood too, but she seems to be healing well. "Shirt up," I order.

"Sure thing." She simply rips it off, leaving her breasts free, and my mouth goes dry and I forget how to move or speak. "Doc?" she purrs.

I duck my head and lift the gauze to check her wound, trying to ignore the way her silken skin feels against my knuckles as I touch her. She's my patient here, after all.

I clean and redress it. "You can put your shirt on now, babe," I say, even as my eyes catch on her breasts, my cock hardening as it always does around my girl. "Now, let's talk about you. How are you feeling?"

"Needy. Want to play doctor?" she whispers. "Because I do."

"This is a perfectly normal response to trauma. You are finding ways to make yourself happy. I love you, Nova, but I don't want you to ignore what happened to you."

"Hmm, sure, you're a great doctor. So smart," she teases, rubbing her bare chest against me. "What else?" She reaches down and grips my cock, making me groan and jerk.

"You—" My head falls back as she starts to massage my hard length. "You need to be able to talk about what happened so you can deal with it and we can be aware of any triggers—fuck it."

She giggles. "Thank God. I thought you would talk all day."

"Nova." I really try to remember why this can't happen, but I've never just been her doctor. I'm her lover as well, and I'm helpless when it comes to her.

Sliding from the bed, she stops before me. "Isaac, I know you worry, but I'm fine. We both know we need this. We need some fun and a whole lot of pleasure, so lay your sexy ass down on the table and let me play nurse." The wicked grin she gives me melts all my defences, and when she slides her leggings down, I'm lost in the beauty that is Nova.

Grabbing her hair when she leans in, I tug on the shorter strands. She stiffens for a moment before relaxing. "I love your shorter hair," I tell her, seeing the edge of panic in her eyes. She probably needs this control, so I kiss her softly before shucking off my joggers and shirt as she watches. I throw myself onto the table and lean back, placing an arm under my head. "Go ahead, Nurse Nova."

Her eyes trace my body, making my cock jerk and stand at attention. I stretch to showcase my muscles, loving the way she moans. I've never been more thankful for the drills Louis puts us through than when I see my girl's appreciation for my body. Sliding on top of me, she straddles my thighs as her eyes sweep over me once more like she doesn't know where to start.

"I'm so goddamn lucky," she murmurs.

"No, that's me, sweetheart," I say without even a moment's hesitation. Sitting on top of me is a goddamn angel, or maybe a devil—all wicked grins, dark hair, tanned muscles, and tattoos. She looks fucking incredible, and as she slides her body across me, I lift so I can kiss around her new scar. The flash of love in her eyes makes me smile as I lie back.

"I'm yours, Nova, have your wicked way with me."

"Oh, I plan to," she promises, pressing her pussy against my bare thigh and grinding into me, letting me feel her wetness. My hands curl into fists so I don't reach for her and drag that pretty pussy up here so she can sit on my face instead. This is her show at her pace. If she wants to be in control, then she's got it.

She could spend hours here, teasing me and working me up, and then leave and I would let her, as long as she keeps looking at me like I'm her goddamn saviour. So despite my need to bend her over and fuck her raw until she screams my name, I wait patiently.

I'm rewarded because my girl isn't cruel. Her lips slide down my throat, and she nips my skin here and there, the sharp pain making me jerk up. Soothing it better, she kisses down and across my chest.

"Nova."

"Shh, you said I could play," she murmurs, rolling her eyes up to mine as her taunting lips slide across my length. I want to throw my arm across my face because it's too much, but I can't look away as she licks up and down my length like it's a fucking ice cream cone. Pleasure spirals through me, and she hasn't even touched me yet.

Giggling, she grips my length and slides her lips down my cock, sucking me all the way to the back of her throat. I see fucking stars. I can't help thrusting into her mouth, trying to take control. She smacks me away, pinning me down as she taunts me, licking and sucking my length until I'm a panting, sweaty mess below her, trying to resist blowing my load before I even get into her glistening pussy.

"Sweetness, swing around. The doctor wants to play too." Her eyes heat and she turns, placing that beautiful ass on my face, and I finally get what I want.

Grabbing her perfect hips, I drag her back, sealing my lips around her engorged clit. Her moans echo around the room as she sucks my cock harder. I'm helpless to do anything but thrust into her hot, wet mouth, fucking it like

I will her pussy. All the while, she grinds against my waiting tongue, her taste exploding across it.

Perfection.

I let her rock onto me, her moans and gasps getting louder, and I know she's close. I want her nice and wet before I get inside her because I know I won't last. I never do, not with her. She makes it impossible.

"Baby, if you don't stop, I'm going to come," I warn her.

"Good," she purrs, sucking my cock like a fucking Hoover.

Fuck.

Fighting back the tightening of my balls, I nip her clit before sucking hard. She falls forward with a cry as she comes, smothering me with her pussy and cum just like I wanted.

When she slumps, I lap at her pussy, tasting as much of her as I can before she turns. "I wanted to play."

"Play now." Circling my length, I hold it for her. "Ride me and see how goddamn crazy you make me, sweetheart. I'm on the verge of spilling as it is, but I want inside you before that, so sit that pretty cunt on my cock and ride."

Pouting, she lifts her pussy over me, dragging it across my cock until I growl. She slides down, sitting on my length before working her hips to take me all the way. My head falls back with a thump, a guttural groan escaping my lips as I fight my release. It's fucking hard, worse than any torture and better than any pleasure. Her tight, wet heat grips me so good, it's painful not to move.

"Eyes on me, Isaac," she commands, not moving, so when I force them open and meet hers, she rewards me by lifting up on her knees and dropping back down, swallowing my cock as she bounces.

"Fuck!" I yell, lifting my hips off the bed to bury myself deeper in her. My chest heaves and sweat pours down my body as I fight to last as long as I can.

My back almost bows from the need to empty my balls inside her. "That's it. Watch me, doctor," she flirts, sliding her hands up her body to grip her swaying tits. My eyes lock on her as she tweaks and twists her nipples, her cunt tightening around me as she chases her own pleasure.

"Feed them to me," I demand breathlessly. "Let me taste them."

"Say please," she purrs, riding me harder.

"Please, sweetheart," I beg.

She leans forward, and my cock slides deeper into her as she feeds me her pretty rosy nipples. I suck and attack them like a madman, unable to stop. She rocks harder on my length before sitting up. I reach for her but she slaps me away, sliding her hand down and rubbing her clit as she lifts and drops.

"I'm so close," she says. "Isaac, I want you to come with me. I want to feel it."

"Baby, I've been there since the moment you walked in here. Make yourself come, use me, I'm yours."

"I know." Her cunt pulses around me, and I know she's close. "God, I love you. I love you so much."

"I love you, sweetheart, now come for me. I want to feel you milk my release. Let go." Whimpering, she closes her eyes and her body jerks. Not a moment later, her pussy clamps down around me and her scream bursts free as she milks my cock, shaking and twisting as she comes.

Snarling, I reach down and grab her thighs, hauling her back and forth on my cock until I follow her into oblivion. My release splashes inside of her as she whines. I keep her there, impaled on my cock, as I fill her, and then she collapses forward onto my chest. Wrapping my arms around her, I try to get my racing heart to slow, even as our bodies are still locked together in bliss.

I kiss her sweaty head and hold her tighter. "We've got the rest of our lives to play, Nova."

Grinning, she places a kiss over my heart. "I can't wait, doctor."

Me fucking too.

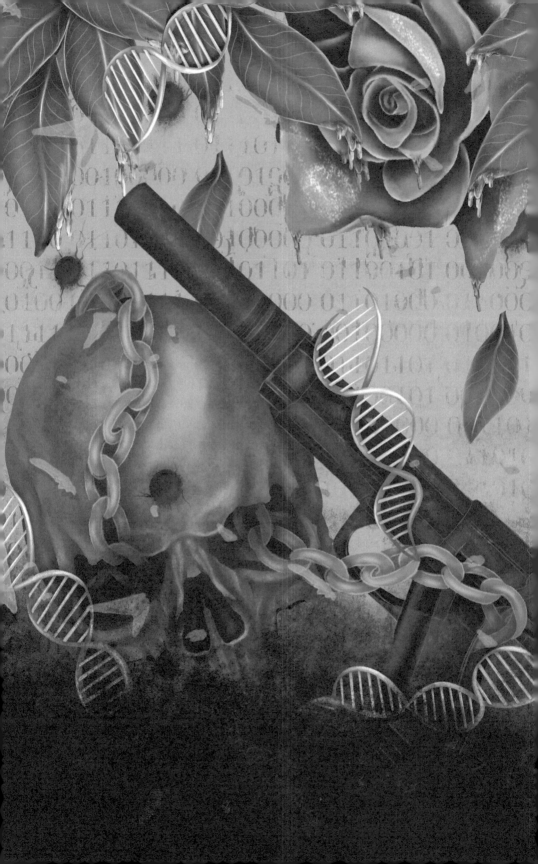

FORTY-SIX

JONAS

"So, Jonas has been working on this for me, but I thought you should all know that I don't plan to give the military what they want."

Nova's head jerks up, but the others don't look surprised as Louis leans back on the sofa.

"I don't like what they plan to use the research for, nor do I like being used for other motives. They won't accept this, so we are planning for the worst-case scenario. They expect us next week, but we are going early—the element of surprise. I'm thinking one last mission, but only if we all agree."

Nico nods. "Fuck yeah."

"I agree." Isaac worries on his lips, glancing at Nova. "I was worried about what it would mean for all of us if they had the research. His notes are substantial, so they could continue where he stopped."

"You know I'm in." Dimitri shrugs.

"Nova?" I ask worriedly. I won't do anything she doesn't want.

"I've been worried but unsure how to bring it up. I think they wanted to take the research from us all along. So, what's the plan?"

Grinning, I lean closer. "We break in, baby. We sneak into the super-secret bunker we helped booby-trap and give them our polite answer of fuck off."

She smiles. "And if he says no to our polite answer?"

"Then we say it not so politely." Louis grins. "We are sneaking in to show them they are weak against us. They have forgotten why they hired us, so it's time to show them. One last mission to protect the research and our family."

"Fuck yeah." Nova nods.

"I get to do the killing!" I call, my hand shooting up.

"No killing," Louis snaps. "We don't need the military on our asses for the rest of our lives."

"Why? I've heard there are some nice no extradition countries," I mutter but deflate. "Fine, no killing unless they try to kill me or you, then all bets are off."

"Thank you." Louis sighs, knowing that's as good as he will get.

"Want to see the project?" I wiggle my eyebrows at Nova, and she grins.

"You know I do."

Rushing around the table, I throw her over my shoulder as the others simply watch us and then continue planning.

Planning is boring anyway. I much prefer this.

I drop her to her feet in the room I claimed. It's a bit of a mess, with weapons and clothes everywhere, but she doesn't care as I wrap my arms around her and show her the device I built to Dimitri's specifications.

"What is it?" she asks, reaching out to touch it.

"An EMP, just in case." I chuckle, running my nose up her neck. "But I really just wanted to have you all to myself."

"Is that right?" She grins up at me. "And what could you want to do all alone up here with me?"

Backing her into the nearest wall, I press my hand above her, grinning down at my girl. I love seeing her so happy. "I can think of some things, but they all lead to the same thing."

"And what's that?" she murmurs as I reach down and hoist her up, wrapping those perfect legs around me as I grind her against my hardness.

I run my nose along her neck once more, inhaling the scent that is all my girl, and when I reach her ear, I bite down on the lobe as she moans. "You screaming for me," I whisper as she shudders.

"Then make me," she demands.

"Oh, I plan to." I grin, rocking into her cunt and letting her feel my desire for her. "I want you on your knees, and I want that pretty ass. I know they have all been in this greedy cunt this week."

"Jonas," she whimpers, rocking into me.

"That's it, get nice and wet for me because you'll be taking my big, fat cock in that pretty little ass until you can't walk. We are taking back every single inch of you, baby, so hold on."

Her eyes flare. She knows what I mean and she wants it. She doesn't want there to be any part of her we have not touched. Turning, I toss her on the bed, watching her bounce, and before she can roll away, I pounce. I roll her onto her stomach, yank her pants down, and slide my fingers through her wet folds.

"So fucking wet," I growl. "Is this all for me, baby? Have you been waiting for me to pin you down and fuck you like you want?"

"Yes." She pushes back into my hand, but I don't let her move as I pinch her clit, her ragged scream filling the air as I abuse it. I keep her there until she's on the verge of coming, and then I pull back, leaving her snarling.

Chuckling, I slide my trousers down, kicking them off the bed before I drag my cock along her pussy. "Don't you dare come yet," I warn her. "I'm going to get my cock nice and wet. If you come, I'll get myself off and leave you here without getting my cock."

"Fucking hell," she grumbles, burying her face in the pillow even as she pushes her ass out.

Sliding my cock along her folds, I get my length nice and wet, purposely bumping her clit until she's whining and fighting not to come. Grinning at how fucking cute she is, I slip my cock inside her, working it into her pussy with slow, soft thrusts that have her rocking back, and when she's about to come again, I slide out.

"Jonas," she screams, pounding her fist into the bed. "If you don't make me come, I'm going to kill you."

"I'd love it, and you know that," I purr as I lift her hips, pressing her ass back and pushing her thighs farther open. "But okay, baby."

Pressing against her ass, I force my cock inside her, watching her stretch around it. She pushes back to take more, and feeling mean, I slam all the way into her. She screams as she tries to jerk away, but I don't let her. I make her feel every hard inch of my cock in her little ass. When I start to move, she whines and fights to get off my cock, but I don't let her, instead sliding my hand down and pinching her clit again.

"Come," I snarl.

She detonates at my command, almost squirting as she cries out. Groaning at the sight, I rub her clit mercilessly as I hammer into her ass, mixing pain and pleasure.

I pummel into her little ass, watching her cheeks jiggle from the force. Her dripping pussy clenches, wanting to be filled too, so I slide my fingers down and work them into her, stretching her with my hand and cock. She cries out and pushes back to take more, fighting me as she claws at the bed.

She's a perfect fucking sight.

I'd win a thousand missions or wars to come back to her.

"Fuck, baby," I growl, hammering into her as I fuck her with my fingers. "I fucking love this so much. I love the way you take me. I love how nothing is ever too much. I'm going to fill you with so much cum, it's going to over-flow, and then later, I'm going to take that pretty mouth too. I will fill every single one of your holes with it. Fuck, I even saw a video where they fucked someone's urethra. I might even try that. I don't want any part of you to go untouched by me. I want to own every inch like you own every inch of me."

"Jonas!" she screams as I work another finger inside her.

My words turn to a growl as she clenches around me. I know she's close, but I want this to last forever. I want to be locked inside of her until the day I die, my name on her lips and her taste on my tongue.

"Don't you fucking dare." I smack her ass hard, making her cry out. "Not yet. Don't you dare. I want you like this."

"Please." Her nails rip at the bedding. "Fuck, J, I can't." Her words slur as she pushes back, impaling herself on my hand and cock. I feel her clenching tighter, needing to come.

"Fuck." I fight my own, feeling it building at the base of my spine. I fight as hard as I can, but I should have known that I always lose when it comes to us. She will always win, and I love it that way.

Roaring, I press into her ass, my release exploding out of me. It sends her off the edge like she was waiting for it, her ass tightening around me and dragging more from me as I spurt and rock into her tight little hole.

Groaning, I pull out and slam back in, fucking my release into her as she whines, her cunt fluttering around my fingers as I pull them out. Her breathing is ragged as she slumps beneath me. I slowly pull my cock out, watching my release spill from her ass, and I almost come again at the sight.

Sliding my fingers through my mess, I watch our combined cum glisten, and I know nothing will ever be more beautiful.

I thrust my fingers into her pussy, coated in her cream, and stroke her as she comes for me again. Groaning, she lies beneath me, shaking with after-shocks, her eyes closed in bliss.

I lie down next to her and let her spoon me, both of us covered in cum and sweat. "That's what I wanted to show you."

"I'm so glad you did." She giggles, burying her head against my neck.

FORTY-SEVEN

NOVA

I t's been a while since I saw the base, months in fact, but so much has changed since then that it feels like a lifetime ago. When I first came here, I was an angry, lost little girl, and now I'm a scarred, hard woman protecting the men she loves. I'm part of a family, a unit, and I'm fighting for something much bigger than petty revenge.

I am fighting for love.

They don't know that we are here this time. Dimitri knows the layout, as well as every trap and alarm in the bunker. Although there is only one way in, we have ways of getting around without being seen. Last time, Jonas happily showed me traps and tricks, but now we are sneaking in.

One last mission together.

One against our very own military.

This won't be like breaking into my father's place. They had soldiers there, sure, but this place is meant to be a fortress, and the soldiers here are active duty and waiting for a fight.

We park as far away as we can so the cameras don't see us beforehand. When we are close enough, Dimitri loops the footage so the alarms don't sound, causing them to go into lockdown. In the darkness, wearing matching black outfits, we share a grin. Adrenaline pumps through me, along with excitement.

I was made for this, and as much as I hate it, it couldn't be more obvious as we effortlessly weave through the many booby traps. We avoid the barn, knowing it's the most heavily guarded area. The scrapyard looks even more abandoned and maze-like in the dark. Jonas points out any areas that are rigged with bombs and sensors and we avoid them, luckily knowing the path through without even making a noise. We simply hop over the landmines and hope they haven't set anymore. Jonas assures me they wouldn't have because before they came along, apparently their security was shit. The guys helped them upgrade it, which works in our favour now.

Once we're through the hill, we head up the sharp incline, which is open ground, to the bunker. We don't spot any guards here, but to be sure, we stay low to the ground. No words are exchanged, since all of us know our roles and how important this is. At the top, I crouch and wait, knowing Dimitri is going to manually open the bunker so we don't alert anyone. I scan our surroundings, watching our backs.

Once we reach the elevator that takes us down, Dimitri pops open a panel as we crouch and protect his back, the night giving us good coverage. We work silently and in a moment, the doors open and we drop to the platform. Unlike last time, there's no escort waiting, and we rush off. We need to find the general before they find us. We want answers, and we want him to understand.

Guns up, we sweep the corridors. Dimitri turned the cameras off, and Jonas plants the EMP while we protect him. We see some soldiers ahead, so we duck into the side rooms and wait for them to pass. My breathing is calm and even as Nico presses against my back. I feel his hardness, even through his suit, and try to focus as desire builds within me.

"Behave," I mutter with a grin.

"Clear," Dimitri murmurs, and I open the door, moving left as Nico moves right, walking backwards to watch our backs. The general should be sleeping at this time, but when we reach the stairs to his room, Dimitri halts us.

"He's in his office. Looks like he fell asleep there. Change of plan."

His office is through the base's hub, but we have no choice. We head that way instead and find a few bored, tired soldiers monitoring the screens, even as they loop.

In the glass office up top, the general reclines back in his chair, his mouth open on a snore. "Target acquired," I murmur. "Five bogies, backs to the door. Unprepared," I report as I move backwards and press my back to the wall.

"Ideas?" Louis asks.

"Three of us sneak in and knock them out." I shrug. "Easy and silent."

Louis frowns, clearly not liking it, but he nods. "Nova, Nico, you're with me. D, you're on cameras. Jonas, watch our backs. Isaac, make sure he doesn't kill anyone."

"Ah, man," Jonas mutters, but we are already moving.

Louis counts down, and when his fist clenches, Nico rips the door open and we move in quickly and silently, sliding behind some desks as one guy turns to look. The door is shut once more and he frowns, searching the room before looking back at the cameras. I point to the two huddled together on the left, playing cards. Nico nods to the middle one, and Louis gestures to the two on the right. I move into position as they do the same.

Once we are all in place, I count down, and on one, I surge into action, stepping behind my two targets and trusting them to do the same. I slam two injections into their necks as they start to turn. "What?" one mumbles before the drug takes hold, and then they slump.

I glance over to see the others were quickly taken care of as well and grin. It's good having a doctor who has access to sedatives on staff. These soldiers should be out cold for a while. The doors open, and the others join us. Isaac and Jonas instantly bar it as we head to the general's office.

We file in and take up our positions. I sit in the opposite chair, lifting my feet and kicking the general's off the desk. They fall with a thump and he windmills his arms to keep his balance as he wakes. His eyes widen when he sees me, and I wave.

"What the fuck is the meaning of this?" he snarls, and when he sees all of us, he looks for his men, all of whom are sleeping. "Why didn't you tell us that you were here?"

"We wanted to have this conversation privately." Louis shrugs, sitting on the edge of the desk. "Ah, don't press that button, sir. I would hate to have to break your hand."

"He will," I say helpfully. "Or I will."

The general moves his hand from the emergency button, crossing his arms as he glares at us. "Where's the research?" he demands, still thinking he's in charge.

The fool.

"Not with us," Louis answers. "We want to know why you want it. Before you snap or answer in anger, know that your life depends on how you answer, general, and we will know if you are lying. After all, we were created to be the best."

"It is none of your business. It's a matter of national security." He huffs. "Now hand over the research. It belongs to the government."

"Do you plan to use it?" I demand, leaning forward. "Think carefully."

"All research will be contained and tested to ensure its safety." He narrows his eyes. "It's better that we use it than some other country. Think of the lives we could save in battle. Dr. Davis went about it wrong, but we can do better—"

"Who else is helping you with it?"

"No one so far. I will present it to the ruling body for testing. You must understand. After all, look at you—"

I lift my gun and blow out his brains before looking at Louis. "No one will ever use that research. This ends with him." Standing, I put my gun away as the alarms blare.

"Fuck, I thought you said no killing. Why did she get to?" Jonas whines just as soldiers burst through the door, and I grin as Louis shakes his head but holds up his hands.

"Do as I say and we'll make it out of this alive," he says.

I grin at him. "Where's the fun in that?" I hold my hands up anyway as soldiers surge into the office. We are ordered to kneel and then handcuffed and led into the room below. A half-dressed man storms into the room. I remember him from our first time here. He's second-in-command, I believe, but I leave the talking to Louis since I tend to shoot first.

"Who the fuck killed the general, and how the fuck did they get in here?" He turns his glare on us. "Answers!" he barks.

Yup, military all the way through.

"We have intelligence that the general was working with Dr. Davis on the banned experimental program to expand the human brain. We were simply doing as we were ordered and executing the mission." Louis is a good liar.

"Do you have proof? You just cannot go around assassinating generals!" he roars.

"We had proof, yes, and we did our mission. Are you going back on your terms now? We did as ordered."

"Dr. Davis?" he asks, his arms crossed. It's clear his general hasn't kept him in the loop.

"Dead."

"The research?"

We all try not to stiffen at that, but it's just genuine curiosity on his part.

"Dead and burned with his body," Louis replies. "It's all gone. The mission is done."

"Fucking hell. This is a clusterfuck. I want these idiots fired" —he points at the drugged men— "and anyone on the perimeter brought up on charges. You six, get the fuck out of my sight. The general might have wanted to work with you, but I sure as shit did not, and when they come around asking questions, I will not protect you. Get out of here now."

"We are free to go?" Louis queries, making damn sure.

"Yes, go before I change my mind. If the general was involved, then you did as ordered. It doesn't mean I fucking like it, but we keep our deals. You're hired mercs, though, and nothing else. Go." Our hands are unlocked, and we are shoved to our feet.

Before we can get into any more trouble, Nico grabs me, and Louis grabs Jonas, and they drag us out. Soldiers escort us up top, where I breathe in the fresh air of the night as sunlight streaks through the sky.

"I guess we didn't need the EMP," I remark.

"Nah, I'll set it off just for fun." Jonas giggles.

Dimitri groans. "Oh, God, get us out of here before we are arrested and thrown into a dark cell somewhere."

The soldiers escort us down the hill just as we see a troop doing early-morning drills and exercises. I guess they didn't hear the alarms, or they have been given the all-clear.

When we get closer, it's clear they are on weapons training, with open crates holding grenades and rocket launchers.

We stop to watch them, but when I glance over, Jonas has a rocket launcher on his shoulder and is pointing it at the drilling soldiers.

"Jonas!" I snap.

He glances between me and the men behind me and pouts. "But they said I could play with it."

I groan. "They didn't mean to shoot them."

"Well, then they should have said that." Pulling the launcher down off his shoulder, he drops it back into the box, still pouting, and stomps away. "I never get to kill anyone anymore."

Wincing at the soldiers who are unsure whether to shoot or laugh, I follow Jonas, and we reach the car in ten minutes. Once there, our escort disappears back up the hill.

We just got away with espionage and murder, but the research is safe and so are we.

When we reach the car, I look over at Louis. "Now what?" I ask.

Before I can react, he grabs the back of my head, yanks me over, and slams his lips to mine. Groaning into the kiss, I return it as the others whistle and cheer, and when he pulls away, he says, "Now, baby? We plan the rest of our lives."

FORTY-EIGHT

NOVA

As I sit at the table, my eyes once more go to the empty chair left for Ana. I love this house and the memories I have here, but in the few days since we have been back, I haven't been able to relax. I wake up with my heart hurting, and I look in every room for her. It almost feels like I'm trapped in the past once more.

Maybe I am.

Maybe I have always been trapped here in one way or another.

As a child, it was my father who kept me here, but as an adult, it was my duty and love for my sister.

Now that both are gone, I'm left in the empty shell and surrounded by ghosts, but the living must live. I don't think I can do that here. I left once, but I was running, knowing the rubber band between me and this place would snap me back one day. This time, I know it won't be a forever good-bye, but it will be an ending. I'll finally be putting my past to rest, which will allow me to move on.

At the moment, we linger in purgatory, but it's time to rejoin the world.

Louis is talking with the guys as they debate house options for the children. Dimitri has found that they are all orphans, either stolen from bad situations, the street, or from a broken system. Nobody misses them, and nobody is looking for them. They have nothing to go back to. We are determined to leave them better off than we found them. Since my father's death, I've become extremely wealthy, not that I give a shit, but now that Ana is . . . Yeah, I'm the sole benefactor of the Davis estate and everything that entails.

Well, fuck him and fuck his money.

An idea comes to me, one that instantly makes me grin and lifts my heart. "I can't stay here." Every eye turns to me, but my focus is on the chair where my sister should sit. "I can't. I can't be trapped here anymore. I have been tied to this house in one way or another since birth. It's time to let go of the ghosts and truly live like you keep telling me." I meet their gazes, seeing their confusion. "I can't stay, but I refuse to leave Annie here alone. If she wasn't here, I'd let this place rot for everything he did, but it's just a house, a house my sister loved and grew up in. A house we became a family in."

I reach over and take Bert's hand. "A house where I learned what love really is. I can't stay, and she can't leave." I look at the maps of choices. "But they can. Let's give him one last fuck you and make this their house. There are enough rooms, and we can get staff for them and fund it with his blood money. He owes them that. Give them a better chance at life and give Annie some company. Let it be filled with laughter and love once more."

"Miss Nova, are you sure?" Bert whispers.

"I want nothing from him. Not this house, not a pound of his money. I've always made my own way, and I always will, but it should be used for good and to make up for what he's done. He'd turn in his grave if he knew, so yeah, I'm sure. Let's bring this old, haunted house back to life. Let's give it a purpose." I smile sadly at Bert. "I know you love this place despite every-thing. You are always welcome to stay and work—"

"My home is where you are," he says. "I only ever stayed for you and Miss Ana. It was never the job or the house; it was you. If you will have me, I will go with you." He looks at my men. "I like to take care of you. You are my family now as much as Miss Nova, as long as it's okay with you."

"You are always welcome wherever we go," I tell him as the others nod.

"You always have a place with us." Louis smiles. "Wherever that is. Nova?"

"I don't know. I just know that there has to be something for us out there. A place where we can learn to live again and heal from the horrors in our pasts. Where we can just . . . thrive." Smiling at them, I reach out and lay my hand on the table. "When I was down in the bunker, it's all I thought about—a place of our own, a place for a family."

"Then we will find it," Louis murmurs.

"We can still . . . work on the side, right?" Jonas asks worriedly.

Laughing, I wink at him. "I think we will need to in order to stop us all from going completely insane. We can't change who we are, but I think we can afford a little slice of peace, don't you? Besides, it's now our mission to protect that research."

"I'm in." Dimitri shrugs. "Where you go, I go."

"I agree. I think I'd like somewhere warm for a change." Isaac grins.

"Fuck it, I'm in. I'd just stalk you anyways." Jonas chuckles.

I look at Nico, who rolls his eyes like he can't believe I have to ask. "We're a family."

"Louis?" I query.

"I agree. Where you go, we go. I think you're right though. We deserve a slice of peace. We have spent so much time tracking your father and getting our revenge, we never truly got to live, not even as kids. We deserve it, and you deserve it as well, Nova. Let's go find our home together."

Their hands cover mine until we are one.

One family.

My eyes go back to the chair, and I know she would like this decision. I know she would be happy with me finally letting go and moving on. It doesn't mean I'll forget her. It just means I'll carry her with me on my adventures, wherever they may take us.

It didn't take us long to pack up our stuff. We are so used to being on the go, everything is already packed and we travel light. Bert, on the other hand, took longer, and we had to help him pack everything, but after Jonas threw his clothes in a bag, he kicked him out, refolding everything and tightly packing it in little cubes that blew my mind. We've set plans into motion for the house. Bert was the one to interview his replacement, and he was happy with the lady he chose. She will help maintain the house and care for the children and report back to us. There will also be other staff on hand, such as teachers and everything they could ever need. They will all turn up tomorrow, and we want to be gone before then.

I leave the guys to pack the car under Bert's watchful gaze and head to the tree, my hands twisting before me. "I can't leave without saying goodbye, though it's not goodbye forever. I'll come back and visit and check on the house . . . and you, but I can't stay here forever, not even for you. I know you'd be happy that I'm putting myself first for once and giving life a go, as you used to say. And of course, they are by my side. I love them, Annie. I really do. I'm glad you got to know that before . . ." Swallowing hard, I close my eyes for a moment and feel the sun on my face. "I'm going to miss you so much. I don't think it will ever stop hurting, but I'm taking you with me. Wherever we wander, wherever we go, you'll be there. I'll live enough for both of us, and when the time comes, I'll meet you beyond." Leaning down, I brush away some dirt from the headstone and smile sadly, tears once more filling my eyes, but I don't let them fall.

"I love you, Annie. I always have. Thank you for being my little sister. Thank you for teaching me that it's okay to love again." Standing, I wipe off my hands and glance over to see them all waiting. Nico is perched at the open door with his shades on. "I promise to show you one hell of a life, and maybe a few more missions." I chuckle. "Watch over them for me, Annie." I glance back down at her. "Take care of Sam. Bye."

I force my feet to the car, each step lighter than the last, and when a light breeze brushes over me, pushing me towards it, I smile, knowing she's there. Nico slides inside, and before I follow, I glance back at the house. I'll come back to check on the kids, but I'll never live here again.

This manor holds so much pain and so many ghosts for me—both good and bad. It's where I lived. It's where I hurt, grieved, and loved. It's where I learned I was unbreakable and where I learned I could be unstoppable. It will always be where I grew up, but now it's time to find a home, not just a house.

It's time to find my forever with them.

With my family.

FORTY-NINE

NICO

"**A**re you sure you want to go this way?" I ask for the tenth time, glancing back at Nova who's staring out of the window. She has a look in her eye that I can't describe, like she knows something we don't. When she turns to me with a soft smile, I know she does.

"I can almost feel it. Keep going," she demands.

Over the last month, we have travelled around Paris so Isaac could see his old home like he never did before, but she didn't want to live anywhere in France. We then explored Spain, Germany, Norway, Poland, and hell, even Iceland. When you have a private plane, you can go wherever you want, and it seems like Nova wants something very specific. She's smiling more, and she's starting to heal. I love seeing my girl so happy, but she hasn't found somewhere to settle down like she wants.

Not until the plane landed in Italy.

The last places were chosen at random, just by placing a finger on the map, but as soon as she stepped out here, something changed in her. It's like she looked out at the view and said this is it. For the last few days, we have been driving around Italy, exploring the scenery, experiencing the culture, and evaluating all it has to offer. Every time, she gets this look in her eye and tells us to keep going.

I don't care where we stay, just as long as it's with her, so I turn down the dirt road she randomly told me to stop at. There's a little village sign posted not far from here. We passed some old chateaus and wineries, and the rolling hills are beyond beautiful. There's something so pure and real about where we are, but this dirt road looks like it leads to nowhere.

Dimitri has a physical map open. She wouldn't even let him use his satellites or computers, which is making him cranky, but we are all determined to find the place where she wants to spend the rest of our lives, to make our family, our future. Fuck, I'll travel the world twice over to find it if that's what it takes.

I just want her to be happy and for us to be together.

Keeping my hands on the wheel as the SUV bumps over the dirt road, I glance to either side of us. I only see rolling fields until we crest a hill, and on the other side is a house. It appears to be an older chateau with a few outbuildings surrounding it. It almost looks like a farm, and up front is a for sale sign.

Nova leans forward, smiling at it. "This is it. I can feel it. Can you?"

I nod as I look at her smiling face. "I can, baby."

"Then let's go!"

I rev the engine and we drive the rest of the way. When we pull up outside of the house, I cringe. It needs a lot of work, but as I get out and survey the land, I realise it clearly has potential.

"It needs work," Louis comments.

"Eh, so do we." Nova shrugs. "Perfect would be boring." She smiles at the house just as the two front doors open and an older lady in a summer dress peers out.

"Are you here for the viewing?" she asks, glancing over at us.

"We are," Nova replies and heads her way. "I hope that's okay. I couldn't just drive past." She peers around. "This place is beautiful."

"It was my grandmother's and hers before it." She smiles at Nova. "It was here before most of the rest of the world was. Come on in."

We troop in after the older lady, and my jaw drops at the inside of the house. It's beautiful. Huge windows framed by old-style curtains with gauze allow the sunlight to hit the brick walls, and the floors are a mix of old styles that somehow seem warm and homey. The lady guides us around, showing us a grand dining room big enough for us. There are old carved fireplaces and even a library with a sitting room, all done in robin's-egg blue and white, with comfy-looking sofas and gorgeous paintings and rugs. I tune out her voice as I walk around, imagining us here. There is room for us outside to spar and train, and there are enough bedrooms for all of us, but the master is my favourite.

Double doors lead out onto a veranda, and the bed itself is huge and up on a small platform. White sofas face a roaring fire with a painting above it. The en suite has a gigantic tub with a window before it, looking out over the hills. Every room is clearly well-loved and has been designed for the people living here. It feels like a fairy tale. Bert gets excited about the kitchen, oohing and aahing over the appliances and talking with the lady about recipes as we wander around and explore.

It's a strange mix of old Italian and updated tastes, and honestly, Nova is right. It's incredible. The outside needs work, but all the best things do. I could imagine us here, curled up together before the fire, laughing and joking at the dining table, and exploring the land.

I could see us here.

I could see Nova here, and when I turn to her, it's clear she can too. She's smiling in a way I've never seen before, appearing almost hopeful.

There's a pool out back, overlooking the valley, surrounded by perfectly manicured bushes and roses, and when we join them again, Bert smiles at us widely. He's clearly already in love with the place, and the older lady showing us looks hopeful.

"This place is incredible," Nova gushes.

"It is. It needs some work, since I've not been able to keep up with it since my husband died, but I just want the next owners to enjoy their lives here like my children and I have. I want it to be filled with laughter again."

"That's exactly what we are looking for," Nova tells her. "A home, a place where we can just live and enjoy life."

"I've raised all my children here, and I can tell you that no matter where you go in the world, there is no place like home, and when you feel it, you know it," she says wisely.

"I couldn't agree more. My name is Nova, by the way. It's nice to meet you." Nova reaches out to shake her hand.

"Hi, Nova, I'm Anabel."

We all freeze, and Nova's eyes widen as she shakes the older lady's hand. "Anabel?" she repeats.

"Yes, Anabel." She seems confused.

"A beautiful name," Nova says and glances back at us with a knowing smile. "Almost like it led us home."

"I'm sorry?" Anabel asks.

"I said we'll take it," Nova replies. "This is where we are meant to be. This is home."

LOUIS

Dimitri is more than happy to buy the house with the money he says is ours. Nova is hesitant, but he insists. Anabel suggested a price that I was pretty sure was nowhere near what we should be paying, but when we asked, she simply said that some things were meant to be, and seeing her family house loved and restored once more would be enough.

We get the keys the very next day.

It only took us a few hours after we moved in to find a place to hide the research. There's a wine cellar under the house, which can only be accessed through a trapdoor in the kitchen. Dimitri starts to heighten security, but we lock the research down there and leave it to be forgotten.

All we ever wanted was to stop this from happening to anyone else. We succeeded, and now we get to live. It won't be easy to settle into civilian life, but we deserve it. That doesn't mean I won't keep my eyes peeled for anything we can help with—after all, old habits die hard—but for now, it's time for us to enjoy our lives.

Here, we are not super soldiers or experiments. Here, we just get to be, and as I sip my coffee, watching the beautiful sunrise, my family's laughter reaching me, I can't help but let the tension roll from my shoulders for the first time ever.

No enemies or missions.

No responsibilities.

My only purpose is to be happy.

Arms slide around me from behind, making me grin as I close my eyes. "Morning, beautiful."

"Morning." She sighs. "I woke up and you were gone."

"I couldn't miss this." Putting down my coffee, I turn and wrap my arms around her, turning us once more to face the sunrise as she picks up my coffee and starts to drink it. We always seem to share, so I've started taking it how she likes it, even if it's too sweet for me. I kiss the top of her head as I hold the love of my life in my arms in our new forever home.

"It's beautiful, isn't it?" she whispers.

"It is, but it will never be as beautiful as you."

She giggles, elbowing me. "Corny bastard."

"You love it." I grin, kissing her head once more. "We get forever, Nova, but I promise it won't be long enough with you." She turns to peer up at me, and I smile softly down at her, my heart leaping with joy. "Promise me this is it—us, this house, our family . . . If you try to leave us again, I'll chain you to us forever."

"It's us, baby. I promise." She leans up, coffee forgotten, and interlaces her hands behind my neck. The feel of her warm body against mine makes my dick harden but I ignore it, soaking in her comfort as I press my head to hers.

"What shall we do with all the time we have?" I grin.

"Oh, I don't know. I can think of a few things," she teases just as the sounds of Jonas's maniacal laughter and Nico's swearing reach us.

I groan as she laughs. "It's a good thing I'm stuck with them," I mutter as she kisses me and grabs the coffee, sliding past me.

"Well, when they get to be too much, you could always just hide away with me," she purrs as she slides backwards into the house. "Like right now, I plan on taking a very long, very hot bath."

Before she can run, I have her draped over my shoulder as I stride through the house. "Bert, the kids are yours for an hour."

"Yay!" Jonas yells as Nico groans loudly.

She laughs as I spank her and bring her back to our bedroom to spend the next fifty years ravishing the love of my life.

FIFTY

ISAAC

"Isaac!"

I jerk awake, and I'm out of the empty bed where my love should be quicker than I can blink. Thundering down the stairs in search of her panicked scream, I pick up a weapon on the way. Jonas has hidden them around the entire house—old habits. We might be settling into civilian life, but we cannot change who we are.

We are still soldiers.

It's been a week since we've moved in and we've settled into bliss, apart from now, when my heart races in worry. I don't hear the guys, only Nova's scream echoing in my head. What if she's hurt? What if someone came after us?

I smash through the front door, frantically searching for her. "Nova!" I scream.

"Isaac!"

I follow the sound around the house and slide to a stop when I find Nova. She's almost crying, staring down at a donkey lying before her with its leg in her lap.

"Isaac. Help him. He broke his leg." She pouts as I continue to stare, my adrenaline pumping through me.

"You screamed because you found a donkey that has a broken leg?" I scrub the back of my head in confusion, sliding my knife into my pants. "Babe, I'm a doctor, not a vet."

"You're a hero." She widens her eyes. "Please, Isaac? We can't leave him in pain."

I blink before dropping to my knees before her. "Okay, go get my bag."

She nods. "It's going to be okay," she tells the donkey, who whines and gently places his foot down as she rushes inside.

Scratching my head, I stare at the donkey. "It can't be too different from a human, right?" I tell him. "I guess we'll find out."

Taking hold of its legs, I wince when it cries. "Shh, it's going to be okay," I say. "I just have to check this fracture." I talk to it like it's one of my patients, and when Nova comes back, I prop up the leg as best as I can and give him some pain meds before leaning back.

"We can move him into the old barn. There's still hay there, and we can give him food until he gets—" My voice cuts off as she knocks me to the floor, kissing my face.

"My hero!" She grins down at me.

"Always," I reply, smiling up at her.

DIMITRI

"Why the fuck is there a donkey in the barn?" I hear Nico yell, and I shake my head with a laugh.

I focus on the screens before me. I've checked on the kids every day. They seem to be settling in well, and I'm glad for that. I also check on my investments. We have enough money for this lifetime and ten over, so our girl will never want for anything since she refuses to touch any of her father's money.

A message comes through just then, an old contact of mine offering us a job. Smiling, I hit accept before turning the computers off and getting to my feet. My eyes linger on the photo of Bas and me. We were so young. Pressing my fingers to my lips, I kiss the tips and then press them to the photo. "Love you," I tell him.

"D, come see this!" Nova laughs.

Grinning, I turn to the stairs. "Coming, my love." Glancing back at Bas, I smile. "I'll take care of her for us." I go to join my family, leaving the screens I once claimed as home behind and joining the real world instead.

FIFTY-ONE

JONAS

Two months later . . .

"I got him." I grin, my eye on the scope. "Let me know when you're clear, baby."

"Got it," she says just before the door bursts open and my girl emerges, a backpack slung over her shoulder with the stolen gear. Nico isn't far behind, and Louis is on their tail, slamming and blocking the door.

Dimitri sighs at my side. "Incoming," he says, and I don't glance away from the scope as I hit the detonator and the building explodes, throwing them to the floor before they roll to their feet and run.

"You were only supposed to distract them, not blow up the building," Isaac deadpans from my left, his first-aid kit ready.

"Oops." I grin just as they burst from the door, and we start picking them off as my girl and brothers race to our vehicle. Once they are clear, we pack up. Slinging the bag over my shoulder, I clap Dimitri on the back and head to meet them.

We don't take missions often anymore, only enough to keep us from growing bored, but this was a fun one for sure. We stole some important documents for the US government, and although no country admits to using us, that's fine. It works well for us.

At the car, Nova grins up at me. "Big fire, babe."

"You know it." I kiss her, moaning as her taste spreads through me. I never thought I could love someone as much as I do her, and my obsession only gets worse the longer we are together.

Sliding her down my body, I let her feet hit the floor as the others climb in and the car roars to life.

"Let's go home." She grins at me. "I've got some new toys to show you." She wiggles her brows, making me groan.

Smacking her ass, I haul her into the car and hit the hood through the window. "Fast as you can, we've got things to do."

"Hopefully not rescuing more animals," Nico grumbles, even though the big bastard is up every morning, feeding every single animal Nova has rescued. She turned our home into a rescue centre. She said they are like us, and we couldn't argue with that, especially when she named the pig Davis.

Otherwise, life is fucking good.

I'm not broken.

I'm not psychotic . . . Okay, I am a little, but only for her.

My girl.

My love.

My family.

Forever.

NOVA

"Don't," I warn, pointing my finger at a grinning Dimitri. I turn to keep Jonas in my sights as he tracks me. Shit. I turn to see Nico at the door, his muscles flexing. Louis is sipping his coffee as he watches with glowing eyes, and Isaac winks at me as he climbs to his feet. "I mean it," I warn. "I just showered."

"I'll clean you . . . with my tongue," Jonas says. "You just look so pretty today."

"It is your own fault, coming down like that and expecting us to behave," Dimitri remarks.

Bert just sings along to his music, carrying on cooking breakfast.

"Bert, I claim sanctuary!" I call.

"Nope, sorry, Miss Nova." He waves a spatula at me. "I will put the food in the oven to stay warm though."

"Fuck!" I snap, turning to the open windows and dashing to them.

I hear them give chase, their laughter urging me on. Gritting my teeth, I run as fast as I can. I slide across dirt as I wind around the house, searching for an advantage. My brain processes like a computer, discarding route options and highlighting better ones, but theirs are doing the same.

I skid to a stop when I see a grinning Nico standing near the pool, waiting for me. Turning, I find Jonas skipping after me, and when there's a thud, I whirl to find Louis landing below the balcony he jumped from. Groaning, I scan for Dimitri and Isaac, and when I don't see them, I start to back away slowly.

"You think I'll make it that easy?" I chuckle. I feint left and then turn and race right, ducking under Louis's reaching hands. They don't want to catch me yet, though. That much is obvious. When I skirt the windows, I see Dimitri and Isaac chatting, holding coffee cups in their hands as they stroll from the kitchen. They blow me kisses as I race by.

Bastards.

Annoyance flares in me. I want to win, even though I know they are five of the best soldiers in the entire world and it's me against them.

I have an advantage though. I know how they think. Louis will hang back, letting them track me while trying to create a net around me to corner me in, and then he will take the kill shot. If I can cause enough chaos and confusion, I might just manage to evade them.

If I want to.

I slow slightly when arms suddenly wrap around me, lifting me into the air. A warm breath wafts over my ear as I shudder with desire, and someone's hard cock grinds into my ass tauntingly.

"Got you."

Jonas.

"Do you?" I purr, leaning back as I relax, and when he lowers me slightly, I slide from his grip, turn, and knee him in the cock. With a howl, he drops to his knees.

"Sorry, babe." I giggle as I back away.

"That was so fucking hot. Shit, baby, my balls," he groans as he stumbles to his feet. "Better run," he growls as he hounds my steps. "She's over by the barn!" he calls to the others.

"Traitor," I hiss.

"For your pussy, baby? Absolutely."

Done with talking, I duck through the barn and burst out of the other end, racing towards the fields. Maybe I can lose them in the overgrown grass. Diving into the long foliage, I hold my arm out to block it as I race forward. I hear some shouts behind me and put on a burst of speed to outrun them, but the grass suddenly parts before me, revealing a grinning Dimitri. "Hey, beautiful."

"Fuck." I start to back away when hands grab me from behind once more.

"Got you," Nico says.

"You put up a good fight, but we both know you wanted to be caught, love," Louis murmurs as he wanders forward and stops before me, jerking his head at Nico. "Take her back."

"Bastards," I hiss as I flail and kick, but I moan when Nico grips my pussy.

"Behave, brat," he warns before tossing me over his shoulder and racing for the house. Part of me wants to give in—after all, it's exactly what I want —but then again, I never did know how to concede.

Once we are out in the open, heading towards Isaac and Jonas, I make my move. I unbalance Nico, which allows me to fall from his shoulder, but before I take two steps, I'm hauled back up.

A hand comes down on my ass in a hard slap. "If you carry on, I'll let Jonas play."

"You are threatening me with a good time," I remind him, wiggling on his shoulder to get him to spank me again, and he does. The sting fades into a burn, making me moan.

I lift my head as we move into the house. Bert waves at me as he sits and reads his paper.

"I claim sanctuary."

"Nope, have fun," he replies without even lifting his head, and when we hit the stairs, I see him putting on some headphones.

We reach our room within seconds, and Nico tosses me on the bed. I bounce and dart to the door, but the others file in, blocking my way. Backing away, I make my way towards the balcony without looking, but Isaac moves behind me, stopping that route too.

"Fine, you caught me." I huff. "Now what do you plan to do?"

The smile Louis aims at me is cruel and possessive. "Clothes," he orders, and I tilt my head in confusion, but my clothes are ripped off from behind. I spin to find Isaac backing away with a grin.

I narrow my gaze on him when my bra and knickers are cut away. Growling, I kick them off, and they hit Jonas's chest where he plucks them up with the knife he used to remove them and stuffs my underwear into his mouth.

The shudder that passes through me isn't healthy, nor the clenching of my thighs as desire hammers through me.

"Bed," Louis commands.

Shit. Before I can dart away, Nico strides over and hauls me to the bed, lying down with me pinned on top of him. His ankles catch my kicking legs and press them down to the bed. One hand grips my throat; the other grabs my hands.

I twist and buck, but he's too fucking strong, and all it does is rub his hard cock against me, leaving me wet and panting. When I still, chest heaving, Louis looks at Dimitri. "You caught her. You get her first."

Chuckling, D grins as he unzips his jeans and palms his hard cock. "The question is, is she wet enough to take us all?"

"Why don't you find out?" I snarl.

His grin widens at my words as he strokes himself. The adrenaline from the chase changes to raw, primal need as I watch him touch himself, and when I can't take it anymore, I widen my thighs to try and entice him. I see the victory in his eyes at my submission before he presses a knee to the bed and crawls between my pinned legs. His eyes are only for me as his hands slide up my thighs and grip them, yanking them farther open.

He lies down between my legs, nudging his wide shoulders there, and drags his tongue across my pussy. I jerk and cry out, twisting in Nico's hold, who tightens his grip on my throat.

"Oh, she's wet, but let me make sure," he coos, and his dark eyes close as he attacks me. His tongue laps at my clit before thrusting inside me, fucking me like we both know he will soon. Groaning, I try to lift my hips and grind into him, but I'm caught between them with no other choice but to take it.

My breath catches as he wraps his lips around my clit and sucks. My back tries to bow, and my eyes close as I cry out. I feel all of their eyes on me, intent on my pleasure and making me theirs.

I fucking want it.

I want it all, dirty, hard, and raw.

Dimitri's fingers slide into me, curling and stroking as he sucks and bites until it's too much. With a scream, I explode, gushing over his fingers and tongue. When the pleasure ebbs, I slump and feel him pull away. I don't even manage to open my eyes before he's driving into me.

Nico's hand keeps me anchored as my eyes snap open, clashing with Dimitri's as he moves above me, and with a growl, he pulls out and slams back in, taking me hard and fast. My name is a hissed word on his lips as his body presses against mine, all hard edges and perfection.

His gaze holds mine, forcing me to see every inch of his love, devotion, and obsession as he fucks me. "Look at you," he growls as I lift my hips to meet his thrusts, wordlessly begging for more.

I only feel alive when I am with them.

"Look at how perfect you are. We caught you, Nova, and we are never letting you go, not ever. You are ours for eternity."

Whimpering his name, I turn my hands and slash my nails into Nico, hearing him grunt, but he still doesn't release me, and I realise that was their plan all along—no escape, not even an inch of space.

"I love you, Nova, so much it hurts, and when I thought I lost you, I didn't see the point of going on. I live only for you. Do you understand? Without you, I am just another computer," he growls, his thrusts speeding up.

It's bordering on painful but so fucking delicious I cry out, clenching around him. It's too much. It's not enough.

I'm lost to it, to him, to them.

"Nova," he whispers as he drives into me. His long, hard thrusts hit that spot inside me, making me see stars.

My heart skips, and fire races through my veins until I can't take any more.

"Come for me again," he demands. "Come with me, together."

As always, they ensure my pleasure first, and his words send me over the edge once more. Crying out my release, I clamp on his cock as he hammers into me twice more before stilling, his forehead hitting mine as he pants and jerks. His cum drips from me as we both breathe raggedly.

"I love you," I tell him.

Grinning, he kisses me softly. "I love you too." He pulls from my body, and with one last, lingering kiss, he moves away.

Isaac crawls up my body, trailing kisses along my skin as he goes. His soft smile is firmly in place when he reaches my lips.

"Hi." He grins.

"Hi." I giggle.

"Are you okay?" he asks with a naughty grin.

"No, but you can make it better by fucking me," I taunt, rubbing against him.

"Gladly," he purrs, sliding down my body. He stops to lick and suck my nipples until I moan loudly. His cock slides across my pussy and the mess there, and then his mouth meets mine once more and he swallows my gasp as he pushes into me.

He kisses me leisurely, softly, and builds the heat inside me with love.

His hips pull back and roll forward.

Unlike Dimitri, Isaac is soft and loving. He rains kisses across every inch of me he can reach. Pleasure arcs through me, leaving me gasping and writhing. His slow thrusts never change, and then I shatter, pulling him with me, his groan echoed in my chest as he fills me with his release.

When I open my eyes, he places a soft kiss over my heart before pulling from my body and sliding away. Their cum drips from me, my legs shake with aftershocks, and I'm covered in sweat, yet they look at me like I'm the most beautiful woman in the world.

Louis is next, which surprises me.

His dark eyes lock me in place like always. Louis has this strange power over me that constantly makes me either want to fight him or give into him. "Be a good girl and ride my cock, love," he purrs, sliding farther up until he consumes my vision. His hands jerk my hips up so I'm rubbing my pussy along his length, and with each rub, his mushroom head smacks my clit, making me groan. I roll my hips, chasing my release, and just when I'm about to come, he pulls away.

"Asshole." I pout.

"Brat," he counters, but it's said lovingly. He frees one leg from Nico, holding it hostage as he tosses it over his shoulder, bending me as his cock presses to my entrance. "Scream for me," he orders.

"How about you make—" My retort ends in a high-pitched howl as he drives into me. The force shifts me back on Nico. Chuckling, Louis tightens his grip on my leg, turning his head to bite my thigh as he pulls out and hammers in.

"What was that?" he taunts, his voice silky against my skin. "Want me to do it again, love?"

"You couldn't even if you tried—" He smacks my clit so hard, I see stars, a scream slipping free once more.

"That's what I thought, brat. Now be a good girl and don't come until I say so." Before I can respond, he's fucking me in earnest. The bed shakes from the force as he rubs my clit, driving me towards my release despite his words.

I hold it back, gritting my teeth as I fight the pleasure spiralling through me as he fucks me.

He grinds me back into Nico, who grunts in pain, his hard cock notched against my ass, and with each thrust, I slide across it.

"I can't," I whine. "Louis, please, I need to—" I can barely speak over the roaring blood in my veins, and with one last twist of his hips, Louis smacks my clit.

"Now," he orders.

Like a perfect soldier, I howl as my release flows through me. My legs kick and shake as he fucks me through it, growling. With a groan, he stills, and his cum splashes inside me.

When he pulls back, he falls to the side. "Go easy on her. No fucked-up shit this time," he warns Jonas, his voice rough, and pleasure fills me at how

I affected him, but I don't have long to think about it because Jonas consumes my vision.

He pouts. "He said we have to behave, Nova."

"When do you ever?" I reply.

"True." He tugs me down, freeing my legs until Nico is just holding my hands. He presses my legs to his chest, lifting me into the air, and with a wicked grin, his cock slides across my pussy. I tense, preparing myself for his invasion, but when he's covered in cum, he slides lower.

My eyes close as he presses to my ass. "If I cannot have your madness, I want your screams," he snarls, and with a brutal twist of his hips, he buries himself in my ass. He works himself as deep as he can, our mixed cum helping him slide inside before he pulls out and thrusts back in, forcing me up and onto his cock.

I cry out from the sharp pain, but then his fingers thrust into my pussy, curling to rub that spot that has my cries turning into screams as he begins to claim my ass. Pain and pleasure mixes like it always does with him.

I close my eyes, unable to handle it, my body his to master, and when I scream my release, he roars his, pumping it into my ass before pulling out and spraying the rest across my chest and pussy.

"Fucking perfect," he praises.

"Isn't she just?" Isaac says.

Their attacks disarm me. They love on every inch of me until all I can do is take their praise and love as it rebuilds every inch of me that has been torn down before them.

Arms drag me back up.

Nico.

Spent, I slump into Nico. "Shh, I've got you, baby," he promises, lifting me slightly, and all I can manage is a whine as he slides me down onto his waiting cock. Arms wrap around me from behind as he fucks me from below.

My breasts bounce with the force, and my eyes close in bliss as I let him carry me away.

"Mine, my Nova."

"Yours," I agree, arching back and rolling into his touch.

His hand slides down my body and across my clit. "I'm close already. Watching you get fucked and feeling it on top of me almost had me spilling, baby," he admits. "So come for me, let me feel it before I can't hold back anymore."

He pinches my clit, making me scream in pain and pleasure as a surprise orgasm slams through me. When I come back to, he's groaning so sexily in my ear and filling me with his release.

I can barely breathe, and I definitely can't move. Long after the sweat starts to cool on my body, Nico pulls free, leaving me sticky and satisfied.

"We've got you," Louis murmurs, climbing onto the bed. Someone wipes my pussy and thighs, but I don't look, just lax with pleasure and so happy I could cry.

Arms wrap around me once more, different ones sliding across my body until they are all touching me.

I want every day to be like this.

I cuddle closer to my men, a satisfied smile on my lips as I close my eyes. My body is sweaty, my pussy is sore in the best way, and my heart is full and overflowing. "I love you all," I murmur.

Louis sighs happily. "I love you too."

"I love you too. Now sleep, you've worn me out," Jonas mumbles, making me giggle as I bury my head deeper into Nico's chest. Isaac pulls me closer as Dimitri presses a kiss to my leg.

I fade into a dreamless sleep, just as I always do when they are here.

The crack of lightning wakes me just before thunder rattles the shutters of our house. My men wake instantly. I smile at them as I slip from the bed. Unlike before, I wait for them. Nico wraps a robe around me, and I put my slippers on as we head downstairs. Opening the veranda doors we installed, we gather on the sofas there. Dimitri wraps blankets around us as Bert makes trays of herbal tea and sets them out, joining us as we watch the storm.

A tradition to honour the woman who gave her life for us.

Somewhere, Ana is watching this storm with us, her grave decorated with flowers and drawings from the kids we saved. We also started a soldiers' rehab program in her and Sam's names, and I know every person there tonight will be looking at the sky, thinking of the woman they owe that to.

Hands hold me close, and although it hurts, a smile tilts my lips as I watch the rain hit the windows of my new home. Storms will always make me think of my sister, of the woman I loved so deeply, I gave up everything for her, but life has a funny way of ripping you apart and putting you back together.

It certainly did that to me. I often wondered when I would break and give into the darkness, and more than once, I debated doing just that. It would have been easier, but I never liked the easy option. It doesn't mean I don't carry my scars with me because I do. I still struggle sometimes, but on nights like this, I remember why I fight to get up every day.

For her.

For every child my father hurt.

For every child they killed.

For the soldiers who were just doing their duty.

I live for them, my family, and for myself.

"Do you remember the night before we met you?" Dimitri murmurs.

It brings me out of my thoughts, and he smiles brightly. "It was a stormy night just like this. I checked. I guess storms have always been our thing as well as hers."

"I guess so," I whisper. "Maybe that's why I always loved them so much."

I take his hand and turn back to the windows, a brighter smile on my face. Somewhere out there, destiny is laughing at me. Only a few years ago, on a night like this, I was trapped in a cheap hotel room, completely alone, guided by anger and revenge, and now here I am, in love and happier than I've ever been.

I have a new life and a new future I plan to fully embrace.

I guess I was just a pretty liar when I said revenge was all there was to live for.

The world still has its dark days, and there are still those who would come for the research, but that is our mission now. We will protect it and those children. My father's experiments end with us. We will never let another suffer under the same experiments, and one day, it will be forgotten just like him. We will be forgotten as well, but that's okay with me. We know what we did, we know what we are capable of, and we will stand here as a reminder and a promise until the very end because we are unbreakable.

We are unstoppable.

EPILOGUE

NOVA

Two years later . . .

Like I do every morning, I sip my coffee as I watch the sunrise. The house and our land are quiet. Not even the animals are awake yet. The dogs are snoring on top of Nico and waiting for him to feed them. Dimitri's computers are turned off and have been for days, since he prefers to spend his time with us now. Jonas continues to build weapons, only now he sells them to the good guys. Louis, as it turns out, is very good at restoration, and we updated our house and started on the property together. Maybe in time, we'll make that a business, but for now, we are just enjoying life. Isaac fully embraced his role as vet and qualified in it. His days of being a doctor are behind him—unless Jonas and I get too rough during sex—and he now spends his days helping animals rather than patching bullet wounds.

And me?

My smile grows as I watch the colours spread across the sky. I got everything I wanted. I'm never alone anymore. I have a family who loves me more than anything else in this world. I have men willing to kill for me. I still train, but not religiously. I'm more than my body and what it's capable of, after all. I still haven't figured out what I'll do with the rest of my life, but I have plenty of time.

"Baby?" comes a sleepy voice behind me.

I open my eyes as I glance down at my ring, the ring they all had made for me, before I turn to see Louis. "Hey," I whisper. "Go back to sleep. I'll be there in a second."

"You better or we'll find you," he warns.

I nod, knowing they will.

They prove how much they love me every day, and I finally started to believe it and let go of my pain and my past. My heart still aches when I think of everything we lost, including my sister, but I'm more determined than ever to enjoy the life we have because nothing is guaranteed.

So, I stop and watch the sunrise, feel the breeze, and dance in storms and remember . . .

Life is so much more than what others want for us. There is a big, wide world out there just waiting for us to find our happiness in whatever shape or form that comes in.

My happiness just so happens to be in an old Italian villa with six incredible men, a father I never lost, five dogs, three cats, a donkey, two horses, a pig, and a llama.

I head inside our home and back to my men where my heart pulls me, the floor under me protecting the very thing that created us.

Our secret we will always protect.

Together.

ACKNOWLEDGMENTS

This book was so hard to write in some places, it took me to a very dark place and as darkness plagued me and my loved ones, I turned the pain into ink. Luckily, for every stormy, shadowed night, there is a bright sunshine morning.

I cannot begin to thank everyone who makes my work possible but for especially trusting me through the process of this one. From my incredible betas who's hearts I break daily to my phenomenal editor and proofreader who make my madness legible. To my PAs who understand the craziness and help me get it out into the world . . . and then finally to you.

My readers.

I would not be here today without you all. I never forget that and I'm truly so thankful every time you take a chance on a book I have written. I hope you love Nova's story as much as I did and remember, Pretty Liars, you are never alone.

ABOUT K.A. KNIGHT

K.A Knight is an USA Today bestselling indie author trying to get all of the stories and characters out of her head, writing the monsters that you love to hate. She loves reading and devours every book she can get her hands on, and she also has a worrying caffeine addiction.

She leads her double life in a sleepy English town, where she spends her days writing like a crazy person.

Read more at K.A Knight's website or join her Facebook Reader Group.
Sign up for exclusive content and my newsletter here
http://eepurl.com/drLLoj

ALSO BY K.A. KNIGHT

THEIR CHAMPION SERIES *Dystopian RH*

The Wasteland

The Summit

The Cities

The Nations

Their Champion Coloring Book

Their Champion - the omnibus

The Forgotten

The Lost

The Damned

Their Champion Companion - the omnibus

DAWNBREAKER SERIES *SCI FI RH*

Voyage to Ayama

Dreaming of Ayama

THE LOST COVEN SERIES *PNR RH*

Aurora's Coven

Aurora's Betrayal

HER MONSTERS SERIES *PNR RH*

Rage

Hate

Book 3 coming soon..

THE FALLEN GODS SERIES _PNR_

Pretty Painful

Pretty Bloody

Pretty Stormy

Pretty Wild

Pretty Hot

Pretty Faces

Pretty Spelled

Fallen Gods - the omnibus 1

Fallen Gods - the omnibus 2

COURTS AND KINGS _PNR RH_

Court of Nightmares

Court of Death (Coming soon!)

FORBIDDEN READS _(STANDALONES)_

CONTEMPORARY

Daddy's Angel

CONTEMPORARY RH

Stepbrothers' Darling

PRETTY LIARS _CONTEMPORARY RH_

Unstoppable

Unbreakable

FORGOTTEN CITY _PNR_

Monstrous Lies

Monstrous Truths

Monstrous Ends

STANDALONES

IN DEN OF VIPERS' UNIVERSE - CONTEMPORARY

Scarlett Limerence

Nadia's Salvation

Alena's Revenge

Den of Vipers *CONTEMPORARY RH*

Gangsters and Guns (Co-Write with Loxley Savage)

CONTEMPORARY

The Standby

Diver's Heart *CONTEMPORARY RH*

SCI FI RH

Crown of Stars

AUDIOBOOKS

The Wasteland

The Summit

Rage

Hate

Den of Vipers *(From Podium Audio)*

Gangsters and Guns *(From Podium Audio)*

Daddy's Angel *(From Podium Audio)*

Stepbrothers' Darling *(From Podium Audio)*

Blade of Iris *(From Podium Audio)*

Deadly Affair *(From Podium Audio)*

Stolen Trophy *(From Podium Audio)*

Crown of Stars *(From Podium Audio)*

Monstrous Lies *(From Podium Audio)*

Monstrous Truth *(From Podium Audio)*

SHARED WORLD PROJECTS

Blade of Iris - Mafia Wars *CONTEMPORARY*

CO-AUTHOR PROJECTS - *Erin O'Kane*

HER FREAKS SERIES *PNR Dystopian RH*

Circus Save Me

Taming The Ringmaster

Walking the Tightrope

Her Freaks Series - the omnibus

STANDALONES

PNR RH

The Hero Complex

Collection of Short Stories

Dark Temptations (contains One Night Only and Circus Saves Christmas)

THE WILD BOYS SERIES *CONTEMPORARY RH*

The Wild Interview

The Wild Tour

The Wild Finale

The Wild Boys - the omnibus

CO-AUTHOR PROJECTS - *Ivy Fox*

Deadly Love Series *CONTEMPORARY*

Deadly Affair

Deadly Match

Deadly Encounter

CO-AUTHOR PROJECTS - *Kendra Moreno*

STANDALONES

CONTEMPORARY RH

Stolen Trophy

PNR RH

Fractured Shadows

PNR

Burn Me

CO-AUTHOR PROJECTS - *Loxley Savage*

THE FORSAKEN SERIES *SCI FI RH*

Capturing Carmen

Stealing Shiloh

Harboring Harlow

STANDALONES

CONTEMPORARY

Gangsters and Guns - IN DEN OF VIPERS' UNIVERSE

OTHER CO-WRITES

Shipwreck Souls *(with Kendra Moreno & Poppy Woods)*

The Horror Emporium *(with Kendra Moreno & Poppy Woods)*

Made in United States
Troutdale, OR
02/01/2024

17348776R00196